倍斯特出版事業有限公司
Best Publishing Ltd.

Just enjo

學校沒教的

趣你的英語單字

A !!

跟著MP3這樣學才有趣!

MP3

郭玥慧
Jin-Ha Woo (하진우) ◎著

Absolutely No Pressure!

「有訣竅的學習」跟「樂趣」結合才能事半功倍
激發潛能、引起好奇心、會持續性去接觸

語言學習需要持之以恆，持之以恆才能將你導向優質學習成效
（即強化記憶力和正向學習能量）
「趣」你的英語單字書，讓你終身受用

835個
趣味英單，讓你...

● 兼顧玩樂跟考試
● 不再淪為填鴨式教育的犧牲品
● 學習無壓力

One language sets you in a corridor for life. Two languages open every door along the way. (Frank Smith, psycholinguist)

一種語言可以為人生開啟一條走廊。兩種語言則會為你開啟這條人生走廊上的每一道門。（弗蘭克史密斯，心理語言學家）

You live a new life for every new language you speak. If you know only one language you live only once. (Czech proverb)

每說一種新的語言，你就過一種新的人生。如果你只說一種語言，那麼你只活過一次。（捷克諺語）

學習語言，不容易，但卻也是一種享受。就像前面的引言所說的，是為人生開啟了另一道門、展開了另一種人生、為你帶來不同的視野。我向來喜愛接觸不同語言，但英文一直都是引領我去另一種語言的基礎。不得不說，透過英文能掌握到的資訊還是比較多。

那麼英語學習可以如何進行？

單字是基礎

「背了馬上忘」是很多人共同的經驗吧？然而單字是基礎。沒有基礎，如何建構出句子、對話、文章？

只有單字卻不夠?!

但大家不要誤會，學語言不能只有背單字。

1. 首先，要會唸。如此，能利用發音與字母之間的關係幫助你記得一個字的拼法。此外，要會唸學了語言才能用。

2. 既然語言是要拿來用的，很多時候只有單字是不行的，也要知道這個
單字怎麼用。這時，利用句子來學習是個很好的方法。

我們整理了高中必備單字，並提供單字的發音註解與其他詳細資訊，讓
你不需再花時間查字典。我們更蒐集了包含這些單字的有趣或振奮人心
的引句，好讓語言學習更輕鬆、有趣，也為您帶來靈感和激勵。衷心希
望這本書不只是一本增加英語能力的單字書，也是給你在學習與人生的
路上帶來微笑、勇氣與希望的一本書。好好享受您的語言學習和您的人
生吧！

Carolin Kuo（郭玥慧）

這本書包含了來自財經、時尚、運動與科學等各個領域的引言，希望能
夠讓讀者有一個引人入勝又有效的字彙學習過程。在每個單字後都有詳
細的說明，包含詞性和單字的變化形，加強讀者對文法知識與認知。我
們也精心選出相關的引言，好讓讀者更能了解如何自然地使用這個單字，
並藉由這些引句增強文化知識、加深洞察力。以更國際化的視野思考與
看待周遭。在本書中的引句會為您帶來娛樂與靈感，您也會從中找到積
極過活的動力。身為一位英語教授，我非常肯定「享受」是英語學習過
程非常重要的成分，我最引以為傲的學生，都是能在課堂外，找到有趣
的方式持續不斷學習英語的人。正因如此，我們編寫了這本書，讓您能
夠在捷運上、咖啡廳裡或周末在家裡，都能利用這本書，有趣的學習。

雖然學習英語的過程充滿挑戰，但也同時深具意義並能讓人感到收穫良
多，未來很可能帶您走上令人驚奇、超乎想像的人生道路。我很感謝我
勤奮的合著者。我也要對我的指導教授— Richard Day 教授以及 Bert
Kimura 教授 — 表達感激，他們教導我一切並不斷的激勵我。最後，我
必須謝謝我最棒的同事— Bella，為我帶來這個機會並給我前所未有的
靈感與鼓舞。

Jin-Ha Woo（하진우）

趣你的英文單字

目　次

Part 1 「趣」你的單字基礎篇

Part 2 「趣」你的單字進階篇

Part 1

趣你的單字基礎篇

Unit 1

人生中常有驚喜

趣味字彙表

1.	abandon *vt.* 拋棄	9.	aggressive *adj.* 有侵略性的、好鬥的
2.	acceptance *n.* [U] [C] 接受	10.	alert *adj.* 警覺的
3.	accompany *vt.* 伴同	11.	amateur *n.* 業餘人士
4.	accuracy *n.* [U] 準確性	12.	ambitious *adj.* 有野心的
5.	acquaintance *n.* [U] [C] 相識、熟人	13.	analysis *n.* [U] [C] 分析
6.	acquire *vt.* 取得、獲得	14.	anxiety *n.* [U] [C] 焦慮
7.	adapt *vt. vi.* 適應	15.	appreciation *n.* [U] [C] 欣賞
8.	adequate *adj.* 適當的、勝任的		

趣味字彙句 🎧 MP3 01

1. abandon [ə'bændən] *vt.* 拋棄 abandoned abandoned

🐸 Art is never finished, only **abandoned**. (Leonardo da Vinci, Artist)
藝術沒有完成的時候，只有被拋棄。

🐸 Steve Job's adopted parents told him he was special not **abandoned**.
賈伯斯的養父母告訴他，他是很特別的而不是被拋棄的。

2. acceptance [ək'sɛptəns] *n.* [U] [C] 接受 acceptances

🐸 Harry Potter received an **acceptance** letter from Hogwarts.
哈利波特收到霍格華滋的入學通知了。

🐸 In his **acceptance** speech, Kanye West said that he would be the next president.
肯伊威思特在他的領獎演說裡提到他會是下一任總統。

3. accompany [ə'kʌmpənɪ] *vt.* 伴同 accompanied accompanied

🐸 Arguments, differences, and conflicts **accompany** true love. (Marshall McLuhan, Philosopher)
真愛伴同著爭執、差異和衝突

🐸 Mark Wahlberg has a human alarm clock **accompany** him on business trips.
馬克華格柏在出差的時候都會帶著一個隨身的人類鬧鐘。

4. accuracy [ˈækjərəsɪ] *n.* [U] 準確性

🐛 Being fast is fine, but **accuracy** is everything. (Wyatt Earp, Public Servant)
速度很快是一回事，可是準確性才是最重要的。

🐛 **Accuracy** is the least significant part of drawing. (Milton Glaser, Graphic Designer)
畫畫時，準確性是最不重要的部分。

5. acquaintance [əˈkwentəns] *n.* [U] [C] 相識、熟人 acquaintances

🐛 The Victoria's Secret Angels started as **acquaintances** and became best friends.
這些薇多利亞的秘密的模特兒一開始只是點頭之交，到現在已經變成最好的朋友了。

🐛 An **acquaintance** would save the last slice of pizza for you, but a friend would eat the last slice and laugh.
一個認識的人會幫你留最後一片披薩，但是一個朋友會把最後一片吃掉然後笑你沒吃到。

6. acquire [əˈkwaɪr] *vt.* 取得、獲得 acquired acquired

🐛 The richest man in India plans to **acquire** a house with six parking floors, three helicopter pads, and 600 staff members.
印度最有錢的富豪計劃要買一棟有六樓停車場，三座直升機起落坪，和六百名員工的房子。

🐛 Beyonce **acquired** a pair of gold leggings for 100,000 dollars.
碧昂絲得到了價值十萬美金的純金內搭褲。

7. adapt [əˋdæpt] *vt. vi.* 適應 adapted adapted

🐸 While filming the Hunger Games, Jennifer Lawrence **adapted** to daily running, biking, and medicine ball exercises.
在飢餓遊戲的拍片過程中，珍妮佛羅倫斯適應了每天跑步、騎腳踏車和做健身實心球的運動。

🐸 The crime novel Black Mass will be **adapted** into a movie starring Johnny Depp.
犯罪小說《黑勢力》將會被改編為由強尼戴普主演的電影。

8. adequate [ˋædəkwɪt] *adj.* 適當的、勝任的

🐸 The actress, Melissa McCarthy, began to lose weight by going on an **adequate** diet.
演員梅利莎麥卡西以適當的飲食來減重。

🐸 Jennifer Aniston was an **adequate** waitress before she became an actress.
珍妮佛安妮斯頓在當演員前，曾經是一個勝任的服務生。

9. aggressive [əˋgrɛsɪv] *adj.* 有侵略性的、好鬥的

🐸 When reporters asked for free concert tickets, Rihanna became **aggressive** and yelled.
蕾哈娜在記者要求免費的演唱會門票後，突然變得很有攻擊性並大叫。

🐸 Gordon Ramsay is an **aggressive** cook who screams and spits out food.
戈登拉姆齊是一個很有侵略性的廚師。他會大叫或是把食物吐出來。

10. alert [əˈlɜt] *adj.* 警覺的

📖 I am an **alert** father who checks to see if my kids are breathing. (Matt Damon, Actor)
我是一個小心的父親，我會確認我的小孩是不是還在呼吸

📖 Patrick Dempsey, the handsome actor, is always **alert** when he races cars.
帥氣的演員帕特里克德姆西在賽車的時候總是很小心。

11. amateur [ˈæməˌtʃʊr] *n.* 業餘人士

📖 A successful writer is an **amateur** who doesn't quit. (Richard Bach, Writer)
成功的作家其實就是一個從不放棄的業餘人士。

📖 When it comes to love, women are experienced but men are **amateurs**. (Francois Truffaut, Director)
在愛情這方面，女人總是比較有經驗，而男人只是業餘的。

12. ambitious [æmˈbɪʃəs] *adj.* 有野心的

📖 Ralph Lauren, the **ambitious** designer, began his career by selling handmade ties to his classmates.
拉夫羅倫這個很有野心的設計師一開始是從賣手作領帶給他的同學而開始他的職業生涯的。

📖 The **ambitious** supermodel, Miranda Kerr, does yoga and only eats organic food.
米蘭達可兒這個充滿野心的超級名模每天都會做瑜伽，並且只吃有機的食物。

13. analysis [əˈnæləsɪs] *n.* [U] [C] 分析 analyses

A good **analysis** can be explained in simple words. (Albert Einstein, Physics)

可以用簡單的話解釋的才是好的分析。

What action will I take once I finish my **analysis**? (Hiten Shah, Entrepreneur)

我分析完之後會做什麼行動呢？

14. anxiety [æŋˈzaɪətɪ] *n.* [U] [C] 焦慮 anxieties

Kate Moss suffered from **anxiety** at her first Calvin Klein photo shoot.

凱特摩絲在第一次幫凱文克萊拍照的時候得到了焦慮症。

Spiderman experienced great **anxiety** when his girlfriend Gwen Stacy died.

蜘蛛人在他的女友關史黛西死掉的時候非常焦慮。

15. appreciation [əˌpriʃɪˈeʃən] *n.* [U] [C] 欣賞 appreciations

My boyfriend is afraid of my great **appreciation** of jewelry. (Ivanka Trump, Businesswoman)

我男友對於我如此欣賞珠寶感到害怕。

The minions have a great **appreciation** for bananas, apples, and frog legs.

小小兵很喜歡香蕉、蘋果，還有蛙腳。

Unit 2

找回自信

趣味字彙表

1.	approval *n.* [U] 贊同、認可	9.	behavior *n.* [U] 行為
2.	artistic *adj.* 藝術的、美術的	10.	blessing *n.* [C] 祝福、幸運的事
3.	assurance *n.* [U] 保證、自信	11.	boast *vt. vi.* 誇耀、吹噓
4.	attraction *n.* [U] [C] 吸引（力）、吸引物	12.	brutal *adj.* 殘忍的
5.	authority *n.* [U] 權力、影響力	13.	calculate *vt. vi.* 計算
6.	awkward *adj.* 笨拙的、尷尬的	14.	calorie *n.* [C] 卡路里
7.	bankrupt *adj.* 破產的	15.	campaign *n.* 活動、競選活動
8.	barrier *n.* [U] 阻礙、障礙		

趣味字彙句 🎵 MP3 02

1. approval [ə`pruvl] *n*. [U] 贊同、認可

🛒 If you're horrible to me, I'm going to write a song about you with or without your **approval**. (Taylor Swift, Singer)

如果你對我很差勁的話,不管你同不同意,我都會寫一首關於你的歌

🛒 You have my **approval** because you're sweet and you even created a dish called Eggs Marshall. (Marshall Eriksen, TV Character)

你有我的認可,因為你人很好,而且你還創造了一道菜叫做「馬修蛋」的料理。

2. artistic [ɑr`tɪstɪk] *adj*. 藝術的、美術的

🛒 Marc Jacobs, the **artistic** designer, created a shirt based on an embarrassing Instagram post.

藝術設計師馬克雅各布斯依據一張他登在 Instagram 上的糗照,設計了一件襯衫。

🛒 Plastic surgery is a harmful form of **artistic** expression. (Lady Gaga, Singer)

整形是一種有害的藝術表現形式。

3. assurance [ə`ʃurəns] *n*. [U] 保證、自信

🛒 Demi Lovato needed **assurance** to beat her eating problems and perform again.

黛咪洛瓦特曾經需要信心才能擊退她的飲食問題,並重回舞台表演。

🛒 Lea Michele, the Glee TV show actor, wanted **assurance** for the unusually shaped nose.

《歡樂合唱團》演員麗婭米雪兒希望能為自己較特異的鼻形找到自信。

4. attraction [əˈtrækʃən] *n.* [U] [C] 吸引（力）、吸引物 attractions

🐛 The **attraction** quickly faded and Drew Barrymore divorced her husband in 19 days.
吸引力很快就消失，茱兒芭莉摩十九天後便與丈夫離婚。

🐛 Disney developed a new **attraction** called Star Wars land.
迪士尼開發了一項名叫「星際大戰主題樂園」的新景點。

5. authority [əˈθɔrətɪ] *n.* [U] 權力、影響力

🐛 Although the CEO of ZARA has a lot of **authority**, he eats lunch with his employees every day.
雖然 ZARA 的總裁握有極大權力，他仍然每天與他的員工一起吃午餐。

🐛 Jackie Chan has used his **authority** to support hundreds of charities.
成龍已善用他的影響力大力支持了無數個慈善機構。

6. awkward [ˈɔkwəd] *adj.* 笨拙的、尷尬的

🐛 The reporters filmed the **awkward** moment when Brad Pitt bumped into his ex-wife.
記者捕捉到布萊德彼特遇到前妻時尷尬的樣子。

🐛 Justin felt **awkward** after he accidentally called his manager 'dad'.
賈斯汀在不小心叫了他的經紀人「爸爸」之後覺得很尷尬。

7. bankrupt [ˈbæŋkrʌpt] *adj.* 破產的

Donald Trump made terrible decisions and went **bankrupt** four times.
唐納德川普曾經下了很不好的決定，結果破產四次。

Although Michael Jackson was a millionaire, he went **bankrupt**.
雖然麥可傑克森曾經是個百萬富翁，他後來也破產了。

8. barrier [ˈbærɪr] *n.* [U] 阻礙、障礙

While filming the movie Titanic, the crew faced many **barriers** including an angry worker who poisoned 50 people.
在拍電影《鐵達尼號》的時候，劇組遇到很多困難，其中包含一位不滿的員工毒害了 50 人。

Stan Lee beat the age **barrier** and created the X-Men comics after he was 40 years old.
史丹李跨越年齡隔閡，並在四十歲後創作了漫畫《X 戰警》。

9. behavior [bɪˈhevjɚ] *n.* [U] 行為

Professor Snape punished Harry Potter for his rude **behavior**.
石內卜教授因為了哈利波特粗魯的行為而處罰他。

Directors will not hire Lindsay Lohan because of her bad **behavior**.
很多導演後來都因為琳賽羅涵的負面行為，拒絕用她。

Part 1 「趣」你的單字基礎篇

Part 2 「趣」你的單字進階篇

10. blessing [ˈblɛsɪŋ] *n.* [C] 祝福、幸運的事 blessings

- Remember your **blessings** and forget what you lost. (Drew Barrymore, Actress)
  要記得發生在你身上的好事，忘記你失去過什麼。

- My troubles are **blessings** because they have made me stronger. (Walt Disney, Entrepreneur)
  很多麻煩其實都是好事，因為它們使我變得更堅強。

11. boast [bost] *vt. vi.* 誇耀，吹噓 boasted boasted

- I don't mean to **boast**, but I finished my 14-day diet in 3 hours.
  我不是想吹牛，但我三小時就完成了我為期十四天的節食（註：三小時內吃了本來十四天應該吃的量）。

- Hip-hop is all about **boasting** and who has the most money. (Two Chainz, Rapper)
  嘻哈就是吹噓與比誰最有錢。

12. brutal [ˈbrutl̩] *adj.* 殘忍的

- On American Idol, Simon Cowell **brutally** told a singer that he looked like a poodle.
  西蒙高維爾在《美國偶像》中殘酷地告訴一位歌手他看起來像一隻貴賓犬。

- Christian Bale went on a **brutal** diet and lost 63 pounds for a movie.
  克里斯汀貝爾為了電影進行了殘酷的節食，並減了六十三磅。

13. calculate ['kælkjə‚let] *vt. vi.* 計算 calculated calculated

🐸 Am I the only one who **calculates** how much sleep I can get before going to bed?

我是唯一睡前會先算可以睡幾小時的人嗎？

🐸 Anna **calculated** the risks and decided to save her sister Elsa.

安娜推估了風險後，決定拯救她的姊姊艾莎。

14. calorie ['kælərɪ] *n.* [C] 卡路里 calories

🐸 America's unhealthiest drink is a 2,000 **calorie** milkshake with chocolate ice cream, milk, and peanut butter.

美國最不健康的飲料是一種由巧克力冰淇淋、牛奶與花生醬做成，含兩千卡的奶昔。

🐸 If stress burned **calories**, I would be a supermodel.

如果壓力會消耗熱量，我現在已經是個名模了。

15. campaign [kæm'pen] *n.* 活動、競選活動 campaigns

🐸 Chanel spent 33 million dollars on a two-minute TV ad **campaign**.

香奈兒為了一個兩分鐘的電視廣告花了三千三百萬美元。

🐸 I like the brand Valentino because they never use actresses in their **campaigns**. (Emma Watson, Actress)

我之所以喜歡瓦倫蒂諾這個品牌是因為他們從不在宣傳活動中使用女演員。

Part 1 「趣」你的單字基礎篇

Part 2 「趣」你的單字進階篇

Unit 3

關鍵時刻

趣味字彙表

1.	candidate *n.* 候選人、應試者	9.	charity *n.* [U] [C] 慈悲、慈善機構
2.	capacity *n.* [U] [C] 能力	10.	chore *n.* [C] 家庭雜務、日常零星事務
3.	career *n.* [C]（終身的）職業	11.	circumstance *n.* [U] 情況、境遇
4.	carve vt. *vi.* 刻、雕刻	12.	civilization *n.* [U] [C] 文明（階段）、文化
5.	cease vt. *vi.* 停止	13.	clarify *vt. vi.*（得到）澄清、淨化
6.	celebration *n.* [U] [C] 慶祝、慶祝活動	14.	clash *vi. vt.*（使）碰撞、牴觸
7.	championship *n.* [C] 冠軍地位、冠軍稱號	15.	classify *vt.* 將…分類、將…歸入某類
8.	characteristic *n.* [C] 特徵、特性		

趣味字彙句 🎧 🎧 💿 MP3 03

1. candidate [ˈkændədet] *n.* 候選人、應試者 candidates

🐤 The superman actor, Henry Cavill, is a **candidate** to play the next James Bond.
出演電影《超人》的亨利卡維爾是下一任詹姆士龐德的候選人之一。

🐤 Carly Fiorina, a **candidate** to be the next U.S. president, was the CEO of Hewlett-Packard.
下任美國總統候選人卡莉費奧莉娜曾任惠普公司總裁。

2. capacity [kəˈpæsətɪ] *n.* [U] [C] 能力 capacities

🐤 Your **capacity** to say no allows you to say yes to great things. (E. Stanley Jones, Missionary)
你說「不」的能力讓你可以對偉大的事物說「好」。

🐤 The **capacity** to feel joy, happiness, and fear are developed at birth.
感受欣喜、幸福與恐懼的能力是在出生時就發展而成。

3. career [kəˈrɪr] *n.* [C]（終身的）職業 careers

🐤 Robert Downey Jr. recovered his acting **career** after he stopped using drugs.
小勞勃道尼在戒毒後重新找到自己的演藝生涯。

🐤 During their **career**, the Kardashians sold energy drinks, exercise shoes, and socks.
卡戴珊家族在他們的職業生涯中，賣過能量飲料、運動鞋與襪子。

4. **carve** [kɑrv] *vt. vi.* 刻、雕刻 carved carved

🐛 Teams from Hawaii, Indonesia, and Italy **carve** ice at the Sapporo Snow Festival.
來自夏威夷、印尼與義大利的團隊在札幌雪祭活動中雕刻冰雪。

🐛 On National Watermelon Day, people **carve** watermelons into impressive art.
在「全國西瓜節」這天，人們將西瓜雕成驚為天人的藝術品。

5. **cease** [sis] *vt. vi.* 停止 ceased ceased

🐛 Facts do not **cease** because they are ignored. (Aldous Huxley, Writer)
事實並不會因為被忽略就不存在。

🐛 AT&T and Gatorade **ceased** their contracts with Tiger Woods after he cheated on his wife.
美國電話電報公司和蓋特瑞飲料兩家公司在老虎伍茲外遇背叛老婆後，終止了合約。

6. **celebration** [sɛləˋbreʃən] *n.* [U] [C] 慶祝、慶祝活動

🐛 Katy Perry had a birthday **celebration** based on Willy Wonka's chocolate factory.
凱蒂佩芮辦了一場模仿威利旺卡的巧克力工廠的慶生會來慶生。

🐛 A couple in Russia had their marriage **celebration** while biking.
一對俄羅斯夫妻一邊騎車一邊慶祝結婚周年。

7. championship [ˈtʃæmpɪənˌʃɪp] n. [C] 冠軍地位、冠軍稱號 championships

- You win the **championship** by fighting one more round. (James Corbett, Boxer)

  繼續再打一回合,你就是冠軍。

- Talent wins games, but teamwork wins **championships**. (Michael Jordan, Basketball Player)

  天賦讓你贏得比賽,團隊合作卻可讓你贏得冠軍。(麥可喬丹,籃球選手)

8. characteristic [kærəktəˈrɪstɪk] n. [C] 特徵、特性 characteristics

- Women think men with honest, caring, and humorous **characteristics** would be the perfect boyfriend.

  女人認為擁有誠實、有愛心、幽默特質的男人會是最完美的男友。

- While wizards in Hufflepuff display kind **characteristics**, wizards in Gryffindor display daring characteristics.

  赫夫帕夫學院的巫師展現了仁慈的特質,葛萊分多學院的巫師則展現了勇敢的特質。

9. charity [ˈtʃærətɪ] n. [U] [C] 慈悲、慈善機構 charities

- An act of **charity**, no matter how small, is never wasted. (Aesop, Story Teller)

  無論多麼微不足道的善行都不會被視而不見。

- Bill Gates is the second richest person in the world and he gave $28 billion to **charity**.

  比爾蓋茲是世界排名第二的富豪,並捐贈了二百八十億美金給慈善團體。

10. chore [tʃor] *n.* [C] 家庭雜務、日常零星事務 chores

- Malia and Sasha Obama's **chores** include cleaning their room and walking their dogs.
  瑪麗亞歐巴馬與莎夏歐巴馬的日常事務包含整理房間與遛狗。

- Strangely enough, I love putting clothes in the washing machine and doing **chores**. (Nicole Kidman, Actress)
  奇怪的是，我熱愛把衣服放進洗衣機與做家事。

11. circumstance [ˈsɝkəmˌstæns] *n.* [U] 情況、境遇 circumstances

- I don't think that love changes, but people and **circumstances** change. (Nicholas Sparks, Writer)
  我不認為愛會改變，但人與環境卻會。

- Shia LaBeouf grew up under difficult **circumstances** of poverty and divorced parents.
  演員西亞李畢福在貧窮與雙親離異的艱困環境中長大。

12. civilization [ˌsɪvl̩əˈzeʃən] *n.* [U] [C] 文明（階段）、文化 civilizations

- In future **civilizations**, engineers believe that robots will replace schools, books, and human workers.
  工程師相信在未來文明中，機器人會取代學校、書本與人工。

- Emma Watson, the actress, aims to improve our **civilization** by encouraging women.
  演員艾瑪華森立志鼓勵女人以改善我們的文明。

13. clarify [ˈklærəˌfaɪ] *vt. vi.* （得到）澄清、淨化 clarified clarified

🦋 Every mistake **clarifies** our minds for greater ideas and possibilities.
每一個錯誤都讓我們的心靈能夠更加清晰地看到更偉大的構想與可能。

🦋 Noah **clarified** his love for Allie by building her dream house.
諾亞為愛莉蓋了她夢想中的房子以闡明他對她的愛。

14. clash [klæʃ] *vi. vt.* （使）碰撞、牴觸 clashed clashed

🦋 Let ideas **clash** but not hearts. (Chandravadan Mehta, Poet)
讓想法，而不是心，相互激盪。

🦋 The Beatles **clashed** with their fans in the Philippines after refusing to meet the President.
披頭四在菲律賓拒絕與總統見面後，與樂迷起了衝突。

15. classify [ˈklæsəˌfaɪ] *vt.* 將…分類、將…歸入某類 classified classified

🦋 I want to **classify** my life as a romantic comedy movie, but it's more of a TV reality show. (Uma Thurman, Actress)
我想把我的人生歸類為愛情喜劇電影，但它卻其實比較像是個實境電視秀。

🦋 Anna Wintour, the editor-in-chief of Vogue, is **classified** as a fashionable ice queen.
VOGUE 雜誌主編安娜溫特被歸類為時尚的冰山女魔。

Unit 4

使自己變得更好

趣味字彙表

1.	clumsy *adj.* 笨拙的	9.	competition *n.* 競爭、比賽
2.	coarse *adj.* 粗的、粗糙的	10.	competitor *n.* 競爭者、對手
3.	collapse *vi. vt.* （使）倒塌、瓦解	11.	complicate *vt.* 使複雜化、使難對付
4.	combination *n.* [U] [C] 結合	12.	compose *vt.* 作（詩，曲等）、構（圖）
5.	comment *n.* [U] [C] 評論、註釋	13.	concentrate *vt. vi.* 聚集、集中
6.	commit *vt.* 犯（罪）、做（錯事等）、使作出保證	14.	concentration *n.* [C][U] 集中、專注
7.	communication *n.* [U] [C] 傳達、交流、訊息	15.	concept *n.* [C] 概念、觀念
8.	companion *n.* [C] 同伴		

趣味字彙句 ♫ ♫ ● MP3 04

1. clumsy [ˈklʌmzɪ] *adj.* 笨拙的

🐞 The **clumsy** smurf accidentally made the smurfs travel through time.
笨手笨腳的藍色小精靈不小心讓所有的小精靈穿越時空。

🐞 I'm not **clumsy**. The floor, tables, and chairs just hate me.
不是我笨手笨腳，地板、桌子跟椅子們就是討厭我。

2. coarse [kors] *adj.* 粗的、粗糙的

🐞 Andy waxed off his **coarse** chest hair to get a girlfriend.
安迪為了交到女友，除掉了他粗糙的胸毛。

🐞 Beyoncé uses hot oil treatments to manage her **coarse** hair.
碧昂絲利用熱油護髮，來管理粗糙的頭髮。

3. collapse [kəˈlæps] *vi. vt.* （使）倒塌、瓦解 collapsed collapsed

🐞 When you feel like **collapsing**, remember that there is still a lot to learn and always great stuff out there. (Robin Williams, Actor)
當你覺得你要崩潰的時候，記得你還有很多要學習的，而且外面總是有美好的事物等著你。

🐞 At the Chloe fashion show, a supermodel **collapsed** and hit her forehead on the runway.
在蔻依的時裝秀上，一位名模在伸展台上跌倒，撞到額頭。

Part 1 「趣」你的單字基礎篇

Part 2 「趣」你的單字進階篇

4. combination [kɑmbəˈneʃən] *n.* [U] [C] 結合 combinations

🐛 Some people enjoy eating the **combination** of Cheetos and chocolate pudding.
有些人享受把芝多士和巧克力布丁配在一起吃。

🐛 Be more creative and reinvent new **combinations** of what you already own. (Karl Lagerfeld, Fashion Designer)
發揮創意，重新組合你已知的。

5. comment [ˈkɑmɛnt] *n.* [U] [C] 評論、註釋 comments

🐛 Maturing is realizing how many things don't require your **comment**. (Rachel Wolchin, Blogger)
成熟就是了解有多少事物不需要你做評論。

🐛 A lady likes to hear praises about her looks but positive **comments** about her personality are much appreciated. (Betty White, Actress)
女人喜歡聽你誇獎她的外表，但比起來還是比較喜歡關於她個性的正面評論。

6. commit [kəˈmɪt] *vt.* 犯（罪）、做（錯事等）、使作出保證 committed committed

🐛 The greatest act anyone could ever **commit** is to be happy. (Patch Adams, Physician and Clown)
一個人能夠做出的最偉大行為就是保持開心。

🐛 If you **commit** to never make a same mistake again, then you get better with every mistake that you make. (Harsha Bhogle, Journalist)
如果你致力於不再犯同樣的錯誤，那你每犯一次錯誤，你就變得更好。

7. communication [kəˌmjunəˈkeʃən] *n.* [U] [C] 傳達、交流、訊息
communications

☝ The most important thing in **communication** is to hear what isn't being said. (Peter Drucker, Author)
溝通過程中最重要的是聽出沒被說出來的話語。

☝ The three fastest ways of **communication** are Twitter, telephone, and telling a woman.
傳達訊息最快的三種方式：推特、電話和告訴女人。

8. companion [kəmˈpænjən] *n.* [C] 同伴 companions

☝ A guitar is the perfect **companion** to the human voice. (Jason Mraz, Singer)
吉他是人類聲音最好的伴侶。

☝ You can go to places with a camera and feel like you're with someone, like you have a **companion**. (Annie Leibovitz, Photographer)
旅行的時候如果帶著相機，你就會覺得好像有人陪你，彷彿你有個伴侶。

9. competition [kɑmpəˈtɪʃən] *n.* 競爭、比賽 competitions

☝ You have to look at the **competition** and say you're going to do it differently, not better. (Steve Jobs, Businessman)
你應該面對競爭，然後說你會用不同的方式進行，而不是更好的方式。

☝ When I go out on the ice, I forget it is a **competition** and just think about skating. (Katarina Witt, Figure Skater)
當我上場的時候，我忘記我是在比賽，我只想著溜冰。

10. competitor [kəmˈpɛtətɚ] *n.* 競爭者、對手 competitors

🐑 We will win if we can keep our **competitors** focused on us, while we stay focused on the customer. (Jeff Bezos, Amazon CEO)
如果我們能讓我們的競爭對手只想著對付我們，同時我們卻專注在客戶上，我們就會贏得勝利。

🐑 Matthew Stonie, one of the top eating **competitors**, ate 62 hot dogs in 10 minutes.
其中一個最厲害的大胃王史托尼（Matthew Stonie）十分鐘內吃了六十二份熱狗。

11. complicate [ˈkɑmpləˌket] *vt.* 使複雜化、使難對付

🐑 Sometimes the questions **complicate** us and the answers are simple (Dr. Seuss, Writer)
有時候問題讓我們難以應付，答案卻很簡單。

🐑 Any fool can make something **complicated**. It takes a smart person to make it simple.
任何一個笨蛋都可以把事情變得複雜，但要把一件事情簡單化卻得靠聰明的人。

12. compose [kəmˈpoz] *vt.* 作（詩，曲等）、構（圖）

🐑 When I **compose** a song, I think about love, life, and death, and other people's situations. (Ed Sheeran, Singer)
我作曲的時候，想著愛、人生、死亡以及其他的人處境。

🐑 Every day after high school, I would run home and **compose** music on the piano. (Josh Groban, Singer)
高中每天放學後，我都會跑回家，用鋼琴作曲。

13. concentrate [ˈkɑnsɛnˌtret] *vt.* *vi.* 聚集、集中 concentrated concentrated

☞ I can't **concentrate** when I am wearing flat shoes. (Victoria Beckham, Fashion Designer)
我穿平底鞋的時候沒辦法集中精神。

☞ Losing weight doesn't seem to work, so I'm going to **concentrate** on getting taller.
減肥似乎沒用，所以我決定要專注在長高。

14. concentration [ˌkɑnsɛnˈtreʃən] *n.* [C][U] 集中、專注 concentrations

☞ **Concentration** comes from a mixture of confidence and hunger.
專注力來自於自信加上飢餓感。

☞ **Concentration** is the ability to think about nothing when it is necessary. (Ray Knight, Baseball Player)
專注力指的是一種每當必要的時候可以什麼都不想的能力。

15. concept [ˈkɑnsɛpt] *n.* [C] 概念、觀念 concepts

☞ Boredom is a **concept** that I don't understand. (Christian Louboutin, Fashion Designer)
「無聊」是個我無法理解的概念。

☞ The **concept** of being sexy is embarrassing and confusing. Dying my hair blonde and wearing a mini-skirt is not me. (Emma Watson, Actress)
「性感」這個概念讓人感到尷尬與困惑。把頭髮染金和穿迷你裙很不像我。

Unit 5

驚人的內在價值

趣味字彙表

1.	confess *vt. vi.* 坦白、承認	9.	consultant *n.* [C] 顧問
2.	confidence *n.* [U] 自信、信心、信任	10.	consumer *n.* [C] 消費者、消耗者
3.	confusion *n.* [U] 混亂、困惑	11.	content *adj.* 滿足的
4.	congratulate *vt.* 恭喜	12.	continuous *adj.* 連續的
5.	conquer *vt. vi.* 攻取、戰勝	13.	contrast *n.* [C][U] 反差
6.	consequence *n.* [U] [C] 後果、重要（性）	14.	contribute *vt. vi.* 捐獻、提出
7.	construct *vt.* 建造、構成	15.	convention *n.* [C][U] 慣例、習俗
8.	constructive *adj.* 建設性的、結構上的		

趣味字彙句 🎧 💿 MP3 05

1. confess [kən'fɛs] *vt. vi.* 坦白、承認 confessed confessed

🐞 I should probably **confess** that ice cream is my favorite food. I'm on a mission to taste every flavor of ice cream out there! (Becca Fitzpatrick, Author)
或許我該承認冰淇淋是我最愛的食物。我給自己的任務是吃遍世界所有的冰淇淋口味。

🐞 Between lovers too much **confessing** is a dangerous thing. (Helen Rowland, Journalist)
在戀愛關係中，過頭的坦誠是很危險的。

2. confidence ['kɑnfədəns] *n.* [U] 自信、信心、信任

🐞 Happiness and **confidence** are the prettiest things you can wear. (Taylor Swift, Singer)
快樂與自信是最美麗的服飾。

🐞 **Confidence** is the ability to fall in front of people. (Craig Swanson, Entrepreneur)
自信就是不怕在人前跌倒、失敗。

3. confusion [kən'fjuʒən] *n.* [U] 混亂、困惑

🐞 Gradually happiness will come, until then laugh at the **confusion** and live for the moment.
漸漸地快樂會到來的，在那之前，對困惑一笑置之，然後活在當下吧。

🐞 I stay in a constant state of **confusion** because I like the expression it leaves on my face. (Johnny Depp, Actor)
我常常處在一個困惑的狀態，因為我喜歡它給我帶來的表情。

Part 1 「趣」你的單字基礎篇

Part 2 「趣」你的單字進階篇

4. congratulate [kənˈgrætʃəˌlet] *vt.* 恭禧 congratulated congratulated

🐞 Katy Perry **congratulated** her husband by giving him a $100,000 ticket to travel to space.

凱蒂佩芮送丈夫一張十萬美金的太空船船票以示祝賀。

🐞 Kanye West **congratulated** Kim Kardashian by buying her ten Burger King stores around the world.

肯伊威斯特在世界各地買了十家漢堡王給金卡戴珊以示祝賀。

5. conquer [ˈkɑŋkɚ] *vt. vi.* 攻取、戰勝 conquered conquered

🐞 Happiness is like those palaces in fairy tales that are guarded by dragons: we must fight in order to **conquer** it. (Alexandre Dumas, Writer)

「快樂」有如童話故事裡由龍守護著的皇宮，我們必須奮鬥才能攻下。

🐞 Give a girl the right shoes, and she can **conquer** the world. (Marilyn Monroe, Actress)

給女人一雙對的鞋，她就能征服世界。

6. consequence [ˈkɑnsəˌkwɛns] *n.* [U] [C] 後果、重要（性）consequences

🐞 It's easy to play a bad girl in movies. You can do anything you want without **consequences**. (Eliza Dushku, Actress)

在電影裡演壞女孩很容易，你可以做任何事情而不用擔心後果。

🐞 I don't speak particularly well. That's one of the **consequences** of being extremely ugly. (Chris Martin, Singer)

我不是非常會說話，這就是長得很醜的後果之一。

7. construct [kən`strʌkt] vt. 建造、構成 constructed constructed

Look closely at what you are **constructing**: it should look like the future you are dreaming. （Alice Walker, Author）
仔細看看你正在建構的，它應該要像你夢想中的未來。

I never stopped thinking about the ideal car. All I had to do was **construct** a factory to build it. (Ferruccio Lamborghini, Car Entrepreneur)
我從沒停止思考怎麼樣的車是最理想的，我唯一需要做的就是建造一座工廠來做出這台車。

8. constructive [kən`strʌktɪv] adj. 建設性的、結構上的

The man who will use his **constructive** imagination to see how much he can make for a dollar will succeed. (Henry Ford, Car Entrepreneur)
一個人如果懂得善用他有建設性的想像力，看自己能用一塊錢賺到多少，他就會成功。

It's not **constructive** for my children to grow up having billions of dollars. (Bill Gates, Businessman)
讓我的孩子在擁有數十億元的情況下長大毫無建設性。

9. consultant [kən`sʌltənt] n. [C] 顧問 consultants

Consultants are wise enough to give advice but not dumb enough to work at your company. (Scott Adams, Cartoonist)
顧問們夠聰明，可以給你意見，而沒有笨到去你的公司上班。

Give a man a fish, and you will feed him for a day. Talk to a hungry man about fish, and you're a **consultant**. (Cartoonist)
給人魚吃，你餵飽他一天，跟個餓肚子的人討論魚，你就是顧問。

10. consumer [kənˈsjumə] *n.* [C] 消費者、消耗者 consumers

🐸 I'm always telling **consumers** to buy less, choose well, and make it last. (Vivienne Westwood, Fashion Designer)
我常常告訴消費者要買少一點，小心選擇，然後讓你買的東西用得久又有價值。

🐸 Your most unhappy **consumers** are your greatest source of learning. (Bill Gates, Businessman)
你最不滿意的客戶是你最佳的學習資源。

11. content [kənˈtɛnt] *adj.* 滿足的

🐸 It's easy to impress me. I'm **content** with good friends, good food, and good laughs. (Maria Sharapova, Tennis Player)
我很容易取悅，只要有好朋友、美食和歡笑，我就滿足了。

🐸 A lot of people are **content** with winning a few games, but we shouldn't focus on the past. We focus on the present.
很多人只要贏幾場比賽就滿足了。但我們不該專注在過去，要專注在當下。

12. continuous [kənˈtɪnjʊəs] *adj.* 連續的

🐸 Hackers are making **continuous** efforts to improve their work. (Mark Zuckerberg, Businessman)
駭客不斷努力改善他們的作品。

🐸 Anyone who has a **continuous** smile on their face is hiding frightening strength inside of them. (Greta Garbo, Actress)
任何永保微笑的人其實都藏著驚人的內在力量。

13. contrast ['kɑn‚træst] n. [C][U] 反差 contrasts

🐞 I always like the **contrast** between being blond and having dark features. (Rita Ora, Singer)
我向來都很喜歡我雖是金髮，卻有著深色人種長相的反差。

🐞 The more conflict and **contrast** you have with a movie character makes acting more interesting. (Chris Hemsworth, Actor)
當電影角色和你有越大的衝突與反差，你越能感受到演戲的趣味。

14. contribute [kən'trɪbjut] vt. vi. 捐獻、提出 contributed contributed

🐞 We need more kindness, joy, and laughter. I really want to **contribute** to that.
我們需要更多的善行、喜悅與笑聲，而我真心想對此有所貢獻。

🐞 The more I travel around the world, the more I see that people want to be happy. I want my music to **contribute** to their happiness. (Jason Mraz, Singer)
去世界越多地方旅行，我越能看出人們希望感到快樂，而我希望我的音樂能成為他們快樂的理由。

15. convention [kən'vɛnʃən] n. [C][U] 慣例、習俗 conventions

🐞 I wasn't looking for marriage, but Paul and I married because of **convention**. (Linda McCartney, Musician/Photographer)
我當時並沒有在尋找婚姻，但保羅和我因為習俗結婚了。

🐞 Most people call me E.C. It's an Irish **convention** to call your first child by their initials. (Elvis Costello, Singer)
大部分的人叫我 E.C.。愛爾蘭人習慣用姓名首字母稱呼他們的長子女。

Unit 6

實現自己的夢想

1.	convince *vt.* 說服	9.	defend *vt. vi.* 保衛、為…辯護
2.	cooperation *n.* [U] 合作、配合	10.	delight *n. vt. vi.* (使)高興 delighted delighted
3.	courageous *adj.* 勇敢的	11.	demand *n.* [C][U] 要求、需求；vt. 要求、請求
4.	courteous *adj.* 禮貌的	12.	departure *n.* [U] [C] 出發、離開
5.	creativity *n.* [U] 創造力	13.	deserve *vt. vi.* 該得、應受賞（罰）
6.	criticism *n.* [C] 評論、批評	14.	desperate *adj.* 情急拼命的、絕望的
7.	curiosity *n.* [U] [C] 好奇（心）、珍奇的人或物	15.	despite *prep.* 儘管、任憑
8.	deadline *n.* [C] 截止期限、最後限期		

趣味字彙句 🎵 MP3 06

1. convince [kən'vɪns] vt. 說服 convinced convinced

🐸 If you can **convince** yourself that you look fabulous, you don't need to dress up.

如果你能說服自己你看起來美翻了，那你就不需要打扮了。

🐸 If you can't **convince** someone, confuse them instead. (Harry S. Truman, President)

當你無法說服某人的時候，那就把他弄糊塗吧。

2. cooperation [koˌɑpə'reʃən] n. [U] 合作、配合

🐸 I often pretended that I knew less than I did to cameramen. I got more **cooperation** that way. (Ida Lupino, Actress)

我面對攝影師，習慣隱藏我的所知，藉此贏得他的配合。

🐸 The **cooperation** of NASCAR is only kept when everyone believes that they have the opportunity to win. (Charles Duhigg, Reporter)

全國運動汽車競賽協會只在大家有贏得比賽的希望的時候才會合作。

3. courageous [kə'reɪdʒəs] adj. 勇敢的

🐸 Being **courageous** is the quiet voice at the end of the day saying that I will try again tomorrow. (Mary Anne Radmacher, Author)

有勇氣就是在一天的尾聲，說著「我明天會再試一次」那微小的聲音。

🐸 Any fool can make things more complex and violent. It takes a **courageous** person to go in the opposite direction. (Albert Einstein, Physicist)

任何一個笨蛋都可以把事情變得複雜且暴力，但我們卻需要有勇氣的人才能把事情帶往另一個方向。

4. courteous [ˈkɝtjəs] *adj.* 禮貌的

🐦 Women are won over by men who are sweet, **courteous**, kind, and funny. (Zooey Deschanel, Actress)
貼心、有禮貌、善良與幽默的男人總是能贏得女人芳心。（柔伊黛絲香奈，演員）

🐦 Men don't know enough about being **courteous** toward women. (Thom Browne, Fashion Designer)
男人對於如何對女人展現禮儀懂得還不夠多。（湯姆布朗，時尚設計師）

5. creativity [krieˈtɪvətɪ] *n.* [U] 創造力

🐦 **Creativity** is inventing, growing, taking risks, breaking rules, making mistakes, and having fun. (Mary Lou Cook, Actress)
「創意」就是發明、成長、冒險、打破成規、犯錯和享受。

🐦 The worst is a fashion designer who talks all the time about their **creativity**. Stop talking and do it. (Karl Lagerfeld, Designer)
只會成天討論他們創意的設計師是最糟的。不要再說了，動手做吧。

6. criticism [ˈkrɪtɪsɪzəm] *n.* [C] 評論、批評 criticisms

🐦 One learns to ignore **criticism** by first learning to ignore clapping. (Robert Brault, Opera Singer)
人想要學會忽略批評前，要先學會忽略讚美。

🐦 All of us could take a lesson from the weather. It pays no attention to **criticism**.
我們都應該跟天氣學習。它從不在意他人的批評。

7. curiosity [kjʊrɪˋɑsətɪ] *n.* [U] [C] 好奇（心）、珍奇的人或物 curiosities

🐞 I have no special talents, but I always have **curiousity**. (Albert Einstein, Physicist)
我沒什麼專長，但我一直都保持好奇心。

🐞 First love is only a little foolishness and a lot of **curiosity**. (George Bernard Shaw, Playwright)
初戀不過就是些許的愚蠢加上大量的好奇。

8. deadline [ˋdɛdˌlaɪn] *n.* [C] 截止期限、最後限期 deadlines

🐞 Television filming moves very fast. You don't have time to shoot many takes because there are strict **deadlines**. (Dev Patel, Actor)
拍攝電視節目的步調是很快的，因為有嚴謹的截止期限，你沒有太多的時間可以錄太多鏡頭。（戴夫帕特爾，演員）

🐞 A goal is a dream with a **deadline**. (Napoleon Hill, Author)
「目標」就是有截止期限的夢想。

9. defend [dɪˋfɛnd] *vt. vi.* 保衛、為…辯護 defended defended

🐞 Beautiful girls should know how to **defend** themselves against gentlemen. (Cassandra Clare, Author)
美女們應該知道如何保護自己，避開紳士。

🐞 I will **defend** anyone as long as a client gives me total control and pays in advance. (Edward Bennett Williams, Lawyer)
不管是誰，我都代表辯護，只要他們控制權都給我，而且先付錢。

10. delight [dɪˋlaɪt] *n.* [C][U] 愉快、樂趣 delights *vt. vi.* (使) 高興 delighted delighted

🐞 Love and magic have a great deal in common. They both **delight** the heart and take practice. (Nora Roberts, Author)

「愛」和「魔法」極度相似，兩者都讓人感到愉悅，也都需要練習。

🐞 Unlike other girls, I wore miniskirts back when no fat girls should have, and with total **delight**. (Maeve Binchy, Author)

和其他女孩不同，當人們都認為胖女孩不該穿迷你裙的時候，我就會很愉悅地把它穿上，並感到極度愉悅。

11. demand [dɪˋmænd] *n.* [C][U] 要求、需求 demands； *vt.* 要求

🐞 I act for free, but I **demand** a huge salary for having no private life. (Michelle Pfeiffer, Actress)

我演戲不收錢，但對於失去隱私，我要求高額薪資。

🐞 Fashion is harder than the film industry. You have to constantly produce hit after hit on **demand**. (Tom Ford, Fashion Designer)

時尚產業比電影產業艱難，你必須不斷地根據要求做出熱門商品。

12. departure [dɪˋpartʃɚ] *n.* [U] [C] 出發、離開 departures

🐞 I took a cab to the airport, looked at the **departure** board, and decided to go to Rome right then and there. (Cory Monteith, Actor)

我搭了計程車去機場，看了一下離境飛機登記板，當場決定去羅馬。

🐞 Visits always give pleasure— if not the arrival, the **departure**.

拜訪總是令人愉悅。就算不是到達的時候感到快樂，離開的時候也會。

13. deserve [dɪˋzɝv] *vt. vi.* 該得、應受賞（罰） deserved deserved

🐾 If you can't handle me at my worst, then you sure as hell don't **deserve** me at my best. (Marilyn Monroe, Actress)
如果你不能接受我最糟的時刻，那你肯定也沒資格我對你展現最好的一面。

🐾 I don't **deserve** any attention. There's nothing but one movie audition that separates me from 2,000 other brown-haired, blue-eyed guys in L.A. (Zac Efron, Actor)
我不值得任何矚目，我與在洛杉磯其他兩千名棕髮碧眼的男人不過就差在一場電影試鏡。

14. desperate [ˋdɛspərɪt] *adj.* 情急拼命的、絕望的

🐾 She's like the white crayon in the box, **desperate** for attention.
她就像在盒子裡的白色蠟筆，渴望得到矚目。

🐾 Do you know how **desperate** and bored I was today? I almost cleaned the house. (Gabrielle Solis, TV Character)
你知道我今天有多無聊嗎？我差點就要整理家裡了。（嘉百莉索利斯，電視劇角色）

15. despite [dɪˋspaɪt] *prep.* 儘管、任憑

🐾 For some reason, bad boys attract attention **despite** the fact that they are jerks. (Alexis Bledel, Actress)
不知道為什麼，壞男人就是能吸引人的注意，即使他們都是渾蛋。

🐾 Hope is being able to see that there is light **despite** all of the darkness. (Desmond Tutu, Leader)
希望即使在黑暗中仍舊能看見光明。

Unit 7

扭轉劣勢

趣味字彙表

1.	devote *vt.* 將……奉獻（給）	8.	distribute *vt.* 分發、分配
2.	digest *vt. vi.* 消化（食物）	9.	dominate *vt. vi.* 支配、統治
3.	diploma *n.* [C] 畢業文憑、學位證書	10.	download *vt.* 下載
4.	diplomat *n.* [C] 外交官、處事圓滑機敏的人	11.	dread *vt. vi.* 懼怕、擔心
5.	disadvantage *n.* [C] 不利條件	12.	drift *vt. vi.* 漂、漸漸趨向、逐漸地睡著了覺
6.	discipline *n.* [U] [C] 紀律、學科；*vt.* 懲罰、訓導	13.	durable *adj.* 經久的、耐用的
7.	dismiss *vt.* 把……打發走、徹底忘掉	14.	dynamic *adj.* 動態的、有活力的、力（學）的
8.	distinguish *vt. vi.* 區別		

趣味字彙句 🎧🎧 ➤ 💿MP3 07

1. devote [dɪˋvot] *vt.* 將……奉獻（給） devoted devoted

🐌 One of the nicest things about life is the way we regularly stop and **devote** ourselves to eating. (Luciano Pavarotti, Musician)
生命中美好的事物之一就是我們偶爾會停下腳步，然後專注於「吃」。

🐌 If you **devote** yourself to being more than just a man, you can change history. (Henri Ducard, Movie Character)
如果你致力於不是只當「一個人」，你就可以改變歷史。

2. digest [daɪˋdʒɛst] *vt. vi.* 消化（食物） digested, digested

🐌 A heart can't be forced to love, just like a stomach can't be forced to **digest** food. (Alfred Nobel, Chemist)
我們無法強迫我們的心去愛，如同我們無法強迫我們的胃去消化食物。

🐌 The reason honey is so easy to digest is because it's already been **digested** by a bee.
蜂蜜之所以好消化，是因為蜜蜂已經先消化過了。

3. diploma [dɪˋplomə] *n.* [C] 畢業文憑，學位證書 diplomas

🐌 Now that I have my **diploma**, I would prefer a job with unlimited internet, cupcakes, and coffee.
既然現在我已經有文憑了，我希望我的工作能提供無限上網、杯子蛋糕和咖啡。

🐌 I would like to thank Google, Wikipedia, and Microsoft Word for my **diploma**.
能拿到文憑，我必須感謝谷歌、維基百科和微軟 Word 軟體。

4. diplomat [ˈdɪpləmæt] *n.* [C] 外交官、處事圓滑機敏的人 diplomats

🐸 A **diplomat** can tell you to go to hell and make you look forward to the trip. (Caskie Stinnett, Travel Writer and Magazine Editor)
一個處事圓滑的人即使叫你下地獄，都可以讓你感到期待。

🐸 A **diplomat** is a man who remembers a woman's birthday but never remembers her age. (Robert Frost, Poet)
一個處事圓滑的人會記得女人的生日，而遺忘她的年紀。

5. disadvantage [dɪsədˈvæntɪdʒ] *n.* [C] 不利條件 disadvantages

🐸 Do you know what's funny? I never thought of being blind and black as **disadvantages**. (Stevie Wonder, Singer)
你知道有趣的是甚麼嗎？我從不覺得身為盲人與黑種人帶給我劣勢。

🐸 As an actress, being beautiful is actually a **disadvantage** because there are not many interesting roles. (Tuppence Middleton, Actress)
身為女演員，如果長得漂亮反而處於劣勢，因為你沒辦法找到太多有趣的角色。

6. discipline [ˈdɪsɪplɪn] *n.* [U] [C] 紀律、學科 disciplines； *vt.* 懲罰、訓導 disciplined disciplined

🐸 The problem is that I eat everything. I don't have any **discipline** when it comes to Caribbean food. (Ricky Martin, Singer)
問題在於我甚麼都吃。面對加勒比海料理，我毫無紀律。

🐸 The best way to **discipline** your kids is to change the Wi-Fi password.
處罰小孩最好的方式，就是更改無線上網的密碼。

7. dismiss [dɪsˈmɪs] *vt.* 把……打發走、徹底忘掉 dismissed dismissed

🛒 As a former street performer, I know what it means to spend eight hours a day practicing something that people just walk by and **dismiss**. (Penn Jillette, Magician)

因為之前當過街頭藝人，所以我知道一天花八小時練習某個東西，而人們根本路過也不會看的感覺是什麼。（潘恩朱列鐵，魔術師）

🛒 I tend to **dismiss** movies that are only good once. I like movies that get better the more you watch them. (Drew Goddard, Director)

我不太看只有第一次讓你覺得好看的電影，我喜歡越看越好看的電影。

8. distinguish [dɪˈstɪŋgwɪʃ] *vt. vi.* 區別 distinguished distinguished

🛒 I don't **distinguish** between being laughed with, and laughed at. I'll take either. (David Sedaris, Comedian)

我不去區分「和我一起笑」跟「嘲笑我」。兩個我都可以接受。

🛒 Healthy human eyes can **distinguish** 17,000 different colors.

健康的人眼可以區分一萬七千種顏色。

9. distribute [dɪˈstrɪbjʊt] *vt.* 分發；分配 distributed distributed

🛒 The actor, Jake Gyllenhaal, helped **distribute** eyeglasses to poor people overseas.

演員傑克葛倫霍協助捐贈眼鏡到貧窮國家。

🛒 Oprah has **distributed** farm animals and training resources to developing countries.

歐普拉捐贈農場動物與訓練資源到發展中國家。

Part 1 「趣」你的單字基礎篇

Part 2 「趣」你的單字進階篇

10. dominate [ˈdɑməˌnet] *vt. vi.* 支配，統治 dominated dominated

🐏 Before every show, I have to put perfume on. When I smell good, I feel like I can **dominate** the room. (Rita Ora, Singer)

每次表演前，我都要噴香水。只要我聞起來很香，我就覺得我可以掌控全場。

🐏 If Shaq can **dominate** the NBA for 19 years using his body, why can't I dominate the music industry for 50 years using my brain? (Rico Love, Musician)

如果俠客（歐尼爾）可以用身體主導 NBA 十九年，為什麼我不能用大腦主導音樂界五十年？

11. download [ˈdaʊnˌlod] *vt.* 下載 downloaded downloaded

🐏 If we all go to prison for **downloading** music, I hope they group us by the music we like.

如果我們都要因為下載音樂被關，那我希望他們能依據我們的音樂喜好分區。

🐏 It is silly go to a restaurant, take pictures of my food, **download** them, and call that a blog. (Jonathan Dee, Novelist)

上餐廳、幫食物拍照、下載照片，然後說這是部落格，這種行為真是愚蠢。

12. dread [drɛd] *vt. vi.* 懼怕、擔心 dreaded dreaded

🐏 I always **dreaded** becoming an inactive passenger in life. (Princess Margaret of England)

我恐懼當一個生命旅程中被動的乘客。

🐏 The moment you **dread** the most, seeing yourself bald, is actually not such a bad moment. (Sylvie Meis, TV Host/Model)

人們最害怕的時刻一看到自己禿頭，其實並沒那麼糟。

13. drift [drɪft] *vt. vi.* 漂、漸漸趨向、逐漸地睡著了覺 drifted drifted

🐸 If I could eat whatever I wanted, I would have pizza with pasta inside every slice. Then, I would **drift** off telling myself that it's okay because I'm going to workout tomorrow. (Robert Downey Jr., Actor)

如果我可以隨便吃，那我想吃每片都夾義大利麵的披薩。然後我會一面入睡，一面告訴自己沒關係，我明天會去運動。

🐸 Most couples **drift** apart because of comparisons. (Sonam Kapoor, Actress)

大部分情侶的感情會因為比較而漸漸變淡。

14. durable [ˈdjʊrəbl̩] *adj.* 經久的、耐用的

🐸 Vampires have always been hot. They are one of the most **durable** monsters. (Justin Cronin, Author)

吸血鬼向來都很熱門。他們是最不會過時的怪物。

🐸 People are too **durable**. They can do too much by themselves, and they last too long. (Bertolt Brecht, Poet)

人太耐用了。他們自己能做的太多，而且活太久。

15. dynamic [daɪˈnæmɪk] *adj.* 動態的、有活力的、力（學）的

🐸 I cannot say that Korean musicians are the best in the world, but they are really **dynamic** and lively. (Psy, Singer)

我不能說韓國藝人是世界最厲害的，但他們真的多變又有活力。

🐸 Always point your finger at the chest of the person with whom you are being photographed. You will appear **dynamic**, and no editor can crop you from the picture. (Ken Auletta, Writer)

記得拍照的時候，手指要指著跟你一起拍照的人的胸口，這樣你才顯得活潑，而且編輯也無法把你切掉。

Unit 8

面對現實

趣味字彙表

1.	earnest *adj.* 誠摯的、熱心的	9.	encounter *vt. vi.* 遭遇困難或危險、偶然遇見
2.	economical *adj.* 經濟的、節儉的	10.	enormous *adj.* 巨大的、龐大的
3.	efficiency *n.* [U] 效率、效能	11.	enthusiasm *n.* [C][U] 熱情、熱忱
4.	elegant *adj.* 雅致的、優美的	12.	envious *adj.* 嫉妒的、羨慕的
5.	eliminate *vt.* 排除、消除	13.	errand *n.* [C] 差事
6.	email *n.* [U] [C] 電子郵件	14.	essay *n.* [C] 論說文、散文、隨筆
7.	embarrass *vt.* 使不好意思、使感到尷尬	15.	essential *adj.* 必要的、不可缺的
8.	emerge *vi.* 浮現、出現		

趣味字彙句 🎧 ⚫ *MP3 08*

1. earnest [ˋɜnɪst] *adj.* 誠摯的、熱心的

🐛 Some **earnest** person is always telling you to keep your knees bent? (Dave Barry, Football Player)
總是有熱心的人告訴你膝蓋要保持彎曲。

🐛 In Los Angeles, people dress with the deep and **earnest** hope that people will do nothing but stare at them. (Ellie Kemper, Actress)
在洛杉磯，人們深刻且真誠地希望自己當天的穿著要能讓路人盯著他們看。

2. economical [ikəˋnɑmɪkl̩] *adj.* 經濟的、節儉的

🐛 Middle age is when a guy keeps turning off lights for **economical** rather than romantic reasons. (Lillian Gordy Carter)
「中年」就是當男人是為了節省而不是浪漫，不斷關掉電燈。

🐛 Every man wants a wife who is beautiful, understanding, **economical**, and a good cook, but the law allows only one wife.
每個男人都希望找到的老婆既美麗、善解人意、不會亂花錢，還很會煮飯，可惜法律規定只能娶一個老婆。

3. efficiency [ɪˋfɪʃənsɪ] *n.*[U] 效率、效能

🐛 **Efficiency** is the smart kind of laziness. (David Dunham)
「效率」是一種聰明的懶惰方式。

🐛 When I am told that I would never make a film on time and on budget, I turn into a powerful force of **efficiency**.
當人家說我絕對沒辦法在期限或預算內完成電影製作，我就會變得很有效率。

4. elegant [ˈɛləgənt] *adj.* 雅緻的、優美的

🐛 An **elegant** woman thinks about how they decorate their house, who they surround themselves with, what books they read, and what their interests are. (Carolina Herrera, Fashion Designer)
優雅的女性會思考如何裝飾她們的房子，該和怎樣的人往來，讀什麼書，自己的興趣是什麼。

🐛 An **elegant** woman knows not only how to be noticed, but also how to be remembered. (Giorgio Armani, Fashion Designer)
優雅的女性不但知道如何引起注意，也知道怎樣能被記住。

5. eliminate [ɪˈlɪməˌnet] *vt.* 排除、消除 eliminated eliminated

🐛 If we **eliminate** risk from our lives, the sad thing is that you also eliminate the future. (Ziad K. Abdelnour, Financier)
假設我們將風險從生命中移除，未來也跟著被移除了，這是很可惜的。

🐛 Can you imagine opening a bottle of champagne with a bottle opener? I can't, it would **eliminate** all the fun!
可以想像用開瓶器打開一瓶香檳嗎？我不行。這樣就不好玩了嘛！

6. email [ˈiˌmel] *n.* [U] [C] 電子郵件 emails

🐛 Men will not read **emails** from women that are over 200 words. (Douglas Coupland, Novelist)
女人如果寄來超過兩百字的電子郵件，男人是不會看的。

🐛 Any **email** that contains the word 'important' never are, and annoy me to the point of not replying. (Markus Persson, Video Game Designer)
所有標注「重要」的電子郵件向來都不重要，而且讓我厭煩到不想回覆。

7. embarrass [ɪmˈbærəs] *vt.* 使不好意思、使感到尷尬

🐛 My grandmother used to **embarrass** me when she picked me up from school wearing a big fuzzy hat. (Adam Sandler, Actor)
我的奶奶以前會戴一頂大毛帽來學校接我，這讓我覺得很丟臉。

🐛 I had many nicknames: V, Nessa, Nessy, and Van. Only my parents call me Van, and I get **embarrassed**. (Vanessa Hudgens, Actress)
我有過很多綽號：V、妮莎、小妮西、凡。只有我父母會叫我「凡」，我都會覺得很丟臉。

8. emerge [ɪˈmɜːdʒ] *vi.* 浮現、出現 emerged emerged

🐛 If you dress up, it helps your personality to **emerge** — if you choose well. (Vivienne Westwood, Fashion Designer)
打扮自己會幫助展露你的個性，如果你有好好選的話。

🐛 Unlike previous first ladies who seemed to wear a uniform, Michelle Obama likes fashion and **emerging** designers. (Anna Wintour, Editor-In-Chief of Vogue)
以前的第一夫人看起來都像穿制服，蜜雪兒歐巴馬就不一樣，她喜歡時尚與新興設計師。

9. encounter [ɪnˈkaʊntə] *vt. vi.* 遭遇困難或危險、偶然遇見

🐛 A business plan won't survive its first **encounter** with reality. The reality will always be different, and the plan has to be changed. (Jeff Bezos, Amazon CEO)
生意計畫在碰到現實後，通常無法倖存。現實會變，計畫一定要跟著做調整。

🐛 I **encountered** coyotes while driving around or returning from clubbing. (Dan Gilroy, Screenwriter)
我開車兜風或是從夜店回家的路上都會遇到郊狼。

Part 1 「趣」你的單字基礎篇

Part 2 「趣」你的單字進階篇

10. enormous [ɪˈnɔrməs] *adj.* 巨大的、龐大的

- Behind every working woman is an **enormous** pile of unwashed laundry.
  在每個成功的職場女性背後，是一堆還沒洗的衣服。

- I don't understand why American kitchens are so **enormous** when they just order pizza. (Marina Abramovic, Performance Artist)
  我不懂美國的廚房為什麼要做那麼大，他們不都是訂披薩來吃。

11. enthusiasm [ɪnˈθjuziˌæzəm] *n.* [C][U] 熱情、熱忱 enthusiasms

- Dogs have so much **enthusiasm** and no shame. I should have a dog as my life coach. (Moby, Musician)
  狗兒充滿熱情而且完全不怕丟臉。我應該請狗當我的生活導師。

- My husband's **enthusiasm** about wine and food helped me to discover my tastes. (Julia Child, Chef)
  我先生對酒與食物的熱情幫助我發現自己的品味。

12. envious [ˈɛnvɪəs] *adj.* 嫉妒的、羨慕的

- I get **envious** of actors. They can walk into a club and they are surrounded by girls in two seconds. (Claire Danes, Actress)
  我有時很羨慕男演員，他們一走進夜店，兩秒內就會被女人包圍。

- I am always **envious** of Johnny Depp's style. If I wore big hats and long coats, I'd look like a homeless person. (Stephen Merchant, Writer)
  我一直很羨慕強尼戴普的造型。如果我戴大帽子，穿長外套，看起來肯定像個流浪漢。

13. errand [ˈɛrənd] *n.* [C] 差事 errands

- I want to spend my time doing **errands** and having arguments. In other words, I want to get married. (Jarod Kintz, Author)

  我想把時間花在做家事跟吵架上，換句話說，我想結婚。

- Any kid will run an **errand** for you, if you ask at bedtime. (Red Skelton, Entertainer)

  任何一個孩子都會很樂意幫你跑腿，如果你是在睡覺時間問他們的話。

14. essay [ˈɛse] *n.* [C] 論說文、散文、隨筆 essays

- When I was ten, I wrote an **essay** on what I would be when I grew up, and said I would be a soccer player and a comedian on the side. (Will Ferrell, Actor)

  我十歲的時候，寫了一篇散文，是關於長大後的夢想，我說我以後想當足球選手，兼差當喜劇演員。

- It takes me forever to finish a ten-page **essay**, but I love it when I finish. It's a confusing relationship. (Chris Abani, Author)

  我寫一篇十頁的散文都會拖很久，但我又很愛寫完的感覺。這是一種令人困惑的關係。

15. essential [ɪˈsɛnʃəl] *adj.* 必要的、不可缺的

- Nothing brings me more happiness than helping those in need. It is a goal and an **essential** part of my life. (Princess Diana of Wales)

  幫助需要幫忙的人帶給我最大的快樂，這是我的目標，也是我生命很重要的一部份。

- Disappointment, although painful at times, is a very positive and **essential** part of success. (Bo Bennett, Former United States Senator)

  失望雖然令人痛苦，卻是成功很正面且重要的一部份。

Unit 9

思考的重要性

趣味字彙表

1.	establish *vt.* 建立、確立	9.	faithful *adj.* 忠實的、忠誠的、忠貞的
2.	evidence *n.* [C][U] 證據、證詞、跡象	10.	fame *n.* [U] 聲譽、名望
3.	exaggerate *vt.* *vi.* 誇張、誇大	11.	fantastic *adj.* 想像中的、【口】極好的
4.	exception *n.* [C] 例外、例外的人或事	12.	fantasy *n.* [U] [C] 空想、幻想
5.	expand *vt.* *vi.* 展開、張開	13.	farewell *n.* [U] [C] 告別、告別辭
6.	explore *vt.* *vi.* 探測、探勘	14.	fierce *adj.* 兇猛的、殘酷的、激烈的
7.	expose *vt.* 揭露、使暴露於、使接觸到	15.	finance *n.* [U] 財政、金融；*vt.* *vi.* 供資、籌措資金
8.	facial *adj.* 臉的、表面的		

趣味字彙句 👂 🎧 **MP3 09**

1. establish [ə`stæblɪʃ] *vt.* 建立、確立 established established

🐝 Heroes need monsters to **establish** themselves as heroes. (Margaret Atwood, Poet)
英雄需要怪獸來把自己塑造成英雄。

🐝 I began wearing hats as a young lawyer because it helped me to **establish** my position. Before that, people would always ask me to get coffee. (Bella Abzug, Lawyer)
剛當律師的時候，我開始戴帽子來建立我的地位。在這之前，大家常常叫我端咖啡來。

2. evidence [`ɛvədəns] *n.* [C][U] 證據、證詞、跡象 evidences

🐝 A bookstore is one of the only pieces of **evidence** we have that people are still thinking. (Jerry Seinfeld, Comedian)
書店是唯一能顯示人們其實還有在思考的證據。

🐝 Really know yourself. Just because your dog admires you, it is not strong **evidence** that you are wonderful. (Ann Landers, Columnist)
要真的去了解自己。你的狗對你的崇拜，並不太能證明你真的很棒。

3. exaggerate [ɪg`zædʒəˌret] *vt. vi.* 誇張、誇大

🐝 Young men may **exaggerate**, but old men pretend.
年輕人或許容易誇大，但老人很會裝。

🐝 I learned how to be a better actor after five years in Hollywood. I learned how to be natural and never to **exaggerate**. (Walter Huston, Actor)
在好萊塢待五年後，我學會怎麼當一個更好的演員，我學會如何保持自然，然後不要太誇張。

4. exception [ɪkˈsɛpʃən] *n.* [C] 例外、例外的人或事 exceptions

- I really prefer personal gifts or ones made by someone for me. Except diamonds, that's the **exception** to the rule. (Minnie Driver, Actress)
  我真的比較喜歡個人化的禮物或是人家親手為我做的禮物，除了鑽石，這是唯一的例外。

- I think a lot of people secretly wish they were a rock star, and I'm no **exception**. (Cindy Crawford, Model)
  我覺得很多人私底下都希望自己是搖滾歌手，我也不例外。

5. expand [ɪkˈspænd] *vt. vi.* 展開、張開 expanded expanded

- Pets, like their owners, eat a lot and **expand** a little over Christmas. (Frances Wright, Writer)
  寵物，跟他們主人一樣，聖誕節時，吃很多，然後身體因此膨脹了一點。

- You can always change a big plan, but you can never **expand** a little plan. I don't believe in little plans. (Harry S Truman, President)
  你總有辦法修改大計畫，但你無法擴展小計畫。我不相信小計畫。

6. explore [ɪkˈsplor] *vt. vi.* 探測、探勘 explored explored

- Grab your running shoes and go **explore**! (Laura Marano, Actress)
  拿起你的慢跑鞋，去探險吧！

- Women can **explore** so much about fashion but if I were a guy I would constantly wear suits with crazy ties. (Helena Christensen, Actress)
  女人可以試各種服飾，但假如我是男人的話，我只能一直穿西裝配瘋狂的領帶。

7. expose [ɪkˈspoz] *vt.* 揭露、使暴露於、使接觸到 exposed exposed

People think I like to **expose** my body, but I don't. It's just because the dance moves require it. (Shakira, Singer)

人們以為我喜歡暴露我的身體，但其實我並不喜歡，只是舞蹈動作需要。

I'm kind of scared of horror films, but my girlfriend always tries to **expose** me to them. (Chris Carmack, Actor)

我有點怕恐怖片，但我女友總是試著讓我看到它們。

8. facial [ˈfeʃəl] *adj.* 臉的、表面的

The Yankees baseball team has strict rules. You cannot have a lot of **facial** hair. (Derek Jeter, Baseball Player)

洋基棒球隊的規定很嚴格，你不太能留鬍子。

Watch how you communicate with a woman because you are always communicating — with your body language, your **facial** expressions, and your eyes. (Orlando Bloom, Actor)

觀察自己怎麼跟女人溝通，因為你其實隨時都在溝通，無論是用肢體語言、臉部表情或你的眼神。

9. faithful [ˈfeθfəl] *adj.* 忠實的、忠誠的、忠貞的

There are three types of **faithful** friends — an old wife, an old dog, and the money you have. (Benjamin Franklin, Founding Father of the United States)

有三種忠實的朋友：結婚已久的老婆、老狗和你擁有的錢。

It's easier to be **faithful** to a restaurant than it is to a woman. (Federico Fellini, Film Director)

對餐廳忠心比對女人忠心還簡單。

10. fame [fem] *n.* [U] 聲譽、名望

🐘 You can't take back **fame**. You can lose all the money, but you'll never lose people knowing you. (J. Cole, Hip-Hop Artist)
出名後就無法回頭了。你可以甩掉所有的錢,但你無法回到人們不認識你的時候。

🐘 My friends are all really nice about my **fame**, they are just curious and ask lots of questions. (Emma Watson, Actress)
我的朋友對於我的名氣處理得很得當,他們只是好奇,會問很多問題。

11. fantastic [fænˈtæstɪk] *adj.* 想像中的、【口】極好的

🐘 It's about making your own future and my wife Kate will do a **fantastic** job at that. (Prince William, Duke of Cambridge)
自己的未來是要靠自己建立的,而我太太凱特會做得很好。

🐘 Photographers have to make clothes look **fantastic**; that's why we get paid. (Patrick Demarchelier, Photographer)
攝影師要讓服裝看起來令人驚艷,人家付錢就是請我們做這個。

12. fantasy [ˈfæntəsɪ] *n.* [U] [C] 空想、幻想 fantasies

🐘 **Fantasy** is a necessary part of our lives. It allows us to laugh at life's realities. (Dr. Seuss, Writer)
幻想是人生很重要的一部分,它讓我們可以笑著看待人生現實面。

🐘 When I have a bad day, I dream about opening up an ice cream shop. Doesn't everyone have a fun escape **fantasy**? (Nancy Lublin, CEO)
當我心情不好的時候,我就會想像我開了一間冰淇淋店。每個人不都有個有趣的幻想能幫助你逃離一切?

13. farewell [ˈfɛrˋwɛl] *n.* [U] [C] 告別、告別辭 farewells

🐦 Saying **farewell** is necessary before meeting again, and meeting again is certainly for those who are friends. (Richard Bach, Writer)
在相遇之前必須道別，而對朋友來說，再次相遇是必然的。

🐦 How lucky am I to have something that makes saying **farewell** so hard? (Winnie the Pooh, Cartoon Character)
能有東西讓我如此難以說出再見，我真的很幸運。

14. fierce [fɪrs] *adj.* 兇猛的、殘酷的、激烈的

🐦 Although being **fierce** is very cool, I must be a strong person and individual first. (Johnny Weir, Figure Skater)
雖然當個兇狠的人很酷，但我必須先成為一個堅強且獨立的個體。

🐦 My mother influenced me the most. I called her the lion because she's so **fierce** and proud. (Christopher Judge, Actor)
我母親給我的影響很大，我都說她是獅子，因為她總是兇狠且驕傲。

15. finance [faɪˋnæns] *n.* [U] 財政、金融； *vt.* financed financed *vi.* 供資、籌措資金

🐦 Our **finances** are like our shoes. They hurt if they are too small, but cause us to fall if they are too large. (John Lockc, Philosopher)
我們的收入好比我們的鞋，如果太小，會引起疼痛，如果太大，我們會跌倒。

🐦 I collected hats my whole life, but I did not have a lot of **finances**. I would buy really cheap hats from the corner store and wear those to school. (Ne-Yo, Singer)
我一輩子都在蒐集帽子，但其實以前我沒有堅強的財力，我會在轉角商店買很便宜的帽子，然後戴去學校。

Unit 10

快樂開啓幸運之門

趣味字彙表

1.	flatter *vt.* 諂媚、奉承	9.	furious *adj.* 狂怒的、猛烈的
2.	flexible *adj.* 可彎曲的、有彈性的	10.	gallery *n.* [C] 畫廊、美術館
3.	fluent *adj.* 流利的、流暢的	11.	gangster *n.* [C] 流氓
4.	fortunate *adj.* 幸運的、僥倖的	12.	generosity *n.* [U] 寬宏大量、慷慨
5.	fragrance *n.* [C][U] 芬芳、香味	13.	genius *n.* [C] 天資、天才
6.	frown *n.* [C] 皺眉; *vi. vt.* 皺眉	14.	genuine *adj.* 真的、真誠的
7.	frustration *n.* [U] [C] 挫折、失敗	15.	giggle *vt. vi.* 咯咯地笑、傻笑
8.	fundamental *adj.* 基礎的、十分重要的		

趣味字彙句 🎧🎧 ⊙ MP3 10

1. flatter [ˋflætɚ] *vt.* 諂媚、奉承 flattered flattered

When your friends begin to **flatter** you on how young you look, it's a sure sign you're getting old. (Mark Twain, Author)
當你的朋友開始諂媚，說你看起來有多年輕，這很明顯地表示你開始變老了。

Flatter me, and I may not believe you. Ignore me, and I may not forgive you. Love me and I may be forced to love you. (William Arthur Ward, Writer)
對我諂媚，我可能不會相信你。忽略我，我可能不會原諒你。愛我，那我可能會被迫愛上你。

2. flexible [ˋflɛksəbl] *adj.* 可彎曲的、有彈性的

I have extremely **flexible** thumbs. (Laura Mennell, Actress)
我的大拇指很柔軟。

Take your risks now, as you grow older, you become less **flexible**. (Amy Poehler, Actress)
現在就去冒險吧，年紀越大，越不柔韌。

3. fluent [ˋfluənt] *adj.* 流利的、流暢的

I wish I could fly or speak **fluent** Chinese. I think both are equally impossible. (Karlie Kloss, Model)
我真希望我會飛，或是中文很流暢，我想兩者都同樣不可能。

I am just like 99% of my friends in France, who say on their resume they can speak **fluent** English. In reality, they can't even count up to three. (Greg Akcelrod, Footballer)
我和我百分之九十九的法國朋友一樣，履歷寫著英語流利，事實上，連數到三都沒辦法。

4. fortunate [ˈfɔrtʃənɪt] *adj.* 幸運的、僥倖的

You have to fight for your dream, but you also have to feel **fortunate** for what you have. (Cesc Fabregas, Footballer)
你要為了你的夢想打拼，但你也應該對你已擁有的感到幸運。

I was very **fortunate** to play sports. All the anger in me went out. If you stay angry all the time, then you really don't have a good life. (Willie Mays, Baseball Player)
可以打球，我感到很幸運，我內在的怨氣得以抒發。如果你一直處於憤怒的狀態，你是無法過圓滿的生活的。

5. fragrance [ˈfregrəns] *n.* [C][U] 芬芳、香味 fragrances

Happiness is like the **fragrance** from a flower, and it pulls good things towards you. (Maharishi Mahesh Yogi, Guru)
快樂有如花香，讓你得以吸引好事發生在你身上。

If you want someone to miss you, go secretly and spray your **fragrance** somewhere. (Blake Lively, Actress)
如果你希望某人想念你，偷偷的去把你的香水噴在某處。

6. frown [fraʊn] *n.* [C] 皺眉 frowns ； *vi. vt.* 皺眉 frowned, frowned

Botox should be banned for actors. Acting is all about expressions, and **frowns** are a necessity. (Rachel Weisz, Actress)
演員應該被禁止使用肉毒桿菌，演戲最重要的就是表情，而皺眉是必要的。

Beauty comes from a life well lived. If you lived well and your **frown** lines aren't too bad, what more do you need? (Jennifer Garner, Actress)
美麗源自於美滿的生活，如果你有好好過活，抬頭紋也不深，那你還有何所求？

7. frustration [frʌsˈtreʃən] *n.* [U] [C] 挫折、失敗 frustrations

🐝 Even though **frustration** is quite painful at times, it is an important part of success. (Bo Bennett, CEO)
雖然挫折有時令人痛苦，但它卻是成功很重要的一部份。

🐝 Don't give up because of your **frustrations**.
不要因為挫折而放棄。

8. fundamental [fʌndəˈmɛntl̩] *adj.* 基礎的、十分重要的

🐝 The most **fundamental** thing about leadership is to be humble enough to continue to get feedback and try to get better. (Jim Yong Kim, Physician)
身為領導者最重要的便是，能謙虛詢問意見，並試著改進。

🐝 Love and hate is **fundamental**. Everyone hates reality television, and everyone's watching it. (Bo Burnham, Comedian)
愛與恨都是基本的。大家都討厭實境電視節目，然而大家都看。

9. furious [ˈfjʊərɪəs] *adj.* 狂怒的、猛烈的

🐝 I accidentally set the kitchen on fire while writing a song. My boyfriend was **furious,** but it was worth it for a song. (Jill Scott, Musician)
我有一次在寫歌，害廚房起火，我男友非常生氣，但為了一首歌，這一切都值得。

🐝 I was always into fashion, and I would shop a lot. My father was **furious**, but I would always say that it was a party emergency. (Carmen Busquets, Fashion Entrepreneur)
我向來都很喜歡時尚，我買很多，而我的父親都會很生氣，但我都跟他說這是為了臨時有派對準備的。

10. gallery [ˈgælərɪ] *n.* [C] 畫廊、美術館 galleries

🐛 If you make bread in a **gallery**, you're an artist. So environment determines what we do. (Marina Abramovic, Performance Artist)
如果你在藝廊做麵包，你就是藝術家，所以環境決定了我們做的是什麼。）

🐛 When I go to an art **gallery**, I want to feel whatever I feel, see whatever I see, and figure out what I figure out. (James Frey)
當我去藝廊的時候，我希望能感受我所感受到的，看到我所看到的，理解出我所理解的。

11. gangster [ˈgæŋstɚ] *n.* [C] 流氓 gangsters

🐛 We had an apartment in New York with very reasonable rent. We found out later that it belonged to a **gangster** named Legs Diamond. (James Stewart, Film Actor)
我們在紐約有間公寓，租金很合理，我們後來才發現公寓為幫派成員雷葛斯戴蒙所有。

🐛 Excuse me, **gangster**? Your pants are falling and your underwear is showing.
流氓，不好意思，你的褲子要掉了，內褲都露出來了。

12. generosity [dʒɛnəˈrɑsətɪ] *n.* [U] 寬宏大量、慷慨

🐛 A couple showed **generosity** by tipping a waiter one hundred dollars for terrible service.
一對情侶展現了他們的慷慨，給了一位服務很不好的服務生一百元美金的小費。

🐛 A dry cleaning shop that offers free dry cleaning for unemployed people going on job interviews is known for its **generosity**.
一間乾洗店的慷慨廣為人知，他們為要去面試的失業人士提供免費的乾洗服務。

13. genius [ˋdʒinjəs] *n.* [C] 天資、天才 geniuses

🛒 The man who invented the hamburger was smart, but the man who invented the cheeseburger was a **genius**. (Matthew McConaughey, Actor)

發明漢堡的人很聰明，但發明起司堡的人是天才。

🛒 Everyone is a **genius**. But if you judge a fish on how well it climbs a tree, it will live its whole life thinking that it is stupid. (Albert Einstein, Physicist)

每個人都是天才。但如果你想要以樹爬得好不好為標準來判斷一隻魚，那牠一輩子都會覺得自己很笨。

14. genuine [ˋdʒɛnjʊɪn] *adj.* 真的、真誠的

🛒 Love is many things, but it never lies. Nothing poisonous comes from **genuine** love.

愛代表很多東西，但它絕不說謊。真誠的愛絕對不會產出有害的東西。

🛒 When anything becomes routine, there's a value lost. Always be **genuine** in your approach, and let good things come.

當事情變成例行公事，便會有價值流失。確定自己的做事方式一直都真誠，讓好事發生。

15. giggle [ˋgɪgl] *vt. vi.* 咯咯地笑、傻笑 giggled giggled

🛒 I'm training to become a **giggle** doctor. It's a kind of hospital clown who makes patients laugh to help them get better. (Nina Conti, Actress)

我在受訓成為一位笑聲醫生，那是一種讓病人發笑以恢復病情的醫院小丑。

🛒 Anything that makes you **giggle**, smile, or laugh, buy it or marry it!

看到任何讓你傻笑、微笑或大笑的事物，買它，不然就跟它結婚！

Unit 11

追尋內在的平靜

趣味字彙表

1.	graceful *adj.* 優美的、雅緻的	9.	guarantee *n.* [C][U] 保證（書）
2.	graduation *n.* [C][U] 畢業（典禮）	10.	handwriting *n.* [U] 書寫、筆跡
3.	grammar *n.* [U] 文法	11.	hardship *n.* [U] [C] 艱難、困苦
4.	gratitude *n.* [U] 感激之情、感恩	12.	habitual *adj.* 習慣的、慣常的
5.	greasy *adj.* 油膩的	13.	harmony *n.* [U] 和睦、融洽
6.	guilt *n.* [U] 犯罪、過失	14.	harsh *adj.* 粗糙的、嚴厲的
7.	greeting *n.* [C][U] 問候、招呼	15.	helicopter *n.* [C] 直升飛機
8.	grief *n.* [U] 悲痛、悲傷		

趣味字彙句 🎧 MP3 11

1. graceful [ˋgresfəl] *adj.* 優美的、雅緻的

🐝 The trick is to be thankful when your mood is high and **graceful** when it is low. (Richard Carlson, Author)

秘訣就是當心情很好的時候,保持感恩,而當心情不好的時候,保持優雅。

🐝 There's a trick to a **graceful** exit. Recognize when a job, a relationship, a life stage is over and let it go. (Ellen Goodman)

要優雅地離開是有秘訣的,要承認工作、感情或人生的某一階段已告一段落並放手。

2. graduation [grædʒʊˋeʃən] *n.* [C][U] 畢業(典禮) graduations

🐝 I learned law so well. The day after **graduation**, I sued the college and won, and got my money back. (Fred Allen, Comedian)

我法律學得很好。畢業隔天,我告了學校,贏了,並把我的錢拿了回來。

🐝 For many, **graduation** marks the end of long spring breaks and of thinking that a 10 am class is too early. (Alexa Von Tobel)

對很多人來說,畢業等於失去為期頗長的春假,也無法再有「十點的課太早」這種想法。

3. grammar [ˋgræmɚ] *n.* [U] 文法

🐝 Ladies, the way to my heart is good spelling and good **grammar**. (John Mayer, Singer)

女士們,要贏得我的心,只需要拼字與文法正確。

🐝 On a first date, I said the wrong word and someone corrected my **grammar**. (Reese Witherspoon, Actress)

在一次的初次約會,我說錯字,而某人糾正我。

4. gratitude [ˈgrætəˌtjud] *n.* [U] 感激之情、感恩

🐦 **Gratitude** is one of the sweetest shortcuts to finding peace and happiness. (Barry Neil Kaufman, Writer)
感激是找到內在平靜與幸福最甜蜜的捷徑之一。

🐦 A designer is like a doctor for women. If he does his job well, he will have the **gratitude** of women for the rest of his life. (Oleg Cassini, Fashion Designer)
設計師就像女人的醫生，如果做得好，女人一輩子都會感激他。

5. greasy [ˈgrizɪ] *adj.* 油膩的

🐦 You can enjoy **greasy** fried butter, beer, and burgers at fairs in America.
在美國市集你可以享用到炸奶油、啤酒及漢堡。

🐦 One of the **greasiest** foods in America is a 7 pound burrito made from seven potatoes, twelve eggs, and a pound of ham.
美國最油膩的食物之一是一種由七顆馬鈴薯、十二顆蛋和一磅的火腿所做成的，重達七磅的墨西哥捲餅。

6. guilt [gɪlt] *n.* [U] 犯罪、過失

🐦 I got a huge, expensive flower arrangement from someone I didn't like, who sent it out of **guilt**. I hated it. (Maeve Binchy, Author)
我曾經從一位我不喜歡的人那裡收過一大束很貴的插花，他是因為愧疚才送花給我，而我恨透了那束花。

🐦 **Guilt** is feeling bad about what you have done and shame is feeling bad about who you are. Don't confuse what you've done with who you are. (Marcus Brigstocke, Comedian)
「罪惡感」是為你的所為感到愧疚，而「羞愧」是對你自身感到愧疚，不要混淆你的所為與你的為人。

7. greeting [grit ɪ ŋ] *n.* [C][U] 問候、招呼 greetings

🐛 Don't tell your friends about your love problems. 'How are you' is used as a **greeting**, it's not a question (Arthur Guiterman, Comedian)

請不要跟你的朋友說戀愛上的困擾，「你好嗎」只是打招呼，並不是個問題。

🐛 I've always acted like a 13 year old girl when **greeting** Justin Bieber. I can't help it. (Anderson Cooper, Journalist)

每次跟小賈斯汀打招呼的時候，我總是表現得像個十三歲的少女，我無法控制自己。

8. grief [grif] *n.* [U] 悲痛、悲傷

🐛 **Grief** is the price we pay for love. (Queen Elizabeth II)

悲痛是我們因愛必須付出的代價。

🐛 **Grief** and sadness brings two hearts closer than happiness ever can; and common sufferings are far stronger than common joys. (Alphonse De Lamarline, Writer)

悲痛與傷心比快樂更能讓兩顆心靠得更近，而共患難比同樂的作用更強烈。

9. guarantee [ˌgærənˋti] *n.* [C][U] 保證（書）guarantees

🐛 The best way to **guarantee** a loss is to quit. (Morgan Freeman)

保證失敗的最好方法就是放棄。

🐛 Invest three percent of your income to develop yourself, in order to **guarantee** a bright future. (Brian Tracey, Author)

把百分之三十的收入用來投資自己，可以保證自己有個明亮的未來。

10. handwriting [ˈhænd͵raɪtɪŋ] *n.* [U] 書寫、筆跡

🐧 As a person with terrible **handwriting**, I love the computer. I've waited all my life for the computer. (Janet Finch, Sociologist/Professor)

身為一個字醜的人，我愛電腦，我等電腦等了好久。

🐧 I don't have bad **handwriting**. I just have my own font.

不是我字寫得醜，我不過是用我自己的字體而已。

11. hardship [ˈhɑrdʃɪp] *n.* [U] [C] 艱難、困苦 hardships

🐧 There is beauty within **hardship**. The prettiest eyes have cried the most, and the kindest hearts have felt the most pain.

艱困中是有美麗的事物的，最美的雙眼總是哭過最多的，最善良的心是感受過最多痛苦的。

🐧 Handle **hardships** like a dog. If you can't eat it or play with it, just pee on it and walk away.

學狗處理困難的方法吧，如果沒辦法吃它或跟它玩，就對它尿尿，然後走開。

12. habitual [həˈbɪtʃʊəl] *adj.* 習慣的、慣常的

🐧 Friendship is the **habitual** desire in two people to promote the good and happiness of one another. (Eustace Budgell, English Politician)

友誼是兩個人之間慣有的渴望，要讓彼此更好、更快樂。

🐧 Meaningless **habitual** behavior is the enemy of new ideas. (Rosabeth Moss Kanter, Harvard Business School Professor)

無意義的習慣是創意的敵人。

13. harmony [ˈhɑrmənɪ] *n.* [U] 和睦、融洽

🐸 What is happiness except the simple **harmony** between a man and the life he leads? (Albert Camus, Author)
快樂就是人與自己的生活間簡單的和諧。

🐸 A wise woman recognizes when her life is out of balance and corrects it. Happiness is a life lived in **harmony**. (Suze Orman)
聰明的女人會看出自己的生活是否已失去平衡，並予以矯正。快樂就是過著和諧的生活。

14. harsh [hɑrʃ] *adj.* 粗糙的、嚴厲的

🐸 Experience is a **harsh** teacher. He gives tests first and then the lessons.
經驗是個嚴苛的老師。它先給你考試，然後再幫你上課。

🐸 Keep the friend who tells you the **harsh** truth, wanting ten times more to tell you a loving lie. (Robert Brault, Author)
會把殘酷的事實告訴你的朋友要留下來，並找十倍多的朋友來告訴你出自愛的謊言。

15. helicopter [ˈhɛlɪkɑptɚ] *n.* [C] 直升飛機 helicopters

🐸 My business partner gave me a small **helicopter** that I can control with my iPhone. I have great fun flying it around the gardens in Portugal. (Christian Louboutin, Fashion Designer)
我生意上的夥伴給我一台可以用 iPhone 控制的小直升機，我會在葡萄牙的花園裡開它，因此得到很多樂趣。

🐸 I do about 90 percent of my own stunts expect for the things I can't do for safety reasons, like jumping out of a flying **helicopter**. (LL Cool J, Rapper/Actor)
百分之九十的特技我都是自己上場，除非因為安全問題無法自己做，例如要從飛行中的直升機跳下來。

Unit 12

心中有夢最好

趣味字彙表

1.	hesitation *n.*[U] [C] 躊躇、猶豫	9.	idle *adj.* 閒置的、懶惰的
2.	honeymoon *n.* [C] 蜜月（假期）	10.	idol *n.* [C] 偶像
3.	hopeful *adj.* 充滿希望的	11.	ignorant [ˈɪgnərənt] adj. 無知的
4.	horrify *vt.* 使恐懼	12.	imaginary *adj.* 虛構的、幻想的
5.	housewife *n.* [C] 家庭主婦	13.	imitate *vt.* 模仿、仿效
6.	humidity *n.* [U] 濕氣、濕度	14.	imitation *n.* [U] 模仿、仿造
7.	identical *adj.* 完全相似的	15.	immigrant *n.* [C] （外來）移民
8.	identify *vt. vi.* 確認、確定		

趣味字彙句 🎧 🎧 ⊙ MP3 12

1. hesitation [hɛzəˋteʃən] *n.*[U] [C] 躊躇、猶豫

🔹 If there are any **hesitations** in the fitting room, just walk away. (L'Wren Scott)

如果在試衣間裡感到猶豫，就走開。

🔹 Act boldly and prepare for consequences. No good is ever done in this world by **hesitation**. (Thomas Huxley, Biologist)

大膽地去做，然後對後果有所準備，世上沒有好事是因為猶豫而產生的。

2. honeymoon [ˋhʌnɪˏmun] *n.* [C] 蜜月（假期） honeymoons

🔹 I danced so crazily that I hurt my knees. The next morning, I had to use a wheelchair at the airport to go on my **honeymoon**. (Casey Wilson)

我跳舞跳得太瘋狂，傷到我的膝蓋。隔天要去度蜜月時，在機場我必須坐輪椅。

🔹 The tans will fade, but the memories from our **honeymoon** will last forever.

曬黑的痕跡會消失，但我們蜜月的記憶卻永存。

3. hopeful [ˋhopfəl] *adj.* 充滿希望的

🔹 To be **hopeful** means to wonder about the future, be open to possibilities, and to be ready to change everything about yourself. (Rebecca Soinit, Writer)

充滿希望表示對未來感到好奇，放開心面對所有可能，並隨時準備改變自己。

🔹 I'm always **hopeful**. I feel like I'm at a party waiting for someone to ask me to dance. (Sarah Dessen, Writer)

我向來都充滿希望。我覺得我像在派對上等待某人邀我共舞。

4. horrify [ˈhɔrəˌfaɪ] *vt.* 使恐懼 horrified horrified

🐾 I think I'm an average-looking guy. Sometimes I look great, and other times I look **horrifying**. (Bradley Cooper, Actor)
我覺得我長相平凡，我有時看起來帥氣，有時看起來很恐怖。

🐾 I did a film once that I was killed in. It was a painful and **horrifying** day. (Leslie Easterbrook, Actress)
有次拍了部電影，在電影中我被殺害，那天真是痛苦且恐怖。

5. housewife [ˈhaʊsˌwaɪf] *n.* [C] 家庭主婦 housewives

🐾 As a **housewife**, I feel that if the kids are still alive when my husband gets home, then I did a good job. (Roseanne Barr, Actress)
身為一位家庭主婦，我認為只要先生到家時小孩還活著，我就算做得很好了。

🐾 I love being a mother but hate being a **housewife**. The cooking and laundry takes away time I could be with my kids. (Marcia Gay Harden, Actress)
我樂於當一位母親，但痛恨當家庭主婦，煮飯和洗衣服剝奪我可以與孩子相處的時間。

6. humidity [hjuˈmɪdətɪ] *n.* [U] 濕氣、濕度

🐾 I'm like a mosquito. I love **humidity**, and I don't sweat. (Shakira, Singer)
我就像蚊子一樣，熱愛潮濕而且不會流汗。

🐾 Books have the same enemies as people: fire, animals, and **humidity**. (Paul Valery, Poet)
書和人有共同的敵人：火、動物及潮溼的天氣。

7. identical [aɪˋdɛntɪkl̩] *adj.* 完全相似的

- I'm glad I have **identical** twin boys because I can save money on photographs. Here's my little boy, and I got another one just like it. (Ray Ramano, Actor)

  我很高興我有長相相似的雙胞胎兒子，因為我可以省照片錢。這個是我的兒子，然後還有另外一個也是長這樣。

- Our days are **identical** boxes. All the same size but some people can pack more into them than others.

  我們的日子都是一樣的箱子，全部的大小都一樣，但有些人就是可以放更多東西在裡面。

8. identify [aɪˋdɛntəˏfaɪ] *vt. vi.* 確認、確定 identified identified

- Every guitar player has something special about their playing. They just have to **identify** and develop it. (Jimmy Page, Musician)

  每個吉他手都有他獨特的彈法，只是需要找出它並持續發展。

- It's easier to **identify** with loss than love, because we had so much more experience of it. (Roger Ebert, Critic)

  認同失去比認同愛更容易，因為我們失去的經驗比較豐富。

9. idle [ˋaɪdl̩] *adj.* 閒置的、懶惰的

- To do something just for money is to be truly **idle**. (Henry David Thoreau, Author)

  只為了錢做事是真正的無所事事。

- I love being on set. The hardest thing for me is dealing with **idle** time, that's when I get in trouble. (Shia LeBeouf, Actor)

  我喜歡到攝影現場，對我來說最痛苦的是面對空閒時間，那是我遇到麻煩的時候。

10. idol [ˈaɪdl̩] *n.* [C] 偶像 idols

🐛 I would love to be a pop **idol** although my fans would now be between 40 and 50 years old. (Kevin Bacon, Actor)
我很想當流行偶像，雖然我的影迷現在都在四十歲到五十歲之間了。

🐛 Every girl creates a dream in her mind; everyone needs an **idol**. (Roberto Cavalli, Fashion Designer)
每個女孩心中都有個夢，每個人都需要一個偶像。

11. ignorant [ˈɪgnərənt] *adj.* 無知的

🐛 We are all born **ignorant**, but one must work hard to remain stupid. (Benjamin Franklin, Founding Father of the United States)
我們生來都是無知的，但維持愚蠢卻要很大的努力。

🐛 It takes a lot of things to prove you are smart, but only one thing to prove you are **ignorant**. (Don Herold, Writer)
證明自己很聰明，需要很多努力，但只需一件事便會證明自己無知。

12. imaginary [ɪˈmædʒəˌnɛrɪ] *adj.* 虛構的、幻想的

🐛 Many children make up **imaginary** languages. I haven't stopped since I could write. (J.R.R. Tolkien, Writer)
很多小孩都會創造自己虛構的語言，我自從會寫字後便沒停過。

🐛 A relationship with an **imaginary** woman is better than a relationship with a real one. (Salman Rushdie, Novelist)
和幻想的女人交往比跟真實的女人交往好多了。

13. imitate [ˈɪmə͵tet] *vt.* 模仿、仿效 imitated imitated

Life doesn't **imitate** art, it imitates bad television. (Woody Allen, Director)
人生不仿效藝術，而是模仿了拙劣的電視節目。

I dress like a doll. I look at doll outfits and **imitate** them. (Taylor Momsen, Actress/Musician)
我把自己打扮得像洋娃娃，我會看洋娃娃的穿著，然後模仿。

14. imitation [ɪməˈteʃən] *n.* [U] 模仿、仿造

Rudeness is a weak person's **imitation** of strength. (Eric Hoffer, Philosopher)
無禮是懦弱的人們試著假裝堅強。

The best **imitation** in the world is not half as good as a poor original. (Luise Rainer, Actress)
世上最好的模仿還不如粗劣的原創一半好。

15. immigrant [ˈɪməgrənt] *n.* [C]（外來）移民 immigrants

My father taught me that **immigrants** must work twice as hard and never give up. (Zinedine Zidane, Footballer)
我的父親教導我，移民必須付出別人兩倍的努力，且永不放棄。

Superman is the greatest **immigrant**. He comes from another world and helps people with his amazing powers. (Bryan Singer, Film Director)
超人是最棒的移民，他來自另一個世界，而且善用他神奇的力量幫助別人。

Unit 13

隨時保持愉快心情

趣味字彙表

1.	impact *n.* [C][U] 衝擊	9.	inspiration *n.* [U] 靈感、鼓舞人心的人或事物
2.	impression *n.* 印象	10.	instinct *n.*[C][U] 本能、直覺
3.	incident *n.* [C] 事件、事變	11.	insult *vt.* 侮辱、羞辱
4.	influential *adj.* 有影響的、有權勢的	12.	intellectual *n.* [C] 知識分子；*adj.* 智力的
5.	informative *adj.* 情報的、見聞廣博的	13.	intend *n.*[U] 意圖、目的
6.	ingredient *n.* [C] 原料、要素	14.	intensity *n.*[U] 強烈、強度
7.	innocence *n.* [U] 清白、純真	15.	intention *n.* [C][U] 意圖、目的
8.	input *n.* [U] [C] 投入、輸入		

趣味字彙句 🔊 **MP3 13**

1. impact [ɪmˋpækt] *n.* [C][U] 衝擊 impacts

🐞 Every day, there are 1,440 minutes. That means we have 1,440 daily opportunities to make a positive **impact**. (Les Brown)
每天有一千四百四十分鐘，表示我們每天有一千四百四十個機會做出正面的影響。

🐞 Being happy makes the biggest **impact** on your appearance. (Drew Barrymore, Actress)
保持愉快對你的外表產生最大的影響。

2. impression [ɪmˋprɛʃən] *n.* [C][U] 印象 impressions

🐞 Looks are just a first **impression**. There are people you talk to and they become the most beautiful thing in the world. (Brad Pitt, Actor)
外表只是第一印象。有些人你和他們講過話之後，發現他們是世上最美麗的。

🐞 The strangest part of being famous is you don't give first **impression** anymore. (Kristen Stewart, Actress)
出名後最奇怪的部分是，人們不再對你有第一印象。

3. incident [ˋɪnsədnt] *n.* [C] 事件、事變 incidents

🐞 If you hear an **incident** about me, don't believe it until you talk to me. (Leonardo DiCaprio, Actor)
如果你聽說了關於我的事情，在跟我談過之前都不要相信。

🐞 My life is a lovely story, happy and full of unexpected **incidents**. (Hans Christian Anderson, Author)
我的人生是個美好的故事，快樂且充滿預期外的事件。

4. influential [ɪnfluˈɛnʃəl] *adj.* 有影響的、有權勢的

❧ You can be much more **influential** if people are not aware of your influence.
當人們不知道你所帶來的影響力時，你其實更有影響力。

❧ If we don't build a company as **influential** as Google or Facebook, then we failed. I am always stressed about this. (Arash Ferdowsi, Dropbox Founder & CTO)
如果我們不設立一間如同 Google 或臉書有影響力的公司，那我們就失敗了，對此我的壓力一直很大。

5. informative [ɪnˈfɔrmətɪv] *adj.* 情報的、見聞廣博的

❧ I like Twitter because it's very funny and **informative**. It's like having your own radio program. (Margaret Atwood, Poet)
我喜歡推特，它很有趣且充滿新消息，好像你有自己的電台節目。

❧ Music is both **informative** and generous. It's like emotional news. (Jim Drain, Artist)
音樂既具有益又豐富，好似充滿感情的新聞。

6. ingredient [ɪnˈgridɪənt] *n.* [C] 原料、要素 ingredients

❧ Fantasy is a necessary **ingredient** in living. (Dr. Seuss, Writer)
幻想是生活中的必要成份。

❧ Strangeness is a necessary **ingredient** in beauty. (Charles Baudelaire, Poet)
怪異是美麗的必要成分之一。

7. **innocence** [ˋɪnəsns] *n.* [U] 清白、純真

I am glad that I rediscovered some of the **innocence** and beauty I had as a child when I started my own family. (Angelina Jolie)
我很高興我能在建立自己的家庭後，重新發現自己當小孩時的一些純真與美麗。

Having a birthday cake thrown into your face? Wearing a Santa suit at Christmas? I always do it because I want to keep my **innocence**. (John Lydon, Singer/Songwriter)
被生日蛋糕砸臉？聖誕節的時候穿聖誕老人的服裝？我常做，因為我想保持純真。

8. **input** [ˋɪnˏpʊt] *n.* [U] [C] 投入、輸入 inputs

Family life is not a computer project that runs on its own; it needs constant **input** from everyone. (Neil Kurshan, Author)
家庭生活不是會自己跑的電腦程式，它需要每個人不斷的輸入東西。

When you are trying to satisfy everybody's **input**, you usually end up with something so boring that has no point of view. (Rob Zombie, Musician)
當你想要滿足每個人提供的意見，成品通常無趣且看不出觀點。

9. **inspiration** [ˏɪnspəˋreʃən] *n.* [U] 靈感、鼓舞人心的人或事物 inspirations

Don't give up trying to do what you really want to do. Where there is love and **inspiration**, you can't go wrong. (Ella Fitzgerald)
不要放棄嘗試做自己真正想做的，只要有愛與靈感，不會錯的。

Inspiration comes from within yourself. When you're positive, good things happen. (Deep Roy, Actor)
靈感來自自身，當你有正面態度的時候，好事就會發生。

10. instinct [ˈɪnstɪŋkt] *n.*[C][U] 本能、直覺 instincts

🐖 Fashion is a language. Some know it, some learn it, and some never will— like an **instinct**. (Edith Head)
時尚是種語言，有些人生來就知道，有些人靠學習，有些人永遠都學不會，像是種本能。

🐖 In life, when stuff happens, the **instinct** is to close off your heart. By leaving your heart open, it leaves room for someone else to come in. (Jane Seymour, Actress)
生命中，當事情發生時，人們的直覺是關上心門，但若你敞開心門，你便留了空間讓人某人進入。

11. insult [ɪnˈsʌlt] *vt.* 侮辱、羞辱 instulted insulted

🐖 Real friends don't get mad when you **insult** them. They smile and call you something ruder.
真正的朋友不會因為你污辱他而生氣。他們會微笑，然後用更狠的話回你。

🐖 I like Frenchmen very much, because even when they **insult** you, they do it so nicely. (Josephine Baker, Dancer)
我很喜歡法國人，因為即使他們在汙辱你，他們也污辱得很有禮貌。

12. intellectual [ˌɪntlˈɛktʃʊəl] *n.* [C] 知識分子 intellectuals；*adj.* 智力的

🐖 An **intellectual** is a person who's found something more interesting to study than women. (Aldous Huxley, Writer)
知識分子是發現有比女人更有趣、更值得研究的東西的人。

🐖 An **intellectual** says a simple thing in a hard way. An artist says a hard thing in a simple way. (Charles Bukowski, Poet)
知識分子用艱難的話語解釋簡單的事物，藝術家用簡單的方式表達艱難的東西。

13. intend [ɪnˋtɛnt] n.[U] 意圖、目的

🐝 I never exercise except for sleeping and resting, and I never **intend** to. (Mark Twain, Writer)

除了睡覺跟休息這兩種「運動」外，其他種運動我一律不做，往後也不打算做。

🐝 If God did not **intend** for us to eat animals, then why did he make them out of meat? (John Cleese, Actor)

如果上帝沒有希望我們吃動物，那為什麼要用肉創造他們？

14. intensity [ɪnˋtɛnsətɪ] n.[U] 強烈、強度

🐝 Hire for passion and **intensity**; there is training for everything else. (Nolan Bushnell, Entrepreneur)

根據一個人的熱情與他的強度來決定要不要雇用他，其他的東西都可以訓練。

🐝 My eyes are so big that I feel like an alien if my eyelashes don't match their **intensity**. I like to curl my lashes and put on tons of mascara. (Sarah Hyland, Actress)

我的眼睛太大，如果我的睫毛沒有配合我的眼睛，我會覺得自己像外星人，我喜歡捲睫毛並塗大量的睫毛膏。

15. intention [ɪnˋtɛnʃən] n. [C][U] 意圖、目的 intentions

🐝 No word is completely wrong. It all depends on the **intention**. (Janet Jackson, Singer)

話語沒有全然錯誤的，一切取決於其意圖。

🐝 I'm very simple when it comes to gifts. The best ones that I've received have love as their main **intention**. (Adriana Lima, Model)

談到禮物，我是很簡單的，我收過最棒的禮物都出自愛。

Unit 14

接受人生所給予的所有經驗

趣味字彙表

1.	interact *vi.* 互相作用、互動	9.	isolation *n.* [U] 隔離、孤立
2.	internet *n.* [U]【電腦】網際網路	10.	jealousy *n.* [U] [C] 妒忌、猜忌
3.	interpret *vt. vi.* 解釋、理解、口譯	11.	keen *adj.* 熱心的、熱衷的、渴望的
4.	interruption *n.*[U] [C] 中止、打擾	12.	landmark *n.* [C] 地標、里程碑
5.	intimate *adj.* 親密的、熟悉的	13.	lately *adv.* 近來、最近
6.	invade *vt. vi.* 侵入、侵略	14.	launch *vt. vi.* 發射、開始
7.	invention *n.* [U] [C] 發明（物）、創造（物）	15.	lecture *vt. vi.* 演講、講課
8.	.invest *vt. vi.* 投資		

趣味字彙句 c c ⊙ MP3 14

1. interact [ˌɪntəˋrækt] *vi.* 互相作用、互動 interacted interacted

☝ If you want a machine to **interact** with people, it better not do things that are surprising to people. (Rodney Brooks)
如果你想要發明會和人類互動的機器，那這個機器最好不要做出會嚇到人們的事情。

☝ When you do video games, you don't **interact** with other actors. You each record on different days and never meet the other characters. (Eliza Dushku, Actress)
當你參與電玩製作時，你和其他演員是沒有互動的，你們各自在不同天錄製，彼此不會碰到面。

2. internet [ˋɪntəˌnɛt] *n.* [U]【電腦】網際網路

☝ It feels like every day or two, people on Twitter and the **Internet** are very angry about something. (Demetri Martin, Comedian)
似乎每一兩天，推特和網路上就有人會對甚麼事情感到極度憤怒。

☝ The **Internet** is just a world passing around notes in a classroom. (Jon Stewart, Comedian)
網路其實只是一個大家在教室裡互傳紙條的世界。

3. interpret [ɪnˋtɜprɪt] *vt. vi.* 解釋、理解、口譯 interpreted interpreted

☝ An actor must **interpret** life by accepting all experiences that life can offer. (Marlon Brando, Actor)
演員必須接受人生所給予的所有經驗，以這種方式解釋人生。

☝ Happiness is not about what happens to you, it's about how you **interpret** what happens.
快樂不是你身上發生了甚麼事，而是你如何解釋這些事。

Part 1「趣」你的單字基礎篇

Part 2「趣」你的單字進階篇

089

4. interruption [ɪntəˈrʌpʃən] *n.* [U] [C] 中止、打擾 interruptions

🐞 Do not cause an **interruption** for someone doing something that you said couldn't be done. (Amelia Earhart, Aviator)
不要阻止別人做你認為做不到的事情。

🐞 We have **interruptions** every 11 minutes on average. (Pico Lyer, Essayist)
我們平均每十一分鐘就會被打擾。

5. intimate [ˈɪntəmɪt] *adj.* 親密的、熟悉的

🐞 A wedding dress is both **intimate** and personal for a woman— it must reflect the personality and style of the bride. (Carolina Herrera, Fashion Designer)
結婚禮服對女人來說既親密又私人，一定要能反映新娘的個性與風格。

🐞 If you kiss on the first date, then there will be no second date. I am a strong believer in kissing being very **intimate**. (Jennifer Lopez, Singer/Actress)
如果第一次約會就親吻，那就不會有第二次約會，我堅信親吻是很親密的。

6. invade [ɪnˈved] *vt. vi.* 侵入、侵略 invaded invaded

🐞 When women are upset, they eat or go shopping. Men **invade** another country. (Elayne Boosler, Comedian)
當女人生氣的時候，她們會吃東西或採購，男人則會侵略另一個國家。

🐞 The best thing you can do for someone is make them a beautiful plate of food. How else can you **invade** someone's body without touching them? (Padma Lakshmi, Author/Cookbook Author)
你能為人做的最棒的事，是為他做一盤美麗的食物。想不碰他人而侵略他的身體，還有其他方法嗎？

7. invention [ɪnˋvɛnʃən] n. [U] [C] 發明（物）、創造（物） inventions

- I never had plastic surgery, but if they made a new **invention** for making people taller, I would be the first to have that surgery. (Alanna Ubach, Actress)
  我從沒整形過，但如果他們發明能讓人變高的手術，我會第一個去做。

- I didn't fail 1000 times. The light bulb was an **invention** with 1000 steps. (Thomas Edison, Inventor)
  我並沒有失敗一千次，燈泡只是個有一千個步驟的發明。

8. invest [ɪnˋvɛst] vt. vi. 投資 invested invested

- **Investing** should be like watching paint dry or watching grass grow. If you want excitement, go to Las Vegas. (Paul Samuelson, Economist)
  投資應該像盯著油漆變乾或看著草長大，如果你想追求刺激，去拉斯維加斯吧。

- Money is a wonderful thing because it enables you to **invest** in ideas. (Steve Jobs, Businessman)
  金錢是個美好的東西，因為它讓你得以投資想法。

9. isolation [ˌaɪsḷˋeʃən] n. [U] 隔離、孤立

- If you want to end your **isolation**, you must be honest about what you want and go after it. (Martha Beck, Author)
  如果你想要終止孤立，你必須誠實面對自己想要的，然後去追求。

- With technology, there is so much **isolation** with people now, that there are very few places where you can connect. (Mireille Giliano, Author)
  隨著科技的發展，人們越來越孤立，越來越少地方讓你能與人有所連結。

10. jealousy [ˈdʒɛləsɪ] *n.* [U] [C] 妒忌、猜忌 jealousies

🐝 I would miss months of school and then return with bright blond hair. There was some teasing and **jealousy**. (Tom Felton, Actor)
我會錯過幾個月的課，回來的時候頂著一頭亮金髮，會聽到一些嘲笑與忌妒。

🐝 The good part about **jealousy** is that it comes from passion. It's also an ugly emotion that hurts. (Matthew McConaughey, Actor)
忌妒好的一面是，它出自於熱情，它也是個傷人的醜陋情感。

11. keen [kin] *adj.* 熱心的、熱衷的、渴望的

🐝 After marriage, a woman's sight becomes so **keen** that she can see right through her husband. (Helen Rowland, Journalist)
結婚後，女人的視力變得銳利到可以看穿她的先生。

🐝 One of the reasons I like a suit is because I've never been **keen** on my body. The body shape a suit presents is always going to be better. (Bill Nighy, Actor)
我喜歡西裝的原因之一是，我向來不是很喜歡自己的身材，西裝呈現出的身材總是好很多。

12. landmark [ˈlændˌmɑrk] *n.* [C] 地標、里程碑 landmarks

🐝 You can't put the Hollywood sign in a movie without paying them. That is a **landmark** in L.A. (Dax Shepard, Actor)
你想在電影中放好萊塢的標誌，你就要付錢，那明明是洛杉磯的地標。

🐝 Eighty is a **landmark** age and people treat you differently. At eighty, people pick things up for you. (Helen Van Slyke, Author)
八十歲是個里程碑，而人們開始以不同方式對待你，人們會幫八十歲的人撿東西。

13. lately [ˈletlɪ] *adv.* 近來、最近

☙ I have lots of shoes, but I have to be comfortable. **Lately**, I've stolen my husband's big, ugly Uggs. (Debi Mazar, Actress)
我擁有很多鞋，但我又必須要感到舒服。最近我偷了我先生又大又醜的雪靴。

☙ The one thing I am crazy with **lately** is new cellphones. I walk about with three phones because I can't choose one. (Bar Refaeli, Model)
我最近瘋的東西是新手機，我出門帶三支手機，因為我無法決定選哪一個。

14. launch [lɔntʃ] *vt. vi.* 發射、開始 launched launched

☙ When **launching** into space, half of the risk is in the first nine minutes. (Chris Hadfield, Astronaut)
當發射進入太空時，大半的風險會發生在前九分鐘。

☙ **Launching** a rocket into space costs about $3 billion on average.
發射太空梭進入太空平均需花費三十億美元。

15. lecture [ˈlɛktʃɚ] *vt. vi.* 演講、講課 lectured lectured

☙ As you **lecture**, you keep watching faces, and information keeps coming back to you all the time. (George Wald, Scientist)
當你演講的時候，你要觀察觀眾的臉，你會一直得到訊息。

☙ When I **lecture**, people can look at their watches. However, I get mad when they raise it to their ear to find out if their watch stopped. (Marcel Achard, Playwright)
我演講的時候，人們可以看他們的錶，但如果他們舉起手來聽錶是不是壞了，我就會生氣。

Unit 15

懂得思考

趣味字彙表

1.	legend *n.* [C][U] 傳奇（故事）、傳奇人物	9.	luxury *n.* [U] [C] 奢華、奢侈（品）
2.	license *n.* [C][U] 許可（證）、特許	10.	machinery *n.* [U] 機器、方法
3.	limitation *n.* [U] [C] 限制（因素）、極限	11.	magnetic *adj.* 磁鐵的、磁性的、有吸引力的
4.	literature *n.* [U] [C] 文學（作品）	12.	makeup *n.* [U] 妝、化妝品
5.	location *n.* [C] 位置、場所	13.	manual *adj.* 手的、手工的
6.	logic *n.* [U] 邏輯、邏輯學、道理	14.	marathon *n.* [C] 馬拉松賽跑
7.	lousy *adj.* 非常糟糕的	15.	maturity *n.* [U] 成熟、完善
8.	loyal *adj.* 忠誠的、忠心的		

趣味字彙句 ⚫⚫ 🎧 **MP3 15**

1. legend [ˈlɛdʒənd] *n.* [C][U] 傳奇（故事）、傳奇人物 legends

🐸 Some people hear their own inner voices with great clearness. Such people become crazy or they become great **legends**. (Jim Harrison, Author)

有些人能清楚聽到內在的聲音，這樣的人可能變精神病，也可能變成偉大的傳奇人物。

🐸 Madonna turned herself into a **legend** by simply never staying the same. (Janice Dickinson, Model)

瑪丹娜只靠著不斷改變，就把自己變為傳奇。

2. license [ˈlaɪsns] *n.* [C][U] 許可（證）、特許 licenses

🐸 I don't like to have my picture taken. My driver's **license** photo looks like a blond Elvis Presley. (Emily Procter, Actress)

我不喜歡照相，我駕照的照片看起來像金髮貓王。

🐸 It was harder to get my driver's **license** than having a baby. (Julie Bowen, Actress)

對我來說，拿到駕照比生小孩還難。

3. limitation [ˌlɪməˈteʃən] *n.* [U][C] 限制（因素）、極限 limitations

🐸 Don't believe what your eyes are telling you, all they show is **limitation**. Look with your understanding, and you'll see the way to fly. (Richard Bach, Writer)

不要相信你的眼睛所告訴你的，它們表現出來的都是有限制的。用你的理解去看，那麼你就會看見飛行的方式。

🐸 Art has **limitations**. The most beautiful part of every picture is the frame. (Gilbert K. Chesterton, Writer)

藝術是有極限的，每幅畫最美的部分是她的畫框。

Part 1 「趣」你的單字基礎篇

Part 2 「趣」你的單字進階篇

4. literature [ˈlɪtərətʃɚ] n. [U] [C] 文學（作品）

🐏 **Literature** is the art of writing something that will be read twice. (Cyril Connolly, Critic)
文學是一門藝術，你需要寫出會讓人看兩次的東西。

🐏 Just like all great stories, we focus on a question that is as important in life as it is in **literature**: What will happen next? (Karen Thompson Walker, Novelist)
有如所有偉大的故事，我們專注於一個在人生或文學中都同樣重要的問題：接下來會發生甚麼事？

5. location [loˈkeʃən] n. [C] 位置、場所 locations

🐏 Food is as much about the event, the **location**, and the people as it is about the taste. (Heston Blumenthal, Chef)
食物和活動、場地、人食物以及它本身味道同樣密切相關。

🐏 Silicon Valley is a way of thinking, not a **location**. (Reid Hoffman, Co-founder of LinkedIn)
矽谷是一種思考方法，不是一個地點。

6. logic [ˈlɑdʒɪk] n. [U] 邏輯、邏輯學、道理

🐏 I buy fancy dresses because I always think I'll wear them a lot, but it's false **logic**. (Alexa Chung, Fashion Model)
我買高級的洋裝，因為我總是認為我會常穿，但這是錯誤的邏輯。

🐏 Love and **logic** are so conflicting, but they are both necessary for a happy balance. (Laura Marling, Singer)
愛與邏輯彼此矛盾，但對快樂的和諧感來說，兩個同樣重要。

7. lousy [ˈlaʊzɪ] *adj.* 非常糟糕的

🛒 Success is a **lousy** teacher. It makes smart people think they can't lose. (Bill Gates, Businessman)
成功是個糟糕的老師，它讓聰明的人自以為他們不可能會失敗。

🛒 Show me a great actor, and I'll show you a **lousy** husband. Show me a great actress, and you've seen the devil. (W.C. Fields, Comedian)
要成為偉大的演員，你就會成為一個糟糕的先生，而站在眼前的偉大的女演員是個惡魔。

8. loyal [ˈlɔɪəl] *adj.* 忠誠的、忠心的

🛒 One **loyal** friend is worth ten thousand aunts, uncles, and cousins. (Euripides, Playwright/Poet)
一個忠實的朋友可抵萬個阿姨、叔叔或堂表兄弟姊妹。

🛒 I'm a very **loyal** person. In a relationship, it's like they are the syrup and I'm a pancake. Their syrup gets into my pancake. (Warren Farrell, Activist/Author)
我是個很忠心的人，在一段關係裡，他們好比楓糖，而我是鬆餅，他們的糖漿滲入我的鬆餅。

9. luxury [ˈlʌkʃərɪ] *n.* [U] [C] 奢華、奢侈（品） luxuries

🛒 Love is a **luxury**. You have no right to it, unless you can afford it. (Anthony Trollope, Novelist)
愛是奢侈的，除非你負擔得起，不然你無權得到。

🛒 Love is like those second-rate hotels where all the **luxury** is in the lobby. (Paul Jean Toulet, Poet)
愛就像二等旅館，所有奢華的東西都放在大廳。

Part 1 「趣」你的單字基礎篇

Part 2 「趣」你的單字進階篇

10. machinery [məˈʃɪnərɪ] *n.* [U] 機器、方法

- If you don't understand how to manage, new **machinery** will just give you new problems in business management. (W. Edwards Deming, Engineer)

  如果你不懂管理，那新機器只會給你新的生意管理問題。

- **Machinery** can only work well if there is someone determined to make it work. (Cordell Hull, Congressman)

  機器只有當有人下定決心要讓它成功運作時，才會運作。

11. magnetic [mægˈnɛtɪk] *adj.* 磁鐵的、磁性的、有吸引力的

- A **magnetic** personality doesn't always indicate a good heart. (Laura Linney, Actress)

  有吸引力的個性並不代表善良的心。

- Listening is a **magnetic** force. When we are listened to, it opens our hearts and minds. (Karl Menninger, Psychiatrist)

  傾聽是個有吸引力的力量，當別人專心聆聽時，我們感性與理性的心都會被打開。

12. makeup [ˈmekʌp] *n.* [U] 妝、化妝品

- I believe that all women are pretty without **makeup**, and can be pretty powerful with the right makeup. (Bobbi Brown, Makeup Artist)

  我相信所有女人沒化妝都是美麗的，而適當化妝後會變得有力量。

- Makeup can only make you look pretty on the outside, but it doesn't help if you're ugly on the inside. Unless you eat **makeup**. (Audrey Hepburn, Actress)

  化妝品只能幫助你外表變漂亮，如果你內在醜陋，它是沒有幫助的，除非你吃下化妝品。

13. manual [ˈmænjʊəl] *adj.* 手的、手工的

🐝 Women are confusing. Their instruction **manual** should be 800 pages. (Hugh Laurie, Actor)

女人真是令人困惑,她們的說明書應該是長達八百頁。

🐝 There's no instruction **manual** on how to handle success, so you just have to rely on having great friends and a good team. (Bryan Adams, Musician)

並沒有說明書教你怎麼面對成功,你只能仰賴好朋友與良好的團隊。

14. marathon [ˈmærəθɑn] *n.* [C] 馬拉松賽跑 marathons

🐝 Making a movie is like a **marathon**, and commercials are like short races— they're equally satisfying, but in different ways. (Tony Scott, Film Director)

拍電影就像跑馬拉松,而拍廣告像跑短跑,兩者都可以以不同的方式帶給我滿足感。

🐝 Career is not about speed but patience. It is a **marathon**, and it takes a lot of time. (Jamie Camil, Actor)

職業非關速度,重要的是耐心,這是一場馬拉松,是需要長期奮戰的。

15. maturity [məˈtjʊrətɪ] *n.* [U] 成熟、完善

🐝 What makes Superman a hero is not that he has power, but that he has the **maturity** to use the powers wisely. (Christopher Reeve, Actor)

超人之所以是英雄,不是因為它有超能力,而是因為他夠成熟,知道怎麼善用他的能力。

🐝 To make mistakes is human; to be able to laugh at yourself is **maturity**. (William Arthur Ward, Writer)

人難免會犯錯,但能嘲笑自己才是真正的成熟。

Unit 16

打造最好的自己

趣味字彙表

1.	maximum *n.* [C] 最大量、頂點；*adj.* 最大的，最多的	9.	misfortune *n.* [C][U] 不幸（的事）、災難
2.	mechanic *n.* [C] 機械工、技工	10.	modesty *n.*[U] 謙遜、虛心
3.	memorable *adj.* 得懷念的、難忘的	11.	mostly *adv.* 大多數地、主要地、一般地
4.	mercy *n.* [U] [C] 慈悲（行為）、憐憫（行為）；*vt.* 值得 merited merited	12.	motivate *vt.* 刺激、激發
5.	merit *n.* [U] [C] 價值、長處、功績	13.	multiple *adj.* 複合的、多樣的
6.	messy *adj.* 混亂的	14.	mustache *n.* [C] 小鬍子
7.	mischief *n.* [U] 淘氣、惡作劇、損害	15.	mysterious *adj.* 神祕的、詭祕的
8.	miserable *adj.* 痛苦的、不幸的、悽慘的		

趣味字彙句 🎧 MP3 16

1. maximum [ˈmæksəməm] *n.* [C] 最大量、頂點 maximums； *adj.* 最大的，最多的

🐝 A newspaper should have the **maximum** amount of information but a tiny amount of comments. (Richard Cobden, Former Statesman)

報紙應該要包含最大量的資訊與最少量的評斷。

🐝 My table seats eight, so that's my **maximum**. That way we have good conversation and the whole house doesn't get destroyed. (Paul Lynde, Comedian)

我的桌子只能坐八個人，所以那是我的極限，如此一來，我們既可以好好談話，房子也不會被搞砸。

2. mechanic [məˈkænɪk] *n.* [C] 機械工、技工 mechanics

🐝 A man too busy to take care of his health is like a **mechanic** too busy to take care of his tools. (Spanish Proverb)

人如果忙到沒空照顧自己的健康，那就像技工忙到沒空維護自己的工具。

🐝 Never trust a **mechanic** who drives new cars. (Patricia Briggs, Writer)

如果技工開著新車，那就不要相信他。

3. memorable [ˈmɛmərəb!] *adj.* 得懷念的、難忘的

🐝 What makes things **memorable** is that they are meaningful, significant, and colorful. (Joshua Foer, Journalist)

事情之所以難忘是因為它有意義、重要且生動。

🐝 If you want to live a **memorable** life, you have to be a person who remembers to remember. (Joshua Foer, Journalist)

如果你想要有個難忘的人生，那你必須成為一個記得要記住事情的人。

Part 1 「趣」你的單字基礎篇

Part 2 「趣」你的單字進階篇

4. mercy [ˋmɝsɪ] *n.* [U] [C] 慈悲（行為）、憐憫（行為） mercies

One night, I drove right through a stop sign because I was busy dipping my French fries into my milkshake. The angry cop showed me no **mercy**. (Arielle Kebbel, Actress)
有一天晚上，我在停止標誌前沒有停下來，因為我忙著拿薯條沾奶昔，那位生氣的警察並沒有放過我。

When I have my portrait painted, I want **mercy** instead of justice. (Billy Hughes, Former Prime Minister of Australia)
當人家畫我的畫像的時候，我比較需要慈悲，而不是正直。

5. merit [ˋmɛrɪt] *n.* [U] [C] 價值、長處、功績 merits ; *vt.* 值得 merited merited

Nature gives you the face you have at twenty; it is up to you to **merit** the face you have at fifty. (Coco Chanel, Fashion Designer)
二十歲的臉蛋是上天給你的，五十歲的時候就要靠自己了。

People are just afraid of things too much. Afraid of things that don't necessarily **merit** fear. (Frank Ocean, Singer)
人們太害怕了，總是害怕不值得恐懼的事情。

6. messy [ˋmɛsɪ] *adj.* 混亂的

At the end of the day, your feet should be dirty, your hair **messy**, and your eyes shining.
在一天的尾聲，你的雙腳應該是骯髒的，頭髮是蓬亂的，而眼睛是閃閃發亮的。

My room is not **messy**. I just have everything on display like a museum.
我的房間並不亂。我只是像博物館一樣，把所有東西都展示出來。

7. mischief [ˈmɪstʃɪf] *n.* [U] 淘氣、惡作劇、損害

🐸 Very few men are clever enough to know all the **mischief** they do. (Francois de La Rouchefoucauld, Author)
很少有人可以聰明到看清自己做的所有壞事。

🐸 The opportunity for doing **mischief** is found a hundred times a day, and the opportunity to do good only once a year. (Voltaire, Writer)
做壞事的機會一天會出現好幾百次，但做好事的機會一年只會出現一次。

8. miserable [ˈmɪzərəbl] *adj.* 痛苦的、不幸的、悽慘的

🐸 A single man's life is a good breakfast, average lunch, and a **miserable** dinner. (Francis Bacon, Philosopher)
一個單身男性的一生是一份豐富的早餐，平凡的午餐，和淒涼的晚餐。

🐸 Only married people understand you can be **miserable** and happy at the same time. (Chris Rock, Actor/Comedian)
只有結婚的人才知道原來人可以既悲慘又快樂。

9. misfortune [mɪsˈfɔrtʃən] *n.* [C][U] 不幸（的事）、災難 mistfortunes

🐸 We lie about **misfortune** and happiness. We are never as bad off or as happy as wc say we are. (Honore de Balzac, Novelist)
我們隱藏不幸與快樂，我們從來沒有像我們說得那樣悲慘或快樂。

🐸 I had the **misfortune** of learning how to read from three years old. In the first grade, I already knew that my teachers were lying to me. (Alan Kay, Scientist)
很不幸的，我三歲就學會閱讀，到一年級的時候，我已經知道我的老師在欺騙我了。

10. modesty [ˋmɑdɪstɪ] *n.*[U] 謙遜、虛心

🐦 I wish I invented jeans. They have **modesty** but still maintain sex appeal. (Yves Saint Laurent, Fashion Designer)
我真希望是我發明牛仔褲的，它們低調但又不失性感。

🐦 Nothing is worse than a beautiful girl asking for praises by saying how gross she is. I find real **modesty** attractive. (Chris Evans, Actor)
當一個美麗的女孩說自己有多噁心來贏得誇獎是最糟的。我覺得真心的謙虛才是吸引人的。

11. mostly [ˋmostlɪ] *adv.* 大多數地、主要地、一般地

🐦 Security is **mostly** a lie. Life is either a daring adventure or nothing. (Helen Keller, Author)
安定大部分時候只是個謊言。人生如果不是場勇敢的冒險，就甚麼都不是。

🐦 Write for yourself, not for an audience. If you do, you'll **mostly** fail, because it's impossible to judge what people want. (Wilbur Smith, Novelist)
為自己而寫作，不要為了觀眾，如果你為觀眾寫作，那你極可能會失敗，因為判定別人想要什麼是不可能的。

12. motivate [ˋmotəˌvet] *vt.* 刺激、激發 motivated motivated

🐦 To **motivate** people, you've got to engage their minds and hearts. (Rupert Murdoch, Business Leader)
要激勵人，你必須使他們用心與腦。

🐦 Goals are not only necessary to **motivate** us. They are needed to really keep us alive. (Robert H. Schuller, Christian Televangelist)
目標是必要的，它不只激勵我們，它讓我們得以活著。

13. multiple [ˋmʌltəpḷ] *adj.* 複合的、多樣的

📺 Research shows you get **multiple** tasks done faster if you do them one at a time. (Shawn Achor, Business Trainer)

研究顯示，有多重任務時，如果你一次做一樣完成速度會比較快。

📺 If you have **multiple** purposes, you'll confuse yourself as a storyteller. If you have one purpose, everything will fall into place. (Andrew Stanton, Film Director)

如果你有數個目的，身為說故事的人也會困惑，但如果你專注在一個目的，一切會自然水到渠成。

14. mustache [ˋmʌstæʃ] *n.* [C] 小鬍子 mustaches

📺 Nowadays, if you have a **mustache** on your face, people look at you like you're crazy. (Kevin Connolly, Actor)

最近如果你臉上留鬍子，人們就會覺得你瘋了。

📺 My **mustache** makes me look like a bad guy. (Jesse Ventura, Professional Wrestler)

我的鬍子讓我看起來像個壞男人。

15. mysterious [mɪsˋtɪrɪəs] *adj.* 神祕的、詭祕的

📺 You can't go wrong with vampires. Vampires are a hit because they're **mysterious**, dangerous, and kind of sexy. (Ashley Greene, Actress)

用吸血鬼就不會錯，吸血鬼很流行，因為他們神秘、危險還有點性感。

📺 Understanding can fix any situation, no matter how **mysterious** it may appear to be. (Norman Vincent Peale, Minister)

諒解可以修正任何情況，不論情況看起來有多不可思議。

Unit 17

生命是經驗的累積

趣味字彙表

1.	neglect *vt.* 忽視、疏於照管；*n.* [C] 忽視、疏忽	9.	operation *n.* [U] [C] 操作、經營、手術
2.	negotiate *vt. vi.* 談判、協商	10.	oppose *vt. vi.* 反對、反抗
3.	nightmare *n.* [C] 惡夢、可怕的事件、難纏的人	11.	orchestra *n.* [C] 管弦樂隊
4.	nonsense *n.* [U] 無意義的話、胡說	12.	organic *adj.* 有機的
5.	nuclear *adj.* 原子核的、核能的	13.	outcome *n.* [U] [C] 結果、後果
6.	obstacle *n.* [C] 障礙（物）、妨礙	14.	outstanding *adj.* 傑出的、顯著的
7.	obtain *vt. vi.* 得到、獲得	15.	overcome *vt. vi.* 戰勝、克服
8.	offend *vt. vi.* 冒犯、引起不舒服		

趣味字彙句 🎧 MP3 17

1. neglect [nɪ'glɛkt] *vt.* 忽視、疏於照管 neglected neglected； *n.* [C] 忽視、疏忽

A man should never **neglect** his family for business. (Walt Disney)
人永遠都不該為了事業而忽略家庭。

Not caring and **neglecting** someone often does the most damage. (Albus Dumbledore, book character)
毫不關心並忽略他人通常是最有破壞力的。

2. negotiate [nɪ'goʃɪet] *vt. vi.* 談判、協商 negotiated negotiated

A lot of business people think their job is to **negotiate** the highest price. However, deals that are too good will end up hurting you. (Ryan Kavanaugh, Film Producer)
很多商人以為他們的工作是談到最高的價錢，然而太完美的交易可能最後會害了你。

85% of your success is due to your personality, and ability to communicate, **negotiate**, and lead.
成功的百分之八十五取決於你的個性以及你溝通、協商和領導的能力。

3. nightmare ['naɪtmɛr] *n.* [C] 惡夢、可怕的事件、難纏的人 nightmares

I never paint dreams or **nightmares**. I paint my own reality. (Frida Kahlo, Painter)
我從不畫夢想或夢魘。我只畫自己的真實生活。

I stopped looking for my dream girl. I just want a girl who isn't a **nightmare**. (Charles Bukowski, Poet)
我已經停止尋找夢中情人了。我現在只想找到一個不是惡夢的女孩。

4. nonsense [ˈnɑnsɛns] *n.* [U] 無意義的話、胡說

🛒 The best part of friendship is talking total **nonsense** and having that nonsense respected.
友誼最棒的部分就是即使說出沒意義的話，那話依舊可以受到重視。

🛒 A little **nonsense** now and then, is enjoyed by the wisest men. (Ronald Dahl, Novelist)
最有智慧的人會享受偶有的愚蠢。

5. nuclear [ˈnjuklɪɚ] *adj.* 原子核的、核能的

🛒 **Nuclear** weapons can be stopped, but they cannot be uninvented.
我們可以阻止核子武器，但無法回到它被發明前。

🛒 A woman would never make a **nuclear** bomb that kills. They'd make a weapon that makes you feel bad for a while. (Robin Williams, Actor/Comedian)
女人從不做出會死人的核子彈，他們做出的武器是會讓你痛苦好一段時間的。

6. obstacle [ˈɑbstəkl̩] *n.* [C] 障礙（物）、妨礙

🛒 A lot of people give up just before they're about to make it. You never know when that next **obstacle** is going to be the last one. (Chuck Norris, Martial Artist)
很多人在他們快要成功前放棄，你永遠不會知道下一個障礙會不會是最後一個。

🛒 Nothing is an **obstacle** unless you say it is. (Wally Amos, Businessman)
世上沒有事物可以成為障礙，除非你認為它是。

7. obtain [əb'ten] *vt.* *vi.* 得到、獲得 obtained obtained

Everyone needs a certain amount of money. Beyond that, we only pursue money because we know how to **obtain** it. (Gregg Easterbrook, Writer)

每個人都需要一筆特定數目的錢,除此之外,人們追求金錢不過因為他們知道怎麼取得它。(格雷格伊斯特布魯克,作家)

I'm done with nicknames. Actually, when I **obtain** my PhD, I will not allow people to call me Shaq anymore. (Shaquille O'Neal)

我受夠綽號了。事實上,等我拿到博士學位的時候,我會開始禁止人家叫我「俠客」。

8. offend [ə'fɛnd] *vt.* *vi.* 冒犯、引起不舒服 offended offended

It's difficult enough to be funny without worrying about what is going to **offend** someone. (Alan King, Actor)

要搞笑已經很難了,還要擔心冒犯別人,真是難上加難。

I think the worst way you can **offend** a Mexican is to insult their mother. (Emiliano)

我覺得冒犯墨西哥人最糟糕的方式就是污辱他的母親。

9. operation [ɑpə'reʃən] *n.* [U] [C] 操作、經營、手術 operations

I have written two medical novels, but I have never seen an **operation**. (Taylor Caldwell, Popular Fiction Novelist)

我已寫過兩本醫學小說,但我連一次手術都沒看過。

If there's one **operation** for a disease, you know it works. If there are 15 operations, you know that none of them works. (Sherwin B. Nuland, Surgeon)

如果治療一項疾病,開了一次刀,那你可以看出這項手術成功了,如果有十五場手術,那你就知道沒有一次手術是有用的。

10. oppose [əˋpoz] *vt. vi.* 反對、反抗 opposed opposed

- Men often **oppose** something because they did not plan it, or because it was planned by someone they dislike. (Alexander Hamilton, U.S. Founding Father)
  人們通常只因為事情不是他們計畫的而反對，或是因為是他們討厭的人計畫的。

- Don't be afraid when people **oppose** you. A kite rises against, not with the wind.
  當別人反對你的時候，不要感到害怕。風箏是逆風而起，而非順風而行。

11. orchestra [ˋɔrkɪstrə] *n.* [C] 管弦樂隊 orchestras

- If you want to lead the **orchestra**, you must turn your back on the crowd. (Max Lucado, Christian Author)
  如果你想要指揮管絃樂隊，那你必須背對觀眾。

- The conductor of an **orchestra** doesn't make a sound. His power comes from making other people powerful. (Benjamin Zander, Conductor)
  管絃樂隊指揮家是不出聲的，他的力量來自給予他人力量。

12. organic [ɔrˋgænɪk] *adj.* 有機的

- I try my best to eat **organic** whenever possible, but it's important not to be too strict about it. Just do the best you can. (Miranda Kerr, Supermodel)
  可以的話，我盡量都吃有機食物，但重要的是不需要太苛求自己，只要盡力就好。

- Yes, **organic** food is expensive, but cancer is pretty expensive, too.
  是的，有機食物是真的很貴。但治療癌症也是挺貴的。

13. outcome [ˈaʊtˌkʌm] *n.* [U] [C] 結果、後果 outcomes

🐸 Don't focus on the **outcome**. If I fight, I know I'm going to go out there and do my best whether I win or lose. (Luke Rockhold, Mixed Martial Artist)

不要只注意結果。當我格鬥的時候，我知道不管我會贏或輸，我都會勇敢面對並盡我所能。

🐸 Success is sometimes the **outcome** of many failures. (Vincent Van Gogh, Artist)

成功有時是許多失敗的結果。

14. outstanding [aʊtˈstændɪŋ] *adj.* 傑出的、顯著的

🐸 Alone also means available for someone **outstanding**. (Greg Behrendt, Comedian)

獨自一人也表示你有空與某個傑出的人接觸。

🐸 The brain is the most **outstanding** organ. It works 24 hours a day from your birth until you fall in love.

大腦是最出色的器官，它不停工作二十四小時，從你出生那刻，直到你陷入戀愛。

15. overcome [ovɚˈkʌm] *vt.* *vi.* 戰勝、克服 overcame overcome

🐸 Real problems can be **overcome**, but invented problems will take you around in circles. (Barbara Sher, Author)

真正的問題是可以克服的，但想出來的問題只會讓你一直繞圈圈。

🐸 I **overcame** my fear of skydiving. My parents already jumped out of the plane, and I jumped out after them because I didn't want to be an orphan. (Mandy Moore, Singer/Songwriter)

我戰勝了我對跳傘的恐懼，看著我父母跳下飛機，我只好跟著跳，因為我不想當孤兒。

Unit 18

懂得選擇

趣味字彙表

1.	overlook *vt.* 眺望、忽略、寬恕、監督	9.	perfection *n.* [U] 完美
2.	oxygen *n.* [U] 氧氣	10.	permanent *adj.* 永久的、永恆的、常在的
3.	pace *n.* [C][U] 一步、步速	11.	persuasive *adj.* 勸說的、有說服力的
4.	participation *n.* [U] 參加、參與	12.	physical *adj.* 身體的、物質的
5.	partnership *n.* [U] [C] 合夥或合作關係	13.	plentiful *adj.* 豐富的、充足的、富裕的
6.	passive *adj.* 被動的、消極的	14.	portable *adj.* 便於攜帶的、輕便的
7.	peculiar *adj.* 特別的、奇怪的、罕見的	15.	possession *n.* [U] [C] 擁有、所有物
8.	penalty *n.* [U] [C] 處罰、罰款		

趣味字彙句 🎧 🎧 🎧 MP3 18

---

1. overlook [ovɚˋluk] *vt.* 眺望、忽略、寬恕、監督 overlooked overlooked

🐸 A friend is one who **overlooks** your broken fence and admires the flowers in your garden.
朋友是會忽略你破掉的柵欄，轉而欣賞你花園裡的花朵。

🐸 Wisdom is learning what to **overlook**. (William James, Philosopher)
智慧是學會甚麼是該被忽略的。

2. oxygen [ˋɑksədʒən] *n.* [U] 氧氣

🐸 After I get up, I take in **oxygen**, then bacon and black coffee, and then bacon again. (Nick Offerman, Actor/Writer)
我起床後，我吸入氧氣，然後是培根和黑咖啡，然後又是培根。

🐸 He is not the reason why your heart's still beating. Love, **Oxygen**.
他並不是你心臟還在跳動的原因，是愛與氧氣。

3. pace [pes] *n.* [C][U] 一步、步速 paces

🐸 It's amazing how the same **pace** feels so much harder during practice than on race day. Stay confident and trust the process. (Sara Hall, Runner)
真的很神奇，同樣的腳步，在練習的時候卻比競賽當天令人感覺更艱難。保持信心並相信過程。

🐸 Life will reveal answers at the **pace** life wishes to do so. You feel like running, but life is on a walk. (Don Miller, Author)
人生會以它想要的腳步揭露答案，你覺得你在賽跑，但生命是在散步。

4. participation [pɑrˌtɪsəˈpeʃən] *n.* [U] 參加、參與

🐾 Life is about experience and **participation**. It is more complex and interesting than what is obvious. (David Libeskind, Architect)
生命是經驗和參與，比那些明顯的事物更複雜且有趣。

🐾 I hate going to magic shows. I love magic and wizards, but going to a show where there is any possibility of audience **participation** is stressful for me. (Aubrey Plaza, Actress)
我討厭看魔術秀，我熱愛魔術和巫師，但去可能觀眾需要參與的秀，給我很大的壓力。

5. partnership [ˈpɑrtnɚˌʃɪp] *n.* [U] [C] 合夥或合作關係 partnerships

🐾 Love isn't ownership. Love is **partnership**. It takes time, effort, and pain to be in love.
愛不是所有關係，愛是一種合作關係，需要時間、努力和痛苦。

🐾 When it comes to **partnership**, humans need other people. It's more like painting, you can't just use the same color in every painting. (Ben Harper, Singer/Songwriter)
談到關係，人類需要其他人。就像畫畫，你不能每幅畫都只用同一種顏色。

6. passive [ˈpæsɪv] *adj.* 被動的、消極的

🐾 I used to be really **passive**, and all I cared about was being in love with my boyfriend. I don't know that person any more. (Gwen Stefani, Singer/Songwriter)
我以前是很被動的，我關心的只有和男友談戀愛，我現在已經不認識那個我了。

🐾 Leaders are always active not **passive** even when observing. (James Humes, Author/Presidential Speechwriter)
領導人即使在觀察過程中也是活躍的、不消極被動。

7. peculiar [pɪˋkjuljɚ] *adj.* 特別的、奇怪的、罕見的

There's something **peculiar** about writing fiction. It requires an interesting balance between seeing the world as a child and having the wisdom of a middle-aged person. (Kazuo Ishiguro, Novelist/ Screenwriter)

寫小說有個詭異的地方，它需要你能用小孩的方式看世界並擁有中年人的智慧，且從中取得有趣的平衡。

Luck has a **peculiar** habit of favoring those who don't depend on it.

運氣有個特別的習慣，它總是偏好不靠著它的人。

8. penalty [ˋpɛnḷtɪ] *n.* [U] [C] 處罰、罰款 penalties

Always keep calm. You can't score from the **penalty** box; and to win, you have to score. (Bobby Hull, Ice hockey player)

隨時保持冷靜，在判罰室是無法得分的，而為了贏得比賽，得分是必要的。

You pay a certain **penalty** for going your own way. A lot of people think you're crazy, and you're not as popular with girls as you should be. (Ray Bradbury, Fiction Author)

走自己的路你需要付代價，很多人會認為你是瘋子，而你也無法從女孩子那得到你該有的關注。

9. perfection [pɚˋfɛkʃən] *n.* [U] 完美

Perfection is shallow, unreal, and dangerously uninteresting. (Anne Lamott, Novelist)

完美既膚淺又不真實，而且危險又無趣。

I don't believe in **perfection**. I only know people with faults worth loving. (John Green, Young Adult Fiction Author)

我不相信完美，我只認識有缺陷的人，而且他們值得我的愛。

10. permanent [ˈpɝmənənt] *adj.* 永久的、永恆的、常在的

🐑 People aren't **permanent**. Remember this and you'll be just fine.
(Rachel Molchin, Blogger)
人不是永恆的，記住這點，那一切就會沒事了。

🐑 Never make a **permanent** decision based on temporary feelings.
(Wiz Khalifa, Rapper)
絕對不要根據瞬間的感受，下會有長久影響的決定。

11. persuasive [pəˈswesɪv] *adj.* 勸說的、有說服力的

🐑 To be **persuasive**, we must be believeable; to be believable, we
must be truthful. (Egbert Murrow, Journalist)
要有說服力，我們必須讓人感到可信，要讓人感覺可信，我們必須坦率。

🐑 Truthful words are not beautiful; and beautiful words are not
truthful. Good words are not **persuasive**; **persuasive** words are not
good. (Lao Tzu, Philosopher)
信言不美，美言不信。善者不辯，辯者不善。

12. physical [ˈfɪzɪkl̩] *adj.* 身體的、物質的

🐑 Beauty is how you feel inside, and it is reflected in your eyes. It is
not something **physical**. (Sophia Loren, Actress)
美麗是你內在的感受，它會反映在你的眼神中，美麗不是肉體上的。

🐑 If you always put a limit on everything you do, **physical** or anything else, it will spread into your life. You must go beyond them.
(Bruce Lee, Martial Artist)
如果對每件事，不論在體能或其他方面，你都設限，它會擴散到你的生
活中，你必須跨越它們。

13. plentiful [ˈplɛntɪfəl] *adj.* 豐富的、充足的、富裕的

🔲 Readers are **plentiful** but thinkers are rare. (Anthony Burgess, Writer/Composer)

讀者很多，但思想家卻很罕見。

🔲 Work is hard, distractions are **plentiful**, and time is short. (Adam Hochschild, Author)

工作很艱難，到處都是讓人分心的事物，但時間卻很不足。

14. portable [ˈportəbl̩] *adj.* 便於攜帶的、輕便的

🔲 I lead a very busy life and don't have a lot of time, so my skincare needs to be **portable**. (Erin O'Conner, Model)

我生活很忙碌，而且沒甚麼時間，所以皮膚保養必須在路上做。

🔲 Books are funny little **portable** pieces of thoughts. (Susan Sontag, Writer)

書本是充滿想法，可攜帶的有趣小東西。

15. possession [pəˈzɛʃən] *n.* [U] [C] 擁有、所有物 possessions

🔲 The **possession** of anything begins in the mind. (Bruce Lee, Martial Artist)

心是擁有任何事物的起點。

🔲 Music is everybody's **possession**. Nobody owns it. (John Lennon, Singer/Songwriter)

音樂是大家的，沒有一個人擁有它。

Unit 19

從小地方累積成功

趣味字彙表

1.	predict *vt. vi.*（作）預言、（作）預料	9.	publish *vt. vi.* 出版
2.	preserve *vt.* 保存、維護	10.	pursuit *n.* [U] 追求、尋求
3.	prime *adj.* 最初的、基本的、主要的	11.	rage *n.* [C][U] 狂怒、強烈的慾望
4.	privacy *n.* [U] 私生活、隱私	12.	rebel *n.* [C] 造反者、反叛者
5.	privilege *n.* [C][U] 特權、恩典、殊榮	13.	reception *n.* [U] 接見、歡迎、反應
6.	proceed *vi.* 繼續進行、著手	14.	recognition *n.* [U] 認出、承認、賞識
7.	production *n.* [U] 生產、製作	15.	recreation *n.* [C][U] 消遣、娛樂
8.	professional *n.* [C] 專家		

趣味字彙句 cc ◎MP3 19

1. predict [prɪˋdɪkt] *vt. vi.* （作）預言、（作）預料 predicted predicted

🐸 Life comes at us in waves. We can't **predict** those waves, but we can learn how to surf. (Daniel Jay Millman, Author/Lecturer)
生命以波浪的形式像我們湧來，我們無法預測那些浪，但我們可以學習如何衝浪。

🐸 You can plan a pretty picnic, but you can't **predict** the weather. (Andre Lauren Benjamin, Rapper/Songwriter)
你可以計畫一次令人愉快的野餐，但你無法預測天氣。

2. preserve [prɪˋzɝv] *vt.* 保存、維護 preserved preserved

🐸 I think it's nice to have a little mystery, and I'd like to **preserve** some of my private life. (Maggie Q, Actress)
我覺得能保有一點神祕感是很好的，而且我希望保護我某部分的隱私。

🐸 I wanted to **preserve** the spirit of my songs in Spanish. I am the same Shakira in English and in Spanish. (Shakira, Singer)
我想要保留我唱西文歌時的精神，我唱英文歌跟西文歌的時候是同一個夏奇拉。

3. prime [praɪm] *adj.* 最初的、基本的、主要的

🐸 Our **prime** purpose is to help others. If you can't help them, at least don't hurt them. (Dalai Lama, Leader)
我們最重要的目的是幫助他人。如果你不能幫助他們，那至少不要傷害他們。

🐸 Forty to sixty years old is your **prime**. (Jerry Seinfeld, Comedian/Actor)
四十歲 到六十歲是人生的高峰。

Part 1 「趣」你的單字基礎篇

Part 2 「趣」你的單字進階篇

119

4. privacy [ˈpraɪvəsɪ] *n.* [U] 私生活、隱私

🐦 I value my **privacy** and my personal life. I don't use my personal life to be famous. (Scarlett Johansson, Actress)
我很重視我的隱私和個人生活，我絕不利用我的私生活賺取名氣。

🐦 The worst thing about being famous is that nobody respects your **privacy**. (Justin Timberlake, Singer/Actor)
出名最糟的部分就是沒人會尊重你的隱私。

5. privilege [ˈprɪvḷɪdʒ] *n.* [C][U] 特權、恩典、殊榮 privileges

🐦 Writing is a **privilege** and a gift. It's a gift to yourself, and it's a gift of giving a story to someone. (Amy Tan, Writer)
寫作是一種殊榮，是一種禮物。它是一種給自己的禮物，是一份把故事給他人的禮物。

🐦 Life is a gift, and it offers us the **privilege** to give something back by becoming more. (Anthony Robbins, Motivational Speaker)
生命是一份禮物，它提供給我們一份殊榮，讓我們能有所成長以回饋社會。

6. proceed [prəˈsid] *vi.* 繼續進行、著手 proceeded proceeded

🐦 If you choose the wrong questions and you **proceed**, you still get a result, but it's not interesting (Bruce Nauman, Artist)
如果你選錯問題，卻還是繼續進行，你會得到一個結果，但它會很無趣。

🐦 For art and dreams, may you **proceed** freely. In life, you need to proceed with balance and careful planning. (Patti Smith, Singer/ Songwriter)
對於藝術和夢想，希望你能自由地進行。人生中，你需要平衡地往前，並小心地計畫。

7. production [prə`dʌkʃən] n. [U] 生產、製作

- The **production** of too many useful things results in too many useless people. (Karl Marx, Philosopher)
  產出太多有用東西，結果就是出現太多沒用的人。

- Every **production** of an artist should be the expression of an adventure of his soul. (W. Somerset Maugham, Playwright)
  藝術家的每個作品都應該表達出他靈魂的冒險。

8. professional [prə`fɛʃən!] n. [C] 專家 professionals

- A **professional** is someone who can do his best work when he doesn't feel like it. (Alistair Cooke, Journalist)
  專家就是不想要的時候也可以做得好的人。

- **Professional** is not a label you give yourself. It's a description you hope others will apply to you. (David Maister, Writer)
  專家這個標籤不是自己給的，而是一種你希望別人會用來形容你的字眼。

9. publish [`pʌblɪʃ] vt. vi. 出版 published published

- Someone recently asked if they could **publish** a book of pictures of me sleeping because there are so many. (Cara Delevingne, Model/Actress)
  最近有個人問我可不可以出一本書，裡面都放我睡覺的照片，因為這樣的照片實在太多了。

- I will carry on with writing, but I don't know if I want to **publish** again after Harry Potter. (J.K. Rowling, Author)
  我會繼續寫作，但我不確定在《哈利波特》之後我會不會還想要再出版書籍。

10. pursuit [pəˈsut] n. [U] 追求、尋求

- Happiness is the **pursuit** of reality. (Parker Palmer, Author)
  快樂就是追求真實。

- Things shouldn't come easily. There should be joy in the chase and excitement in the **pursuit**. (Branch Rickey, Baseball player)
  事情不該輕鬆到手，在追求過程中應該有喜悅與激動。

11. rage [redʒ] n. [C][U] 狂怒、強烈的慾望 rages

- As a child, it took me 10 months to learn how to tie my shoe laces. I must have cried with **rage**. (George Steiner, Literary Critic)
  我小時候花了十個月才學會綁鞋帶，我肯定有憤怒的大哭。

- After you forgive someone, you feel sadness instead of **rage**. You have nothing left to say about it at all. (Clarissa Pinkola Estes, Author)
  在你原諒人之後，你會感受到悲傷，而不是憤怒，你對這件事再也沒話可說了。

12. rebel [ˈrɛbl̩] n. [C] 造反者、反叛者 rebels

- The only people who ever called me a **rebel** were people who wanted me to do what they wanted. (Nick Nolte, Actor)
  有些人說過我是反叛者，但他們都想要我做他們想要的事。

- Other people will call me a **rebel**, but I just feel like I'm living my life and doing what I want to do. (Joan Jett, Guitarist/Singer)
  人們可能會說我是個反叛者，但我覺得我只不過是過我的日子，做我想做的事。

13. reception [rɪˋsɛpʃən] *n.* [U] 接見、歡迎、反應

🐝 It's impossible to control the **reception** of your work. The only thing you can control is the work you create. (Kim Edwards, Author)
你無法控制你的作品得到的反應，但你可以控制你創造的作品。

🐝 When you write, you can't think about the **reception**. It has to be worth it even if no one reads it. (Ta-Nehisi Coates, Writer)
寫作的時候，你不能想著他人的反應，作品即使沒人看也必須要有價值。

14. recognition [rɛkəgˋnɪʃən] *n.* [U] 認出、承認、賞識

🐝 People work hard for money but do their best for **recognition** and praise. (Dale Carnegie, Writer)
人們為了錢努力工作，但為了認同和讚賞會使盡全力。

🐝 Love is the joy of **recognition** from those who matter most. (Alexander Smith, Poet)
愛是因為在意的人表示認同的時候所產生的快樂。

15. recreation [rɛkrɪˋeʃən] *n.* [C][U] 消遣、娛樂 recreations

🐝 If bread is the first necessity of life, **recreation** is a close second. (Edward Bellamy, Author)
如果麵包是生命的首要條件，那娛樂是緊隨在後的第二。

🐝 My job is what millions of people do for fun and **recreation**. How can you not like that? (Paula Creamer, Golfer)
我的工作是數百萬人平常為了有趣和消遣才做的，你怎麼能不喜歡這樣的生活？

Part 1 「趣」你的單字基礎篇

Part 2 「趣」你的單字進階篇

Unit 20

從事自己想做的事

趣味字彙表

1.	reform *n.* [C][U] 改革、改良；*vt.* 改革、改造	9.	severe *adj.* 嚴重的、劇烈的
2.	refresh *vt. vi.* 使清新、恢復精神	10.	significance *n.* [U] 重要（性）、意義、含義
3.	regarding *prep.* 關於、就……而論	11.	slight *adj.* 輕微的、微小的、脆弱的
4.	ruin *vt. vi.* （使）毀滅、（使）變成廢墟	12.	spare *adj.* 多餘的、剩下的
5.	reward *n.* [C][U] 報答、報償	13.	spiritual *adj.* 精神（上）的、心靈的、神聖的
6.	route *n.* [C] 路線、途徑	14.	split *vt. vi.* （被）切開、（被）撕裂
7.	sacrifice *n.* [C] [U] 犧牲；*vt.* 犧牲	15.	strengthen *vt. vi.* 加強、增強
8.	satisfaction *n.* [U] [C] 滿足、快樂、樂事		

趣味字彙句 MP3 20

1. reform [rɪˈfɔrm] *n.* [C][U] 改革、改良 reforms；*vt.* 改革、改造 reformed reformed

🐛 People who care too much about what other people think can never begin a **reform**. (Susan B. Anthony, Women's Rights Activist)
太擔心別人想法的人永遠都開始一項改革。

🐛 At twenty, a man is full of fight and hope. He wants to **reform** the world. (Rodney Dangerfield, Comedian)
二十歲的時候，男人充滿鬥志與希望，想要改變世界。

2. refresh [rɪˈfrɛʃ] *vt. vi.* 使清新、恢復精神 refreshed refreshed

🐛 You can **refresh** what you're thinking about. (Ernesto Bertarelli, Businessman)
你可以翻新你的想法。

🐛 Rest when you are tired. **Refresh** and renew yourself, and then get back to work. (Ralph Marston, American Football Player)
疲累的時候，就休息吧。重新提起精神、重新振作，然後回去工作。

3. regarding [rɪˈgɑrdɪŋ] *prep.* 關於、就……而論

🐛 The amazing thing is, we have a choice everyday **regarding** the attitude we will have for that day. (Charles R. Swindoll, Pastor)
驚人的是，我們每天都要做一個決定，要以甚麼態度面對那一天。

🐛 I always tried to do things by example, even though I was not a very good mother **regarding** routines and family life. (Vivienne Westwood, Fashion Designer)
我做事時盡量以身作則，雖然以例行公事和家庭生活來說，我不是個很好的母親。

Part 1 「趣」你的單字基礎篇

Part 2 「趣」你的單字進階篇

4. ruin [ˈruɪn] *vt. vi.* （使）毀滅、（使）變成廢墟 ruined ruined

🐞 Traveling **ruins** happiness! You cannot look at another building after seeing Italy. (Fanny Burney, Novelist)
旅行毀了快樂，看過義大利之後，你眼裡容不下其他建築物。

🐞 The roads to **ruin** are women and gambling. The most pleasant way is women and the quickest way is gambling. (Georges Pompidou, French Statesman)
自我毀滅的途徑是女人與賭博，最令人愉快的路是女人，而最快的路是賭博。

5. reward [rɪˈwɔrd] *n.* [C][U] 報答、報償 rewards

🐞 The **reward** for work well done is the opportunity to do more. (Jonas Edward Salk, Medical Researcher)
工作做得好的獎賞就是擁有可以再做更多的機會。

🐞 To gain profit without risk, experience without danger, and **reward** without work is impossible.
想要不經冒險得到利潤，不經危險得到體驗，不工作就得到獎勵，這些都是不可能的。

6. route [rut] *n.* [C] 路線、途徑

🐞 The surest **route** to jealousy is to compare. (Dorthy Corkille Briggs, Writer)
「忌妒」的確定途徑就是「比較」。

🐞 I've run the Boston Marathon six times before. The best part is the beautiful changes of the view along the **route**. (Haruki Murakami, Writer)
我跑過波士頓馬拉松六次了，其中最棒的部分就是路途上景色的變化。

7. sacrifice [ˈsækrəˌfaɪs] *n.* [C] [U] 犧牲 sacrifices；*vt.* 犧牲 sacri-ficed sacrificed

🐸 I will not give up. Freedom can only be won through hardship and **sacrifice**. (Nelson Mandela, President)
我不會放棄，只有經過艱困和犧牲才能贏得自由。

🐸 Football is like life— it requires hard work, **sacrifice**, and respect for others. (Vince Lombardi, Football Coach)
橄欖球就像人生，需要努力、犧牲和互相尊重。

8. satisfaction [sætɪsˈfækʃən] *n.* [U] [C] 滿足、快樂、樂事 satisfac-tions

🐸 Success is finding **satisfaction** in giving a little more than you take. (Christopher Reeve, Actor)
成功是比你得到的多付出一點，並從中找到滿足。

🐸 Basketball has been everything to me. It's where I experienced the strongest sense of pain, joy, and **satisfaction**. (Michael Jordan, Basketball Player)
籃球是我的一切，它讓我感受到最強烈的痛苦、喜悅和滿足感。

9. severe [səˈvɪr] *adj.* 嚴重的、劇烈的

🐸 I might look successful and happy to you, but I once suffered from **severe** hopelessness. (Ji-Hae Park, Violinist)
在你看來，我可能成功、快樂，但我曾經陷入嚴重的絕望中。

🐸 I have a **severe** addiction to the game 'Angry Birds'. I always play one game after another and another. (Kevin Nealon, Comedian)
我玩「憤怒鳥」玩到嚴重上癮，我一場接著一場地玩。

10. significance [sɪgˋnɪfəkəns] *n.* [U] 重要（性）、意義、含義

🐸 Being able to care is the thing that gives life its deepest **significance**. (Pau Casals I Defillo, Cellist & Conductor)
關懷的能力給生命最深的意義。

🐸 Art teaches nothing, expect the **significance** of life. (Michael Korda, Writer/Novelist)
藝術沒有教我們任何東西，除了人生的意義之外。

11. slight [slaɪt] *adj.* 輕微的、微小的、脆弱的

🐸 I always wanted to find true love without any fake or **slight** moments. (Angelina Jolie, Actress)
我一直都很想要不需經過虛假或脆弱的時刻就可以找到真愛。

🐸 All my dreams came true. I became Mr. Universe, and I became a top actor even though I speak with a **slight** accent. (Arnold Schwarzenegger, Actor/Politician)
我所有的夢想都已成真，我當上了環球先生，而且雖然我有點口音，我還是成為了數一數二的演員。

12. spare [spɛr] *adj.* 多餘的、剩下的

🐸 Playing video games is something I enjoy in my **spare** time. I've always been a gamer. (Kevin Maurice Garnett, Basketball Player)
我空閒時間都愛打電動，我一直以來都是個電玩家。

🐸 Even working actors have a lot of **spare** time. I often go sit at a Starbucks and wait for my agent to call me. (Nick Offerman, Actor)
即使專業演員都會有很多空閒時間，我常常坐在星巴克等我的經紀人打電話給我。

13. spiritual [`spɪrɪtʃʊəl] *adj.* 精神（上）的、心靈的、神聖的

Happiness is the **spiritual** experience of living every minute with love, grace, and thankfulness. (Denis E. Waitley, Motivational Speaker/Writer)

快樂就是每分鐘都過得充滿愛、優雅與感激的一種心靈經歷。

Sometimes you struggle so hard to feed your family one way, you forget to feed them in a **spiritual** sense. (James Brown, Singer/Musician)

有時候你努力掙扎著用一種方法養活你的家，你卻忘了在精神層面上供給他們。

14. split [splɪt] *vt.* *vi.* （被）切開、（被）撕裂 split split

We were pretty good friends until the Beatles started to **split** up and Yoko came into it. (Paul McCartney, Singer/Songwriter)

我們本來是很好的朋友，直到披頭四開始分裂，然後洋子介入。

If people have **split** views about your work, I think it's a compliment. (Stephen Joshua Sondheim, Composer)

如果人們對你的作品有不同的意見，我認為那是讚美。

15. strengthen [`strɛŋθən] *vt.* *vi.* 加強、增強 strengthened strengthened

A man and a woman must support and **strengthen** each other. They just can't do it by themselves. (Marilyn Monroe, Actress/Model)

男人和女人應互相扶持，並幫助對方變強大，只靠自己是無法達成的。

Some people **strengthen** society just by being the kind of people they are. (John W. Gardner, Educator)

有些人只靠做自己就可以強化社會。

Unit 21

承擔責任且愛自己

趣味字彙表

1.	suggestion *n.* [C][U] 建議	9.	thoughtful *adj.* 深思的、細心的、體貼的
2.	surrender *vt. vi.* 放棄、（使）投降、（使）自首	10.	tolerance *n.* [U] [C] 寬容、忍耐（力）
3.	sway *vi. vt.* 搖擺，動搖	11.	tough *adj.* 棘手的、嚴格的、堅韌的
4.	syllable *n.* [C] 音節	12.	tragic *adj.* 悲劇的
5.	tendency *n.* [C] 癖性、傾向、趨勢	13.	unique *adj.* 唯一的、獨一無二的
6.	tense *adj.* 繃緊的、（心理或神經）緊張的	14.	volunteer *n.* [C] 志願者、義工
7.	terrify *vt.* 使害怕、使恐怖	15.	abide *vt.* 忍受、頂住、等候
8.	theme *n.* [C] 話題、主題		

趣味字彙句 🎧🎧 🔘 MP3 21

1. suggestion [səˋdʒɛstʃən] *n.* [C][U] 建議 suggestions

🦗 If you're the greatest, it's okay to say you're the greatest. My **suggestion** to everybody is to be their own greatest fan. (Chaim Witz)
如果你是最好的，說自己是最好的是沒關係的。我給每個人的建議是當他們自己最大的粉絲。

🦗 Negative criticism is the cheapest of all comments because it does not require effort like **suggestions**. (Charles Martin Jones, Animator)
負面的批評是最沒價值的評論，因為他不像建議還要付出努力。

2. surrender [səˋrɛndə] *vt. vi.* 放棄、（使）投降、（使）自首

🦗 When you go through hardships and decide not to **surrender**, that is strength. （Arnold Schwarzenegger, Actor/Politician）
當你經歷艱苦時，決定不妥協，那就是力量。

🦗 As president, the two happiest days of my life were entering the office and my **surrender** of it. (Martin Van Buren, President)
當總統的時候，我生命中最快樂的兩天就是入駐總統府的那天以及交接的那一天。

3. sway [swe] *vi. vt.* 搖擺，動搖 swayed swayed

🦗 Trees love to toss and **sway**. They make such happy noises. (Emily Carr, Artist)
樹木喜歡搖擺，它們總發出如此令人快樂的聲音。

🦗 Don't let the opinions of the average man **sway** you. (Robert Gray Allen, Businessman)
不要因為平凡人的意見而動搖了。

4. syllable [ˋsɪləbḷ] *n.* [C] 音節 syllables

The audience needs to understand every **syllable** to grasp the meaning of the song. (Kathryn Elizabeth Smith, Singer)
觀眾需要懂每個音節才能真的懂這首歌的意思。

With network shows, writers can be so protective of every **syllable**. (Michael Garrett Shanks, Actor)
在電視網節目裡，作家對每個音節都很保護。

5. tendency [ˋtɛndənsɪ] *n.* [C] 癖性、傾向、趨勢 tendencies

I love to sleep. My life has a **tendency** to fall apart when I'm awake. (Ernest Miller Hemingway, Novelist)
我愛睡覺。我的生活好像在我醒著的時候特別容易瓦解。

Anyone who has lost track of time when using a computer knows the **tendency** to miss lunch. (Sir Timothy John Berners-Lee, Computer Scientist)
有用電腦用到忘記時間的人都知道玩電腦的時候很容易錯過午飯。

6. tense [tɛns] *adj.* 繃緊的、（心理或神經）緊張的

Exercise helps me whenever I feel **tense** or stressed. I will go to the gym or out on a bike ride with the girls. (Michelle Obama, First Lady)
每當我感到緊繃或壓力大的時候，運動是很有幫助的。我會去健身房或是跟女兒一起去騎腳踏車。

Every year of playing, I try to relax one more muscle. The **tenser** you are, the less you can hear. (Yo-Yo Ma, Cellist)
每年演奏，我都試著再放鬆一個肌肉。你越緊繃，能聽到的越少。

7. terrify [ˈtɛrəˌfaɪ] *vt.* 使害怕、使恐怖 terrified terrified

🐛 I'm strongly independent, but I'm also **terrified** of being alone. (Adam Levine, Singer)

我十分獨立，但同時我也害怕一個人。

🐛 I've been **terrified** every moment of my life, and I've never let it keep me from doing a single thing I wanted to do. (Georgia O' Keeffe, Artist)

我一生沒有一個時刻是不害怕的，但我從不讓恐懼阻礙我做我想做的事。

8. theme [θim] *n.* [C] 話題、主題 themes

🐛 The **theme** for me is love and the lack of it. We all want love, but we don't know how to get it. (Ryan Gosling, Actor)

對我來說，主題是愛以及愛的缺乏，我們都想要愛，但我們不知道怎麼得到它。

🐛 You can't tell any kind of story without having some kind of **theme**, something to say between the lines. (Robert Earl Wise, Director)

講故事的時候不能沒有某個主題，或沒有隱藏在字裡行間的訊息。

9. thoughtful [ˈθɔtfəl] *adj.* 深思的、細心的、體貼的

🐛 My rules for life are to be honest, **thoughtful**, and caring. (Prince William, Duke of Cambridge)

我人生的原則是做個誠實、體貼和有愛心的人。

🐛 Writing in a journal reminds you of your goals and your lessons in life. It is a place where you can hold a **thoughtful** conversation with yourself. (Robin Sharma, Writer)

寫日記讓你得以提醒自己你的目標和人生的教訓，在日記裡你能夠跟自己進行深刻的對話。

Part 1 「趣」你的單字基礎篇

Part 2 「趣」你的單字進階篇

10. tolerance [ˈtɑlərəns] *n.* [U] [C] 寬容、忍耐（力）tolerances

🐾 When traveling with someone, take large doses of **tolerance** and understanding with your morning coffee. (Helen Hayes MacArthur, Actress)

當你要和某人一起旅行時，配一大劑量的包容心與理解心搭你的早晨咖啡。

🐾 **Tolerance** is giving everyone else the rights that you claim for yourself. (Robert Green Ingersoll, Lawyer)

包容就是讓每個人都有你主張你該有的權利。

11. tough [tʌf] *adj.* 棘手的、嚴格的、堅韌的

🐾 **Tough** times never last, but tough people do. (Robert Harold Schuller, Televangelist)

艱難的時光不會太久，但堅強的人會走到最後。

🐾 There's no changing your mind about whom you love. That's the **tough** part of being in love. (Piper Perabo, Actress)

對於愛上誰，我們無法改變，這就是陷入戀愛的困難處。

12. tragic [ˈtrædʒɪk] *adj.* 悲劇的

🐾 It's **tragic** that we put off living. We are all dreaming of some magical rose garden instead of enjoying the roses outside our windows today. (Dale Carnegie, Writer)

可悲的是，我們都在拖延過生活。我們都夢想有座神奇的玫瑰花園，而不去看當下在我們窗外的玫瑰花。

🐾 Life would be **tragic** if it weren't funny. (Stephen Hawking, Physicist/Author)

人生如果不好笑，那就太悲慘了。

13. unique [juˋnik] *adj.* 唯一的、獨一無二的

🐞 The more you like yourself, the less you are like anyone else, which makes you **unique**. (Walt Disney, Entrepreneur)
只要你越愛自己，你就越不像其他人，而你也因此獨特。

🐞 Never stop fighting until you find your **unique** self. Continuously acquire knowledge and realize the great things in your life. (Avul Pakir Jainulabdeen, President)
在你找到獨特的自我以前，不要停止奮鬥。不斷地增進自己的知識，以實現生命中更偉大的事物。

14. volunteer [ˌvɑlənˋtɪr] *n.* [C] 志願者、義工 volunteers

🐞 I love to make travel plans! I **volunteer** to plan trips for everyone I know. (Lauren Weisberger, Novelist)
我喜歡計畫旅行！我常常自願幫我認識的人計畫。

🐞 We all have a responsibility to **volunteer** somewhere. I'm lucky that I get to see what's out there and what's happening. (Jennifer Garner, Actress)
我們都有責任當義工，哪都可。我很幸運可以看到外面的世界有甚麼、發生甚麼事。

15. abide [əˋbaɪd] *vt.* 忍受、頂住、等候 abided abided

🐞 A wise person decides slowly but **abides** by these decisions. (Arthur Ashe, Tennis player)
智者做決定緩慢，但謹守這些決定。

🐞 Those who trust to chance must **abide** by the results of chance. (Calvin Coolidge, President)
靠運氣的人，就要忍受靠運氣的結果。

Unit 22

相信希望

趣味字彙表

1.	abolish *vt.* 廢除、廢止、徹底破壞	9.	altitude *n.* [U] [C] 高度、高處、海拔
2.	abrupt *adj.* 突然的、魯莽的	10.	ample *adj.* 豐富的、足夠的
3.	absurd *adj.* 荒謬的、可笑的	11.	ascend *vi. vt.* 上升
4.	accustom *vt.* 使習慣（於）	12.	beware *vt. vi.* 當心
5.	affection *n.* [U] [C] 愛、情愛	13.	barren *adj.* 貧瘠的、缺乏的
6.	agony *n.* [C][U] 極度痛苦	14.	beneficial *adj.* 有益的、有利的
7.	allergy *n.* [C] 過敏症	15.	blur *vi. vt.* 變模糊；*n.* [C] 模糊
8.	allergic *adj.* 過敏的		

趣味字彙句 　🅲🅲　⊙MP3 22

1. abolish [ə'bɑlɪʃ] *vt.* 廢除、廢止、徹底破壞 abolished abolished

To be creative is to **abolish** the gap between the body, the mind and the soul, between science and art, between fiction and nonfiction. (Nawal El Saadawi, Feminist writer)

想要有創意就要消除身體、頭腦與心靈之間，科學與藝術之間，以及想像與現實之間的隔閡。

The only way to **abolish** war is to make peace seem heroic. (John Dewey, Philosopher)

消滅戰爭的唯一方法是讓和平變成一件英勇的事。

2. abrupt [ə'brʌpt] *adj.* 突然的、魯莽的

Revolution— in politics, an **abrupt** change in the form of misgovernment. (Ambrose Bierce, Journalist)

造反：在政治上，是以惡政的形式帶來的劇變。

At first I probably seem very **abrupt**, but I like efficiency. I always think, 'Let's get the work over with so we can thoroughly enjoy the play. (Kathy Reichs, Writer)

我可能第一眼看起來很魯莽，但我喜歡效率。我總是想：「我們趕快把工作做完好真正的享受玩樂吧」。

3. absurd [əb'sɝd] *adj.* 荒謬的、可笑的

If at first the idea is not **absurd**, then there is no hope for it. (Albert Einstein, Physicist)

一個新的想法在一開始如果不顯得荒謬，那它就沒希望了。

It's really a wonder that I haven't dropped all my ideals, because they seem so **absurd**. (Anne Frank, Writer)

我沒有把我的理想全都拋棄，也是奇事，因為它們看起來似乎很荒謬。

4. accustom [əˈkʌstəm] *vt.* 使習慣（於） accustomed accustomed

❦ If you **accustom** yourself to speak well of others, you are always in a paradise. (Rumi, Poet)
如果你讓自己習慣對人常常說好話，那麼你將常常感覺身處天堂。

❦ **Accustom** yourself continually to make many acts of love, for they enkindle and melt the soul. (Saint Teresa of Avila, Saint)
要讓你自己不斷地做許多有愛心的行動，因它們點燃且融化靈魂。

5. affection [əˈfɛkʃən] *n.* [U] [C] 愛、情愛 affections

❦ I was born with an enormous need for **affection**, and a terrible need to give it. (Audrey Hepburn, Actress)
我天生渴求被愛，也迫切想去愛人。

❦ The wrong person makes you beg for attention, **affection**, love, and commitment. The right person gives you these things because they love you.
錯的人讓你懇求注目、關愛、愛情以及承諾，對的人會因為愛你給你這些東西。

6. agony [ˈægənɪ] *n.* [C][U] 極度痛苦 agonies

❦ One of the greatest **agonies** is being in one sided love with someone.
最大的痛苦莫過於單戀了。

❦ Only in the **agony** of parting do we look into the depths of love. (Goerge Eliot, Author)
只有在面對離別的痛苦，我們才會了解到對彼此的愛有多深。

7. allergy [ˈælədʒɪ] *n.* [C] 過敏症 allergies

Please manifest my **allergies** into human form so I can punch them in the face.

拜託讓我的過敏以人類的形式顯現吧，好讓我可以揍他們一拳。

The only thing I like about my **allergy** face is using it to frighten my misbehaving children.

我唯一喜歡我過敏的臉的地方就是可以用它來嚇我頑皮的小孩。

8. allergic [əˈlɜdʒɪk] *adj.* 過敏的

In school, I learned about artists and how they were free to express themselves. I was **allergic** to conformity, and the lifestyle attracted me. (Grace Slick, Musician)

學生時期我學到許多藝術家與他們如何自由表達自己，我對順從過敏，而他們的生活方式很吸引我。

My daughter couldn't care less about me being famous. She finds it revolting and, like a lot of teenagers, is virtually **allergic** to me. (Dawn French, Comedian)

我女兒對我出名這件事一點都不關心，覺得這很噁心，而且和大多數的青少年一樣，她實際上是對我過敏。

9. altitude [ˈæltətjud] *n.* [U] [C] 高度、高處、海拔

Your attitude, not your aptitude, will determine your **altitude**. (Zig Ziglar, Author)

決定你人生高度的，不是你的才能，而是你的態度。

Because of the high **altitude**, you get drunk really fast. So everyone's drunk all the time. (Clea Duvall, Actress)

因為海拔高，你很快就會醉，所以大家隨時都處在喝醉的狀態。

10. ample [ˈæmpl̩] *adj.* 豐富的、足夠的

🐾 Do not be fooled into believing that because a man is rich he is necessarily smart. There is **ample** proof to the contrary. (Julius Rosenwald, Businessman)

不要誤以為有錢的人就一定很聰明，有大量的證據證明事實不是這樣的。

🐾 Whoever does not regard what he has as most **ample** wealth, is unhappy, though he be master of the world. (Epictetus, Philosopher)

那些不覺得他所擁有的是最足夠的財富的人，是不幸的，即便他擁有全世界。

11. ascend [əˈsɛnd] *vi. vt.* 上升 ascended ascended

🐾 As we **ascend** the social ladder, viciousness wears a thicker mask. (Erich Fromm, Psychologist)

我們在社會上地位爬得越高，我們的罪惡戴的面具就越厚。

🐾 I'll lift you and you lift me, and we'll both **ascend** together. (John Greenleaf Whittier, Poet)

我扶持你，你扶持我，我們將可一起向上提升。

12. beware [bɪˈwɛr] *vt. vi.* 當心 bewared bewared

🐾 **Beware** of the man who knows the answer before he understands the question.

小心在真正了解問題之前就知道答案的人。

🐾 **Beware** the barrenness of a busy life. (Socrates, Philosopher)

小心忙碌生活帶來的空洞。

13. barren ['bærən] *adj.* 貧瘠的、缺乏的

🛒 Friends make life dynamic, motivating and interesting. Without true friends life is **barren**.

朋友讓生活變得有活力、有動機和有趣，沒有真朋友的人生是很貧乏的。

🛒 Revenge is **barren** of itself: it is the dreadful food it feeds on; its delight is murder, and its end is despair. (Friedrich Schiller, Dramatist)

報復的本身是貧乏的：復仇只會滋生更多復仇，殺害是復仇快樂的來源，然而絕望是它的結局。

14. beneficial [bɛnə'fɪʃəl] *adj.* 有益的、有利的

🛒 Happiness is **beneficial** for the body, but it is grief that develops the powers of the mind. (Marcel Proust, Author)

快樂對身體有益，但發展內心能量的卻是悲痛。

🛒 Jogging is very **beneficial**. It's good for your legs and your feet. It's also very good for the ground. If makes it feel needed. (Charles M. Schulz, Cartoonist)

慢跑是很有益的，他對你的腿和腳都很好。慢跑對土地也很好，它讓地板有被需要的感覺。

15. blur [blɜ] *vi. vt.* 變模糊 blurred blurred； *n.* [C] 模糊 blurs

🛒 The supreme accomplishment is to **blur** the line between work and play. (Arnold J. Toynbee, Historian)

最大的成就莫過於模糊工作與玩樂的界線。

🛒 I'd been round the world a hundred times and had started to forget where I'd been. It was a massive **blur**. (Bryan Adams, Musician)

我去過世界各地好幾百遍，然後已經開始忘記我去過哪裡，一切都很模糊。

Part 1 「趣」你的單字基礎篇

Part 2 「趣」你的單字進階篇

Unit 23

別依賴物質使自己成長

趣味字彙表

1.	bribe *n.* 賄賂、行賄物； *vt. vi.* 行賄	9.	compel *vt.* 強迫
2.	bully *n.* [C] 惡霸； *vt. vi.* 威嚇、霸凌	10.	compliment *n.* [C] 讚美的話、恭維
3.	carefree *adj.* 無憂無慮的、輕鬆愉快的	11.	compound *vt. vi.* 使混合、【經】以複利計算
4.	cautious *adj.* 十分小心的、謹慎的	12.	comprehend *vt.* 理解、領會
5.	ceremony *n.* [C] 儀式、典禮	13.	compromise *vi.* 妥協、讓步
6.	commute *n.* [C] 通勤	14.	conceal *vt.* 隱藏，、隱瞞
7.	compact *n.* [C][U] 契約； *adj.* 簡潔的、緊湊的	15.	conceive *vt. vi.* 想像、抱有
8.	compassionate *adj.* 有同情心的，慈悲的		

趣味字彙句 🔊 MP3 23

1. bribe [braɪb] *n.* 賄賂、行賄物 bribes ; *vt. vi.* 行賄 bribed, bribed

🐏 It's really difficult working with kids and with babies because they are not cooperative subjects: they're not like undergraduates, who you can **bribe** with beer money or course credit. (Paul Bloom)
和小孩和寶寶合作真的很困難，他們不是很合作的實驗對象：他們不像大學生，你無法用啤酒錢和課程學分賄賂他們。

🐏 Though the **bribe** be small, yet the fault is great. (Edward Coke)
雖然賄賂的金額小，罪惡卻很大。

2. bully [ˋbʊlɪ] *n.* [C] 惡霸 bullies ; *vt. vi.* 威嚇、霸凌 bullied bullied

🐏 I realized that **bullying** never has to do with you. It's the bully who's insecure. (Shay Mitchell, Actress)
我了解到霸凌不一定是因為你，不安的是霸凌者。

🐏 People talk about **bullying**, but you can be your own bully. You can be the person who is standing in the way of your success. (Katy Perry, Singer)
人們常常談論霸凌，但你可能是自己的霸凌者，你可能是阻礙自己成功的人。

3. carefree [ˋkɛrˏfri] *adj.* 無憂無慮的、輕鬆愉快的

🐏 I want my kids to grow up and enjoy their childhood and be **carefree**. (Jim Morris, Athlete)
我希望我孩子的成長享受他們的童年，並能無憂無慮。

🐏 I love the way little kids dress themselves! They're completely **carefree** about how others perceive them. (Gillian Zinser, Actress)
我好喜歡小孩裝扮自己的方式，他們對別人的眼光毫不在意。

4. cautious [ˈkɔʃəs] *adj.* 十分小心的、謹慎的

🐸 The **cautious** seldom err. (Confucius, Philosopher)
以約失之者，鮮矣。

🐸 Let's be **cautious** about relying so much on material things that we have no energy left for the spiritual aspects of our lives. (James A. Forbes, Clergyman)
我們要小心，不要太依賴物質的東西，導致我們沒有力氣追求我們人生的精神層面。

5. ceremony [ˈsɛrəˌmonɪ] *n.* [C] 儀式、典禮 ceremonies

🐸 There are few hours in life more agreeable than the hour dedicated to the **ceremony** known as afternoon tea. (Henry James, Writer)
人生很少有比用來進行叫「下午茶」的這個儀式更令人愉悅的時間了。

🐸 A graduation **ceremony** is an event where the commencement speaker tells thousands of students dressed in identical caps and gowns that "individuality" is the key to success. (Robert Orben, Entertainer)
畢業典禮就是演講者告訴一群穿著一模一樣的學位帽與學位袍的學生「獨特性」是成功的關鍵。

6. commute [kəˈmjut] *n.* [C] 通勤 commutes

🐸 The only reason I come to work is to complain about the com-mute.
我來上班的唯一理由就是我可以抱怨交通。

🐸 President Bush has said that the economy is growing, that there are jobs out there. But you know, it's a long **commute** to China to get those jobs. (Tom Daschle, Politician)
布希總統說經濟在成長中，而且是有工作機會的。但你知道吧，到中國做那些工作的通勤時間是很長的。

7. compact [kəmˋpækt] *n.* [C][U] 契約 compacts；*adj.* 簡潔的、緊湊的

🐛 Justice is a kind of **compact** not to harm or be harmed. (Epicurus, Philosopher)
正義是一種不傷害別人否則你就會被傷害的契約。

🐛 My stories are very **compact**. I want them to say the most complex things in the simplest way. (Etgar Keret, Writer)
我的故事都很簡潔，我想用最簡單的方式述說最複雜的事。

8. compassionate [kəmˋpæʃənet] *adj.* 有同情心的、慈悲的

🐛 I haven't lost faith in human nature and I haven't decided to be less **compassionate** to strangers. (Armistead Maupin, Novelist)
我還沒對人性失望，而且我也還沒決定要對陌生人減少我的同情心。

🐛 One must be **compassionate** to one's self before external compassion. (Dalai Lama, Leader)
人在對外展現憐憫之前要先對自己慈悲。

9. compel [kəmˋpɛl] *vt.* 強迫 compelled compelled

🐛 To advise is not to **compel**. (Anton Chekhov, Dramatist)
給人建議並不是強迫。

🐛 While early childhood experiences may impel, they do not **compel**. In the end, evil is a matter of choice. (Andrew Vachss, Author)
童年的經驗或許會驅使，但不會強迫，到最後邪惡是一種選擇。

10. compliment [ˈkɑmpləmənt] *n.* [C] 讚美的話、恭維 compliments

🐛 Being taken for granted can be a **compliment**. It means that you've become a comfortable, trusted element in another person's life. (Joyce Brothers, Psychologist)

被當作理所當然也可能是個誇獎，這表示你在另一個人的生命裡已經變成一個舒服、值得信任的元素。

🐛 If you're not the one cooking, stay out of the way and **compliment** the chef. (Michael Strahan, Athlete)

如果你不是下廚的人，不要擋路，然後稱讚主廚吧。

11. compound [kɑmˈpaʊnd] *vt. vi.* 使混合、【經】以複利計算

🐛 **Compound** interest is the eighth wonder of the world. (Albert Einstein)

複利是世界第八大奇蹟。

🐛 By pouring money and goods into devastated regions, foreign aid workers sometimes **compound** the disruption and debauch the survivors. (James Buchan, Novelist)

因為傾倒金錢與物資遭摧毀的區域，國際救援人員有時加深分裂並使倖存者墮落。

12. comprehend [kɑmprɪˈhɛnd] *vt.* 理解、領會

🐛 As with real reading, the ability to **comprehend** subtlety and complexity comes only with time and a lot of experience. (Jeffrey Kluger, Writer)

就像閱讀一樣，要讀懂言語中的細微差異以及複雜是需要時間與經驗的。

🐛 I would rather not live in a world so small that my mind could **comprehend** it. (Harry Emerson Fosdick, Clergyman)

我寧可不活在一個我的大腦可以完全理解的小世界。

13. compromise [ˈkɑmprəˌmaɪz] *vi.* 妥協、讓步 compromised compromised

☕ When developing an idea, I remind myself not to start with **compromise**. (Janet Echelman, Artist)

當孕育一個想法的時候，我提醒自己不要以妥協為起點。

☕ If you set out to be liked, you would be prepared to **compromise** on anything at any time, and you would achieve nothing. (Margaret Thatcher, Leader)

如果你以得到喜愛為起點，那麼你就要準備好你會一直對所有事情妥協，也會因此無法完成任何事情。

14. conceal [kənˈsil] *vt.* 隱藏、隱瞞 concealed concealed

☕ True friendship ought never to **conceal** what it thinks. (St. Jerome, Saint)

真正的友誼，從不應該有隱瞞。

☕ It is harder to **conceal** ignorance than to acquire knowledge. (Arnold H. Glasow, Author)

嘗試隱藏無知比學得知識更難。

15. conceive [kənˈsiv] *vt. vi.* 想像、抱有 conceived conceived

☕ Most men today cannot **conceive** of a freedom that does not involve somebody's slavery. (W. E. B. Du Bois, Writer)

現在大部分的人無法想像一個不需要奴役他人的自由方法。

☕ Whatever the mind of man can **conceive** and believe, it can achieve. (Napoleon Hill, Writer)

人類可以達成任何他們想得到與相信的事。

Part 1 「趣」你的單字基礎篇

Part 2 「趣」你的單字進階篇

Unit 24

讓自己走的更遠

趣味字彙表

1.	condemn *vt.* 責備、宣告 ... 有罪	9.	contemplate *vt. vi.* 思量、仔細考慮
2.	conduct *n.* [U] 行為、品行	10.	contemporary *adj.* 當代的
3.	confront *vt.* 正視、對抗	11.	contend *vt. vi.* 爭奪、爭辯、奮鬥
4.	considerate *adj.* 體貼的、體諒的	12.	continuity *n.* [U] 連續性、持續性
5.	console *vt.* 安慰	13.	convert *vt. vi.* 轉變、使皈依
6.	constitutional *adj.* 憲法的、本質的	14.	corporation *n.* [C] 法人、股份（有限）公司
7.	contagious *adj.* 接觸傳染性的、會蔓延的	15.	copyright *n.* [C][U] 版權、著作權
8.	contaminate *vt.* 汙染、毒害		

趣味字彙句 🎧 🎧 💿 MP3 24

1. condemn [kənˋdɛm] *vt.* 責備、宣告 ... 有罪

🐸 Any fool can criticize, **condemn** and complain — and most fools do. (Benjamin Franklin, Politician)

任何笨蛋都會批評、責備與抱怨，而大部分的笨蛋實際上都會這樣做 。

🐸 To pursue a goal which is by definition unattainable is to **condemn** oneself to a state of perpetual unhappiness. (Emile Durkheim)

如果追求一個在定義上是不可能達成的目標，那麼人將註定陷入永久的不幸。

2. conduct [kənˋdʌkt] *n.* [U] 行為、品行

🐸 I have only two rules which I regard as principles of **conduct**. The first is, have no rules. The second is, be independent of the opinions of others. (Albert Einstein, Physicist)

我只有兩個我視為行為規範的準則，第一個是沒有規定，第二個是不要受他人意見的影響。

🐸 Circumstances are beyond human control, but our **conduct** is in our own power. (Benjamin Disraeli, Statesman)

人無法控制環境，但可以控制自己的品行。

3. confront [kənˋfrʌnt] *vt.* 正視、對抗 confronted confronted

🐸 When you **confront** a problem, you begin to solve it. (Rudy Giuliani, Politician)

當你正視一個問題時，你已開始解決這個問題。

🐸 The Holocaust forces us to **confront** the ramifications of indifference and inaction. (Tim Holden, Politician)

大屠殺強迫我們面對冷漠與坐視不管的後果。

4. considerate [kənˋsɪdərɪt] *adj.* 體貼的、體諒的

🛒 Being **considerate** of others will take you and your children further in life than any college degree. (Marian Wright Edelman)
對他人體諒會比任何大學文憑都能讓你與你的小孩在人生中走得更遠。

🛒 It is great to be **considerate** of others, but think before sacrificing your own needs to please them.
體諒他人是很好的，但在犧牲自己需求之前先想想吧。

5. console [ˋkɑnsol] *vt.* 安慰 consoled consoled

Imagination was given to man to compensate him for what he is not; a sense of humor to **console** him for what he is. (Francis Bacon, Philosopher)
想像力是讓人類補償他的所不是，而幽默感是來安慰他的所是。

🛒 If the career you have chosen has some unexpected inconvenience, **console** yourself by reflecting that no career is without them. (Jane Fonda, Actress)
如果你選擇的職業生涯有些預料外的不便，那麼安慰自己所有職業都是這樣的。

6. constitutional [ˌkɑnstəˋtjuʃənl̩] *adj.* 憲法的、本質的

🛒 A **constitutional** democracy is in serious trouble, if its citizenry does not have a certain degree of education and civic virtue. (Phillip E. Johnson, Educator)
在一個憲政民主國家中，如果人民沒有達到一定的教育與公民德行程度，那麼會出現嚴重的問題。

🛒 I have an inalienable, **constitutional** and natural right to love whom I may. (Victoria Woodhull, Activist)
我有不可剝奪、憲法規定的自然權利，可以愛我想愛的人。

7. contagious [kənˋtedʒəs] *adj.* 接觸傳染性的、會蔓延的

🐸 You don't always get what you ask for, but you never get what you don't ask for unless it's **contagious**! (Beverly Sills, Musician)
你無法每次得到你要求的，但你永遠得不到你沒要求的，除非那是會傳染的。

🐸 A healthy attitude is **contagious** but don't wait to catch it from others. Be a carrier. (Tom Stoppard, Dramatist)
健康的態度是會傳染的，但不要等到別人傳染給你，當帶菌者吧。

8. contaminate [kənˋtæməˌnet] *vt.* 汙染、毒害 contaminated contaminated

🐸 Glue actually **contaminates** recyclables. We throw things in a landfill just because they're glued together. (Janine Benyus, Writer)
黏著劑其實汙染了可回收物，我們把東西丟在垃圾掩埋場只因為他們是用黏著劑組合的。

🐸 **Contaminated** food is a major cause of diarrhea. (Gro Harlem Brundtland, Politician)
受汙染的食物是腹瀉的主要原因。

9. contemplate [ˋkɑntɛmˌplet] *vt. vi.* 思量、仔細考慮 contemplated contemplated

🐸 We need time to defuse, to **contemplate**. (Laurie Colwin, Author)
我們都需要時間解除武裝、思考。

🐸 For one minute, walk outside, stand there, in silence, look up at the sky, and **contemplate** how amazing life is.
花一分鐘，走出戶外，就站在那裡，靜靜的，抬頭看天空，思考人生有多美好。

10. contemporary [kənˈtɛmpəˌrɛrɪ] *adj.* 當代的

🐑 It's a mystery to me the way that **contemporary** art galleries function. (Steve Martin, Comedian)
現代藝廊運作的方式對我是個謎。

🐑 The problem, when comparing **contemporary** television to television in 1974, is that TV has become not just bad but sad. (P. J. O'Rourke, Comedian)
當比較現代電視與一九七四年的電視時,問題在於電視不是變得更糟,而是更悲哀。

11. contend [kənˈtɛnd] *vt. vi.* 爭奪、爭辯、奮鬥 contended contended

🐑 It is hard to **contend** against one's heart's desire; for whatever it wishes to have it buys at the cost of the soul. (Heraclitus, Philosopher)
對抗內心慾望是很困難的,慾望想要的將以靈魂為代價。

🐑 I **contend** that the strongest of all governments is that which is most free. (William Henry Harrison, President)
我強烈認為最自由的政府是最強大的。

12. continuity [kɑntəˈnjuətɪ] *n.* [U] 連續性、持續性

🐑 Libraries are reservoirs of strength, grace, and wit, reminders of order, calm and **continuity**, lakes of mental energy, neither warm nor cold, light nor dark. (Germaine Greer, Activist)
圖書館是力量、優雅與智慧的蓄水池,是秩序、平靜與延續提示,是一池池的心靈能量,不暖不冷,也不明不暗。

🐑 To walk through the ruined cities of Germany is to feel an actual doubt about the **continuity** of civilization. (George Orwell, Author)
走過德國的城市廢墟,就會真正感受到對人類文明能延續的懷疑。

13. convert [kənˋvɝt] *vt. vi.* 轉變、使皈依 converted converted

Adopting the right attitude can **convert** a negative stress into a positive one. (Hans Selye, Scientist)
採用正確的態度，可以讓你將負面的壓力轉變成正面的。

The freedom to **convert** is fundamental to freedom of religion. (Bob Inglis, Politician)
轉變宗教的自由是宗教自由的基礎。

14. corporation [ˌkɔrpəˋreʃən] *n.* [C] 法人、股份（有限）公司

Corporation: An ingenious device for obtaining profit without individual responsibility.(Ambrose Bierce, Journalist)
企業是一種不經個人責任得到利益的精明手段。

When you're a **corporation**, you're going to stick with what works. That's why every McDonald's is the same. (Will.i.am, Musician)
當你是一個企業的時候，你會堅持做可行的，這就是為什麼每間麥當勞都是一樣的。

15. copyright [ˋkɑpɪˌraɪt] *n.* [C][U] 版權、著作權 copyrights

I have always found it interesting that there are people who regard **copyright** infringement as a form of flattery. (Tom Lehrer, Musician)
我一直都覺得很有趣，有些人把侵犯著作權當作一種諂媚。

Actually, attorneys say, copying a purchased CD for even one friend violates the federal **copyright** code most of the time. (Charles Duhigg, Journalist)
事實上，根據律師的說法，拷貝一張買回來的 CD，就算只給一個朋友，大部分時候也是違反了聯邦著作權法。

Unit 25

社會的腐化、不平

趣味字彙表

1.	correspondence *n.* [U] 通信、符合	9.	declaration *n.* [C][U] 宣布、宣告
2.	corrupt *adj.* 腐敗的、貪汙的；*vt. vi.* （使）腐敗	10.	delegate *vt. vi.* 委託、授（權）
3.	counsel *n.* [U] 忠告、商議	11.	denial *n.* [C][U] 否認、拒絕
4.	cozy *adj.* 舒適的	12.	despair *n.* [U] 絕望
5.	currency *n.* [C][U] 貨幣	13.	despise *vt.* 鄙視、看不起
6.	curriculum *n.* [C] 學校的全部課程、（一門）課程	14.	destination *n.* [C] 目的地、目的
7.	decay *vt. vi.* （使）腐朽、衰敗	15.	destiny *n.* [C] 命運
8.	deceive *vt. vi.* 欺騙、蒙蔽		

趣味字彙句 🎧 📀 MP3 25

1. correspondence [kɔrəˋspɑndəns] *n.* [U] 通信、符合

🐾 I have enjoyed reading the **correspondence** between Gustav Mahler and Richard Strauss. The genuine friendship, competitiveness and support that thread through their communications are life lessons for us all. (Jessye Norman, Musician)

我很喜歡閱讀古斯塔夫·馬勒與理查•史特勞斯之間的通信，充斥在他們溝通之間的那真誠的友誼、競爭與支持對我們每個人都是人生的課程。

🐾 It's a shame that we've lost the art of letter-writing and saving **correspondence**. (Elizabeth McGovern, Actress)

我們已經失去寫信和保存信件的藝術，非常可惜。

2. corrupt [kəˋrʌpt] *adj.* 腐敗的、貪汙的； *vt. vi.* （使）腐敗

🐾 It's easy to view politicians as **corrupt** and voting essentially an act of picking the lesser of two evils. (Macklemore, Musician)

我們容易覺得政治人物都是腐敗的，而投票不過是從兩個惡魔中選擇比較不腐敗的。

🐾 Power doesn't corrupt people, people **corrupt** power. (William Gaddis, Novelist)

權力不會使人腐敗，人使權力腐敗。

3. counsel [ˋkaʊnsḷ] *n.* [U] 忠告、商議

🐾 Never take **counsel** from your fears. (Stonewall Jackson, Soldier)

不要接受你恐懼的忠告。

🐾 When we turn to one another for **counsel** we reduce the number of our enemies. (Khalil Gibran, Poet)

當我們向別人請求忠告時，我們也減少了我們的敵人。

4. cozy [ˈkozɪ] *adj.* 舒適的

It's the best feeling when you wake up and it's warm and **cozy**, and you don't have to go to work. (Emmy Rossum, Actress)
最棒的感覺莫過於當你起床的時候，天氣溫暖又舒服，然後你不用去上班。

I love to wear hoodies because you can get **cozy** and eat some food and your belly doesn't show! (Jared Padalecki, Actor)
我喜歡穿帽 T，因為你可以放鬆、吃東西，然後你的肚子不會跑出來。

5. currency [ˈkɝənsɪ] *n.* [C][U] 貨幣 currencies

Money is my military. I never send my money into battle unprepared and undefended. I send it to conquer and take **currency** prisoner back to me. (Kevin O'Leary, Businessman)
錢是我的軍隊，我從不讓我的錢在準備與防備不全的狀況下上戰場，我送它們出去是去征服敵方，並帶回貨幣囚犯。

Trust is a core **currency** of any relationship. (Kris Carr, Author)
信任是任何關係中最重要的流通貨幣。

6. curriculum [kəˈrɪkjələm] *n.* [C] 學校的全部課程、（一門）課程 curricula/curriculums

Real education is not about making sure every 7th grader has memorized all the facts some bureaucrats have put in the 7th grade **curriculum**. (Aaron Swartz, Businessman)
真正的教育不是確保每個七年級生都記得所有官僚放進七年級課程的事實。

I discovered Deborah Ellis's books after my head teacher encouraged me to go beyond the school **curriculum**. (Malala Yousafzai, Activist)
在我的導師鼓勵我超越學校課程後，我發現了黛伯拉艾里斯的書。

7. decay [dɪ'ke] *vt.* *vi.* （使）腐朽、衰敗 decayed decayed

Writing a novel is a terrible experience, during which the hair often falls out and the teeth **decay**. (Flannery O'Connor, Author)

寫小說是個糟糕的經驗，過程中頭髮時常掉落、牙齒蛀蝕。

Reality TV to me is the museum of social **decay**. (Gary Oldman, Actor)

實境節目對我來說展現了社會的潰敗。

8. deceive [dɪ'siv] *vt.* *vi.* 欺騙、蒙蔽 deceived, deceived

It is double pleasure to **deceive** the deceiver. (Niccolo Machiavelli, Writer)

欺騙騙子給人雙倍的愉悅感。

Nature never **deceives** us; it is we who deceive ourselves. (Jean-Jacques Rousseau, Philosopher)

大自然從不欺騙我們，是我們欺騙自己。

9. declaration [dɛklə'reʃən] *n.* [C][U] 宣布、宣告 declarations

Nature has never read the **Declaration** of Independence. It continues to make us unequal. (Will Durant, Historian)

大自然從沒讀過獨立宣言。她還是一直把我們造得不平等。

The UN **declaration** on human rights must always be first in line before religion or other cultural habits, in case of any conflict between them. (Bjorn Ulvaeus, Musician)

當有爭議的時候，聯合國世界人權宣言一定要先於宗教或其他文化習慣。

Part 1 「趣」你的單字基礎篇

Part 2 「趣」你的單字進階篇

10. delegate [ˈdɛləˌget] *vt. vi.* 委託、授(權) delegated delegated

🐾 Surround yourself with the best people you can find, **delegate** authority, and don't interfere as long as the policy you've decided upon is being carried out. (Ronald Reagan, President)

讓自己周遭充斥著你能找到的最棒的人才，授權，然後只要你決定的政策有被執行就不要干涉。

You can **delegate** authority, but you cannot delegate responsibility. (Byron Dorgan, Politician)

你可以授權，但你不能委託你的責任。

11. denial [dɪˈnaɪəl] *n.* [C][U] 否認、拒絕 denials

🐾 Delay is the deadliest form of **denial**. (C. Northcote Parkinson, Historian)

拖延是否認最致命的形式。

🐾 **Denial** helps us to pace our feelings of grief. There is a grace in denial. (Elisabeth Kubler-Ross, Psychologist)

否認幫助我們調整我們悲傷的腳步，否認中是有一種優雅的。

12. despair [dɪˈspɛr] *n.* [U] 絕望

🐾 Every time I see an adult on a bicycle, I no longer **despair** for the future of the human race. (H. G. Wells, Author)

每次我看到大人騎腳踏車，我就不再為人類的未來感到絕望。

🐾 If you look for comfort you will not get either comfort or truth only soft soap and wishful thinking to begin, and in the end, **despair**. (C. S. Lewis, Author)

如果你尋找安慰，那麼你不會找到安慰或事實，一開始只能找到奉承與一相情願，而最終則是找到絕望。

13. despise [dɪˋspaɪz] *vt.* 鄙視、看不起 despised despised

I **despise** formal restaurants. I find all of that formality to be very base and vile. I would much rather eat potato chips on the sidewalk. (Werner Herzog, Director)

我厭惡高級餐廳，我覺得全部的禮節都很糟糕與卑劣，我寧願在路邊吃洋芋片。

If we don't believe in freedom of expression for people we **despise**, we don't believe in it at all. (Noam Chomsky, Activist)

如果我們不相信我們討厭的人可以有言論自由，那麼我們其實完全不相信言論自由。

14. destination [dɛstəˋneʃən] *n.* [C] 目的地、目的 destinations

There's no **destination**. The journey is all that there is, and it can be very, very joyful. (Srikumar Rao, Educator)

目的地並不存在，只有過程，而這可能是非常、非常愉悅的。

All you need is the plan, the road map, and the courage to press on to your **destination**. (Earl Nightingale, Entertainer)

你只需要計畫、地圖以及勇氣就可以向你的目標奮勇前進。

15. destiny [ˋdɛstənɪ] *n.* [C] 命運 destinies

It is not in the stars to hold our **destiny** but in ourselves. (William Shakespeare, Dramatist)

掌握我們命運的並非星宿，而是我們自己。

It is in your moments of decision that your **destiny** is shaped. (Tony Robbins, Author)

我們做決定的那一刻，我們的命運就形成了。

Unit 26

擁有熱情

趣味字彙表

1.	destructive *adj.* 毀滅性的	9.	dreadful *adj.* 可怕的
2.	devotion *n.* [U] 奉獻	10.	duration *n.* [C][U] 持續時間
3.	devour *vt.* 吞沒、毀滅	11.	dwell *vi.* 居住
4.	dialect *n.* [C][U] 方言、（屬同一語系的）同源語	12.	ego *n.* [C][U] 自尊、自我
5.	disbelief *n.* [U] 懷疑	13.	elaborate *adj.* 精密的、複雜的
6.	discriminate *vi. vt.* 區別、歧視	14ã	elevate *vt.* 提升
7.	distinctive *adj.* 有特色的、特殊的	15.	embrace *vt. vi.* 擁抱、欣然接受
8.	dormitory *n.* [C] 宿舍		

趣味字彙句 MP3 26

1. destructive [dɪˋstrʌktɪv] *adj.* 毀滅性的

What you don't do can be a **destructive** force. (Eleanor Roosevelt)
我們所沒做的可能成為具毀滅性的威力。

Every man must decide whether he will walk in the light of creative altruism or in the darkness of **destructive** selfishness. (Martin Luther King, Jr., Leader)
每個人都需要決定他是要走在創造性利他主義的光明中，或是毀滅性利己主義的黑暗中。

2. devotion [dɪˋvoʃən] *n.* [U] 奉獻

To succeed in your mission, you must have single-minded **devotion** to your goal. (A. P. J. Abdul Kalam, Statesman)
要成功完成任務，你必須對你的目標有全心全意的奉獻。

The best gift you can give to a girl is your **devotion**, not some Louboutins. But buy those if you're busy, for sure. (Diplo)
你能給女人最好的禮物是你的忠誠，而不是紅底鞋。但如果你很忙還是要確保你有買那些鞋。

3. devour [dɪˋvaʊr] *vt.* 吞沒、毀滅 devoured devoured

Let my enemies **devour** each other. (Salvador Dali, Artist)
讓我的敵人互相毀滅吧。

But if we allow it to **devour** our time with vain, unproductive, and sometimes destructive pursuits, it becomes an entangling net. (Joseph B. Wirthlin, Businessman)
但如果我們允許他用虛無、沒有生產力且有時具毀滅性的事物吞沒我們的時間，那麼電腦可能變成牽絆我們的網。

4. dialect ['daɪəlekt] *n.* [C][U] 方言、（屬同一語系的）同源語 dialects

🐸 Each dancer has a different **dialect** that they speak. (Jon M. Chu, Director)

每個舞者都有他自己的語言。

🐸 This African American Vernacular English is more different from standard English than any other **dialect** spoken in continental North America. (William Labov, Writer)

非洲裔美國黑人英語和其他在北美洲使用的方言比起來，與標準英語更不同。

5. disbelief [dɪsbɪ'lif] *n.* [U] 懷疑

🐸 I'm a great audience. I cry very easily. I suspend **disbelief** in two seconds. (Stephen Sondheim, Composer)

我是個很棒的觀眾，我很容易哭，我兩秒內就會擱置我的懷疑。

🐸 It is now life and not art that requires the willing suspension of **disbelief**. (Lionel Trilling, Critic)

現在是人生，而不是藝術，需要你心甘情願地擱置你的懷疑。

6. discriminate [dɪ'skrɪmɪneɪt] *vi. vt.* 區別

🐸 Whether you're a mother or father, or a husband or a son, or a niece or a nephew or uncle, breast cancer doesn't **discriminate**. (Stephanie McMahon, Businesswoman)

不論你是母親或父親，先生或兒子，姪女、姪子或叔叔，乳癌都不會有差別待遇的。

🐸 I don't **discriminate** against anybody for their sexual preference, for their skin color. That's immature. (ASAP Rocky, Musician)

我不因為一個人的性取向或膚色而歧視他，那是很幼稚的。

7. distinctive [dɪˋstɪŋktɪv] *adj.* 有特色的、特殊的

In Australia, we don't have a **distinctive** Australian food, so we have food from everywhere all around the world. (Hugh Jackman)
澳洲沒有自己獨特的食物，所以我們有來自世界各地的食物。

Every man and woman is born into the world to do something unique and something **distinctive** and if he or she does not do it, it will never be done. (Benjamin E. Mays, Educator)
每個男人和女人生來都是要成就一件特殊的事情，如果他們不去做的話，那麼這件事便永遠不會被完成。

8. dormitory [ˋdɔmɪtri] *n.* [C] 宿舍 dormitories

In China, I lived in a **dormitory**, and the government paid for everything— food, buses. (Liang Chow, Athlete)
在中國的時候，我住宿舍，而且政府支付一切，包含食物、公車。

Wouldn't it be nice if all the people who are lonesome could live in one big **dormitory**, sleep in beds next to each other, talk, laugh, and keep the lights on as long as they want to? (Lenny Bruce)
如果孤獨的人可以一起住在一間大宿舍，床都挨在一起，聊天、歡笑、不關燈，到多晚都可以，這樣不是很好？

9. dreadful [ˋdredfl] *adj.* 可怕的

One travels to run away from routine, that **dreadful** routine that kills all imagination and all our capacity for enthusiasm. (Ella Maillart, Writer)
人們旅行是為了逃離例行公事，那些抹殺想像力和我們展現熱情的能力的可怕例行公事。

Every murderer when he kills runs the risk of the most **dreadful** of deaths. (Albert Camus, Philosopher)
每個殺人犯在殺人的時候，都冒著面對恐怖死亡的風險。

Part 1 「趣」你的單字基礎篇

Part 2 「趣」你的單字進階篇

10. duration [djʊ'reɪʃn] *n.* [C][U] 持續時間 durations

🐾 The value of life is not in its **duration**, but in its donation. You are not important because of how long you live, you are important because of how effective you live. (Myles Munroe, Clergyman)
生命的價值不在他的長短，而是它的貢獻，你重要不是因為你活得久，而是因為你的影響力。

🐾 We do not live to experience death. If we take eternity to mean not infinite temporal **duration** but timelessness, then eternal life belongs to those who live in the present. (Ludwig Wittgenstein, Philosopher)
我們活著不是要體驗死亡。如果我們不是把永恆看成無限的時間長度，而是不受時間影響的，那麼永生是屬於活在當下的人。

11. dwell [dwel] *vi.* 居住 dwelled dwelled

🐾 Do not **dwell** in the past, do not dream of the future, concentrate the mind on the present moment. (Buddha, Leader)
不要留戀過去，不要空想未來，讓心專注在當下。

🐾 Don't **dwell** on what went wrong. Instead, focus on what to do next. (Denis Waitley, Writer)
不要沉緬在錯誤，相反的，專注在接下來的動作。

12. ego [ˋigo] *n.* [C][U] 自尊、自我 egos

🐾 All my **ego** wants is to be sitting by a lake in Italy. It doesn't want to be backstage, warming up. (Chet Faker, Musician)
我的自我只想要坐在義大利的湖邊，它不想待在後台暖身。

🐾 The minute you start compromising for the sake of massaging somebody's **ego**, that's it, game over. (Gordon Ramsay, Chef)
你一旦開始妥協好滿足某人的自尊，就這樣了，結束了。

13. elaborate [ɪˈlæbərət] *adj.* 精密的、複雜的

- Acting is like lying. The art of lying well. I'm paid to tell **elaborate** lies. (Mel Gibson, Actor)

  演戲就像說謊，好好說謊的藝術。人家付錢給我說精細的謊言。

- Psychologists really aim to be scientists, white-coat stuff, with **elaborate** statistics, running experiments. (Daniel Kahneman, Psychologist)

  心理學家其實致力於成為科學家，穿白袍，用複雜的數據做實驗。

14. elevate [ˈɛlɪveɪt] *vt.* 提升 elevated elevated

- The role of a clown and a physician are the same— it's to **elevate** the possible and to relieve suffering. (Patch Adams, Author)

  小丑和醫生的角色是一樣的，都是提昇可能，減緩痛苦。

- I wish I had known that education is the key. I'm seeing how knowledge can **elevate** you. (Mary J. Blige, Musician)

  真希望我早一點知道教育是關鍵、知識就是力量。我漸漸看出教育可以讓你提升。

15. embrace [ɪmˈbreɪs] *vt. vi.* 擁抱、欣然接受 embraced embraced

- **Embrace** your differences and the qualities about you that you think are weird. They're going to be the only things separating you from everyone else. (Sebastian Stan, Actor)

  擁抱你的不同與你覺得怪異的特質，它們是唯一讓你跟其他人不同的原因。

- Some people don't like change, but you need to **embrace** change, if the alternative is disaster. (Elon Musk, Businessman)

  有些人不喜歡改變，但如果另一個選擇是個災難的話，你需要擁抱改變。

Part 1 「趣」你的單字基礎篇

Part 2 「趣」你的單字進階篇

Unit 27

關心周遭事、物

趣味字彙表

1.	enthusiastic *adj.* 熱情的	9.	exclude *adj.* 排除
2.	erupt *vi.* 噴發、爆發	10.	extension *n.* [U] [C] 擴展、延長部分、延期
3.	esteem *n.* [U] 尊重	11.	external *adj.* 外在的、表面的
4.	eternal *adj.* 永遠的、永恆的	12.	extinct *adj.* 滅絕的
5.	evergreen *adj.* 常青的、長盛不衰的	13.	extraordinary *adj.* 非凡的、驚人的
6.	exaggeration *n.* [U] [C] 誇大（的言語）	14.	fascinate *vt.* 迷住
7.	exceed *vt.* 超過、超出	15.	feminine *adj.* 女性的
8.	exceptional *adj.* 例外的、不同尋常的		

趣味字彙句 ⊂ ⊂ ◉ MP3 27

1. enthusiastic [ɪnˌθjuzɪ'æstɪk] *adj.* 熱情的

When you are **enthusiastic** about what you do, you feel this positive energy. It's very simple. (Paulo Coelho, Novelist)
當你對自己在做的事情展現熱情的時候,你就會感受到正面的能量。這是很簡單的。

Latins are tenderly **enthusiastic**. In Brazil they throw flowers at you. In Argentina they throw themselves. (Marlene Dietrich)
拉丁美洲人都有著溫柔的熱情,在巴西,他們丟花給你,在阿根廷,他們將自己投入你的懷抱。

2. erupt [ɪ'rʌpt] *vi.* 噴發、爆發 eruted, erupted

A volcano has **erupted** in southern Japan, sending an orange burst into the sky and lava rolling down the mountain.
在日本南部有座火山爆發,橘色的噴發物被噴入空中,熔岩流下火山。

It goes without saying that when survival is threatened, struggles **erupt** between peoples, and unfortunate wars between nations result. (Hideki Tojo, Soldier)
不用說,當生命受到威脅時,民族間的鬥爭與國際間令人遺憾的戰爭便會爆發。

3. esteem [ɪ'stim] *n.* [U] 尊重

I don't have the best self **esteem**; mine wavers month to month, but I know how to pick myself up. (Tyra Banks, Model)
我沒有最高的自信,我的自信每個月都會動搖,但我知道怎麼讓自己重新振作。

Esteem without love is languid and cold. (Jonathan Swift, Writer)
沒有愛的尊重無聊且冷淡。

4. eternal [ɪˈtɜnl] *adj.* 永遠的、永恆的

I'm not fashionable, and I know nothing about fashion, but I have my individual style, and style is **eternal**. (Vidya Balan, Actress)
我不時尚，我完全不懂時尚，但我有個人的風格，而風格才是永恆的。

Hatred does not cease by hatred, but only by love; this is the **eternal** rule. (Buddha, Leader)
仇恨無法停止仇恨，只有愛可以，這是永久不變的法則。

5. evergreen [ˈɛvəˌgrin] *adj.* 常青的、長盛不衰的

An **evergreen** is a plant that has leaves throughout the year, always green.
常綠植物是一種長年都有樹葉的植物，而且常保綠色。

Christmas Holly is an **evergreen** shrub that grows up to 15 inches tall.
冬青樹是一種會長到十五英吋高的常綠植物。

6. exaggeration [ɪɡˌzædʒəˈreɪʃn] *n.* [U] [C] 誇大（的言語） exaggerations

There are some people so addicted to **exaggeration** that they can't tell the truth without lying. (Josh Billings, Comedian)
有些人沉迷於誇大，無法不說謊講出事實。

Resume: a written **exaggeration** of only the good things a person has done in the past, as well as a wish list of the qualities a person would like to have. (Bo Bennett, Businessman)
履歷是誇大的寫作，只包含一個人過去做過事情好的一面，它也是一個列滿一個人希望自己擁有的特質的清單。

7. exceed [ɪk'sid] *vt.* 超過、超出 exceeded exceeded

🐛 The thing I loved the most about teaching is that you can connect with an individual or a group, and see that individual or group **exceed** their limits. (Mike Krzyzewski, Coach)
關於教育我最愛的部分就是你可以跟個人或團體有連結，然後看著他們超越自己的極限。

🐛 No matter who you are or what you intend to do, you should not **exceed** the boundaries of the rule of law. (Li Keqiang, Politician)
不論你是誰、想做甚麼，你都不該超越法律的界線。（李克強，政治家）

8. exceptional [ɪk'sepʃənl] *adj.* 例外的、不同尋常的

🐛 What characterizes a member of a minority group is that he is forced to see himself as both **exceptional** and insignificant, marvelous and awful, good and evil. (Norman Mailer, Novelist)
弱勢族群成員的特徵是，他們被迫同時認為自己不平凡也不重要，了不起但也糟糕，善良也邪惡。

🐛 The thing that makes you **exceptional**, is inevitably that which must also make you lonely. (Lorraine Hansberry, Playwright)
讓你不平凡的事，也無可避免地會讓你感到孤單。

9. exclude [ɪk'sklud] *adj.* 排除

🐛 I don't want my books to exclude anyone, but if they have to, then I would rather they **excluded** the people who feel they are too smart for them! (Nick Hornby, Writer)
我不希望我的書排斥任何人，但如果一定要，那我寧願它們排除那些覺得它們自己很聰明，我的書配不上他們的人。

🐛 I don't believe that fashion should **exclude** people. (Kimora)
我不相信時尚應該把任何人排除在外。

10. extension [ɪk'stenʃn] *n.* [U] [C] 擴展、延長部分、延期 extensions

🐦 The makeup is simply an **extension** of the personality and colors. Clothing and makeup all express something. (Gene Simmons, Musician)

化妝品只是人的個性與膚色的延伸。服裝和妝容都表達了一些東西。

🐦 Inner beauty is great and all, but a few eyelash **extensions** never hurt anyone.

內在美是很棒的，但稍微接一下睫毛也沒甚麼大礙。

11. external [ɪk'stɜnl] *adj.* 外在的、表面的

🐦 Happiness doesn't depend on any **external** conditions, it is governed by our mental attitude. (Dale Carnegie, Writer)

快樂不是來自外在條件，而是由你內心的態度來決定。

🐦 In North America, the greatest threat to the Jewish people is not the **external** force of antisemitism, but the internal forces of apathy, inertia and ignorance of our own heritage. (Michael Steinhardt, Businessman)

在北美，猶太人最大的威脅不是外來的反猶太主義，卻是內在的、對我們文化的不關心、惰性與無知。

12. extinct [ɪk'stɪŋkt] *adj.* 滅絕的

🐦 Many native species have become endangered or **extinct** because they have been killed for food or their fur.

很多當地的物種因為被殺害以作為食物或取得牠們的皮毛，已瀕臨絕種或已絕種。

🐦 If man doesn't learn to treat the oceans, and the rain forest with respect, man will become **extinct**. (Peter Benchley, Author)

如果人不學著尊重海洋和雨林，那麼人類便會絕種。

13. extraordinary [ɪkˈstrɔːdnri] *adj.* 非凡的、驚人的

🐸 A positive attitude causes a chain reaction of positive thoughts, events, and outcomes. It is a catalyst and it sparks **extraordinary** results. (Wade Boggs, Athlete)
正面態度會造成正面想法、事件和結果的連鎖反應，它是種催化劑，而且會激發驚人的結果。

🐸 Mathematics has beauty and romance. It's not a boring place to be, the mathematical world. It's an **extraordinary** place; it's worth spending time there. (Marcus du Sautoy, Mathematician)
數學有它的美好與浪漫，數學的世界並不無聊，那是個美妙非凡的世界，值得你花時間。

14. fascinate [ˈfæsɪneɪt] *vt.* 迷住 fascinated fascinated

🐸 In general, all art forms **fascinate** me— art is the way human beings express what we can't say in words. (Andrea Bocelli)
大致來說，所有藝術形式都讓我強烈地吸引我，藝術是人類用來表達無法說出的。

🐸 I have learned through time that not everyone is interested in the kinds of things that **fascinate** me. (Anthony Braxton, Musician)
隨著時間過去，我學到不是大家都會對我所著迷的東西感到有興趣。

15. feminine [ˈfemənɪn] *adj.* 女性的

🐸 Being strong can be also **feminine**. I don't think feminine equals being weak. Being strong is very sexy. (Sanaa Lathan, Actress)
堅強也可以很女人，我不認為女人等同弱，堅強是很性感的。

🐸 I love being able to wear dresses and clothes that make me feel **feminine** and beautiful. (Portia de Rossi, Actress)
我喜歡我可以穿洋裝和衣裳，讓我覺得自己具女人味且漂亮。

Unit 28

勇於接受改變

趣味字彙表

1.	flourish *vi.* 繁榮、茂盛	9.	gravity *n.* [U] 重力
2.	forgetful *adj.* 健忘的、疏忽的	10.	greed *n.* [U] 貪婪
3.	foul *adj.* 污穢的、惡劣的、犯規的	11.	guideline *n.* [C] 指導方針
4.	fraction *n.* [U] [C] 小部分、片段	12.	hearty *adj.* 豐盛的、熱誠的
5.	gender *n.* [C] 性別	13.	heavenly *adj.* 天堂的、極好的
6.	geographical *adj.* 地理學的、地理的	14.	heighten *vt. vi.* 加高、增強
7.	glacier *n.* [C] 冰川	15.	heroic *adj.* 英勇的
8.	gorgeous *adj.* 華麗的、非常漂亮的		

趣味字彙句 🎧 ⊙ **MP3 28**

1. flourish [ˈflʌrɪʃ] *vi.* 繁榮、茂盛 flourished flourished

🐸 For evil to **flourish**, it only requires good men to do nothing. (Simon Wiesenthal, Activist)
若要邪惡昌盛，只需要好人沉默。

🐸 If you don't let people **flourish** in their jobs, why are they going to stay? (Joel Osteen, Clergyman)
如果你不讓人在他們的工作中興盛，他們怎麼會想留下來？

2. forgetful [fəˈgetfl] *adj.* 健忘的、疏忽的

🐸 I'm so **forgetful**. I'm pretty sure roughly one-third of my life has been spent standing in the middle of the room wondering what I came in here for.
我好健忘，我很確信我大概三分之一的人生都耗在站在房間中間思考我進來做甚麼。

🐸 I'm not **forgetful**. I'm just too lazy to remember.
我不是健忘，只是懶得記。

3. foul [faʊl] *adj.* 污穢的、惡劣的、犯規的

🐸 It is better to use fair means and fail, than **foul** and conquer. (Sallust, Historian)
使用正當的方法而失敗，比使用惡劣的方法而戰勝好。

🐸 A **foul** tongue reveals a lot more about you than the one you are using it against.
惡劣的言語相對於你用來對付的人，反而大大顯露出你的為人。

4. fraction ['fræk∫n] *n.* [U] [C] 小部分、片段 fractions

🐛 When enough people care about autism or diabetes or global warming, it helps everyone, even if only a tiny **fraction** actively participate. (Seth Godin, Writer)
當足夠的人關心自閉症、糖尿病或地球暖化,對每個人都會有幫助,即使只有一小部份的人會主動參與。

🐛 No one who has understood even a **fraction** of what science has told us about the universe can fail to be in awe of both the cosmos and science. (Julian Baggini, Author)
沒有人可以在了解科學告訴我們宇宙相關的事物後,即使只是一小部分,還不對宇宙和科學感到敬畏。

5. gender ['dʒendə(r)] *n.* [C] 性別 genders

🐛 A **gender**-equal society would be one where the word 'gender' does not exist: where everyone can be themselves. (Gloria)
在性別平等的社會裡,「性別」這個字眼是不存在的,而每個人都可以做自己。

🐛 The problem with **gender** is that it prescribes how we should be rather than recognizing how we are. (Chimamanda Ngozi Adichie)
性別的問題在於它指定了我們應該有的樣子,而不是認可我們原有的樣子。

6. geographical [dʒiə'græfɪkəl] *adj.* 地理學的、地理的

🐛 Why should Ireland be treated as a **geographical** fragment of England. (Charles Stewart Parnell, Politician)
為什麼愛爾蘭要被看作英國地理上的一部份。

🐛 The **geographical** isolation and lack of television made world happenings and problems seem remote. (Paul D. Boyer, Scientist)
地理隔離和沒電視讓世界上發生的事與問題顯得遙遠。

7. glacier ['glæsɪə(r)] *n.* [C] 冰川 glaciers

🔊 **Glaciers** all over the world have been melting for at least the last 50 years, and the rate of melting is speeding up.

世界各地的冰河在過去至少五十年間不斷地在融化，而融化速度在加快中。

🔊 I grew up in the mountains in Wyoming, and all the water is **glacier** runoff and cold. (Matthew Fox, Actor)

我從小住在懷俄明的山裡，水都是冰河逕流所以很冰。

8. gorgeous ['gɔrdʒəs] *adj.* 華麗的、非常漂亮的

🔊 The music starts, you're wearing these **gorgeous** clothes and you're nervous about your high heels. (Karlie Kloss, Model)

音樂開始，你穿著美麗的衣服，擔心你的高跟鞋。

🔊 That was the whole point in forming a band. Girls. Absolutely **gorgeous** girls. (Simon Le Bon, Musician)

那就是組樂團的重點：女孩，絕美的女孩。

9. gravity ['grævəti] *n.* [U] 重力

🔊 You can't blame **gravity** for falling in love. (Albert Einstein, Physicist)

你陷入愛情不是重力的錯。

🔊 I can choose to sit in perpetual sadness, immobilized by the **gravity** of my loss, or I can choose to rise from the pain and treasure the most precious gift I have— life itself. (Walter Anderson, Writer)

我可以選擇陷入無止盡的悲痛中、因遺失的重力無法行動，或者我也可以選擇從痛苦中站起，並珍惜我最寶貴的禮物，也就是生命本身。

10. greed [grid] *n.* [U] 貪婪

🐛 **Greed** is a bottomless pit which exhausts the person in an endless effort to satisfy the need without ever reaching satisfaction. (Erich Fromm, Psychologist)

貪婪是個無底洞，讓人耗盡精力，無止盡努力滿足自己的需求，卻永遠無法感到滿足。

🐛 There is a sufficiency in the world for man's need but not for man's **greed**. (Mahatma Gandhi, Leader)

對於人類的需求世界有足夠可以提供的，但對於人類的貪婪卻不是這樣的。

11. guideline ['gaɪdˌlaɪn] *n.* [C] 指導方針 guidelines

🐛 Problems are not stop signs, they are **guidelines**. (Robert H. Schuller, Clergyman)

問題不是停止標誌，而是指導方針。

🐛 Traffic signals in New York are just rough **guidelines**. (David Letterman, Comedian)

交通號誌在紐約只是大概的指導方針而已。

12. hearty ['hɑrtɪ] *adj.* 豐盛的，熱誠的

🐛 Breakfast is the most important meal of the day and I definitely have a **hearty** breakfast before I do anything. (Mayer Hawthorne, Musician)

早餐是一天最重要的一餐，我總是確保我做任何事情之前先吃了豐盛的早餐。

🐛 The big question is whether you are going to be able to say a **hearty** yes to your adventure. (Joseph Campbell, Author)

最重要的問題是你會不會對冒險熱誠地說「好」。

13. heavenly [ˈhɛvənlɪ] *adj.* 天堂的、極好的

Many people say that durian has an awful smell but has a **heavenly** taste.
很多人說榴槤聞起來很臭，但吃起來卻像天堂般美好。

This CD features some of the most **heavenly** music ever written.
這張 CD 收錄了一些至今被創作出來的最美好的音樂。

14. heighten [ˈhaɪtn] *vt.* *vi.* 加高、增強 heightened heightened

The quality of life decreases with **heightened** security. (Rebecca Miller, Director)
生活品質會因為安全措施增強而降低。

The cinema is there to **heighten** the imagination; I have always tried to make sure it does so. (Ken Adam, Desginer)
電影是為了提升想像力，我總是確保自己有做到。

15. heroic [hɪˈrəʊɪk] *adj.* 英勇的

I think that we all do **heroic** things, but hero is not a noun, it's a verb. (Robert Downey, Jr., Actor)
我認為我們都會做英勇的事，但「英雄」不該是個名詞，而是個動詞。

I think the real **heroic** teachers are the ones who work with kids. (David Duchovny, Actor)
我覺得最勇敢的老師是教幼童的老師。

Unit 29

不怕面對未來

1.	horizontal *adj.* 水平的	9.	interpretation *n.* [U] [C] 解釋
2.	hostage *n.* [C] 人質	10.	justify *vt. vi.* 證明⋯是正當的、為⋯辯護
3.	hostile *adj.* 有敵意的	11.	juvenile *adj.* 少年的、未成熟的
4.	impulse *n.* [C][U] 衝動	12.	knowledgeable *adj.* 有知識的、博學的
5.	indifferent *adj.* 漠不關心的	13.	lawmaker *n.* [C] 立法者
6.	indispensable *adj.* 不可或缺的	14.	legislation *n.* [U] 立法、法律
7.	initiate *vt.* 開始、創始	15.	lifelong *adj.* 終身的
8.	innumerable *adj.* 無數的、數不清的		

趣味字彙句 ●● ● MP3 29

1. horizontal [hɑrɪ'zɑntl] *adj.* 水平的

With the widespread **horizontal** distribution of social media, terrorists can identify vulnerable individuals of all ages in the United States. (James Comey)

有了社群媒體普遍的水平分布，恐怖份子可以找出美國各年齡層脆弱的對象。

Company training aims at two types of development: **horizontal** development and vertical development.

公司訓練通常專注在兩種發展：水平發展與垂直發展。

2. hostage ['hɑstɪdʒ] *n.* [C] 人質 hostages

You can't let your past hold your future **hostage**. (LL Cool J)

你不能讓你的過去抓住你的未來當人質。

Three **hostages** being held by militants in the Philippines have appeared in a video pleading for their governments to meet the captors' demands.

被菲律賓激進分子綁架的三名人質出現在影片中，請求他們的政府滿足俘虜者的要求。

3. hostile ['hɑstaɪl] *adj.* 有敵意的

Hostile people live in a hostile world. (Wayne Dyer)

有敵意的人會活在充滿敵意的世界。

For all of nature's wonder and beauty, it is also **hostile** and unpredictable. (Liam Neeson, Actor)

大自然充滿驚奇與優美，但也充滿敵意且無法預測。

4. impulse ['ɪmpʌls] *n.* [C][U] 衝動 impulses

Great things are not done by **impulse**, but by a series of small things brought together. (George Eliot, Author)
偉大的事情不是因為衝動而成功，是許多小事集結而成。

If you have an **impulse** to kindness, act on it. (Douglas Coupland, Author)
如果你有衝動想做好事，就去做吧。

5. indifferent [ɪn'dɪfrənt] *adj.* 漠不關心的

What makes men **indifferent** to their wives is that they can see them when they please. (Ovid, Poet)
男人對太太漠不關心的原因是，他們隨時都可以看到她們。

How should we begin to make amends for raising a generation obsessed with the pursuit of material wealth and **indifferent** to so much else? (Tony Judt, Historian)
我們如何開始補償養育出一代如此執著於追求物質財富而對其他所有事情毫不關心？

6. indispensable [ɪndɪ'spensəbl] *adj.* 不可或缺的

Environmental education is an **indispensable** part of creating a sustainable society in harmony with nature.
要創造一個能與自然和諧共存、持續發展的社會，環境教育是不可或缺的。

Everyone's job is important, but no one is **indispensable**. (Chuck Noll, Coach)
每個人的工作都很重要，但沒人是不可或缺的。

7. initiate [ɪˋnɪʃɪ‚et] *vt.* 開始、創始 initiated initiated

Those who **initiate** change will have a better opportunity to manage the change that is inevitable. (William Pollard, Clergyman)
起始改變的人，更有機會駕馭無法避免的變化。

I want to **initiate** a change in society in the long term. (Francois Hollande, Statesman)
我最終想要帶動一項社會中的改變。

8. innumerable [ɪˋnjumərəbl̩] *adj.* 無數的、數不清的

The young must be prepared to experience **innumerable** disappointments and yet not fail. (Ellen Key, Writer)
年輕人要準備好經歷數不清的失望卻不會一蹶不振。

The rich culture and heritage of Bihar is evident from the **innumerable** ancient monuments that are dotted all over the state.
比哈爾邦豐富的文化和遺產從這邦裡散佈四處數不清的歷史遺址就可以看出來。

9. interpretation [ɪn‚tɝprɪˋteʃən] *n.* [U] [C] 解釋 interpretations

The **interpretation** of dreams is the royal road to a knowledge of the unconscious activities of the mind. (Sigmund Freud, Psychologist)
夢的闡釋是得到內心潛意識活動相關知識的莊嚴道路。

I do not have much patience with a thing of beauty that must be explained to be understood. If it needs additional **interpretation** by someone other than the creator, then I question whether it has fulfilled its purpose. (Charlie Chaplin, Actor)
我對需要經過解釋才有辦法被理解的美麗東西沒耐心，如果它需要作者之外的人多加闡釋，那我會懷疑它到底有沒有達到它的目的。

10. justify [ˈdʒʌstəˌfaɪ] *vt.* *vi.* 證明⋯是正當的、為⋯辯護 justified, justified

🐑 A creator needs only one enthusiast to **justify** him. (Man Ray)
一個創造者只需要一個熱衷的人來為他辯護。

🐑 We live in a world where everyone thinks they do the right thing, so they are entitled to do the wrong thing. So ends can **justify** the means. (Alex Gibney, Director)
我們住在一個每個人都認為他們做了對的事情,所以他們有權做錯事,因此人確實會為達目的不擇手段。

11. juvenile [ˈdʒuvənl] *adj.* 少年的、未成熟的

🐑 When the students are occupied, they're not **juvenile** delinquents. I believe that education is a capital investment. (Arlen Specter)
當學生有事情做的時候,他們就不會變成少年犯罪者。我相信教育是種資本投資。

🐑 An alcoholic father, poverty, my own **juvenile** diabetes, all these things intrude on what most people think of as happiness. (Sonia)
酗酒的父親、貧窮與我自己的兒童糖尿病,這些事情都阻止我得到大部分人認為的快樂。

12. knowledgeable [ˈnɑlɪdʒəbl] *adj.* 有知識的、博學的

🐑 They don't think a fashionable woman can love food and be **knowledgeable** and actually cook. (Padma Lakshmi, Chef)
他們不覺得一個時尚的女人會熱愛食物、博學並實際下廚。

🐑 I had the opportunity to study philosophy, the history of architecture, economics, and Russian history in courses taught by extraordinarily **knowledgeable** professors. (Stanley B. Prusiner)
我還有機會在由極為博學的教授們指導的課程中研讀哲學、建築史、經濟學和俄羅斯歷史。

13. lawmaker [ˈlɔˌmekɚ] *n.* [C] 立法者 lawmakers

🛒 As federal **lawmakers**, we have a responsibility to set a precedent for energy efficient practices. (Greg Walden, Politician)
身為聯邦議員，我們有責任為實踐節能開出先例。

🛒 We need **lawmakers** to provide more funding to local communities to help them protect their clean water supply from pollution.
我們需要立法者提供更多資金給地方社區，幫助他們保護他們乾淨的水源，使其免於受汙染。

14. legislation [ˌlɛdʒɪsˈleʃən] *n.* [U] 立法、法律

🛒 Years ago, we all talked about recycling and not dumping things down your drain and all of that, but talking doesn't help much. Basically, it's going to have to be **legislation**. (Ted Danson, Actor)
多年前，我們都在談論回收以及不把垃圾丟下水管等，但談論並沒有太大的幫助，最終還是需要立法。

🛒 Inflation is taxation without **legislation**. (Milton Friedman, Economist)
通貨膨脹是未經立法的課稅。

15. lifelong [ˈlaɪfˌlɔŋ] *adj.* 終身的

🛒 To love oneself is the beginning of a **lifelong** romance. (Oscar Wilde, Dramatist)
愛自己是一段為期一輩子的戀愛的開始。

🛒 We now accept the fact that learning is a **lifelong** process of keeping abreast of change. And the most pressing task is to teach people how to learn. (Peter Drucker, Businessman)
我們現在已經接受學習是趕上變化的終生事實，而最迫切的任務就是教導人們如何學習。

Part 1 「趣」你的單字基礎篇

Part 2 「趣」你的單字進階篇

Unit 30

讓生活變得更好

趣味字彙表

1.	likelihood *n.* [U] 可能性	9.	motive *n.* [C] 動機
2.	lottery *n.* [C] 獎券、樂透	10.	muscular *adj.* 肌肉發達的、健壯的
3.	mayonnaise *n.* [U] 美乃滋	11.	naive *adj.* 天真的、幼稚的
4.	mermaid *n.* [C] 美人魚	12.	nostril *n.* [C] 鼻孔
5.	migrant *adj.* 移居（尤指移出國境）的	13.	noticeable *adj.* 顯而易見的、值得注意的
6.	milestone *n.* [C] 里程碑	14.	oatmeal *n.* [U] 燕麥粥、燕麥片
7.	modify *vt.* 修改	15.	obstinate *adj.* 頑固的
8.	motherhood *n.* [U] 母親的身分		

趣味字彙句 　 📀 MP3 30

1. likelihood [ˈlaɪklɪˌhʊd] *n.* [U] 可能性

📺 Past performance speaks a tremendous amount about one's ability and **likelihood** for success. (Mark Spitz, Athlete)
過去的表現可以大大地看出一個人的能力以及成功的可能性。

📺 Our planet is warming due to pollution from human activities. And a warming climate increases the **likelihood** of extreme weather. (Gloria Reuben, Actress)
因為人類活動造成的汙染，我們的地球正在持續暖化中，而暖化的氣候增加極端氣候的可能性。

2. lottery [ˈlɑtərɪ] *n.* [C] 獎券、樂透 lotteries

📺 Here's something to think about: How come you never see a headline like "Psychic Wins **Lottery**"? (Jay Leno, Comedian)
這是個值得思考的一點：怎麼從沒聽過頭條新聞說「靈媒贏得樂透」？

📺 Time is running out for the mystery **lottery** winner to claim their £1 million prize.
神秘的樂透贏家快沒時間領取他們的一百萬歐元獎金了。

3. mayonnaise [meəˈnez] *n.* [U] 美乃滋

📺 I mix **mayonnaise**, ketchup and brandy and a little bit of mustard. This is a good sauce for seafood. (Jose Andres Puerta, Chef)
我混合美乃滋、番茄醬、白蘭地和一點芥末醬，這是個配海鮮很好的醬料。

📺 The only exercise I got was trying to twist off the cap of a jar of **mayonnaise**. (Richard Simmons, Celebrity)
我唯一的運動就是嘗試轉開美乃滋罐頭的蓋子。

Part 1 「趣」你的單字基礎篇

Part 2 「趣」你的單字進階篇

4. mermaid [ˈmɝˌmed] *n.* [C] 美人魚 mermaids

🐸 I was a **mermaid** in my past life. I just feel a connection there between me, and the water, and the fish. (Ella Henderson, Musician)

我前世是個美人魚,我就是可以感受到我與海水和魚之間的連結。

🐸 Linden's love of science led to a career as a professional **mermaid**, which she uses to help kids learn about the ocean in a unique, fun way.

琳登對科學的愛引領她踏上專業美人魚的職涯,她這個工作幫助兒童用獨特有趣的方式學習海洋相關的知識。

5. migrant [ˈmaɪgrənt] *adj.* 移居(尤指移出國境)的

🐸 The next time you hear about **migrant** children near the border, just picture them as your own. Then think what you would want our government to do. (Al Sharpton, Activist)

下次你聽到關於國界附近移居的小孩的消息,想像他們是你的小孩,然後想想你希望我們的政府怎麼做。

🐸 Both my parents were **migrant** workers who came to the U.K. to better themselves. (Sanjeev Bhaskar, Comedian)

我的雙親都是移民工作者,他們來到英國讓自己過得更好。

6. milestone [ˈmaɪlˌston] *n.* [C] 里程碑 milestones

🐸 What looks like a mistake to others has been a **milestone** in my life. (Amisha Patel, Actress)

別人看起來是錯誤的,對我來說是人生的里程碑。

🐸 Direction is more important than speed. We are so busy looking at our speedmeters that we forget the **milestone**.

方向比速度更重要,我們都太忙著看車速表而忘了里程碑。

7. modify [ˈmɑdəˌfaɪ] *vt.* 修改 modified modified

Some of our eating habits consist of things we can't change, but if we **modify** it a little and put some exercise in there, we can really make a difference. (Doug E. Fresh, Musician)

我們有些飲食習慣包含我們無法改變的部分，但如果我們一點一點地修改，並加入運動，那我們絕對能改變。

A round man cannot be expected to fit in a square hole right away. He must have time to **modify** his shape. (Mark Twain, Author)

你不能期盼一位圓的人可以馬上合適地放進一個方形的洞，必須要給他時間修改形狀。

8. motherhood [ˈmʌðɚˌhʊd] *n.* [U] 母親的身分

Motherhood is a great honor and privilege, yet it is also synonymous with servanthood. (Charles Stanley)

當母親是個榮耀與特權，但也等同傭人。

Motherhood is the biggest gamble in the world. It is the glorious life force. It's huge and scary—it's an act of infinite optimism. (Gilda Radner, Comedian)

當母親是世上最大的賭博，那是個輝煌的生命力量，強大也恐怖，它也是個無限正面的行為。

9. motive [ˈmotɪv] *n.* [C] 動機 motives

Every action needs to be prompted by a **motive**. (Leonardo da Vinci, Artist)

每個行動都需要有動機激勵。

Getting ahead cannot be the only **motive** that motivates people. (Henry Giroux, Critic)

跑在前面不能是唯一激勵人的動機。

Part 1 「趣」你的單字基礎篇

Part 2 「趣」你的單字進階篇

10. muscular [ˈmʌskjələ] *adj.* 肌肉發達的、健壯的

🔊 I'm naturally a **muscular** gal with some curves, so eating a Mediterranean diet makes my body happy. (Debi Mazar, Actress)
我是個天生健壯、有點豐腴的女孩,所以吃地中海飲食讓我的身體感到比較快樂。

🔊 Happiness is seeing the **muscular** lifeguard all the girls were admiring leave the beach hand in hand with another muscular lifeguard. (Johnny Carson, Comedian)
快樂就是看到所有女人都在欣賞的健壯救生員和另一個健壯的救生員手牽手離開海邊。

11. naive [nɑˈiv] *adj.* 天真的、幼稚的

🔊 It would be **naive** to think that the problems plaguing mankind today can be solved with means and methods which were applied or seemed to work in the past. (Mikhail Gorbachev, Statesman)
如果以為今天苦惱著全人類的問題,可以用過去適用且成功的手段與方式解決,那就太天真了。

🔊 I think it's **naive** to pray for world peace, if we're not going to change the form in which we live. (Godfrey Reggio, Director)
我認為如果我們只求世界和平,卻沒有要改變我們生活的型態,那就太天真了。

12. nostril [ˈnɑstrɪl] *n.* [C] 鼻孔 nostrils

🔊 You just don't appreciate breathing out of both **nostrils** until one suddenly is taken away from you.
直到一個鼻孔無法呼吸,你才會感恩能從兩個鼻孔呼吸的好。

🔊 The **nostrils** of fish are not used for breathing.
魚的鼻孔不是用來呼吸的。

13. noticeable [ˈnotɪsəbl̩] *adj.* 顯而易見的、值得注意的

🐸 I'm a very basic dresser. I'm not interested in calling too much attention to myself. I like to look cool without being too **noticeable**. (Julianne Moore, Actress)

我穿著很基本，我不想吸引太多注意，我喜歡看起來很酷，但不是太顯眼。

🐸 My most **noticeable** physical trait is, hands down, to my hair. It's big, unruly and curly, and you can spot it from a mile away. (Becca Fitzpatrick, Author)

大家都會同意我最顯眼的身體特徵就是我的頭髮，又大、又亂、又捲，你從一哩外就可以看到。

14. oatmeal [ˈotˌmil] *n.* [U] 燕麥粥、燕麥片

🐸 To me, breakfast is my most important meal. I make sure I have **oatmeal**, milk, and fruit. (Andrew Luck, Athlete)

對我來說，早餐是最重要的一餐，我總是確保我有吃燕麥、牛奶和水果。

🐸 As a kid, I got three meals a day. **Oatmeal**, miss-a-meal and no meal. (Mr. T, Actor)

小時候，我一天吃三餐，燕麥早餐、錯過一餐、沒吃晚餐。

15. obstinate [ˈɑbstənɪt] *adj.* 頑固的

🐸 The liberally educated person is one who is able to resist the easy and preferred answers, not because he is **obstinate** but because he knows others worthy of consideration. (Allan Bloom, Philosopher)

受過自由開明教育的人是可以抗拒簡單、大家喜愛的答案，不是因為他頑固，而是因為他知道其他的答案也值得考慮。

🐸 Life is **obstinate** and clings closest where it is most hated. (Mary Shelley, Author)

人生很頑固，總是緊握最令人討厭的部分。

Unit 31

慢慢步向軌道

趣味字彙表

1.	octopus *n.* [C] 章魚	9.	overwhelm *vt.* 戰勝、淹沒
2.	odds *n.* 可能性、投注賠率	10.	participant *n.* [C] 參與者
3.	olive *n.* [C] 橄欖	11.	passionate *adj.* 熱情的
4.	opponent *n.* [C] 對手	12.	pastime *n.* [C] 消遣、娛樂
5.	optimism *n.* [U] 樂觀、樂觀主義	13.	pastry *n.* [C][U] 酥皮點心
6.	ostrich *n.* [C] 駝鳥	14.	patent *n.* [C] 專利、專利權
7.	outgoing *adj.* 直率的、外向的	15.	perceive *vt.* 察覺、感知
8.	overall *adj.* 總的、全部的		

趣味字彙句 ⒸⒸ 🔘 MP3 31

1. octopus [ˋɑktəpəs] *n.* [C] 章魚 octopuses

🐙 Talent without discipline is like an **octopus** on roller skates. There's plenty of movement, but you never know if it's going to be forward, backwards, or sideways. (H. Jackson Brown, Jr., Writer)
沒有受過教養的天賦就像穿溜冰鞋的章魚，有很多動作，但你不知道會向前、向後或向旁邊。

🐙 **Octopus** can fish for prey while deciding what color and pattern to turn, what shape to make their bodies, be on alert for predators and aware how far away their dens are. (Sy Montgomery, Writer)
章魚在引誘獵物的時候，還可以同時決定要變甚麼顏色與樣式、身體要變甚麼形狀、留意獵食者與自己離巢穴多遠。

2. odds [ˋɑdz] *n.* 可能性、投注賠率

🐙 If you fall behind, run faster. Never give up, never surrender, and rise up against the **odds**. (Jesse Jackson, Activist)
如果你落後了，跑快一點，不要放棄，不要投降，以黑馬姿態升起吧。

🐙 When something is important enough, you do it even if the **odds** are not in your favor. (Elon Musk, Businessman)
當某件事情夠重要時，即使機率對你不利你還是會去做。

3. olive [ˋɑlɪv] *n.* [C] 橄欖

🐙 **Olives** are a very traditional garnish used by bartenders to add a slightly savory flavor to a drink.
傳統上酒保都用橄欖來裝飾酒，以加上一點美味強烈的味道。

🐙 I always have a good quality extra virgin **olive** oil. (Nadia Giosia, Chef)
我總是使用高品質的特級初榨橄欖油。

Part 1 「趣」你的單字基礎篇

Part 2 「趣」你的單字進階篇

4. opponent [ə`ponənt] *n.* [C] 對手 opponents

🐦 Don't underestimate your **opponent**, but don't overestimate them, either. (Nancy Pelosi, Politician)
不要低估你的對手，但也不要高估他們。

🐦 In tennis, it is not the **opponent** you fear; it is the failure itself. (Andy Murray, Athlete)
在網球界，令人害怕的不是你的對手，而是失敗本身。

5. optimism [`ɑptəmɪzəm] *n.* [U] 樂觀、樂觀主義

🐦 **Optimism** is the faith that leads to achievement. Nothing can be done without hope and confidence. (Helen Keller, Author)
樂觀是通往成功的信念。如果沒有希望與信心，事情是無法完成的。

🐦 There's a lot of **optimism** in changing scenery, in seeing what's down the road. (Conor Oberst, Musician)
在不斷變換的景觀中、看到路上接下來是甚麼時，人可以強烈感受到樂觀。

6. ostrich [`ɑstrɪtʃ] *n.* [C] 駝鳥 ostriches

🐦 He behaved like an **ostrich** and put his head in the sand, thereby exposing his thinking parts. (George Carman, Lawyer)
他表現得像隻駝鳥，並把他的頭埋進沙裡，因此露出他思考的部位。

🐦 The **ostrich** is not hiding its head in the sand— it shows us its ass.
駝鳥不是把頭埋在沙裡，牠是展現牠的屁股給我們看。

7. outgoing [`aʊtˏgoɪŋ] *adj.* 直率的、外向的

🐛 I've always been spontaneous and **outgoing**. I've tried lots of things so I've got some good life experiences. (Leonardo DiCaprio)
我向來都很隨興且外向，我試過很多東西，所以得到很多很好的人生經驗。

🐛 Like a typical Gemini I'm changeable. I can be very **outgoing**, but sometimes very shy. (Denise Van Outen, Actress)
就像典型的雙子座，我很多變，我可以很外向，但有時候又很害羞。

8. overall [`ovɚˏɔl] *adj.* 總的、全部的

🐛 People who use time wisely spend it on activities that advance their **overall** purpose in life. (John C. Maxwell, Clergyman)
懂得善用時間的人，會把時間用在提升他們人生總體目標的活動上。

🐛 Cell phones, mobile e-mail, and all the other cool gadgets can cause massive losses in our creative output and **overall** productivity. (Robin S. Sharma, Lawyer)
手機、流動電子郵件和其他酷炫的工具可能會大量減少我們的創意輸出和總體生產率。

9. overwhelm [ovɚˋhwɛlm] *vt.* 戰勝、淹沒 overwhelmed, overwhelmed

🐛 Too many choices can **overwhelm** us and cause us to not choose at all. (Sheena Iyengar, Educator)
太多的選擇可能會使我們不知所措，並讓我們決定不選擇。

🐛 We can pretend that China is not there. But China is there, and unless we put our economy on the right track, it is going to **overwhelm** us completely. (Salman Khurshid, Politician)
我們可以假裝中國不存在，但事實不是這樣，而除非我們讓我們的經濟上軌道，否則我們會被完全淹沒。

10. participant [pɑrˈtɪsəpənt] *n.* [C] 參與者 participants

🐸 You can't be a full **participant** in our democracy, if you don't know our history. (David McCullough, Historian)
你如果不懂我們的歷史，那你就無法完全參與我們的民主。

🐸 In life, be a **participant**, not a spectator. (Lou Holtz, Coach)
人生中，當參與者，不是旁觀者。

11. passionate [ˈpæʃənɪt] *adj.* 熱情的

🐸 Passion is one great force that unleashes creativity, because if you're **passionate** about something, then you're more willing to take risks. (Yo-Yo Ma, Musician)
熱情是釋放創意的一大力量，因為如果你對某件事熱情，那麼你會比較願意冒險。

🐸 When you're surrounded by people who share a **passionate** commitment around a common purpose, anything is possible. (Howard Schultz, Businessman)
當你被與你對共同目標有共同熱衷的人包圍時，所有事情都有可能。

12. pastime [ˈpæsˌtaɪm] *n.* [C] 消遣、娛樂 pastimes

🐸 When you're growing up, you play dress-up— it's a game, a **pastime**. And then as you get older, getting ready and looking nice becomes this constant stress. I want to make it fun again. (Lauren Conrad, Designer)
成長過程，你會玩裝扮，那是一種遊戲、一種消遣。你長大後，準備出門與打扮好變成一種壓力。我想要讓它再次變得有趣。

🐸 Some say our national **pastime** is baseball. Not me. It's gossip. (Erma Bombeck, Journalist)
有些人說國民消遣是棒球，對我來說不是棒球，是八卦。

13. pastry [ˈpestrɪ] *n.* [C][U] 酥皮點心 pastries

🛒 There are divisions between a culinary chef and a dessert chef, also called a **pastry** chef. (Ron Ben-Israel, Chef)
料理廚師和甜點廚師，或稱作糕餅廚師是不同的。

🛒 You don't have to do everything from scratch. Nobody wants to make puff **pastry**! (Ina Garten, Author)
不需要所有事情都從頭做，沒人想做酥皮糕點！

14. patent [ˈpætnt] *n.* [C] 專利、專利權 patents

🛒 Microsoft, Apple, Facebook all bought huge **patent** portfolios to further their strategic game. They're doing what I'm doing! (Nathan Myhrvold, Businessman)
微軟、蘋果和臉書都在買大量的專利組合，把他們的策略遊戲更推進一步，他們都在做我正在做的！

🛒 Every piece of software written today is likely going to infringe on someone else's **patent**. (Miguel de Icaza, Scientist)
現在寫得每個軟體都可能侵犯到某個人的專利。

15. perceive [pɚˈsiv] *vt.* 察覺、感知 perceived perceived

🛒 To effectively communicate, we must realize that we are all different in the way we **perceive** the world and use this understanding as a guide to our communication with others. (Tony Robbins, Author)
要有效的溝通，那麼我們就要了解到每個人看世界的方式都不同，並把這份理解當作我們與他人溝通之間的引導。

🛒 I love the way little kids dress themselves! They're completely carefree about how others **perceive** them. (Gillian Zinser, Actress)
我喜歡小孩裝扮自己的樣子！他們完全不管別人的眼光。

Unit 32

展現活力、努力生活

趣味字彙表

1.	permissible *adj.* 可允許的	9.	qualify *vt.* 使合格、授權予
2.	persist *vt. vi.* 堅持、存留	10.	reckless *adj.* 魯莽的、不顧後果的
3.	precaution *n.* [C][U] 預防（措施）	11.	recommend *vt. vi.* 推薦
4.	preference *n.* [C][U] 偏愛	12.	refuge *n.* [C][U] 庇護（所）
5.	prehistoric *adj.* 史前的、非常古老的	13.	resident *n.* [C] 居民
6.	priority *n.* [C][U] 優先（考慮的事）	14.	ridiculous *adj.* 荒謬的
7.	prolong *vt.* 延長	15.	salmon *n.* [C] 鮭魚
8.	purchase *vt.* 購買		

趣味字彙句 🎧 🎧 ⊙ *MP3 32*

1. permissible [pəˋmɪsəbḷ] *adj.* 可允許的

🐸 When artists make art, they shouldn't question whether it is **permissible** to do one thing or another. (Sol LeWitt, Artist)
當藝術家在做藝術的時候,不該質問做的事情是否被允許。

🐸 Those who think it is **permissible** to tell white lies soon grow color-blind. (Austin O'Malley, Actress)
覺得可以說善意謊言的人很快就會變得無法區分色彩。

2. persist [pəˋsɪst] *vt. vi.* 堅持、存留 persisted persisted

🐸 As long as poverty, injustice and gross inequality **persist** in our world, none of us can truly rest. (Nelson Mandela, President)
只要貧窮、不公與明顯的不平等還續存在我們的世界,那麼我們都不能真正的停下來休息。

🐸 Vitality shows in not only the ability to **persist,** but the ability to start over. (F. Scott Fitzgerald, Author)
活力不只出現在堅持的能力裡,也在重新開始的能力裡展現。

3. precaution [prɪˋkɔʃən] *n.* [C][U] 預防(措施) precautions

🐸 If every conceivable **precaution** is taken at first, one is often too discouraged to proceed at all. (Archer John Porter Martin, Scientist)
如果每個想到的預防措施都先被執行,那麼人通常都會感到太挫敗,完全無法前進。

🐸 **Precaution** is better than cure. (Johann Wolfgang von Goethe, Poet)
預防勝於治療。

4. preference [ˈprɛfərəns] n. [C][U] 偏愛 preferences

🔖 Music is a personal **preference**. Everyone's free to connect and like whatever they want. (Natalie Maines, Musician)
音樂是個人喜好，每個人都有自由喜歡自己想要的並做連結。

🔖 I have a **preference** for film just because of the familiarity. It's what I know, and I sort of have nostalgia for it. (Vince Vaughn)
我對電影有偏好，因為它給我一種熟悉感，那是我知道的東西，它有點讓我感到懷舊。

5. prehistoric [prihɪsˈtɔrɪk] adj. 史前的、非常古老的

🔖 In **prehistoric** times, mankind often had only two choices in crisis situations: fight or flee. (Robert Orben, Entertainer)
在古老時代，人類在危急情況下通常只有兩種選擇：戰鬥或逃跑。

🔖 Drawing is still basically the same as it has been since **prehistoric** times. It brings together man and the world. (Keith Haring, Artist)
畫畫還是和古老時代一樣，連結人類和這個世界。

6. priority [praɪˈɔrətɪ] n. [C][U] 優先（考慮的事） priorities

🔖 Time is beyond our control, and the clock keeps ticking regardless of how we lead our lives. **Priority** management is the answer to maximizing the time we have. (John C. Maxwell, Clergyman)
我們無法控制時間，不論我們怎麼過生活，時鐘還是繼續轉動，優先管理才是增加我們擁有時間的解答。

🔖 Climate change is a terrible problem, and it absolutely needs to be solved. It deserves to be a huge **priority**. (Bill Gates)
氣候變遷是個嚴重的問題，絕對需要被解決，它值得最被優先考慮。

7. prolong [prəˈlɔŋ] *vt.* 延長 prolonged prolonged

The proper function of man is to live, not to exist. I shall not waste my days in trying to **prolong** them. I shall use my time. (Jack London, Novelist)

人類正確的功能是生活，而不是存在，我不該把日子浪費在延展它們，我應該好好利用我的時間。

Prescription: A physician's guess at what will best **prolong** the situation with least harm to the patient. (Ambrose Bierce, Journalist)

處方：醫生猜測可以完美的延長這個情況，但對病人造成最小的傷害。

8. purchase [ˈpɝtʃəs] *vt.* 購買 purchased, purchased

The day, water, sun, moon, night — I do not have to **purchase** these things with money. (Plautus, Playwright)

白天、水、陽光、月亮或夜晚，我不需要用錢來買這些東西。

My eating habits are the only behavior of mine that are still manic. I can't walk by a restaurant, a bakery, an ice-cream store or a candy store without making a **purchase**. (Andy Behrman, Writer)

我的飲食習慣是我唯一還很瘋狂的行為，我經過餐廳、麵包店、冰淇淋店或糖果店無法不買東西。

9. qualify [ˈkwɑləˌfaɪ] *vt.* 使合格、授權予 qualified, qualified

I'm just an individual who doesn't feel that I need to have somebody **qualify** my work in any particular way. (David Bowie)

我只是個不覺得我需要別人在任何方面來認同我的作品的人。

Today, if you look at financial systems around the globe, more than half the population of the world do not **qualify** to take out a loan from a bank. This is a shame. (Muhammad Yunus, Economist)

今天你如果觀看全球的經濟系統，超過世界一半的人口沒有向銀行借款的資格，這多令人羞愧。

10. reckless [ˈrɛklɪs] *adj.* 魯莽的、不顧後果的

🐛 I've never been **reckless**— it's always calculated. I'm mischievous, but I'm calculated. (Drake, Musician)
我向來一點都不莽撞，都是有預先計畫過的，我很調皮，但都是有算好的。

🐛 When you're young, you're very **reckless**. Then you get conservative. Then you get reckless again. (Clint Eastwood, Actor)
你年輕的時候，你很魯莽，然後你變得保守，然後又再次變得魯莽。

11. recommend [rɛkəˈmɛnd] *vt.* *vi.* 推薦 recommended recommended

🐛 People often say that motivation doesn't last. Well, neither does bathing - that's why we **recommend** it daily. (Zig Ziglar, Author)
人們常說動機無法持久。其實洗澡也是，所以我們才推薦每天都洗。

🐛 **Recommend** virtue to your children; it alone, not money, can make them happy. (Ludwig van Beethoven, Composer)
向你的小孩推薦美德吧。不是錢，而是美德本身就可以讓他們快樂。

12. refuge [ˈrɛfjudʒ] *n.* [C][U] 庇護（所）refuges

🐛 A true friend encourages us, comforts us, supports us like a big easy chair, offering us a safe **refuge** from the world. (H. Jackson Brown, Jr., Author)
真正的朋友會鼓勵我們、安慰我們、像大張的休閒椅一樣支撐著我們，提供我們一個逃離世界的庇護。

🐛 There are two means of **refuge** from the miseries of life: music and cats. (Albert Schweitzer, theologian)
人生苦難的庇護有兩種：音樂和貓。

13. resident [ˈrɛzədənt] *n.* [C] 居民 residents

🐛 If you are a married man **resident** in Cuba, you cannot get a passport to go to the next town without your wife's permission in writing. (Edward Burnett Tylor, Scientist)

如果你是個在古巴的已婚男性居民，沒有太太的書寫同意書，你是無法拿到去另一個城鎮的護照的。

🐛 Hate crimes impact not just individuals but every **resident** of that neighborhood. (James Comey, Public servant)

仇恨犯罪不只影響個人也會影響整個社區的每個居民。

14. ridiculous [rɪˈdɪkjələs] *adj.* 荒謬的

🐛 Imperfection is beauty, madness is genius and it's better to be absolutely **ridiculous** than absolutely boring. (Marilyn Monroe, Actress)

缺陷是一種美，瘋狂是天才，而且荒謬到極點比無聊透頂好。

🐛 The idea of forever is kind of **ridiculous**, but it's a nice thing to say. (Conor Oberst, Musician)

永遠這個概念是有點荒謬的，但說出它的感覺很好。

15. salmon [ˈsæmən] *n.* [C] 鮭魚 salmons

🐛 If I had the choice between smoked **salmon** and tinned salmon, I'd have it tinned. With vinegar. (Harold Wilson, Statesman)

如果要我在煙燻鮭魚以及罐頭鮭魚之間選擇，那我會選罐頭鮭魚，配上酒醋。

🐛 I love a massage. I don't need to be wrapped in herbs like a **salmon** fillet, but I do love a massage. (Jason Bateman, Actor)

我喜歡按摩，我不需要被像鮭魚排一樣包在香草裡，但我是真的喜歡按摩。

Unit 33

計畫隨時有可能改變

趣味字彙表

1.	scandal *n.* [C][U] 醜聞	9.	straightforward *adj.* 坦率的、簡單的
2.	sensation *n.* [C][U] 感覺、轟動（的事件）	10.	substantial *adj.* 實在的、重要的、大量的
3.	sensitivity *n.* [C][U] 敏感（度）	11.	superficial *adj.* 表面的
4.	shortage *n.* [C][U] 不足	12.	sympathize *vi.* 同情、相互理解
5.	shortcoming *n.* [C] 缺點	13.	temptation *n.* [C][U] 誘惑（物）
6.	slaughter *vt.* 屠宰、屠殺	14.	tentative *adj.* 暫時性的、猶豫的
7.	specialist *n.* [C] 專家	15	toxic *adj.* 有毒的
8.	statistics *n.* 統計、統計資料		

趣味字彙句 👂👂 🎧 *MP3 33*

1. scandal [ˈskænd!] *n.* [C][U] 醜聞 scandals

🐸 You find out who your real friends are when you're involved in a **scandal**. (Elizabeth Taylor, Actress)
當你身處醜聞中時,你就可以看出你的真朋友是誰。

🐸 **Scandal** dies sooner of itself than we could kill it. (Benjamin Rush, Scientist)
醜聞自己消逝的速度,比我們湮滅它的速度還快。

2. sensation [sɛnˈseʃən] *n.* [C][U] 感覺、轟動(的事件) sensations

🐸 At night, when the sky is full of stars and the sea is still you get the wonderful **sensation** that you are floating in space. (Natalie Wood, Actress)
在夜晚,當天空布滿星星,而海洋十分平靜,你會有種飄在太空中的美妙感覺。

🐸 The great art of life is **sensation**, to feel that we exist, even in pain. (Lord Byron, Poet)
人生最偉大的藝術就是感覺,感受我們的存在,即使是在痛苦中。

3. sensitivity [sɛnsəˈtɪvətɪ] *n.* [C][U] 敏感(度) sensitivities

🐸 My biggest weakness is my **sensitivity**. I am too sensitive a person. (Mike Tyson, Athlete)
我最大的弱點是我敏感的個性,我這個人太過敏感。

🐸 I marvel at their **sensitivity** over certain passages that just anyone, even if he knows German well, would not appreciate. (Heinrich Boll, Writer)
我對他們的敏感度感到驚訝,連那些即使德文很好的人也無法理解的特定文章段落他們也可以感受出來。

4. shortage [ˈʃɔrtɪdʒ] *n.* [C][U] 不足 shortages

If people concentrated on the really important things in life, there'd be a **shortage** of fishing poles. (Doug Larson, Journalist)
如果人們專注在人生真正重要的事情上，那麼將會產生魚竿的短缺。

If you put the federal government in charge of the Sahara Desert, in 5 years there'd be a **shortage** of sand. (Milton Friedman)
如果你讓聯邦政府負責撒哈拉沙漠，那五年內沙子就會短缺。

5. shortcoming [ˈʃɔrtˌkʌmɪŋ] *n.* [C] 缺點 shortcomings

One of my few **shortcomings** is that I can't predict the future. (Lars Ulrich, Musician)
我少數的缺點之一就是我無法預測未來。

It's human nature to blame someone else for your **shortcomings** or upsets. (Robert Kiyosaki, Author)
對自己的缺點或氣憤怪罪他人是人性。

6. slaughter [ˈslɔtɚ] *vt.* 屠宰，屠殺 slaughtered slaughtered； *n.* [U] 屠宰

Years of global negotiations and declarations have failed utterly to end Iceland's illegal **slaughter** of whales. (Pierce Brosnan, Actor)
多年的全球談判與宣言仍無法完全停止冰島非法屠殺鯨魚。

I've noticed that the few times I've traveled first class. You've already got your drink by the time the rest of the passengers file on, and you feel sorry for them. They're sort of trooping past you like cows to **slaughter**. (Walter Kirn, Novelist)
幾次搭頭等艙的時候我注意到，你早已經拿到你的飲料，這時其他的旅客才排隊前進，你開始覺得他們可憐，他們成隊經過你，像要進屠宰場的豬隻。

7. specialist [ˈspɛʃəlɪst] *n.* [C] 專家 specialists

🐸 A **specialist** is someone who does everything else worse. (Ruggiero Ricci, Musician)

專家就是在所有其他事情做得更差的人。

🐸 I don't look at a man who's expert in one area as a **specialist**. I look at him as a rookie in ten other areas. (Conor McGregor, Athlete)

我不把在一個領域很專業的人看作專家，我把他看成是在其他十個領域裡的菜鳥。

8. statistics [stəˈtɪstɪks] *n.* 統計、統計資料

🐸 **Statistics** is used much like a drunk uses a lamppost: for support, not illumination. (Vin Scully, Celebrity)

人們使用統計數據，就像喝醉酒的人使用路燈：是用來支撐、不是照明。

🐸 There are two ways of lying. One, not telling the truth and the other, making up **statistics**. (Josefina Vazquez Mota, Politician)

說謊有兩種方式：不說真話或是捏造數據。

9. straightforward [stretˈfɔrwəd] *adj.* 坦率的、簡單的

🐸 And me being who I am, I'm very **straightforward**. (Zayn Malik, Musician)

而我的為人，我是很直接的。

🐸 I think if you show up and you work hard and you're **straightforward**, you can always create your own opportunities. (Cory Monteith, Actor)

我認為如果你出現、認真工作、態度坦率，那麼你就會為自己創造機會。

10. substantial [səbˈstænʃəl] *adj.* 實在的、重要的、大量的

🐝 When I was working, and when I was making **substantial** amounts of money, I always filed and paid my taxes. (Lauryn Hill)
當我有工作，而且收入很高的時候，我總是會報稅並繳稅。

🐝 I have had friends who have acted kindly towards me, and it has been my good fortune to have it in my power to give them **substantial** proofs of my gratitude. (Giacomo Casanova, Celebrity)
我交過對我很好的朋友，而我也很幸運有能力可以對他們展現我感激的豐富證據。

11. superficial [ˈsupɚˈfɪʃəl] *adj.* 表面的

🐝 I suppose if you're really lonely you can call a **superficial** friend. (Courteney Cox, Actress)
我猜如果你很孤單你可以打電話給膚淺的朋友。

🐝 People in this world of **superficial** communication find themselves lonely and have difficulty in talking about personal things that really matter to them. (Theodore Zeldin, Philosopher)
生存在這個表面溝通的世界的人們覺得自己孤單，且無法談論對自己真正重要的私事。

12. sympathize [ˈsɪmpəˌθaɪz] *vi.* 同情、相互理解 sympathized sympathized

🐝 The ability to **sympathize** with those around us seems crucial to our survival. (Jay Parini, Writer)
能同情周遭人的能力似乎對我們的生存很重要。

🐝 All born to encounter suffering and sorrow, and therefore bound to **sympathize** with each other. (Albert Pike, Lawyer)
所有人生來都會遭遇苦難與悲痛，因此必定要彼此同情。

13. temptation [tɛmpˋteʃən] *n.* [C][U] 誘惑（物）temptations

🐸 I can resist everything except **temptation**. (Oscar Wilde, Dramatist)

我能抗拒一切事物，除了誘惑之外。

🐸 Do not worry about avoiding **temptation**. As you grow older, it will avoid you. (Joey Adams, Comedian)

不要擔心避免誘惑，隨著你長大，它會主動避開你。

14. tentative [ˋtɛntətɪv] *adj.* 暫時性的、猶豫的

🐸 I've made a **tentative** plan for the coming month, but it may change at any minute.

我為下個月做了暫時的計畫，但它隨時會變。

🐸 Right now people seem to be very **tentative** about the positive benefits of capitalism. (Jeb Bush, Politician)

現在人們好像對資本主義的正面好處感到十分猶豫。

15. toxic [ˋtɑksɪk] *adj.* 有毒的

🐸 If you have **toxic** emotions of fear, guilt, and depression, it is because you have wrong thinking, and you have wrong thinking because of wrong believing. (Joseph Prince, Clergyman)

如果有恐懼、罪惡和憂鬱這些毒性情緒，是因為你有著錯誤的想法，而你有錯誤的想法是因為你有錯誤的信任。

🐸 When there is an accident involving fire, in most cases death is caused by the inhalation of the **toxic** smoke. (Jackie Stewart, Athlete)

大部分情況下在牽涉到火的意外中，都是因為吸入有毒煙霧造成死亡。

Unit 34

富足的人生

趣味字彙表

1.	transparent *adj.* 透明的、顯而易見的	9.	wildlife *adj.* 野生生物的；*n.* [U] 野生生物
2.	undergraduate *n.* [C] 大學生	10.	worthwhile *adj.* 值得做的
3.	underneath *prep.* 在……下面	11.	abnormal *adj.* 不正常的，畸形的
4.	understandable *adj.* 可理解的	12.	absentminded *adj.* 心不在焉的
5.	vague [veg] *adj.* 模糊不清的	13.	abundance *n.* [U] 豐富，充足
6.	via *prep.* 經由、透過	14.	accelerate *vt. vi.* 加快；增長
7.	wholesome *adj.* 有益於身心健康的	15.	accessible *adj.* 可（或易）接近的
8.	widespread *adj.* 普遍的、廣泛的		

趣味字彙句 MP3 34

1. transparent [trænsˋpɛrənt] *adj.* 透明的、顯而易見的

By giving people the power to share, we're making the world more **transparent**. (Mark Zuckerberg, Businessman)
藉由給人們分享的力量，我們也讓這個世界變得更透明。

I wish that every human life might be pure **transparent** freedom. (Simone de Beauvoir, Writer)
希望每個人的生命都能是純淨透明的自由。

2. undergraduate [ʌndəˋgrædʒʊɪt] *n.* [C] 大學生 undergraduates

By the time you graduate, **undergraduate** or graduate, that field would have totally changed from your first day of school. (Leigh Steinberg, Businessman)
等你畢業的時候，不論是從大學或研究所畢業，你研讀的領域會跟你進去的第一天完全不同。

I can find in my **undergraduate** classes, bright students who do not know that the stars rise and set at night, or even that the Sun is a star. (Carl Sagan, Scientist)
我可以在我的大學課堂中發現不知道星星夜晚會有升落或是太陽是個星體的聰明學生。

3. underneath [ʌndəˋniθ] *prep.* 在……下面

I'm fascinated by human behavior, by what's **underneath** the surface, by the worlds inside people. (Johnny Depp)
我被人類行為、表面下隱藏的，與人的內心世界所吸引。

Be like a duck. Calm on the surface, but always paddling like crazy **underneath**. (Michael Caine, Actor)
像鴨子一樣，表面上安靜，但底下總是瘋狂地踢水。

Part 1 「趣」你的單字基礎篇

Part 2 「趣」你的單字進階篇

4. understandable [ˌʌndɚˈstændəbl̩] *adj.* 可理解的

🐝 Making a wrong decision is **understandable**. Refusing to search continually for learning is not. (Phil Crosby, Businessman)
做錯決定是可以理解的，但拒絕為了學習而不斷尋找是不可被理解的。

🐝 I go to bed normally between midnight and 1 o'clock, so it is **understandable** that I cannot be an early bird. (Dieter Rams, Designer)
我通常半夜到一點間睡覺，可以理解為什麼我無法早起。

5. vague [veg] *adj.* 模糊不清的

🐝 The changing of a **vague** difficulty into a specific, concrete form is a very essential element in thinking. (J. P. Morgan, Businessman)
將模糊的困難轉為確切、具體的形式是思考很重要的一環。

🐝 People who know very little about ancient Egypt are most likely to have at least a **vague** idea about the Pharaoh Akhenaten. (Pamela Sargent, Author)
即使對古埃及的了解很有限的人也很有可能至少有點概念知道法老阿肯那頓。

6. via [ˈvaɪə] *prep.* 經由、透過

🐝 I am annoyed by people that send messages **via** Facebook because I get an e-mail telling me there is a message on Facebook— so I end up processing two messages for every one sent. (Vint Cerf, Scientist)
我討厭人們用臉書傳訊息給我，因為我會收到電子郵件說臉書上有訊息，所以我最終每個訊息都要處理兩次。

🐝 Music's the best drug for me to get away from the everyday pressures just for a second **via** a good song. (Ville Valo, Musician)
音樂是最好的藥，讓我能透過一首歌稍微逃離每天的壓力。

7. wholesome [ˈholsəm] *adj.* 有益於身心健康的

Periods of **wholesome** laziness, after days of energetic effort, will wonderfully tone up the mind and body. (Grenville Kleiser, Author)

偶爾在幾天充滿精力的努力之後，健康的懶惰可以美好的強化身心。

I really want women to know their power, to understand that nothing has been more **wholesome** in the political process than the increased involvement of women. (Nancy Pelosi, Politician)

我真的希望女人知道她們的力量，了解到沒有東西比她們在政治過程中的參與更健康有益了。

8. widespread [ˈwaɪdˌsprɛd] *adj.* 普遍的、廣泛的

Policies that can make commuting shorter and more convenient can reduce minor but **widespread** suffering. (Nassim Nicholas Taleb, Scientist)

可以讓通勤變得更短、更方便的政策能減少微小但廣泛的痛苦。

There is a **widespread** belief in the U.S. and Western Europe that young people have less of a commitment to work and a career than their parents and grandparents had.

在美國和西歐，人們普遍認為年輕人對工作與職涯的承諾不如他們的父母與祖父母。

9. wildlife [ˈwaɪldˌlaɪf] *adj.* 野生生物的； *n.* [U] 野生生物

All over the world the **wildlife** that I write about is in grave danger. (Gerald Durrell, Writer)

世界各地我寫過的野生動物都處在極大的危險中。

There is something wonderful about those strange country and **wildlife** noises. (Jasmine Guinness, Designer)

那些奇怪的鄉下和野生動物的聲音有某些美好的地方。

Part 1 「趣」你的單字基礎篇

Part 2 「趣」你的單字進階篇

10. worthwhile [ˈwɝθˈhwaɪl] *adj.* 值得做的

🐱 Love doesn't make the world go round. Love is what makes the ride **worthwhile**. (Franklin P. Jones, Journalist)
愛不會讓世界運轉，但愛讓人生旅程有價值。

🐱 Even a mistake may turn out to be the one thing necessary to a **worthwhile** achievement. (Henry Ford, Businessman)
即使錯誤也可能變成完成值得的成就必要的一部份。

11. abnormal [æbˈnɔrml] *adj.* 不正常的、畸形的

🐱 The size of my head though is pretty **abnormal**. (Philip Seymour Hoffman, Actor)
不過，我頭的大小是有點不正常。

🐱 My characters all have problems, but I don't see that as weird or **abnormal**. In real life, there are very few normal people. (Sophie Hannah, Poet)
我的角色全部都有問題，但我不認為那是奇怪或不正常的。現實生活中，很少有正常的人。

12. absentminded [ˈæbsntˈmaɪndɪd] *adj.* 心不在焉的

🐱 **Absentminded** people get a lot of exercise looking for things they can't find.
不專心的人因為找他們找不到的東西而做了很多運動。

🐱 I'm not the greatest boyfriend, but I'm not a creep. I'm more **absentminded**. (Matt Dillon, Actor)
我不是最完美的男朋友，但我也不是個變態，我比較算是心不在焉。

13. abundance [ə`bʌndəns] *n.* [U] 豐富、充足

🐸 People are happy in India. When I came back home, people were surrounded with **abundance**, but they were not happy. (Goldie Hawn, Actress)
印度人很快樂。當我回到家鄉後，人們擁有的很多，但卻不快樂。

🐸 Beauty has to do with confidence, proper fit, and an **abundance** of self-love. (Mary Lambert, Singer/Songwriter)
美麗源自自信，適當的健身與充足的自愛。

14. accelerate [æk`sɛləˌret] *vt. vi.* 加快、增長 accelerated acceslerated

🐸 When things begin **accelerating** wildly out of control, sometimes patience is the only answer. Press pause. (Douglas Rushkoff)
當事情開始瘋狂失控的時候，耐心是唯一的解決方法。按暫停吧。

🐸 I really think that technology can **accelerate** happiness in the world. The companies that find a way to help people find love or health will do well. (Ashton Kutcher, Actor)
我真的覺得科技可以增加世界的快樂指數。找到方法幫助人找到愛或者保持健康的公司，將會經營的很好

15. acccssible [æk`sɛsəbl̩] *adj.* 可（或易）接近的

🐸 When you give a speech, you try to make eye contact with the audience. It communicates that you are **accessible** and interested in them. (Simon Mainwaring, Blogger)
當你在演講的時候，你會盡量跟觀眾有眼神接觸，這讓觀眾覺得你容易親近，而且你對他們有興趣。

🐸 I gained a little weight, so I could be more **accessible** to people. (Adam DeVine, Actor/Comedian)
我稍微增重好讓人們覺得我容易親近。

Unit 35

與心靈對話、溝通

趣味字彙表

1.	accessory *n.* [C] 附件、配件	9.	affirm *vt. vi.* 斷言、證實
2.	accommodation *n.* [U] [C] 住處	10.	alienate *vt.* 使疏遠、離間
3.	accountable *adj.* 有解釋義務的、應負責任的	11.	alongside *prep.* 在……旁邊、沿著……的邊
4.	accumulate *vt. vi.* 累積	12.	alternative *n.* [C][U] 選擇、供選擇的東西
5.	activist *n.* [C] 激進主義分子、行動主義者	13.	ambiguous *adj.* 含糊不清的
6.	addiction *n.* [C] 沉溺、成癮	14.	amplify *vt. vi.* 擴大、增強
7.	advocate *n.* [C] 提倡者	15.	analytical *adj.* 分析的、善於分析的
8.	affectionate *adj.* 充滿深情的、溫柔親切的		

趣味字彙句 ● ● ● **MP3 35**

1. accessory [æk`sɛsərɪ] *n.* [C] 附件、配件 accessories

For me, hair is jewelry. It's an **accessory**. (Jill Scott, Singer)
對我來說，頭髮是首飾，是一種配件。

Eyeglasses are like makeup. It's the most amazing **accessory** that can change your whole appearance. (Vera Wang, Fashion Designer)
眼鏡就像化妝品一樣，是可以改變整個外表的，最神奇的飾品。

2. accommodation [əˌkɑmə`deʃən] *n.* [U] [C] 住處 accommodations

One of the most expensive **accommodations** is the Royal Villa in Greece.
最貴的住宅之一是希臘的「皇家村」。

The Hilltop Estate **accommodation** in Fiji costs $40,000 a night.
在斐濟的山頂地產住宅，一晚要價四萬美元。

3. accountable [ə`kaʊntəbl̩] *adj.* 有解釋義務的、應負責任的

People change. I don't want to be **accountable** for the interviews I've done, or the person I was when I was 20. (Robbie Williams, Singer/Songwriter)
人們是會改變的。我不想為我做過的訪問，或是二十歲的我負責任。

A company is not **accountable** just to its owners, but to its workers and its customers. (Ed Miliband, British Politician)
一間公司不是只需對所有人負責，也需對員工與客戶負責。

4. accumulate [əˈkjumjəˌlet] *vt. vi.* 累積 accumulated accumulated

🐝 The more money a person **accumulates**, the less interesting he becomes. (Gore Vidal, Writer)
一個人累積越多財富，他就變得更無趣。

🐝 Travel becomes a strategy for **accumulating** photographs. (Susan Sontag, Writer/Filmmaker)
旅行變成一種累積照片的策略。

5. activist [ˈæktəvɪst] *n.* [C] 激進主義分子、行動主義者 activists

🐝 Leonardo DiCaprio is a well-known environment **activist**. He donated 7 million dollars to save the ocean.
李奧納多狄卡皮歐是個有名的環境保護主義者，他捐贈了七百萬美元拯救海洋。

🐝 Emma Watson is a passionate **activist** for women's rights who works with the United Nations.
愛瑪沃森是個充滿熱情的女權運動家，她和聯合國合作。

6. addiction [əˈdɪkʃən] *n.* [C] 沉溺、成癮 addictions

🐝 Models, actresses, everyone smokes! Don't they realize that it's gross? I understand it's an **addiction**, but it still pains me to see my friends do it. (Kirsten Dunst, Actress)
不論是模特兒或演員，大家都在抽煙。難道他們都沒意識到那有多噁心嗎？我明白他們已上癮，但看到我的朋友抽煙我仍舊感到心痛。

🐝 People should watch out for three things: avoid a major **addiction**, don't go deeply into debt, and don't start a family before you're ready. (James Taylor, Singer/Songwriter)
人們應該注意三件事：避開重大癮頭、不要背負太多債務，還有在準備好之前不要建立家庭。

Part 1 「趣」你的單字基礎篇

Part 2 「趣」你的單字進階篇

7. advocate [ˈædvəkɪt] *n.* [C] 提倡者 advocates

🐝 I still drink vodka. I'm not an **advocate** of drinking, but I'm not an angel. (Calvin Klein, Fashion Designer)
我還是喝伏特加，我並不提倡喝酒，但我也不完美。

🐝 The wisest thing I can do is be on my own side, be an **advocate** for myself and others like me. (Maya Angelou, Author)
我能夠做出最明智的事，就是支持我自己，當我自己以及像我的那些人的提倡者。

8. affectionate [əˈfɛkʃənɪt] *adj.* 充滿深情的、溫柔親切的

🐝 Turkeys know their names, come when you call, and are totally **affectionate**. They're better than teenagers. (Elayne Boosler, Comedian)
火雞知道牠們的名字，你叫牠們會過來，而且非常溫柔，牠們比青少年好多了。

🐝 A correct answer is like an **affectionate** kiss. (Johann Wolfgang von Goethe, Writer)
正確的解答好似溫柔的吻。

9. affirm [əˈfɜm] *vt. vi.* 斷言、證實 affirmed affirmed

🐝 Conflicts are not a sign you're dating the wrong person. They simply **affirm** you are human. (Dr. Gary Chapman, Author)
衝突並不代表你和錯的人在一起，那只不過證明你是人類。

🐝 It is not necessary to deny another's reality to **affirm** your own. (Anne Wilson Shaef, Author/Spiritual Teacher)
不需要否定別人的現實世界來擁護自己的。

10. alienate [ˈeljənˌet] *vt.* 使疏遠、離間 alienated alienated

🐛 If you **alienate** people and just focus on your own, it just becomes lonely and it's not fun anymore. (Julianne Hough, Dancer/Actress)
如果你孤立別人，只注重自己，那麼一切會變得孤單，不再有趣。

🐛 I hid my singing talent from my friends at school because I didn't want to **alienate** anyone. However, we should own the things that make us really unique. (Idina Menzel, Actress/Singer)
我對學校朋友隱藏我的唱歌天份，因為我不想孤立任何人。然而，我們應該要有讓我們變得獨特的事物。

11. alongside [əˈlɔnˌsaɪd] *prep.* 在……旁邊、沿著……的邊

🐛 Filmmaking has always involved pairs: a director **alongside** a producer, a director alongside an editor. (Luc Dardenne, Filmmaker)
電影製作總是涉及兩個人：導演與製片人，或導演與編輯。

🐛 With the fight scenes, they would take a video camera and shoot **alongside** the camera, so we could piece it together on the computer. (Kelly Hu, Actress)
拍武打鏡頭時，他們會同時使用攝影機與照相機，我們之後才能用電腦把他們接在一起。

12. alternative [ɔlˈtɜnətɪv] *n.* [C][U] 選擇、供選擇的東西

🐛 Magic speaks to the child in all of us. There's still a part of us who wants to believe in an **alternative** reality where anything can happen. (Criss Angel, Magician)
魔術會觸碰到每個人內心的小孩。我們內心還是有一部分想要相信另一個什麼都可能發生的世界。

🐛 It's so much easier to like people and let people in. The **alternative** is being an iceberg. (Taylor Swift, Singer/Songwriter)
喜歡別人、接納別人簡單多了。另一個選擇是把自己當作冰山。

13. ambiguous [æm'bɪgjʊəs] *adj.* 含糊不清的

🐸 I left the ending **ambiguous**, because that is the way life is. (Bernardo Bertolucci, Film Director)
我刻意讓結局顯得模稜兩可，因為人生就是這樣。

🐸 Humor is very **ambiguous**. You have it, or you don't. You can't attain it. (Heinrich Boll, Writer)
幽默是很模稜兩可的，你可能天生有，不然就沒有，你是無法習得的。

14. amplify ['æmpləˌfaɪ] *vt. vi.* 擴大、增強 amplified amplified

🐸 Money and success don't change people; they merely **amplify** what is already there. (Will Smith, Actor)
財富與成功並不會改變一個人，它們僅僅突顯了原有的內在。

🐸 A face is a road map of one's life. Without any need to **amplify** it, the face communicates who the person is and what their life has been like. (Chuck Close, Photographer)
臉是顯示一個人一生的地圖。不需突顯，從臉就可以看出這是個怎麼樣的人，以及他的人生到目前如何度過。

15. analytical [ænə'lɪtɪk(ə)l] *adj.* 分析的、善於分析的

🐸 There are people who are just **analytical** because of your genes or too much coffee. (Sabrina Lloyd, Actress)
有些人就是容易分析過頭，可能是天生的，或是喝太多咖啡。

🐸 Art is really lively when it seems to dance off the paper. Art has to hit you on an emotional level rather than just the **analytical**. (Jerry Yang, Businessman)
當藝術似乎在紙上舞動起來時，真的顯得很生動。藝術必須能在情感上打動一個人，而不是只在分析的層面上。

Unit 36

懂得省思

1.	annoyance *n.* [U] [C] 惱怒、使人煩惱的事	9.	attain vt. *vi.* 獲得
2.	anonymous *adj.* 匿名的	10.	authentic *adj.* 真實的、可靠的
3.	anticipate *vt.* 預期	11.	awesome *adj.* 令人敬畏的、令人驚嘆的
4.	arrogant *adj.* 傲慢的、自大的	12.	betray *vt.* 背叛、洩漏
5.	articulate *vt.* 清晰地吐（字）、明確有力地表達	13.	beverage *n.* [C] 飲料
6.	assert *vt.* 斷言、聲稱	14.	bizarre *adj.* 奇異的
7.	assess *vt.* 估價、評價	15.	bleak *adj.* 荒涼的、淒涼的、無希望的
8.	assumption *n.* [U] [C] 假定		

趣味字彙句 🎧 🎧 **◎MP3 36**

1. annoyance [əˋnɔɪəns] *n.* [U] [C] 惱怒、使人煩惱的事 annoyances

🐝 People who think they know everything are a great **annoyance** to those of us who do. (Isaac Asimov, Scientist)
自以為什麼都懂的人對真正懂一切的人來說真是極度討人厭。

🐝 Our love for our children is sometimes mixed with anger and **annoyance**. (Bruno Bettelheim, Writer)
我們對小孩的愛有時混著憤怒與不耐煩。

2. anonymous [əˋnɑnəməs] *adj.* 匿名的

🐝 When I saw teenagers using the Internet to gossip about each other, I wanted to develop a book series about an **anonymous** high-school blogger. (Cecily von Ziegesar, Author)
當我看到青少年用網路聊對方八卦時，我想到了可以寫一系列關於一位高中匿名部落客的書。

🐝 When I had dark hair, I definitely felt more **anonymous**. (Naomi Watts, Actress)
當我的頭髮是黑色的時候，我確實比較有大家不認識我的感覺。

3. anticipate [ænˋtɪsəˌpet] *vt.* 預期 anticipated, anticipated

🐝 My life has taken some turns that I didn't **anticipate**. (Tom Ford, Fashion Designer)
我的人生出現了幾次預期外的改變。

🐝 The more confused you are and the more uncertain you are, then you can get something that you did not **anticipate**. (Elia Kazan, Director)
你越困惑，且越不確定，你越能得到預料外的東西。

4. arrogant [ˈærəgənt] *adj.* 傲慢的、自大的

🐸 A lot of NBA stars are **arrogant** and like to spend lots of money and have lots of girlfriends. (Andrew Bogut, Basketball Player)
很多美國職籃明星都很自大，喜歡花很多錢並交很多女朋友。

🐸 I thought acknowledging praise meant you were **arrogant**, but I've learned that knowing your strengths enables you to use them. (Donna Brazile, Politician)
我原本以為接受讚美代表你很自大，但後來我學到，了解你的強項是什麼讓你能夠善用它。

5. articulate [ɑrˈtɪkjəˌlet] *vt.* 清晰地吐（字）、明確有力地表達

🐸 I'm not too **articulate** when it comes to explaining how I feel about things. But my music does it for me, it really does. (David Bowie, Musician)
我不是很會表達我的感受，但我的音樂會為我表達，真的。

🐸 If you can clearly **articulate** your dream or goal, it's time to start. (Simon Sinek, Author)
如果你能清楚表達你的夢想或目標，那就該開始執行了。

6. assert [əˈsɜt] *vt.* 斷言、聲稱 asserted, asserted

🐸 I think man buns are used to **assert** yoga skills. (Russell Smith, Author)
我覺得男人的包頭是用來聲明他們的瑜伽技術的。

🐸 A child must say no to find out who she is. A teenager must say no to **assert** who she is not. (Louise J. Kaplan, Author)
孩子必須透過說「不」才能尋找自我。青少年必須透過說「不」才能宣稱他不是。

7. assess [əˋsɛs] *vt.* 估價、評價 assessed, assessed

If I was in a situation where it wasn't working and I had a choice with another man, I am going to **assess** it like a business deal: who is the better person for me? (Patti Stanger, Businesswoman)
如果我身處的情況已行不通，而我又有另一個男人可以選擇，那麼我會把它當作一筆生意來評估：誰對我來說比較有利？

Everyone takes a pause at 40 years old. It's the age you have to **assess** everything in your life. (Paul Feig, Director)
每個人在四十歲的時候都會暫停一下，在這個年紀，你必須重新省視人生中的一切。

8. assumption [əˋsʌmpʃən] *n.* [U] [C] 假定 assumptions

It's a false **assumption** that people with a lot of money have a lot of free time to shop. (Natalie Massenet, Businesswoman)
以為有錢人有很多時間買東西是個錯誤的假設。

When I see a fan coming over, I can't help but make an **assumption** about what they want to talk about.
當我看到影迷走過來，我總是忍不住預測他們想要討論的事。

9. attain [əˋten] *vt. vi.* 獲得 attained, attained

It occurred to me that eating is the only form of professionalism most people ever **attain**. (Don DeLillo, Novelist)
我發現吃東西是大部分人唯一習得的專業。

As much experience, education, and awareness as one can **attain** is important for a comedian. (Shelley Berman, Comedian)
對一個喜劇演員來說，能取得最大量的經驗、教育和知名度是很重要的。

10. authentic [ɔˋθɛntɪk] *adj.* 真實的、可靠的

🐑 Cornbread is the most **authentic** type of bread. It's good, hot, and made with love and fresh ingredients. (Jeremy Jackson, Actor)
玉米麵包是最正統的麵包，它好吃，溫熱，由愛及新鮮的食材製作而成。

🐑 Whether I am cooking dinner or selling a product, I try to do it in an **authentic** way by speaking like how I want to be spoken to. (Khloe Kardashian, Entertainer)
不論我是在煮晚餐或是賣產品，我都試著用最正統的方式，以我希望別人對我的方式與對方說話。。

11. awesome [ˋɔsəm] *adj.* 令人敬畏的、令人驚嘆的

🐑 Everyone I know is getting married or pregnant. I'm just getting more **awesome**. (Barney Stinson, TV character)
我認識的每個人都在結婚和懷孕，而我是一直變得更令人驚豔。

🐑 Think of me like Yoda, but instead of being little and green, I wear suits and I'm **awesome**. (Barney Stinson, TV Character)
把我想成尤達吧，但我不矮小也不是綠色的，相反的，我穿西裝，而且我很優秀。

12. betray [bɪˋtre] *vt.* 背叛、洩漏 betrayed betrayed

🐑 Some people are willing to **betray** years of friendship just to get a little bit of the spotlight. (Lauren Conrad, Reality TV Star/Designer)
有些人願意背叛多年的友誼，只為了贏得一丁點的矚目。

🐑 The love of a dog is a pure thing. He gives you total trust, and you must not **betray** it.
狗兒的愛是很純真的，牠們對你完全信任，而你不該背叛這種信任。

13. beverage [ˈbɛvərɪdʒ] *n.* [C] 飲料 beverages

The world's most consumed **beverage** is tea.
全世界最常被飲用的飲料是茶。

Pouring espresso is an art that requires the barista to care about the quality of the **beverage**. (Howard Schultz, Businessman)
倒濃縮咖啡是一項藝術，需要咖啡師關注這種飲料的品質。

14. bizarre [bɪˈzɑr] *adj.* 奇異的

It's so **bizarre**. I'm not scared of snakes or spiders but I'm scared of butterflies. (Nicole Kidman, Actress)
很奇怪，我不怕蛇或蜘蛛，但我怕蝴蝶。

I have a **bizarre** thing that I do. I'll turn on a foreign-language TV station and watch a whole show, even though I have no idea what anyone is saying. (John Travolta, Actor)
我有個奇怪的習慣，我會轉到外語電視台，觀看整個節目，雖然我完全不知道他們在說什麼。

15. bleak [blik] *adj.* 荒涼的、淒涼的、無希望的

Your attitude is like a box of crayons that color your world. Constantly color your picture gray, and your picture will always be **bleak**. (Allen Klein, Author)
你的態度有如一盒為你世界帶來色彩的蠟筆。如果你時常塗上灰色，那你的圖畫則會總是顯得荒涼。

Women always try to see the good in weird guys because the dating world is so **bleak**. Women will say, "He's creepy, but he makes good pancakes!" (Zoe Lister-Jones, Actress)
女人總是試著專注在怪男人好的一面，因為約會的世界實在太慘淡，女人會說：「他很奇怪，但他很會做鬆餅」。

Unit 37

抱持希望

趣味字彙表

1.	blunt *adj.* 鈍的、直率的	9.	catastrophe *n.* [C] 災難
2.	boost *n.* [C] 推動、促進	10.	cater *vt. vi.* 承辦宴席、滿足需要（或慾望）
3.	breakdown *n.* [C] 崩潰	11.	certainty *n.* [C] 確實、必然
4.	breakup *n.* [C] 中斷、分離	12.	chaos *n.* [U] 混亂
5.	brew *vt. vi.* 釀造、泡（茶）、煮（咖啡）	13.	cholesterol *n.* [U] [C] 膽固醇
6.	canvas *n.* [C][U] 帆布、油畫布	14.	chuckle *vi. vt.* 咯咯地笑
7.	caption *n.* [C] 標題、照片說明	15.	clarity *n.* [C][U] 清楚、明晰
8.	carbohydrate *n.* [C][U] 碳水化合物		

趣味字彙句 🎧 MP3 37

1. blunt [blʌnt] *adj.* 鈍的、直率的

🐛 My haircut is **blunt** and modern, and Nicki Minaj started wearing that bob on her head after she came to my show. I'm a trendsetter. (Lil Mama, Musician)

我的髮型很直接且摩登，而妮奇米納看過我的表演後竟然也剪了同樣的鮑柏頭。我是潮流領導者。

🐛 Steve Jobs was very **blunt** about products. (Evgeny Morozov, Writer)

談到產品相關的事，史帝芬賈柏斯是很直接的。

2. boost [bust] *n.* [C] 推動、促進 boosts；*vt.* 促進

🐛 If you ever want an ego **boost**, leave your job and then, six months later, come back for a day. People will treat you like a princess. (Natalie Zea, Actress)

如果你想要增加自信心，那麼離職，然後六個月後，找一天回去，人們會把你當公主一樣對待。

🐛 Snowboarding has really done a lot to **boost** that feeling in me. (Craig Kelly, Snowboarder)

雪地滑板真的為我增加了這種感覺。

3. breakdown [ˈbrekˌdaʊn] *n.* [C] 崩潰 breakdowns

🐛 With a suit, even if you're having a nervous **breakdown**, you still look like you're in charge. (Paul Feig, Director)

只要穿著西裝，即使你面臨精神崩潰，你看起來還是掌控著一切。

🐛 Medically speaking, there is no such thing as a nervous **breakdown**. (Marian Keyes, Writer)

醫學上來說，精神崩潰並不存在。

4. breakup [ˈbrekˌʌp] n. [C] 中斷、分離 breakups

🐛 I am never writing a **breakup** record again. I'm done with being a bitter witch. (Adele, Musician)

我再也不作分手唱片了，我受夠當個充滿仇恨的壞女人了。

🐛 The craziest thing I've done to get over a **breakup** is skydiving. I needed to do something different to start over again. (Shay Mitchell, Actress)

為了遺忘分手，我做過最瘋狂的事就是跳傘了，我需要做件不一樣的事好重新來過。

5. brew [bru] vt. vi. 釀造、泡（茶）、煮（咖啡） brewed, brewed

🐛 Forever: the time it takes to **brew** the first pot of coffee in the morning.

永遠：是煮早晨第一壺咖啡所需花費的時間。

🐛 Give a man a beer, waste an hour. Teach a man to **brew**, and waste a lifetime! (Bill Own, Actor)

給人一瓶啤酒，你浪費了一個小時，教一個人釀啤酒，浪費了一輩子。

6. canvas [ˈkænvəs] n. [C][U] 帆布、油畫布 canvases

🐛 Women are not in love with me but with the picture of me on the screen. I am merely the **canvas** on which women paint their dreams. (Rudolph Valentino, Actor)

女人不是愛上我的人，而是愛上我畫面上的照片，我不過是塊女人會畫上她們夢想的畫布。

🐛 I have no features without makeup. Since I am pale and have blond lashes, you can just paint my face like a blank **canvas**. (Amy Adams, Actress)

沒有化妝的時候，我是沒有特徵的，因為我很白，睫毛又是金色的，你可以把我當作空白畫布來畫。

7. caption [ˈkæpʃən] *n.* [C] 標題、照片說明 captions

🐑 I wish there were **captions** on red-carpet photos that say, This girl trained for two weeks, she went on a juice diet, and has a professional hair and makeup person. It just isn't the truth. (Emilia Clarke, Actress)

我真希望紅地毯照片上的說明會說，這個女孩訓練了兩週，她做了果汁節食，還請了專業的髮型師與化妝師。可惜事實上沒有這種說明。

🐑 I'm afraid that I'm overly involved. I like to check every **caption** in the magazine. (Anna Wintour, Editor)

我擔心我太投入了，我喜歡檢查雜誌裡每個照片說明。

8. carbohydrate [kɑrbəˈhaɪdret] *n.* [C][U] 碳水化合物 carbohydrates

🐑 If I could eat only one **carbohydrate** for the rest of my life, I'd go for rice. I eat that more than anything else. (Nobu Matsuhisa, Chef)

如果我剩下的日子只能吃一種澱粉食物，那我會選米飯，所有食物中我米飯吃最多。

🐑 Happiness is eating **carbohydrates** without putting on weight.

快樂便是可以吃碳水化合物卻不會增胖。

9. catastrophe [kəˈtæstrəfɪ] *n.* [C] 災難 catastrophes

🐑 When a man meets **catastrophe** on the road, he looks in his bag, but a woman looks at her mirror. (Margaret Turnbull, Scientist)

當男人在路上遇到災難時，他會翻他的包包，女人則會看鏡子。（瑪格麗特‧杜布爾，科學家）

🐑 I love cooking without recipe books. It might be amazing or a **catastrophe**. (Trinny Woodall, Designer)

我熱愛不看食譜下廚，結果可能會驚為天人，或是場災難。

10. cater [ˈketɚ] *vt. vi.* 承辦宴席、滿足需要（或慾望） catered catered

🔲 You will fail if you worry too much about your fans. I'm going to always write about what I want, even if it doesn't **cater** to my fans. (Ed Sheeran, Musician)

如果你太擔心你的歌迷，那你注定會失敗。我會一直寫我想要寫的，即使不符合我歌迷的喜好。

🔲 I've done everything from **catering**, waiting tables, teaching painting, selling hair, to being Cinderella, Elmo, and a clown. (Diora Baird, Actress)

我做過所有工作，宴會服務、餐廳服務生、教畫畫、賣頭髮、扮灰姑娘、艾蒙和小丑。

11. certainty [ˈsɝtəntɪ] *n.* [C] 確實、必然 certainties

🔲 Hope is not being sure that something will turn out well but the **certainty** that something makes sense despite the result. (Vaclav Havel, Leader)

希望不是深信事情的結果會很好，而是確信不管結果如何，事情都會是有意義的。

🔲 A woman's guess is much more accurate than a man's **certainty**. (Rudyard Kipling, Writer)

女人的猜測比男人的肯定準確多了。

12. chaos [ˈkeɑs] *n.* [U] 混亂

🔲 My life at the moment is a bit like my closet. Organized **chaos**. (David Wenham, Actor)

我人生的現階段有點像我的衣櫥，亂中有序。

🔲 I accept **chaos**, but I'm not sure whether it accepts me. (Bob Dylan, Musician)

我接受混亂，但我不確定混亂是否接受我。

13. cholesterol [kə'lɛstərol] *n.* [U] [C] 膽固醇 cholesterols

🐸 It is a scientific fact that your body will not absorb **cholesterol** if you take it from another person's plate. (Dave Barry, Journalist)
科學已證明，如果你吃的膽固醇是來自別人的盤子，那你的身體就不會吸收。

🐸 I want a schedule-keeping, waking-up-early, wallet-carrying, picture-hanging man. I don't care if he takes medicine for **cholesterol** or hair loss. (Mindy Kaling, Actress)
我想要有個男人會紀錄行程、早起、帶錢包、幫你掛相片，他有沒有因為膽固醇過高要吃藥或是掉頭髮我都不管。

14. chuckle ['tʃʌkl̩] *vi. vt.* 咯咯地笑 chuckled chuckled

🐸 I **chuckle** when twenty-four year olds say that they are no longer young. A man is still young at sixty and not old before eighty. (Oliver Wendell Holmes Jr., Judge)
當我聽到二十四歲的人說他們不再年輕時，我暗自發笑。人到六十歲都還屬年輕，八十歲前都不算老。

🐸 Mirrors don't lie. Thankfully, they can't **chuckle** either.
鏡子不會說謊，好險，他們也無法嘲笑。

15. clarity ['klærətɪ] *n.* [C][U] 清楚、明晰 clarities

🐸 3D should be used for films like Avatar. 3D animation has such **clarity** and depth of focus. (Steven Spielberg, Director)
像「阿凡達」的這類電影確實應該使用 3D。3D 動畫有高度的清晰度與焦點深度。

🐸 Rain is good for me. I feel like I achieve **clarity** when it rains. (Venus Williams, Tennis Player)
雨對我是有幫助的。下雨讓我覺得思緒更清晰。

Unit 38

洗滌心靈、轉好

趣味字彙表

1.	cleanse *vt.* 使清潔、淨化	9.	complement *n.* [C] 補充物
2.	closure *n.* [U] [C] 關閉、終止	10.	complexion *n.* [C] 膚色、氣色
3.	coincidence *n.* [U] [C] 巧合、巧事	11.	concise *adj.* 簡潔的、簡要的
4.	collector *n.* [C] 收藏家	12.	conform *vi.* 遵守、符合
5.	columnist *n.* [C] 專欄作家	13.	contradict *vt. vi.* 發生矛盾、抵觸
6.	commitment *n.* [U] [C] 託付、承諾	14.	controversial *adj.* 有爭議的
7.	companionship *n.* [U] 友誼、伴侶關係	15.	coordinate *vt.* 協調、調節
8.	compatible *adj.* 能共處的、適合的		

趣味字彙句 🔊 **MP3 38**

1. cleanse [klɛnz] *vt.* 使清潔、淨化 cleansed cleansed

🦗 The most important thing is to **cleanse** your face twice a day. If you look good in a magnifying mirror, you are set to go. (Tom Ford, Fashion Designer)

最重要的是一天洗臉兩次。如果你在放大鏡裡看起來狀況很好，那你就可以出門了。

🦗 I love to eat an apple after a meal, just to **cleanse** my teeth. (Catherine Zeta Jones, Actress)

我喜歡飯後吃一顆蘋果，好來清洗我的牙齒。

2. closure [ˈkloʒɚ] *n.* [U] [C] 關閉、終止 closures

🦗 It's important to have **closure** in any relationship that ends. You need to understand why it began and why it ended. (Jennifer Aniston, Actress)

在每段結束的感情中有個了結是很重要的，你需要知道感情為什麼開始，為什麼結束。

🦗 Forgiving people isn't always about giving them another chance. It's for **closure** so you can move on. (Sonya Parker, Writer)

原諒人的重點不完全是再給別人一次機會，而是給你自己一個了結，你才能繼續向前。

3. coincidence [koˈɪnsɪdəns] *n.* [U] [C] 巧合、巧事 coincidences

🦗 It's no **coincidence** that these people get out of Hollywood. (Boyd)

這些人都逃離好萊塢並不是個巧合。

🦗 It is not a **coincidence** that the Superbowl commercial break is twelve minutes. (Erma Bombeck, Journalist)

超級盃廣告休息時間是十二分鐘的事實不是個巧合。

4. collector [kəˈlɛktə] *n.* [C] 收藏家 collectors

- In Japan, there are many **collectors** of anime, robots, idol posters, military uniforms, and model trains.
  日本有很多收藏動漫、機器人、偶像的海報、軍服和模型火車收藏家。

- Model train **collectors** usually take pictures of trains, record train sounds, read train schedules.
  在日本，模型火車收藏者通常會拍火車的照片、錄火車的聲音、看火車時刻表。

5. columnist [ˈkɑləmɪst] *n.* [C] 專欄作家 columnists

- It is the gossip **columnist's** business to write about what is none of his business. (Louis Kronenberger, Critic)
  八卦專欄作家的工作就是寫他不該干涉的事。

- All coffee shops now have Wi-Fi. Why bring a book when you could be attacking some **columnist** on Twitter or responding to date requests, or posting a picture of your foot? (Russell Smith, Novelist)
  現在全部的咖啡店都有無線上網，如果你可以在推特上攻擊某個專欄作家、回覆邀約或放上你腳的照片，你怎麼會想帶書呢？

6. commitment [kəˈmɪtmənt] *n.* [U] [C] 託付、承諾 commitments

- When you step on the treadmill, make a **commitment**. (Tyrese Gibson, Actor)
  當你踏上跑步機的時候，許下承諾吧。

- Write that novel. Start that business you've always wanted to. The best part of life is the **commitment** to pursuing something. (Diana Nyad, Author)
  寫那本小說吧，開始你一直都想做的那個生意吧，人生最棒的部分就是追求某樣事物的承諾。

7. companionship [kəmˋpænjənˌʃɪp] *n.* [U] 友誼、伴侶關係

The first time you marry for love, the second for money, and the third for **companionship**. (Jackie Kennedy, Former First Lady)
第一次你是因為愛情而結婚，第二次是因為金錢，第三次是為了有人陪伴。

People want to marry me for **companionship**. No thanks! I've got my cats for that! (Ruth Rendell, Writer)
人們想為了有伴與我結婚，不用了，謝謝，我的貓就可以陪我了。

8. compatible [kəmˋpætəbḷ] *adj.* 能共處的、適合的

We are all a little weird and life's a little weird. When we find someone whose weirdness is **compatible** with ours, we call it love. (Dr. Seuss, Writer)
我們都有點奇怪，而人生也有點奇怪，當我們找到某個人奇怪的點跟我們合適的時候，我們就說那是愛。

It's great when you find somebody you're **compatible** with, but I'm really into separate bedrooms. You live your life and I live mine. (Claudia Christian, Actress)
可以找到跟你合適的人是很棒的，但我真的很喜歡分房，你過你的生活而我過我的。

9. complement [ˋkɑmpləmənt] *n.* [C] 補充物 complements

People tell me I'm tall and I always take it as a **complement**. (Maria Sharapova, Tennis Player)
人們都說我很高，而我總是把這當成是一種讚美。

Teaching is a great **complement** to writing. (Eleanor Catton, Author)
教學是寫作很好的補充物。

10. complexion [kəmˋplɛkʃən] *n.* [C] 膚色、氣色 complexions

🐛 I layer my moisturizers, which makes my **complexion** so fresh, I can wear less foundation. (Bobbi Brown, Businesswoman)
我層層塗上我的潤膚產品，讓我的氣色變好，我就可以上少一點粉底。

🐛 People always say you can't wear red lipstick if you have red hair, but you can absolutely do that. It's more about **complexion**. (Kate Walsh, Actress)
人們常說紅髮的人不能塗紅色口紅，但是你當然可以，這跟膚色比較有相關。

11. concise [kənˋsaɪs] *adj.* 簡潔的、簡要的

🐛 I am an enthusiastic and **concise** shopper. (Zac Posen, Fashion Designer)
我是個狂熱且簡潔的購物者。

🐛 There is no truth which cannot be given in fifty words; the truth is always **concise**. (Barry Malzberg, Writer)
沒有甚麼事實是不能用五十個字說完的，事實都是簡要的。

12. conform [kənˋfɔrm] *vi.* 遵守、符合 conformed conformed

🐛 I wouldn't even have braces on my teeth. This idea that everyone should **conform** and be perfect is ridiculous. (Georgia Jagger, Model)
我甚至不戴牙套，大家都應該一樣、都該完美的想法是很荒謬的。

🐛 In New York, you can look at someone and pretty much determine where they live. Everyone seems to want to **conform**. (Iris Apfel, Businesswoman)
在紐約，你可以看一個人就知道他們住在哪，每個人好像都想要一樣。

13. contradict [kɑntrəˋdɪkt] *vt. vi.* 發生矛盾、抵觸 contradicted contradicted

🐸 I always love to quote Albert Einstein because nobody **contradicts** him. (Studs Terkel, Journalist)

我總是喜歡引述阿爾伯特愛因斯坦，因為沒人會牴觸他。

🐸 It is bad manners to **contradict** a quest. You must never insult people in your own house— always go to theirs. (Myrtle Reed, Author)

反駁客人是不禮貌的，你不該在自己家裡污辱別人，記得想那麼做的時候要去他們的家裡。

14. controversial [kɑntrəˋvɝʃəl] *adj.* 有爭議的

🐸 The most **controversial** people of 2015 include the presidential candidate Donald Trump, the football player Tom Brady, and reality TV star Kylie Jenner.

二零一五年最有爭議的人包含總統候選人唐納川普、橄欖球選手湯姆布萊迪以及實境節目明星凱莉詹娜。

🐸 If you've got a big mouth and you're **controversial**, you're going to get attention. (Simon Cowell, Entertainer)

如果你嘴巴很大而且你是個有爭議的人，那麼你一定會受到注目。

15. coordinate [koˋɔrdnɪt] *vt.* 協調、調節 coordinated coordinated

🐸 I **coordinate** stunts and memorize them. (Kurt Angle, Professional Wrestler)

我協調特技動作並把它們記起來。

🐸 My room was clean but then I had to **coordinate** my outfit to match my shoes.

我房間是很乾淨，但我必須調整我的衣服，好配我的鞋子。

Unit 39

寬心面對未知

趣味字彙表

1.	cordial *adj.* 熱忱的、友好	9.	cultivate *vt.* 培育、陶冶
2.	corporate *adj.* 法人（組織）的	10.	dandruff *n.* [U] 頭皮屑
3.	cosmetics *n.* 化妝品、美容品	11.	deadly *adj.* 致命的
4.	covet *vt. vi.* 貪圖、渴望	12.	decent *adj.* 體面的、正派的
5.	credible *adj.* 可信的、可靠的	13.	decline *vt. vi.* 下跌、婉拒
6.	criterion *n.* [C] 標準、準則	14.	defect *n.* [C] 缺點、缺陷
7.	crucial *adj.* 決定性的、重要的	15.	delinquent *n.* [C] 青少年罪犯、違法者
8.	crust *n.* [C][U] 麵包皮、派餅皮		

趣味字彙句 ⚡⚡ 🔴 MP3 39

1. cordial [ˈkɔrdʒəl] *adj.* 熱忱的、友好的

🦗 Banks try to be **cordial** and friendly. (Alan Kings, Comedian)
銀行都試著表現熱心與友善。

🦗 A lot of times their daughters are very **cordial**, but the moms tend to grab you and want to kiss you. (Zac Efron, Actor)
大部分的時候他們的女兒都很友好，但媽媽通常會抓你的手，然後想親你。

2. corporate [ˈkɔrpərɪt] *adj.* 法人（組織）的

🦗 I dated a guy but I didn't like him. That was my first match that led to me leaving my **corporate** job. (Patti Stanger, Businesswoman)
我和一個男人交往過，但我並不喜歡他，那是讓我離開公司的第一次配對。

🦗 I've never laughed as much as I did when I was a **corporate** lawyer. When you're working 16 hours a day, everything and everyone seems funny. (Susan Cain, Writer)
當我是事務所律師的時候，我笑最多，當你一天工作十六個小時，所有事情和所有的人看起來都好笑。

3. cosmetics [kɑzˈmɛtɪks] *n.* 化妝品、美容品

🦗 As women grow older, they rely more on **cosmetics**. (George Jean Nathan, Editor)
女人年紀越大，越依賴化妝品。

🦗 **Cosmetics** makers have always sold 'hope in a jar'. (Virginia Postrel, Writer)
化妝品製造商賣的向來是「瓶裝希望」。

4. covet [ˈkʌvɪt] *vt. vi.* 貪圖、渴望 coveted coveted

🐾 Whenever teenage girls and CEOs **covet** the same new technology, something extraordinary is happening. (Michael J. Saylor, Businessman)
每當青少女和總裁們都渴望一樣的新科技時,非凡的事就正在發生。

🐾 Do I **covet** Madonna's body? Yes! (Salma Hayek, Actress)
我渴望擁有瑪丹娜的身材嗎?是的。

5. credible [ˈkrɛdəbl̩] *adj.* 可信的、可靠的

🐾 If you look good, people assume you aren't **credible**. It's a battle you'll always fight if you're on TV. (Lisa Guerrero, Journalist)
如果你長得好看,人們自動認為你不可靠,如果你在電視圈,這是場你永遠都要參與的戰役。

🐾 The only person you need to be **credible** to is yourself. When you stand in front of the mirror, are you happy with yourself? (Afrojack, Musician)
你唯一需要展現可靠的人就是你自己,當你站在鏡子前,你對自己滿意嗎?

6. criterion [kraɪˈtɪrɪən] *n.* [C] 標準、準則 criterions/criteria

🐾 Time is the fairest and toughest **criterion**. (Edgar Quinet, Historian)
時間是最公平也最嚴苛的判斷準則。

🐾 Do not mind anything that anyone tells you about anyone else. Set your own **criterion** and judge everything for yourself. (Henry James, Writer)
不要在意別人對另一個人的評論,設立自己的標準,一切自己評斷。

7. crucial [ˈkruʃəl] *adj.* 決定性的、重要的

My dad would tell me bedtime stories, and he used to always leave them open-ended at a **crucial** point with the words, 'dream on'. (Hannah Kent, Writer)

我的父親會說睡前故事給我聽，然後他時常在重要時刻停止，說了「繼續作夢吧」，留下開放的結局。

Being at ease with not knowing is **crucial** for answers to come to you. (Eckhart Tolle, Author)

找到答案的關鍵就是寬心面對未知。

8. crust [krʌst] *n.* [C][U] 麵包皮、派餅皮 crusts

I worked as a taxi driver, truck driver, and many other jobs that would get me a **crust** of bread. (Morgan Freeman, Actor)

我做過計程車司機、貨車司機和很多其他可以讓我有塊麵包屑吃的工作。

A pie **crust** promise: easily made, easily broken. (Mary Poppins, Movie Character)

像派皮一樣空洞的保證：易做也易破。

9. cultivate [ˈkʌltəˌvet] *vt.* 培育、陶冶 cultivated cultivated

It's great to have your own label; you can **cultivate** your own artists. I've worked with pretty much everyone I wanted to. (Brian McKnight, Musician)

能有自己的品牌是很好的，你可以培養自己的藝人，而且我已經差不多和所有我想合作的人合作過了。

We're all given different things in life. It's up to you to **cultivate** whatever you were given. (Pharrell Williams, Musician)

人生中我們都得到不同的東西，一切都取決於自己要怎麼培育你得到的東西。

10. dandruff [ˈdændrəf] *n.* [U] 頭皮屑

🐦 You're like **dandruff**; I can't get you out of my head.

你就像頭皮屑一樣，我怎麼都沒辦法把你從我頭上消除。

🐦 One in five people have **dandruff**, and one in four people have mental health problems. I've had both. (Ruby Wax, Actress)

每五個人，就有一個人有頭皮屑，每四個人，就有一個人有精神問題。我兩樣都有。

11. deadly [ˈdɛdlɪ] *adj.* 致命的

🐦 Candy Man is a **deadly** movie character who can control bees and has a hook hand.

糖果人是個致命的角色，能控制蜜蜂，且擁有手鉤。

🐦 Freddy Krueger is a **deadly** movie character who only has power in the dream world.

弗萊迪克魯格是個致命的角色，但只在夢的世界有能力。

12. decent [ˈdisnt] *adj.* 體面的、正派的

🐦 Somewhere deep down, there's a **decent** man in me, but he just can't be found. (Eminem, Rapper/Musician)

我內心深處，有個體面的男人，只是找不到他而已。

🐦 Hip-hop saved my life. It's the only thing I've ever been **decent** at. I don't know how to do anything else. (Eminem, Rapper/Musician)

饒舌音樂救了我，那是我唯一還做得不錯的事，除此之外我甚麼都不會。

13. decline [dɪˋklaɪn] *vt. vi.* 下跌、婉拒 declined declined

In New York, if you **decline** even just a cookie at a party, women will assure you that you are not fat. (Sloane Crosley, Writer)
在紐約，如果你在派對上，即使只是謝絕了一塊餅乾，其他女人也會要你放心，說你並不胖。

Be able to **decline** a date so gracefully that the person isn't embarrassed that he or she asked. (Marilyn vos Savant, Writer)
要能以優雅的方式拒絕邀約，要能讓人不覺得他問了很丟臉。

14. defect [dɪˋfɛkt] *n.* [C] 缺點、缺陷 defects

It is an actor's **defect**. I want everybody to like me, so I'll say what I think will please them. (Jean Reno, Actor)
這是演員的缺點，我想要每個人都喜歡我，所以我選擇說會讓對方開心的話語。

I'm used to always deciding everything myself. It's a blessing, but also a terrible **defect**. (Robert Cavalli, Fashion Designer)
我習慣一切自己做決定，這是一種恩典，但也是個糟糕的缺點。

15. delinquent [dɪˋlɪŋkwənt] *n.* [C] 青少年罪犯、違法者 delinquents

Before a priest helped him, Mark Wahlberg used to be a **delinquent** who used drugs and went to prison.
在得到牧師幫助之前，馬克瓦伯是個吸毒且坐牢的青少年犯罪者。

As a **delinquent** in high school, Snopp Dogg sold drugs and joined a gang. After a few years, he decided to rap about his experiences and become famous.
在高中，歌手史奴比狗狗是個青少年犯罪者，他販售毒品，加入幫派。幾年後，他決定用饒舌音樂，道出他的經驗，並變有名。

Unit 40

相信自己可以

趣味字彙表

1.	descendant *n.* [C] 子孫、後裔	9.	disclose *vt.* 揭發、透露
2.	destined *adj.* 命中注定的	10.	discomfort *n.* [U] [C] 不適、使人不舒服的事物
3.	diagnose *vt.* 診斷	11.	dismay *n.* [U] 沮喪、氣餒
4.	dictate *vt. vi.* 口述、要求	12.	disposable *adj.* 可任意處理的、一次性使用的
5.	dilemma *n.* [C] 困境、進退兩難	13.	dissolve *vt. vi.* 分解、溶解
6.	diplomacy *n.* [U] 外交、交際手段	14.	distort *vt.* 扭曲
7.	disability *n.* [C][U] 無能、殘疾	15.	distraction *n.* [C][U] 分心、分散注意的事物
8.	disastrous *adj.* 災難性的、悲慘的		

趣味字彙句 🎧 🎧 💿 *MP3 40*

1. descendant [dɪˈsɛndənt] *n.* [C] 子孫、後裔 descendants

🐸 Tom Hanks is a **descendant** of Abraham Lincoln, the U.S. President who abolished slavery.
湯姆漢克是廢止奴隸制的美國總統亞伯拉罕林肯的後裔。

🐸 George Clooney is also a **descendant** of Abraham Lincoln, which means Tom Hanks and George Clooney are distantly related.
喬治克隆尼也是亞伯拉罕林肯的後裔，這表示湯姆漢克和喬治·克隆尼是遠親。

2. destined [ˈdɛstɪnd] *adj.* 命中注定的

🐸 I hate the phone, and I don't want to call anybody back. If I go to hell, I will be **destined** to return phone calls forever. (Drew Barrymore, Actress)
我討厭電話，而且我不想回任何人電話，如果我下地獄，我一定被懲罰一直回電話。

🐸 I always knew I was **destined** for greatness. (Oprah Winfrey)
我一直都知道我註定會成為偉大的人。

3. diagnose [ˈdaɪəgnoz] *vt.* 診斷 diagnosed diagnosed

🐸 What person doesn't search online about their disease after they are **diagnosed**? (Howard Rheingold, Critic)
誰不會在被診斷之後，上網查自己疾病的相關資訊呢？

🐸 I know there are many women being **diagnosed** with breast cancer. (Kylie Minogue, Musician)
我知道很多女性被診斷出罹患乳癌。

Part 1 「趣」你的單字基礎篇

Part 2 「趣」你的單字進階篇

4. dictate [ˈdɪktet] *vt. vi.* 口述、要求 dictated dictated

🐾 I really feel like life will **dictate** itself. (Shania Twain, Musician)
我真心相信生命會自己找出路。

🐾 So many people feel that once you reach a certain age then it's time to retire from a sport you love. I don't think that's true. Age should not **dictate** that. (Alonzo Mourning, Basketball Player)
很多人以為你一旦到了一個年紀，你就必須從你愛的運動退休，我不那麼認為，我不覺得年紀有那樣的代表。

5. dilemma [dəˈlɛmə] *n.* [C] 困境、進退兩難 dilemmas

🐾 I hate violence, yes I do. It's kind of a **dilemma**. (Jackie Chan, Actor)
我討厭暴力，是的，我討厭。這讓我有點進退兩難。

🐾 Our **dilemma** is that we hate change and love it at the same time; what we really want is for things to remain the same but get better. (Sydney J. Harris, Journalist)
我們的兩難是我們討厭改變，但同時也愛它，我們真正想要的是，事情不變，但卻更好。

6. diplomacy [dɪˈploməsɪ] *n.* [U] 外交、交際手段

🐾 Trying to get a couple of kids to watch the same TV show requires serious **diplomacy**. (Dee Dee Myers, Political Analyst)
讓幾個小孩看同一個電視節目是需要極高段的交涉手腕。

🐾 To say nothing, especially when speaking, is half the art of **diplomacy**. (Will Durant, Historian)
甚麼都不說，尤其是說話時，也是半個交際的藝術。

7. disability [dɪsə'bɪlətɪ] *n.* [C][U] 無能、殘疾 disabilities

🐛 The world worries about **disability** more than disabled people do. (Warwick Davis, Actor)

大家比殘障人士還擔心殘疾。

🐛 I have terrible handwriting. I now say it's a learning **disability**, but a nun used to hit me with a ruler because my writing was so bad. (Andrew Greeley, Priest)

我寫字很醜，我現在稱它是學習障礙，但以前有個修女因為我寫字實在太醜，會用尺打我。

8. disastrous [dɪz'æstrəs] *adj.* 災難性的、悲慘的

🐛 Life is a series of **disastrous** moments that will break your heart. In between those moments, that's when you enjoy, enjoy, enjoy. (Sandra Bullock, Actress)

就是一連串會讓你心碎的災難片刻，而在那樣的片刻間，就是你享受、享受、再享受的時候。

🐛 I'm often criticized for what I wear. That's my main label in the press now: **disastrous** dresser! (Helena Bonham Carter, Actress)

我時常因為我的穿著被批評。那現在是我在媒體上被貼上的主要標籤：穿著災難者。

9. disclose [dɪs'kloz] *vt.* 揭發、透露 disclosed disclosed

🐛 If you want to keep something concealed from your enemy, don't **disclose** it to your friend. (Solomon Ibn Gabirol, Poet)

如果你不希望你的敵人得知，那就不要告訴你的朋友。

🐛 The only people who don't want to **disclose** the truth are the people with something to hide. (Barack Obama, U.S. President)

唯一不想揭露真相的，就是有所隱瞞的那些人。

10. discomfort [dɪsˈkʌmfɚt] *n.* [U] [C] 不適、使人不舒服的事物
discomforts

🐝 I think **discomfort** is funny, partly because I experience discomfort a lot. (Joaquin Phoenix, Actor)
我覺得不適很搞笑，部分原因是我時常感到不適。

🐝 We all tend to laugh at others' **discomfort**. When someone slips on a banana skin and falls, it's funny. (Shah Rukh Khan, Actor)
我們都喜歡嘲笑別人的不適，如果有人踩到香蕉皮而跌倒，那是很好笑的。

11. dismay [dɪsˈme] *n.* [U] 沮喪、氣餒
🐝 I don't have any children. I just have a cat, to my parents' **dismay**. (Jenna Bush, Daughter of Former U.S. President)
我沒有小孩。讓我父母很沮喪的，我只有一隻貓。

🐝 I obviously have a great appreciation of jewelry much to the **dismay** of both my father and my boyfriends. (Ivanka Trump, Businesswoman)
很明顯的，我非常欣賞珠寶，這讓我的父親與男友感到很沮喪。

12. disposable [dɪˈspozəbl̩] *adj.* 可任意處理的、一次性使用的
🐝 I can read a four-page script and have it memorized. It's a skill you learn in school: **disposable** cramming. (Blake Lively, Actress)
我可以看了四頁的劇本，然後就背起來，這是你能在學校學到的技巧：隨時遺忘的速讀。

🐝 Men should be like Kleenex, soft, strong and **disposable**. (Cher, Musician)
男人應該像舒潔，柔軟、強壯，而且用完即丟。

13. dissolve [dɪˋzɑlv] *vt. vi.* 分解、溶解 dissolved dissolved

🐛 Everything is a miracle. It is a miracle that one does not **dissolve** in one's bath like a lump of sugar. (Pablo Picasso, Artist)
每件事都是奇蹟，人不會像一團糖一樣溶解在澡盆中也是個奇蹟。

🐛 If we were all given magic powers to read each other's thoughts, I suppose all friendships would **dissolve**.
如果每個人都有讀出別人想法的超能力，我猜所有的友情都會瓦解。

14. distort [dɪsˋtɔrt] *vt.* 扭曲 distorted distorted

🐛 Self-pity is never useful. It tends to **distort** like a fun-house mirror. (Anne Roiphe, Journalist)
自憐一點用都沒有，它會像哈哈鏡一樣扭曲你。

🐛 I think plastic surgery is great. But I don't think it's alright to **distort** yourself. (Sharon Stone, Actress)
我認為整形手術是很好的，但我不認為人應該扭曲自己。

15. distraction [dɪˋstrækʃən] *n.* [C][U] 分心、分散注意的事物 distractions

🐛 You can always find a **distraction** if you're looking for one. (Tom Kite, Athlete)
如果你在尋找分散你注意力的事物，那麼你便會分心。

🐛 Girls were always my biggest **distraction** in school. (Channing Tatum, Actor)
女孩一直都是我在學校最大的分心原因。

Unit 41

得忍耐、抱持正面態度

趣味字彙表

1.	diverse *adj.* 不同的、多種多樣的	9.	editorial *n.* [C] 社論
2.	documentary *n.* [C] 紀錄影片	10.	eligible *adj.* 有資格當選的、合適的
3.	donate *vt.* 捐獻、捐贈	11.	eloquence *n.* [U] 雄辯、（流利的）口才
4.	drastic *adj.* 激烈的、極端的	12.	endurance *n.* [U] 忍耐、耐久力
5.	dreary *adj.* 令人沮喪的、枯燥的	13.	enhance *vt.* 提高、增加
6.	dynamite *n.* [U] 炸藥	14.	episode *n.* [C] 連續劇的一集
7.	eccentric *adj.* 古怪的	15.	equivalent *adj.* 相等的、等價的
8.	edible *adj.* 可食的、食用的		

趣味字彙句 🔊 MP3 41

1. diverse [daɪ`vɝs] *adj.* 不同的、多種多樣的

🐛 What makes the world such a wonderful place is the diversity. I always filled my home, my office and my hotels with the most **diverse** crowds possible. (Petter Stordalen, Businessman)
世界如此美好的原因是它的多樣化，我總是讓我的家、辦公室及飯店充滿不同的人。

🐛 Leaders come in many styles and **diverse** qualities. (John W. Gardner, Educator)
領袖有很多種特質，有安靜的領袖，也有鄰國都能聽見的領袖。

2. documentary [dɑkjə`mɛntərɪ] *n.* [C] 紀錄影片 documentaries

🐛 Doing a **documentary** is about discovering, being open, learning, and following curiosity. (Spike Jonze, Director)
拍紀錄片的重點是探索、放開心、學習並跟隨你的好奇心。

🐛 Most people see a **documentary** about the meat industry and then they become a vegetarian for a week. (Jason Reitman, Director)
大多數的人看了屠宰場的紀錄片，然後就變身為素食主義者，為期一週。

3. donate [`donet] *vt.* 捐獻、捐贈 donated donated

🐛 I like being able to **donate** my comedy to charity. I'm not a millionaire, and I can't write checks. (Judy Gold, Comedian)
我喜歡捐贈喜劇給慈善機構，我不是百萬富翁，我無法開支票。

🐛 I think you should **donate** your organs. I would donate whatever anybody would take. (George Clooney, Actor)
我覺得人應該捐贈器官，只要有人要，我會捐贈任何器官。

4. drastic [ˈdræstɪk] *adj.* 激烈的、極端的

There are **drastic** changes when you become a mother. All of my pictures on my cellphone used to be of me, but now every single picture is of Mason. (Kourtney Kardashian, Celebrity)
成為母親後，會有劇烈的改變，以前我手機裡的照片都是我，但現在每一張照片都是梅森。

It's important to still look like yourself on your wedding day, so I didn't do anything **drastic**. (Lily Aldridge, Model)
婚禮上看起來還是你自己是很重要的，所以我沒有做什麼極端的裝扮。

5. dreary [ˈdrɪərɪ] *adj.* 令人沮喪的、枯燥的

Nobody needs a smile so much as the one who has none to give. So get used to smiling heart-warming smiles and spreading sunshine in a sometimes **dreary** world. (Lawrence Lovasik, Clergyman)
沒有笑容可以展現的人最需要笑容，所以在這個有時令人沮喪的世界，隨時準備好展現可以溫暖人心的笑容並傳播陽光吧。

Superheroes have gotten so ugly that even their muscles have muscles. Things have gotten so **dreary**. (Frank Miller, Artist)
超級英雄逐漸變得醜陋，連他們的肌肉都有肌肉了，事情變得很令人沮喪。

6. dynamite [ˈdaɪnəˌmaɪt] *n.*[U] 炸藥

You can touch a stick of **dynamite**, but if you touch a snake, it'll kill you so fast. It's not even funny. (Steve Irwin, Wildlife Expert)
你可以去碰炸藥，但如果你碰蛇，牠會瞬間把你殺死，這不是搞笑的。

Deficits are like putting **dynamite** in the hands of children. (Nassim Nicholas Taleb, Scientist)
赤字好比將炸藥交給小孩。

7. eccentric [ɪkˋsɛntrɪk] *adj.* 古怪的

🐸 When I was losing, they called me nuts. When I was winning, they called me **eccentric**. (Al McGuire, Coach)
我輸的時候，他們說我是瘋子，我贏的時候，他們說我古怪。

🐸 I love Dolce & Gabbana. I love Versace. I love the crazy, more **eccentric** stuff. (Lady Gaga, Musician)
我愛杜嘉班納，我愛范思哲，我愛瘋狂、古怪的東西。

8. edible [ˋɛdəbḷ] *adj.* 可食的、食用的

🐸 The only thing you can do to make catfish **edible** is fry them. (Blake Shelton, Musician)
要讓鯰魚變得可食用的唯一方法就是油炸了。

🐸 Never doubt the courage of the French. They were the ones who discovered that snails are **edible**. (Doug Larson, Columnist/Editor)
決不要懷疑法國人的勇氣，是他們發現蝸牛是可以吃的。

9. editorial [ɛdəˋtɔrɪəl] *n.* [C] 社論 editorials

🐸 They'd rather see SpongeBob than Daddy talking about the latest Wall Street Journal **editorial**. You do what you have to do to get your kids ready for school. (Joe Scarborough, Politician)
他們寧願看海綿寶寶，而不是吹牛老爹，討論華爾街日報社論，你盡一切所能讓你的小孩為學校做好準備。

🐸 Most people don't read **editorial** pages. I think I must have been 40 years old before I even looked at an editorial page. (Tom Wolfe, Journalist)
大部分的人不看社論版，我想我好像四十歲前，社論版面連一眼都不看。

10. eligible [ˈɛlɪdʒəbl̩] *adj.* 有資格當選的、合適的

🕮 The most **eligible** bachelor in the world is Stavros Niarchos III. The 29 year old comes from a Greek shipping dynasty.
世上最搶手的黃金單身漢是史塔沃斯尼亞科斯三世，二十九歲，出身希臘船運王朝。

🕮 One of the most **eligible** bachelorette is Pauline Ducruet. She is a professional diver and the granddaughter of Princess Grace of Monaco.
最搶手的黃金單身女之一是寶琳杜克魯特，她是職業跳水選手，也是摩納哥格雷絲公主的孫女。

11. eloquence [ˈɛləkwəns] *n.* [U] 雄辯、（流利的）口才

🕮 Action is **eloquence**. (William Shakespeare, Poet/Playwright)
行動就是雄辯。

🕮 Talking and **eloquence** are not the same: to speak and to speak well are two different things. (Ben Jonson, Poet)
說話與雄辯是不同的：說話和說得好是兩個不同的東西。

12. endurance [ɪnˈdjʊrəns] *n.* [U] 忍耐、耐久力

🕮 Heroism is **endurance** for one moment more. (George F. Kennan, Historian)
英雄氣概就是再多忍耐一下。

🕮 The length of a film should be directly related to the **endurance** of the human bladder. (Alfred Hitchcock, Director)
電影的片長應該直接和人類膀胱的忍耐力有關。

13. enhance [ɪnˈhæns] *vt.* 提高、增加 enhanced enhanced

🐾 I have always believed that chemistry can't be created between two people. You either have it or you don't. The script can only **enhance** it. (Deepika Padukone, Actress)
我一直都相信兩人間的化學反應是無法創造出來的，有就是有，沒有就是沒有，劇本只是增加那化學反應。

🐾 Travelling can only **enhance** happiness if you are happy inside before you leave. (Andrea Bocelli, Musician)
你要能在出發前發自內心的快樂，旅遊才能為你增加幸福感。

14. episode [ˈɛpəˌsod] *n.* [C] 連續劇的一集 episodes

🐾 When movie people go over into television, it's a little bit of a shock. You won't know your schedule for the next **episode** until the last minute. (Charisma Carpenter, Actress)
當電影明星轉入電視界時，會有點受到衝擊，你最後一秒才會知道自己下一集的行程。

🐾 Plan for each **episode** to be a satisfying experience, but still leave the audience thinking, 'Oh, my God! Now what?' (Andrew Davies, Writer)
計畫讓每一集都是個令人滿足的經驗，但還是要讓觀眾想「喔，天啊！接下來是甚麼？」

15. equivalent [ɪˈkwɪvələnt] *adj.* 相等的、等價的

🐾 A good picture is **equivalent** to a good deed. (Vincent Van Gogh, Artist)
一幅好圖等同一項善行。

🐾 Being on Broadway is the modern **equivalent** of being a monk. I sleep a lot, eat a lot, and rest a lot. (Hugh Jackman, Actor)
現在在百老匯等同當和尚，我睡得多、吃得多，也休息很多。

Unit 42

成長、迎向未來

趣味字彙表

1.	eternity *n.* [U] [C] 永恆	9.	feasible *adj.* 可行的、可能的
2.	ethnic *adj.* 種族（上）的	10.	feedback *n.* [U] 回饋
3.	evolve *vt. vi.* 發展、成長	11.	finite *adj.* 有限的
4.	excessive *adj.* 過度的、過分的	12.	flicker *vt. vi.* 閃爍、搖曳
5.	exclusive *adj.* 唯一的、排外的	13.	foresee *vt.* 預見
6.	expire vt. *vi.* 屆期	14.	formidable *adj.* 可怕的、難對付的
7.	eyesight *n.* [U] 視力	15.	fragile *adj.* 易碎的、脆弱的
8.	familiarity *n.* [U] 熟悉、親近		

趣味字彙句 <!-- MP3 42 -->

1. eternity [ɪ'tɜnətɪ] *n.* [U] [C] 永恆 eternities

Eternity's a terrible thought. I mean, when's it all going to end? (Tom Stoppard, Dramatist)

永恆是個糟糕的想法。我的意思是，到底甚麼時候會結束？

What love we've given, we'll have forever. What love we fail to give, will be lost for all **eternity**. (Leo Buscaglia, Author)

我們付出的愛，將永遠為我們所有，而未及付出的愛，將永遠失落。

2. ethnic ['εθnɪk] *adj.* 種族（上）的

I've been to over 95 countries, so I love **ethnic** food, different types of cuisine. (Larry Fitzgerald, Football Player)

我去過超過九十五個國家，所以我很愛不同種族的食物、不同種類的料理。

I have never felt any **ethnic** connection with the Greeks other than how hairy I am. (George Michael, Musician)

我從不覺得自己和希臘人有種族上的關聯，除了我毛很多的事實。

3. evolve [ɪ'vɑlv] *vt. vi.* 發展、成長 evolved evolved

The whole point of being alive is to **evolve** into the complete person you were intended to be. (Oprah Winfrey, Entertainer)

活著的重點是發展成自己原來注定該成為的完整的個人。

What's dangerous is not to **evolve**. (Jeff Bezos, Amazon CEO)

危險的是永不成長。

4. excessive [ɪkˈsɛsɪv] *adj.* 過度的、過分的

My biggest weakness is that I'm **excessive**. (Mel Gibson, Actor)
我最大的弱點就是太過頭了。

Sometimes I take a while to get ready to go out. It's not **excessive**, but it takes me some time to find clean clothes that match. (Zac Efron, Actor)
有時候我會花一點時間準備出門，不過分，但要找到相配的乾淨衣服有點花時間。

5. exclusive [ɪkˈsklusɪv] *adj.* 唯一的、排外的

Fashion does not need to be **exclusive** to be fashionable. (Marc Jacobs, Fashion Designer)
時尚不需要是排外的才是時髦的。

Once a Bond girl, always a Bond girl. It's an **exclusive** club. (Carey Lowell, Actress)
一旦當過龐德女郎，永遠都是龐德女郎，這是個貴賓俱樂部。

6. expire [ɪkˈspaɪr] *vt.* *vi.* 屆期 expired expired

If I planned everything out in advance, I'd **expire** of boredom. (Peter Straub, Writer)
如果我所有事情都事先計畫好，那我會因為無聊而死。

I am here to inspire before I **expire**. (Kal-El, Comic Book Character)
我在這的目的是在死前鼓舞他人。

7. eyesight [ˈaɪˌsaɪt] *n.* [U] 視力

🐹 Whatever you may look like, marry a man your own age— as your beauty fades, so will his **eyesight**. (Phyllis Diller, Comedian)

不管你看起來怎麼樣，嫁給一位和你年紀相近的男人，當你的美麗逝去，他的視力也是如此。

🐹 I like using snapshot cameras because they're idiot-proof. I have bad **eyesight**, and I'm no good at focusing big cameras. (Terry Richardson, Photographer)

我喜歡用快拍相機，因為傻瓜也可以輕鬆用。我的視力不好，我不太會用大台相機聚焦。

8. familiarity [fəˌmɪlɪˈærətɪ] *n.* [U] 熟悉、親近

🐹 I would like for my kids to at least have some **familiarity** with who I am: 'It's the man from TV!' (Steve Carell, Actor)

我希望我的小孩可以至少稍微了解我是誰：「是電視裡的那個男人！」

🐹 It wasn't love at first sight exactly, but it was **familiarity**. Something like oh, hello, it's you. It's going to be you. (Mhairi McFarlane, Author)

不真的是一見鍾情，而是種熟悉感，有點像「喔，你好，是你。就是你了。」

9. feasible [ˈfizəbl̩] *adj.* 可行的、可能的

🐹 I could never convince the investors that Disneyland was a **feasible** dream. (Walt Disney, Entrepreneur)

我那時一直無法說服投資者迪士尼樂園是個可行的夢。

🐹 Divide each difficulty into as many parts as is **feasible** and necessary to resolve it. (Rene Descartes, Mathematician)

把困難依可行度與必須的程度分成最多的部分，好解決這個問題。

10. feedback [ˈfidˌbæk] *n.* [U] 回饋

- We all need people who will give us **feedback**. That's how we improve. (Bill Gates, Businessman)
  我們都需要會給我們意見的人，這是我們進步的方法。

- Negative **feedback** is better than none. I would rather have a man hate me than overlook me. (Hugh Prather, Writer)
  負面意見比沒有意見好，我寧願有人恨我，也不想要有人忽略我。

11. finite [ˈfaɪnaɪt] *adj.* 有限的

- We must accept **finite** disappointment but never lose infinite hope. (Martin Luther King Jr., Minister)
  我們必須要接受有限的失望但絕不失去無限的希望。

- I believe every human has a **finite** number of heartbeats. I don't intend to waste any of mine. (Neil Armstrong, Astronaut)
  我相信每個人都只有特定數目的心跳數，我並不打算浪費任何一下。

12. flicker [ˈflɪkɚ] *vt. vi.* 閃爍、搖曳 flickered flickered

- Do not worry if all the candles in the world **flicker** and die. We have the spark that starts the fire. (Rumi, Poet)
  不要擔心，即使全世界的燭火都在搖曳與滅去，我們還有點燃火的火花。

- I love having candles. I could just go to sleep seeing the flame **flicker** with the lights off. (Kellan Lutz, Actor)
  我熱愛蠟燭。只要看著在黑暗中閃爍的燭光，我就可以安眠。

13. foresee [for`si] *vt.* 預見 foresaw foreseen

🐾 You can always change a big plan but you can never expand a little one. Plans should be big enough for situations, which we can't **foresee**. (Harry S. Truman, President)
你總有辦法修改大計畫，但你無法擴展小計畫。計畫應該要依情況而有夠大的規模，而那個情況我們是無法預測的。

🐾 Since I do seven different styles of martial arts, I don't **foresee** myself fighting the same way in any two movies. (Michael Jai White, Actor)
因為我學了七種不同形式的武術，我不覺得我會在不同電影裡用相同的方式搏鬥。

14. formidable [`fɔrmɪdəbl] *adj.* 可怕的、難對付的

🐾 A good head and a good heart are always a **formidable** combination. (Nelson Mandela, President)
好頭腦與善良的心不論何時都是個令人畏懼的組合。

🐾 No problem is so **formidable** that you can't walk away from it. (Charles M. Schulz, Cartoonist)
再難以對付的問題，你也是可以直接走開。

15. fragile [`frædʒəl] *adj.* 易碎的、脆弱的

🐾 Your heart is a very **fragile** muscle. You have to take care of it. (Anne-Marie Duff, Actress)
你的心是個脆弱的肌肉，你必須好好照料它。

🐾 I break a lot of drums. They're actually somewhat **fragile** instruments. (Damien Chazelle, Director)
我弄壞了好幾個鼓，它們其實是有點脆弱的樂器。

Unit 43

良性互動

趣味字彙表

1.	fraud *n.* [C][U] 欺騙、騙局、騙子	9.	hospitable *adj.* 好客的、宜人的
2.	generate *vt.* 產生、引起	10.	humanitarian *n.* [C] 人道主義者、慈善家
3.	genetic *adj.* 起源的、基因的、遺傳的	11.	humiliate *vt.* 羞辱
4.	glamour *n.*[U] 魅力	12.	hurdle *n.* [C] 欄、跨欄賽跑
5.	gloomy *adj.* 陰暗的、憂鬱的	13.	hygiene *n.* [U] 衛生
6.	grill *n.* [C] 烤架、燒烤的肉類食物； *vt. vi.*（用烤架）烤（魚、肉等）	14.	hysterical *adj.* 歇斯底里的
7.	heritage *n.*[U] 遺產、傳統	15.	immune *adj.* 免疫的
8.	highlight *n.*[C] 最突出（或最精彩）的部分		

趣味字彙句 🎧 🎧 MP3 43

1. fraud [frɔd] *n.* [C][U] 欺騙、騙局、騙子 frauds

🐸 Things gained through **fraud** are never secure. (Sophocles, Poet)
欺騙得來的東西無法永遠留在身邊。

🐸 I feel like a **fraud**. My name is not even actually Ashton; it's my middle name. (Ashton Kutcher, Actor)
我覺得自己像個騙子。我的名字其實根本不是艾希頓，那是我的中間名。

2. generate [ˈdʒɛnə˛ret] *vt.* 產生、引起 generated generated

🐸 You can only **generate** ideas when you put pencil to paper, and brush to canvas. (Twyla Tharp, Dancer)
唯有在紙上用鉛筆，在畫布上用筆刷，你才有辦法產生創意。

🐸 Having a small number of guests is the only way to **generate** good conversation. (Paul Lynde, Comedian)
唯有賓客的數量少，才能產生良好的對話。

3. genetic [dʒə˛nɛtɪk] *adj.* 起源的、基因的、遺傳的

🐸 Your social networks matter more than your **genetic** networks. Get healthy friends because if your friends have healthy habits you are more likely to as well. (Mary Hyman, Author)
你的人脈比你的基因重要多了，結交健康的朋友，如果你的朋友有健康的習慣，那你很可能也會有。

🐸 I think the genetics of being Irish are that you prefer when it's rainy and cloudy. It's just **genetic**. (Kate Flannery, Actress)
我覺得愛爾蘭的基因遺傳之一就是你比較喜歡下雨天和陰天，這是基因問題。

4. glamour [ˋglæmɚ] *n.*[U] 魅力

One thing about this world of **glamour** is that it is better to have people talking about you than not being talked about at all. (Sonakshi Sinha, Actress)
在這個魅力的世界，被人討論比完全沒人討論你更好。

Glamour is something you can't be without once you're used to it. (Loretta Young, Actress)
你一旦習慣了魅力，你就不能沒有它。

5. gloomy [ˋglumɪ] *adj.* 陰暗的、憂鬱的

Half the fight is won if you never allow yourself to say anything **gloomy**. (Lydia M. Child, Activist)
如果你從不允許自己說出陰沉的話，那麼你的戰爭已經贏了一半。

People ask me to smile for the camera, but somehow it always comes out **gloomy**. (Stephen Rea, Actor)
人們要我拍照的時候微笑，但不知道為什麼，照片出來我總是看起來陰沉。

6. grill [grɪl] *n.* [C] 烤架、燒烤的肉類食物 grills； *vt. vi.*（用烤架）烤（魚、肉等） grilled, grilled

Summer is a completely different experience when you know how to **grill**. (Taylor Swift, Musician)
如果你知道怎麼烤肉，那麼夏天會變得完全不同。

I'm good with a **grill**. I like to make cheeseburgers— you're only supposed to flip a burger once. (Noah Baumbach, Writer)
我很會燒烤，我喜歡做起司堡，漢堡肉應該要只翻一次。

7. heritage [ˈhɛrətɪdʒ] *n.*[U] 遺產、傳統

I have never denied my culture. I taught my child to embrace her Mexican **heritage**, to learn Spanish, and to love the Mexican candy I grew up with. (Salma Hayek, Actress)
我從沒否認我的文化，我教我的小孩要真心接受他是墨西哥裔，學西班牙語並要愛陪我一起成長的墨西哥糖果。

My nose was part of my **heritage**. If I had talent to sing and to act, why should I change my nose? (Barbra Streisand, Actress)
我的鼻子是我繼承的傳統之一，如果我有唱歌或演戲的天分，為什麼我要改變我的鼻子。

8. highlight [ˈhaɪˌlaɪt] *n.*[C] 最突出（或最精彩）的部分 highlights

The **highlight** of my childhood was making my brother laugh so hard that food came out of his nose. (Garrison Keillor, Writer)
我童年時期最精彩的部分就是讓我的哥哥笑到食物從鼻子跑出來。

If you're going to lose weight, you have to change your way of thinking about food. It cannot be the **highlight** of your life. (Jean Nidetch, Businessman)
如果你想要減肥，你就要改變你對食物的看法，食物不能是你生命的高潮。

9. hospitable [ˈhɑspɪtəbl̩] *adj.* 好客的、宜人的

Being **hospitable** is possible when you believe that the other person is on your side. (Danny Meyer, Restaurateur)
當你相信對方是站在你這邊的，那麼表現好客是有可能的。

Being **hospitable** cannot be taught. It's all about hiring the right people. (Danny Meyer, Restaurateur)
招待周到是教不來的，重要的是要請對人。

10. humanitarian [hjuˌmænəˈtɛrɪən] *n.* [C] 人道主義者、慈善家
humanitarians

🐝 Before Angelina Jolie became a **humanitarian**, she was best
known for wearing a vial of blood around her neck and kissing her
brother. (Stephen Rodrick, Journalist)
在安潔莉娜裘莉變成慈善家之前，她是以脖子上的一瓶血以及和哥哥親
嘴聞名。

🐝 In my mid-30s, I realized that I wanted to be a **humanitarian**.
(Angelina Jolie, Actress)
在我三十歲幾歲中期時，我發現我想要當慈善家。

11. humiliate [hjuˈmɪlɪˌet] *vt.* 羞辱 humiliated humiliated

🐝 True basketball coaches are great teachers and do not **humiliate**.
(Morgan Wootten, Basketball Coach)
真正的籃球教練是偉大的導師，且不羞辱人。

🐝 I jumped off a roof in a bee costume. This is my business; I have to
humiliate myself. (Jerry Seinfeld, Comedian)
我曾穿著蜜蜂服裝從屋頂跳下，這是我的工作，我必須羞辱我自己。

12. hurdle [ˈhɝdl̩] *n.* [C] 欄、跨欄賽跑 hurdles

🐝 There is always a **hurdle**. There is always something you have to
go over. (Gail Devers, Track and Field Athlete)
在人生中，不管哪裡都有柵欄，總是會有你需要跨越的。

🐝 I had little legs, so I had to take 50 steps between each **hurdle**.
(Chris Kirkpatrick, Musician)
我的腿很短，所以每個柵欄間我需要跨五十步。

13. hygiene [ˈhaɪdʒin] *n.* [U] 衛生

🐛 My mom is at my house every day, and she nags me about every-thing, especially **hygiene**. (Shia LeBeouf, Actor)
我母親每天都來我家,她甚麼都可以唸我,尤其是衛生相關的。

🐛 **Hygiene** is two thirds of health. (Lebanese Proverb)
衛生是達到健康的三分之二原因。

14. hysterical [hɪsˈtɛrɪkl̩] *adj.* 歇斯底里的

🐛 Trying to express yourself to the press is often like arguing with a **hysterical** person. (Ezra Koenig, Musician)
試著跟媒體解釋自己,就像跟個歇斯底里的人吵架一樣。

🐛 I turn into a crying, **hysterical** crazy person when I see a spider. (Kate Dickie, Actress)
我看到蜘蛛的時候,便會變成一個大哭、歇斯底里的瘋子。

15. immune [ɪˈmjun] *adj.* 免疫的

🐛 Everybody has to deal with tough times. A gold medal doesn't make you **immune** to that. (Dorothy Hamill, Figure Skater)
每個人都需要面對艱困,金牌並不會讓你避開這些。

🐛 The cells in your body react to everything that your mind says. Negativity brings down your **immune** system.
你身體的每個細胞都會對你內心所想的有反應,負面想法會削弱你的免疫系統。

Part 1 「趣」你的單字基礎篇

Part 2 「趣」你的單字進階篇

Unit 44

展現獨創精神、個人特色

趣味字彙表

1.	implement *vt.* 履行、實施	9.	integrity *n.* [U] 正直、完善
2.	incentive *n.* [U] [C] 刺激、鼓勵	10.	intimacy *n.* [U] [C] 熟悉、親密（的行為）
3.	inevitable *adj.* 不可避免的、必然的	11.	intimidate *vt.* 威嚇、脅迫
4.	infectious *adj.* 傳染的、有感染力的	12.	invaluable *adj.* 非常貴重的、無價的
5.	ingenuity *n.* [U] 獨創性、精巧	13.	IQ *abbr.* 智力商數
6.	initiative *n.* [U] [C] 主動的行動、首創精神	14.	irritate *vt. vi.* 使煩躁、引起惱怒
7.	innovation *n.* [U] [C] 革新、新方法	15.	joyous *adj.* 快樂的、高興的
8.	insight *n.* [U] [C] 洞察力、眼光		

趣味字彙句 👂👂 🎧 MP3 44

1. implement [ˈɪmpləmənt] *vt.* 履行、實施

🐾 Always prefer direct promises to long, vague ones. Don't **implement** promises, but keep them. (C.S. Lewis, Author)
選擇直接的承諾而不是又長又模稜兩可的承諾，不要履行承諾，但要遵守承諾。

🐾 It's not necessarily size that matters; it's how fast you **implement** your strategy. (Bryan Clay, Olympic Athlete)
身形大小並不是絕對重要的，你實施策略的速度才是關鍵。

2. incentive [ɪnˈsɛntɪv] *n.* [U] [C] 刺激、鼓勵 incentives

🐾 There is no medicine like hope, no **incentive** so great as the expectation of tomorrow. (Orison Swett Marden, Writer)
沒有比希望更好的藥，也沒有比對明天的期待更好的鼓勵了。

🐾 The best move you can make in a deal is to think of an **incentive** the other person hasn't thought of— and then meet it. (Eli Broad, Entrepreneur)
在一場交易中，最好的策略就是想出別人想不到的獎勵，然後實現它。

3. inevitable [ɪnˈɛvətəbl] *adj.* 不可避免的、必然的

🐾 Success is often achieved by those who don't know that failure is **inevitable**. (Coco Chanel, Fashion Designer)
不知道失敗是必然的人常常就是成功的那些人。

🐾 Expect trouble as an **inevitable** part of life and repeat that to yourself, the most comforting words of all; this, too, shall pass. (Ann Landers, Journalist)
要知道錯誤是人生不可避免的一部份，並重複提醒自己，這是最能安慰自己的話語，這一切都會過去。

4. infectious [ɪnˈfɛkʃəs] *adj.* 傳染的、有感染力的

Your enthusiasm will be **infectious** and attractive to others. (Norman Vincent Peale, Minister)
你的熱忱對他人是有感染力跟吸引力的。

I love living. I think that's **infectious**, it's something you can't fake. (Will Smith, Actor)
我喜歡生活，我覺得那是很有傳染力的，也不是你可以裝出來的。

5. ingenuity [ˌɪndʒəˈnuətɪ] *n.* [U] 獨創性、精巧

Never tell people how to do things. Tell them what to do and they will surprise you with their **ingenuity**. (George S. Patton)
不要告訴別人做事的方法，告訴他們做甚麼事，人們反而會發揮讓你驚訝的創意。

Ingenuity, plus courage, plus work, equals miracles. (Bob Richards, Olympic Athlete)
獨創，加上勇氣和行動等於奇蹟。

6. initiative [ɪˈnɪʃətɪv] *n.* [U] [C] 主動的行動、首創精神 initiatives

I will not start an **initiative** until I've spent my own money. If I spend my own money, people will know that I am serious about it. (Will.i.am, Musician)
直到我花自己錢之前，我不會開始一項創新計劃，但一旦花了自己的錢，人們就會知道我是認真的。

I've always had confidence. It came because I have lots of **initiative**. I wanted to make something of myself. (Eddie Murphy, Comedian)
我向來都很有自信，我的自信來自我滿滿的創新，我想要創立自己的東西。

7. innovation [ɪnəˈveʃən] *n.* [U] [C] 革新、新方法 innovations

So many cartoonists draw the same year after year. With no **innovation**, they become boring. (Pat Oliphant, Cartoonist)
很多漫畫家每年都畫一樣的東西，不革新，他們也因此變得無趣。

The most important thing to remember, if you are trying something that is an **innovation**, is not to think too much about it. (Sandro Veronesi, Novelist)
如果你在嘗試一個革新的事物，要記得的重點是不要想太多。

8. insight [ˈɪnˌsaɪt] *n.* [U] [C] 洞察力、眼光 insights

Einstein liked to play the violin, and I like to go ice-skating. It helps me to forget my problems and gain fresh new **insight**. (Michio Kaku, Physicist)
愛因斯坦喜歡拉小提琴而我喜歡溜冰，這幫助我忘記我的問題，並得到新的觀點。

If one understands one thing well, one has at the same time, **insight** into and understanding of many things. (Vincent Van Gogh, Artist)
如果一個人真正了解一件事，那麼他同時也洞察到並了解到許多其他事。

9. integrity [ɪnˈtɛɡrətɪ] *n.* [U] 正直、完善

Greatness is not about wealth; it is about **integrity** and ability to positively affect others. (Bob Marley, Musician)
偉大與財富無關，重點是正直和正面影響他人的能力。

Live so that when your children think of fairness, caring, and **integrity**, they think of you. (H. Jackson Brown, Jr., Author)
好好過活，讓你的小孩想到公平、關愛和正直，他們就會想到你。

10. intimacy [ˈɪntəməsɪ] *n.* [U] [C] 熟悉、親密（的行為）intimacies

👑 If you age with somebody, you go through so many roles — you're lovers, friends, enemies, strangers, and brother and sister. That's what **intimacy** is. (Cate Blanchett, Actress)

如果你和某人一起變老，那麼你會經歷很多角色，你是愛人、朋友、敵人、陌生人，或兄弟姊妹，這就是親密關係。

👑 For a dinner date, I eat light all day to stay hungry, then I go all in. There's a beautiful **intimacy** in a meal like that. (Anthony Bourdain, Chef/Author)

我有晚餐約會的時候，我當天會吃很少，保持飢餓，然後晚餐全力進食，這樣的晚餐有種美麗的親密感。

11. intimidate [ɪnˈtɪməˌdet] *vt.* 威嚇、脅迫 intimidated intimidated

👑 I don't try to **intimidate** anybody before a fight. That's nonsense. (Mike Tyson, Professional Boxer)

開打前我不會威脅任何人，那是沒有意義的。

👑 I have done scenes with owls, with bats, with special effects, and in the freezing cold. There's honestly nothing that's going to **intimidate** me! (Emma Watson, Actress)

我和貓頭鷹、蝙蝠、特效一起拍過戲，也在極冷的環境下拍過，說真的，沒有甚麼東西可以威脅到我了。

12. invaluable [ɪnˈvæljəbl̩] *adj.* 非常貴重的、無價的

👑 A man who is available for lunch, is interested in everything, and talks well is **invaluable**. (Elizabeth Bibesco, Poet)

一個有時間吃午餐、對甚麼事都好奇，又會講話的人是很有價值的。

👑 Be sure to read a recipe all the way through before you cook. The time it saves you is **invaluable**. (Tom Douglas, Chef)

煮飯之前，一定要把食譜從頭看到尾，這為你省下的時間是無價的。

13. IQ [ˈaɪˈkju] *abbr.* 智力商數

- Americans automatically add 10 points to someone's **IQ** when they hear an English accent. (Rachel Johnson, Author)
  美國人只要聽到對方是英國口音，就會為他的智商多加十分。

- Do you want to increase your **IQ**? Be uncomfortable and learn something from the beginning. (Nolan Bushnell, Businessman)
  你想要提升你的智商嗎？即使感到不自在，也從頭學樣新東西吧。

14. irritate [ˈɪrəˌtet] *vt. vi.* 使煩躁、引起惱怒 irritated irritated

- I **irritate** my wife because of my private dancing. (Brian McDermott, Soccer Player)
  我私下跳舞總是會惹惱我太太。

- It **irritates** me when people talk about every single girl I'm with because it's a complete pain for the girls. (Prince William, Duke of Cambridge)
  當人們討論每個我交往過的女孩，我就會覺得很生氣，因為這對女孩來說是一種痛。

15. joyous [ˈdʒɔɪəs] *adj.* 快樂的、高興的

- The two most **joyous** times of the year are Christmas morning and the end of school. (Alice Cooper, Musician)
  一年最令人開心的時節便是聖誕節早晨和學期末。

- A romance novel should leave readers **joyous**. My books all have happy endings. (Judith McNaught, Author)
  愛情小說應該要讓讀者看完感到愉悅，我的書都有美好的結局。

Part2

趣你的單字進階篇

Unit 45

舒緩負面情緒

1.	kidnap *vt.* 誘拐、綁架	14.	meditate *vi. vt.* 沉思、打算
2.	layout *n.* [C][U] 安排、版面設計	15.	melancholy *n.* [U] 憂鬱
3.	legendary *adj.* 傳說的、傳奇的	16.	mellow *adj.* 圓熟的、老練的
4.	legitimate *adj.* 合法的、正當的	17.	mentality *n.* [C][U] 智力、心性
5.	lengthy *adj.* 長的、冗長的	18.	merchandise *n.* [U] 商品、貨物
6.	liable *adj.* 會……的、有義務的	19.	miraculous *adj.* 神奇的、奇蹟般的
7.	literal *adj.* 照字面的、不誇張的	20.	mobilize *vt.* 動員、使流通
8.	longevity *n.*[U] 長壽	21.	mold [mold] *n.* [C] 模子、模式
9.	lunatic *n.* [C] 瘋子	22.	momentum *n.* [U] [C] 動量、衝力
10.	lyric *n.* [C] 抒情詩、歌詞	23.	monotonous *adj.* 無抑揚頓挫的、單調的
11.	magnitude *n.* [U] 巨大、重、大量	24.	morale *n.*[U] 士氣、鬥志
12.	mastery *n.*[U] 熟練、優勢、支配	25.	motto *n.* [C] 座右銘、格言
13.	mechanism *n.* [C] 機械裝置、結構、辦法		

趣味字彙句 🌙🌙 ⊙MP3 45

1. kidnap [ˈkɪdnæp] *vt.* 誘拐、綁架 kidnapped, kidnapped
🐸 Every time I went out of the house, my nanny was next to me to stop me from being **kidnapped**. (J.G. Ballard, Author)
每次我離開屋子，我的保母都會在我旁邊，確保我不會被綁架。

2. layout [ˈleˌaʊt] *n.* [C][U] 安排、版面設計 layouts
🐸 All my inspiration comes from nature, whether it's an animal or the **layout** of a leaf. (Diane von Furstenberg, Fashion Designer)
我的靈感都來自大自然，不論是動物或樹葉的結構。

3. legendary [ˈlɛdʒəndɛrɪ] *adj.* 傳說的、傳奇的
🐸 I have **legendary** massive breakfasts at hotels. (Calvin Harris)
我在飯店吃過傳奇性的大型早餐。

4. legitimate [lɪˈdʒɪtəmɪt] *adj.* 合法的、正當的
🐸 For dating websites, if you're **legitimate** about it and know what you're looking for, it's definitely effective. (Nev Schulman, Producer)
如果你是以正當方式使用交友網站，而且知道你要找甚麼，那麼它確實是很有效的。

5. lengthy [ˈlɛŋθɪ] *adj.* 長的、冗長的
🐸 The first recipe for happiness is: avoid **lengthy** reflection on the past. (Andre Maurois, Writer)
快樂的第一個秘訣就是：避免沉溺在過去過久。

6. liable [ˈlaɪəbl̩] *adj.* 會……的、有義務的

🐸 If you spend all of your time racing ahead to the future, you're **liable** to discover you've left a great present behind. (Tom Wilson, Cartoonist)
如果你把所有的時間都花在要朝未來跑去，那麼你絕對會發現你遺留了大半的現在。

7. literal [ˈlɪtərəl] *adj.* 照字面的、不誇張的

🐸 I enjoy every climb — maybe it's because it's a **literal** dance between life and death. (Alain Robert, Rock Climber)
每次攀岩我都很享受，也許因為它真的是在生與死之間來回。

8. longevity [lɑnˈdʒɛvətɪ] *n.*[U] 長壽

🐸 If you ask what is the single most important key to **longevity**, I would have to say it is avoiding worry, stress, and tension. (George Burns, Comedian)
如果你問長壽一個最重要的關鍵，我會說要避開擔心、壓力和緊張。

9. lunatic [ˈlunəˌtɪk] *n.* [C] 瘋子 lunatics

🐸 When I was 26 years old, I was running a kitchen in New York, and I acted like a **lunatic**. (Tom Colicchio, Chef)
我二十六歲的時候，在紐約管理餐廳廚房，我像個瘋子一樣。

10. lyric [ˈlɪrɪk] *n.* [C] 抒情詩、歌詞 lyrics

🐸 I have them say the **lyric** until it sounds like something they really believe, like an actor. (Margaret Whiting, Musician)
我會叫他們唸歌詞，唸到他們聽起來真的相信內容，像演員一樣。

11. magnitude [ˈmæɡnəˌtjud] *n.* [U] 巨大、重、大量

☞ It is often said that the **magnitude** of a person is measured by their ability to know how to win. (Jose Eduardo Dos Santos, President of Angola)

人們常說，衡量一個人的重要的方式，是他們知道如何贏得勝利的能力。

12. mastery [ˈmæstərɪ] *n.* [U] 熟練、優勢、支配

☞ If people knew how hard I worked to get my **mastery**, it wouldn't seem so wonderful at all. (Michelangelo, Artist)

如果人們知道我多努力才達到精通狀態，那就不會覺得這有多美好了。

13. mechanism [ˈmɛkəˌnɪzəm] *n.* [C] 機械裝置、結構、辦法 mechanisms

☞ Bad things happen and the brain is able to remember these events. This is a **mechanism** important for survival. (David Perlmutter, Scientist)

壞事發生後大腦會記住這些事，這是個為了生存的重要機制。

14. meditate [ˈmɛdəˌtet] *vi. vt.* 沉思、打算 meditated meditated

☞ I've tried to **meditate**, but it's really hard to stay still. (Ellen DeGeneres, Comedian)

我試過冥想，但靜靜待著實在太難。

15. melancholy [ˈmɛlənˌkɑlɪ] *n.* [U] 憂鬱

☞ You can't be **melancholy** in fashion because people don't respond to it. (Isaac Mizrahi, Fashion Designer)

在時尚中你不該加入憂鬱，人們不會有反應。

16. mellow [ˈmɛlo] *adj.* 圓熟的、老練的

🐾 **Mellow** doesn't always make for a good story, but it makes for a good life. (Anne Hathaway, Actress)

人變得老練不會帶來好故事，但會帶來美好的人生。

17. mentality [mɛnˈtælətɪ] *n.* [C][U] 智力、心性 mentalities

🐾 You begin to take on the **mentality** of your coach. If he feels confident, then I feel confident. (D' Brickashaw Ferguson)

你逐漸受到你的教練心態的影響，如果教練有自信，那我也會有自信。

18. merchandise [ˈmɝtʃənˌdaɪz] *n.* [U] 商品、貨物

🐾 Always be prepared if someone asks you what you want for Christmas. Give brand names, the store that sells the **merchandise**, and the exact model numbers. (John Waters, Director)

隨時準備好回答你聖誕節禮物想要甚麼，要講出品牌、賣這個產品的商店和確切的型號。

19. miraculous [mɪˈrækjələs] *adj.* 神奇的、奇蹟般的

🐾 The most **miraculous** process is watching a song go from a tiny idea in the middle of the night to something that 55,000 people are singing back to you. (Taylor Swift, Musician)

最神奇的過程就是看著一個在深夜出現的微小想法轉變為五萬五千個人在對你回唱的東西。

20. mobilize [ˈmobḷˌaɪz] *vt.* 動員、使流通 mobilized, mobilized

🐾 Take the first step, and your mind will **mobilize** to your aid. (Robert Collier, Author)

跨出第一步，那麼你的心會動員一切來幫你。

21. mold [mold]　*n.* [C] 模子、模式 molds

🐸 I know that some Disney stars want to break out of the Disney **mold**, but no, if they let me, I would work with Disney until I die. (Olesya Rulin, Actress)

我知道有些迪士尼明星想要脫離迪士尼的模子，但不，如果他們願意，我會一輩子在迪士尼工作，直到死去。

22. momentum [mo`mɛntəm]　*n.* [U] [C] 動量、衝力 momentums

🐸 Sometimes thinking too much can destroy your **momentum**. (Tom Watson, Professional Golfer)

有時想太多會摧毀你的動力。

23. monotonous [mə`nɑtənəs]　*adj.* 無抑揚頓挫的、單調的

🐸 I always find cardio the most **monotonous**. Running on a treadmill shows me why hamsters are so crazy. (Luke Evans, Actor)

我常認為有氧運動很單調，在跑步機上跑步讓我了解到為什麼倉鼠那麼瘋狂。

24. morale [mə`ræl]　*n.* [U] 士氣、鬥志

🐸 You can tell a person's **morale** from their Twitter feed. I like that; it's so honest. (Jessie Cave, Actress)

你能從一個人的推特看出他的士氣。我喜歡，一切是很坦率的。

25. motto [`mɑto]　*n.* [C] 座右銘、格言 mottos

🐸 My **motto** is never be ashamed of what you feel. (Demi Lovato, Musician)

我的座右銘是，決不要因為你的感覺感到丟臉。

多練習並嘗試

趣味字彙表

1.	mute *adj.* 沉默的、啞的	14.	ordeal *n.* [C][U] 嚴峻考驗、折磨
2.	mythology *n.* [U]（總稱）神話	15.	originate *vt. vi.* 發源、來自
3.	negotiation *n.* [C] 談判、協商	16.	outfit *n.* [C] 全套服裝
4.	neutral *adj.* 中立的	17.	outlook *n.* [C] 觀點、前景
5.	nomination *n.* [C][U] 提名、任命	18.	outrageous *adj.* 可憎的、粗暴的
6.	norm *n.* [C][U] 基準、規範	19.	paralyze *vt.* 使麻痺、使癱瘓
7.	notorious *adj.* 惡名昭彰的	20.	pact *n.* [C] 契約、協定
8.	nourish *vt.* 養育、培育	21.	pathetic *adj.* 可悲的
9.	nuisance *n.* [C][U] 討厭的人（或事物）	22.	pedestrian *n.* [C] 行人
10.	nutritious *adj.* 有營養的	23.	pension *n.* [C] 退休金
11.	obligation *n.* [C][U] 義務、責任	24.	persevere *vi.* 堅持不懈
12.	opposition *n.* [U] 反抗、對抗	25.	persistent *adj.* 堅持不懈的、持續的
13.	option *n.* [C][U] 選擇、選擇權		

趣味字彙句 🔊 MP3 46

1. mute [mjut] *adj.* 沉默的、啞的

I had to sit in silence for nine days like a naughty kid or a **mute**. (Adele, Musician)

我必須像個頑皮的小孩或啞巴安靜地待九天。

2. mythology [mɪˈθɑlədʒɪ] *n.* [U] （總稱）神話

According to Greek **Mythology**, there is a man named Prometheus who stole fire from the gods and gave it to humans.

根據希臘神話，有個名叫普羅米修斯的男人從眾神手中偷了火給人類。

3. negotiation [nɪˌgoʃɪˈeʃən] *n.* [C] 談判、協商 negotiations

So much of life is a **negotiation**. (Kevin O' Leary, Businessman)

人生很多部分都是談判。

4. neutral [ˈnjutrəl] *adj.* 中立的

Gray is great. People think gray is a **neutral** color, but I think it's intense, dramatic, and sexy. (Bryan Batt, Actor)

灰色很棒。人們以為灰色是中性色，但我覺得灰色很強烈、戲劇化且性感。

5. nomination [nɑməˈneʃən] *n.* [C][U] 提名、任命 nominations

I went from everyone saying, she can't act she can't act she can't act, to an Oscar **nomination**. (Keira Knightley, Actress)

大家原本給我的評論都是「她不會演、她不會演、她不會演」，但我後來卻得到奧斯卡提名。

6. norm [nɔrm] *n.* [C][U] 基準、規範 norms

When I was a kid, being outside was the **norm**. Rain or shine, our parents would tell us to get out of the house. (David Suzuki, Scientist)

小時候，外出是常規，不管下雨或出太陽，我們的父母都會叫我們離開屋子。

7. notorious [noˈtorɪəs] *adj.* 惡名昭彰的

I'm **notorious** for giving a bad interview. (Rock Hudson, Actor)

我接受的訪談都是出了名的糟。

8. nourish [ˈnɜɪʃ] *vt.* 養育、培育 nourished, nourished

Let us **nourish** beginnings. Not all things are good, but the seeds of all things are good. (Muriel Rukeyser, Poet)

讓我們養育起始吧。不是所有事情都是好的，但所有事情的種子都是好的。

9. nuisance [ˈnjʊsns] *n.* [C][U] 討厭的人（或事物） nuisances

No guest is so welcome in a friend's house that he will not become a **nuisance** after three days. (Plautus, Playwright)

再受歡迎的朋友，在家裡作客超過三天後，也會成為令人討厭的人。

10. nutritious [njuˈtrɪʃəs] *adj.* 有營養的

The most **nutritious** types of food in the world include seaweed, garlic, shellfish, and dark chocolate.

最有營養的食物種類有海帶、大蒜、甲殼類生物與黑巧克力。

11. obligation [ɑblə`geʃən] *n.* [C][U] 義務、責任 obligations

🐦 Every opportunity implies an **obligation**. (John D. Rockefeller, Businessman)

每個機會都意味著一項責任。

12. opposition [ɑpə`zɪʃən] *n.*[U] 反抗、對抗

🐦 What has kept me going is one word— care. If you care enough, you will do whatever you have to do, the **opposition** does not matter. (Allan Savory, Scientist)

我前進的動力就兩個字─在意，如果你夠在意，那你會盡你所能，阻礙一點也不重要。

13. option [`ɑpʃən] *n.* [C][U] 選擇、選擇權 options

🐦 I'm kind of comfortable with getting older because it's better than the other **option**, which is being dead. (George Clooney, Actor)

對於漸漸變老我還算感到自在，因為這比另一個選擇，也就是死亡，好多了。

14. ordeal [ɔr`diəl] *n.* [C][U] 嚴峻考驗、折磨 ordeals

🐦 During a terrible snowstorm, a man survived the **ordeal** of being trapped in his car for two months by eating snow.

在一場嚴重的暴風雪中，一名男性經歷被困在車裡兩個月的考驗，靠吃雪活了下來。

15. originate [ə`rɪdʒə‚net] *vt. vi.* 發源、來自 originated originated

🐦 Black Day **originated** in South Korea for singles.

黑色情人節源自於南韓，是因單身者而生。

16. outfit [ˈaʊtˌfɪt] *n.* [C] 全套服裝 outfits

It's not about the **outfit** you wear, but the life you lead in that outfit. (Diana Vreeland, Fashion Editor)
你穿的衣服不重要，重要的是你怎麼穿著那衣服過人生。

17. outlook [ˈaʊtˌlʊk] *n.* [C] 觀點、前景 outlooks

It's your **outlook** on life that counts. (Betty White, Actress)
重要的是你對人生的觀點。

18. outrageous [aʊtˈredʒəs] *adj.* 可憎的、粗暴的

Old age is an excellent time for outrage. My goal is to say or do at least one **outrageous** thing every week. (Louis Kronenberger, Critic/Author)
老年是個從事瘋狂行為的好時機，我的目標是一週至少說或做一件瘋狂的事。

19. paralyze [ˈpærəˌlaɪz] *vt.* 使麻痺、使癱瘓 paralyzed paralyzed

I don't worry about being compared, because I think that **paralyzes** you. (Kenneth Branagh, Actor)
我不擔心被比較，因為我覺得那會讓你無法行動。

20. pact [pækt] *n.* [C] 契約、協定

Every New Year's Eve, I have a **pact** to do something I never thought I'd do. (Carl Lewis, Track and Field Athlete)
每個新年前夕，我發誓我會做一件我從沒想到我會做的事。

21. pathetic [pəˈθɛtɪk] *adj.* 可悲的
🐾 The most **pathetic** person in the world is someone who has sight, but has no vision. (Helen Keller, Author)
世上最可悲的人是看得見，卻看不遠的人。

22. pedestrian [pəˈdɛstrɪən] *n.* [C] 行人 pedestrians
🐾 I always envied rock stars. Writing is a **pedestrian** job that is done while sitting in coffee-stained pajamas. (Kate Christensen, Novelist)
我向來都很羨慕搖滾明星。寫作只是個一般人穿著沾到咖啡的睡衣做的工作。

23. pension [ˈpɛnʃən] *n.* [C] 退休金 pensions
🐾 Chase your passion, not your **pension**. (Denis Waitley, Writer)
追隨你的熱情，不是你的退休金。

24. persevere [ˌpɝsəˈvɪr] *vi.* 堅持不懈 persevered persevered
🐾 Sometimes things aren't clear right away. That's where you need to be patient and **persevere** and see where things lead. (Mary Pierce, Tennis Player)
有時事情不會馬上清晰，這時你需要保持耐心與堅持，觀察事情的走向。

25. persistent [pɚˈsɪstənt] *adj.* 堅持不懈的、持續的
🐾 You need to follow your heart and choose a job you're passionate about. If you haven't found it yet, be **persistent** until you do. (Steve Kerr, Basketball Player)
你要跟隨你的心，選擇你熱衷的工作，如果你還沒找到的話，在你找到之前要持續尋找。

Unit 47

通過考驗

趣味字彙表

1.	perspective *n.* [U] [C] 看法、觀點	14.	prone *adj.* 有……傾向的、易於……的
2.	phase *n.* [C] 階段	15.	propaganda *n.* [U] 宣傳、宣傳活動
3.	pitcher *n.* [C] 投擲者、投手	16.	prospective *adj.* 預期的、即將發生的
4.	ponder *vt. vi.* 仔細考慮、反思	17.	provoke *vt.* 煽動、激怒
5.	posture *n.* [C][U] 姿勢、姿態	18.	punctual *adj.* 準時的
6.	prejudice *n.* [C][U] 偏見、歧視	19.	purity *n.* [U] 純淨
7.	prescription *n.* [C] 處方、法規	20.	qualification *n.* [C] 資格、能力
8.	presidency *n.* [C] 公司總裁（大學校長、會長、美國總統等）的職位（職權、任期）	21.	questionnaire *n.* [C] 問卷
9.	presume *vt. vi.* 假設、推定	22.	racism *n.* [U] 種族主義、種族歧視
10.	preventive *adj.* 預防的	23.	radiant *adj.* 光芒四射的、容光煥發的
11.	productivity *n.* [U] 生產力、生產率	24.	radical *adj.* 根本的、極端的
12.	profound *adj.* 深刻的、深切的	25.	random *adj.* 任意的
13.	projection *n.* [U] [C] 設計、規劃、投射		

趣味字彙句 MP3 47

1. perspective [pɚˈspɛktɪv] *n.* [U] [C] 看法、觀點 perspectives

I like to turn things upside down, to watch pictures and situations from another **perspective**. (Ursus Wehrli, Comedian)
我喜歡翻轉事物,好以另一觀點看圖片或情況。

2. phase [fez] *n.* [C] 階段 phases

Being the first to cross the finish line makes you a winner in only one **phase** of life. It's what you do after that really counts. (Ralph Boston, Retired Track Athlete)
當第一個到達終點線的人,只不過意味你是人生某一階段的勝利者,你在這之後的行為才是重要的。

3. pitcher [ˈpɪtʃɚ] *n.* [C] 投擲者、投手 pitchers

Guessing what the **pitcher** is going to throw is 80% of being a successful hitter. (Hank Aaron, Baseball Player)
能成為成功的打者,百分之八十的原因是要能猜出投手投出的球。

4. ponder [ˈpɑndɚ] *vt. vi.* 仔細考慮、反思 pondered, pondered

Life is a mirror and will reflect back to the thinker what he **ponders** into it. (Ernest Holmes, Theologian)
人生是面鏡子,會反映一個人對人生所作的思考。

5. posture [ˈpɑstʃɚ] *n.* [C][U] 姿勢、姿態 postures

When a woman puts on heels, she has a different **posture** and a different attitude. (Christian Louboutin, Fashion Designer)
當女人穿上高跟鞋時,她會有不同的姿勢及不同的態度。

6. prejudice [ˈprɛdʒədɪs] *n.* [C][U] 偏見、歧視 prejudices

There is no **prejudice** that the work of art does not finally overcome. (Andre Gide, Novelist)
藝術品最終總是可以克服偏見。

7. prescription [prɪˈskrɪpʃən] *n.* [C] 處方、法規 prescriptions

You may not be able to read a doctor's handwriting and **prescription**, but you'll notice his bills are neatly typed. (Earl Wilson, Journalist)
你也許沒辦法讀懂醫生的筆跡與處方，但你會發現，他的帳單總是整齊得打出來。

8. presidency [ˈprɛzədənsɪ] *n.* [C] 公司總裁（大學校長、會長、美國總統等）的職位（職權、任期） presidencies

For the **presidency**, the two happiest days of my life were entering the office and my surrender of it. (Martin Van Buren)
針對總統任職，我人生最快樂的兩天便是總統任職那天與交接的那天。

9. presume [prɪˈzum] *vt. vi.* 假設、推定 presumed, presumed

Most people **presume** my mustache is not real because it's much darker than my regular hair. (John Hodgman, Comedian)
大部分的人都推測我的鬍子不是真的，因為我的鬍子比我平常的頭髮黑多了。

10. preventive [prɪˈvɛntɪv] *adj.* 預防的

Coffee is a **preventive** factor against depression and cancer. (Chris Kilham, Businessman)
咖啡可以預防憂鬱症與癌症。

11. productivity [prodʌkˈtɪvətɪ] *n.* [U] 生產力、生產率

🐝 **Productivity** is being able to do things that you were never able to do before. (Franz Kafka, Novelist)

生產力是能夠做你以前從來無法做的事。

12. profound [prəˈfaʊnd] *adj.* 深刻的、深切的

🐝 Dreams are often most **profound** when they seem the most crazy. (Sigmund Freud, Psychologist)

當夢看似最瘋狂的時候，是最有深度的。

13. projection [prəˈdʒɛkʃən] *n.* [U] [C] 設計、規劃、投射 projections

🐝 Compliments and criticism are all based on some form of **projection**. (Billy Corgan, Musician)

讚美與批評都是基於某種形式的投射。

14. prone [pron] *adj.* 有……傾向的、易於……的

🐝 As a typical native New Yorker, I'm **prone** to wearing the city's unofficial color: black. (Amanda Hearst, Editor)

身為典型的紐約本土人，我傾向穿這個城市非正式的顏色：黑色。

15. propaganda [prɑpəˈgændə] *n.* [U] 宣傳、宣傳活動

🐝 Fashion pictures and travel pictures always look amazing, right? Most of the pictures we see are **propaganda**. (Martin Parr, Photographer)

時尚的與旅行的照片總是令人驚艷，對吧？我們看到的大部分照片都只是種宣傳。

16. prospective [prəˈspɛktɪv] *adj.* 預期的、即將發生的

🐸 I don't know how to change people, but still I keep a long list of **prospective** candidates to change. (David Sedaris, Writer)
我不知道怎麼改變人們，但我還是有一長串可能的候選人。

17. provoke [prəˈvok] *vt.* 煽動、激怒 provoked, provoked

🐸 If you want to provoke, you should **provoke** someone who is stronger than you, or you are misusing your power. (Lars von Trier, Director)
如果你想要激怒某人，那麼激怒比你強大的人，否則你就是在濫用你的權力。

18. punctual [ˈpʌŋktʃʊəl] *adj.* 準時的

🐸 Be **punctual**, never give up, and achieve your goals even when everything goes bad. (Steve Jobs, Entrepreneur)
在一切不順的狀態下，也保持準時、永不放棄，並達成你的目標。

19. purity [ˈpjʊrətɪ] *n.* [U] 純淨

🐸 There has to be evil so that good can prove its **purity** above it.
邪惡的存在才能讓善良證明它在邪惡之上的純淨。

20. qualification [kwɑləfəˈkeʃən] *n.* [C] 資格、能力 qualifications

🐸 My **qualification** to talk about happiness comes from knowing unhappiness. (Alastair Campbell, Journalist)
我能談論幸福的資格來自我對不幸的所知。

21. questionnaire [kwɛstʃənˋɛr] *n.* [C] 問卷 questionnaires

When I was younger, I actually wanted to be a CIA agent. I even completed the online application **questionnaire**. (Lizzy Caplan, Actress)

年輕的時候，我真的想要當一位美國中央情報局探員，我甚至填寫了線上報名問卷。

22. racism [ˋresɪzəm] *n.* [U] 種族主義、種族歧視

Sometimes I feel like rap music is the key to stopping **racism**. (Eminem, Rapper)

有時我覺得饒舌音樂是終止種族歧視的關鍵。

23. radiant [ˋredjənt] *adj.* 光芒四射的、容光煥發的

One of my style rules is to always have beautifully **radiant** skin. (Brad Goreski, Fashion Stylist)

我的造型法則之一就是永保美麗、散發光芒的皮膚。

24. radical [ˋrædɪkl̩] *adj.* 根本的、極端的

Hats are **radical**; only people that wear hats understand that. (Philip Treacy, Hat Designer)

帽子是很基本的，只有戴帽子的人才懂這點。

25. random [ˋrændəm] *adj.* 任意的

I have a giant baking book, so I close my eyes and pick a **random** page. Whatever it is, I try to bake it! (Nina Dobrev, Actress)

我有本很大本的烘培書，所以我會閉上眼，隨便選一頁，不管是甚麼，我就試著烤出來。

贏得信賴

趣味字彙表

1.	rational *adj.* 理性的	14.	relevant *adj.* 有關的、恰當的
2.	realization *n.* [U] 領悟	15.	reliance *n.* [U] 信賴、依靠
3.	rebellion *n.* [C][U] 造反、叛亂	16.	relish *n.* [U] 滋味、愛好； *vt.* 品味
4.	recipient *n.* [C] 接受者、接受器	17.	removal *n.* [U] [C] 搬遷、除去
5.	recommendation *n.* [C][U] 推薦（信）、建議	18.	renaissance *n.* [U] 新生、文藝復興；*adj.* 文藝復興（時代）的
6.	reconcile *vt.* 調停、使和解	19.	rental *adj.* 租賃（業）的
7.	recruit *vt. vi.* 徵募、吸收	20.	repress *vt. vi.* 壓制
8.	redundant *adj.* 多餘的	21.	resemblance *n.* [U] [C] 相似（點）
9.	refine *vt. vi.* 精鍊	22.	resistant *adj.* 抵抗的
10.	reflective *adj.* 反射的、沉思的	23.	resolute *adj.* 堅定的
11.	refreshment *n.* [C][U] 精力恢復、茶點	24.	restoration *n.* [U] 恢復、修復
12.	refund *n.* [C][U] 退還（金額）	25.	restraint *n.* [U] [C] 抑制、克制
13.	rehearse *vt. vi.* 排練		

趣味字彙句 MP3 48

1. rational [ˈræʃənl] *adj.* 理性的

I'm not emotional about investments. Investing is something where you have to be purely **rational**. (Bill Ackman, Businessman)
投資時我不情緒化，投資的時候，你必須百分之百理性。

2. realization [realization] *n.* [U] 領悟

There is joy in work. There is no happiness except in the **realization** that we have accomplished something. (Henry Ford)
工作是有樂趣的，只有在領悟到自己完成了一件事的時候才是快樂的。

3. rebellion [rɪˈbɛljən] *n.* [C][U] 造反、叛亂 rebellions

In ninth grade, I came up with a new form of **rebellion**. I decided to get all A's without taking a book home. (Bill Gates)
國三的時候，我想出了一種新的叛逆方式，我決定一本書都不帶回家就全科拿 A。

4. recipient [rɪˈsɪpɪənt] *n.* [C] 接受者、接受器 recipients

My dad is handsome and my mom is beautiful. I've definitely been the lucky **recipient**. (Ashton Kutcher, Actor)
我的父親很帥，我的母親很美，而我確實是幸運的領受者。

5. recommendation [rɛkəmɛnˈdeʃən] *n.* [C][U] 推薦（信）、建議

Nothing influences people more than a **recommendation** from a trusted friend. (Mark Zuckerberg, Businessman)
來自信任的朋友的建議對人的影響力最大。

6. reconcile [ˈrɛkənsaɪl] *vt.* 調停、使和解 reconciled, reconciled

🐾 I could sooner **reconcile** all of Europe than two women. (Louis XIV, Former King of France)
我讓整個歐洲和解的速度比讓兩個女人和解的速度快。

7. recruit [rɪˈkrut] *vt. vi.* 徵募、吸收 recruited, recruited

🐾 As I was only the third NBA player to come from Africa, I felt I had to **recruit** more young Africans and find a way to bring the NBA to Africa. (Dikembe Mutombo, Basketball Player)
因為我只是第三位來自非洲的美國職籃球員，我覺得我有責任招募更多非洲的年輕人，並找到把他們從非洲帶入美國職籃的方法。

8. redundant [rɪˈdʌndənt] *adj.* 多餘的

🐾 Good coaches make themselves **redundant**. (Paul Strikwerda, Voice Actor/Coach)
好教練會讓自己變成多餘的。

9. refine [rɪˈfaɪn] *vt. vi.* 精鍊 refined, refined

🐾 Deadlines **refine** the mind. (Adam Savage, Industrial Designer)
期限精煉內心。

10. reflective [rɪˈflɛktɪv] *adj.* 反射的、沉思的

🐾 The heart is the best **reflective** thinker. (Wendell Phillips, Activist)
心是最棒的反省思考者。

11. refreshment [rɪˋfrɛʃmənt] *n.* [C][U] 精力恢復、茶點 refreshments

New York is where I go for **refreshment**. It's a place where you're not going to be bitten by a goat. (Brendan Behan, Poet)

我去紐約恢復精神，那是個你不會被羊咬的地方。

12. refund [ˋriˏfʌnd] *n.* [C][U] 退還（金額） refunds

There should be a calorie **refund** for things that didn't taste as good as you expected.

食物若不如你預期的好吃，應該要可以退還卡路里。

13. rehearse [rɪˋhɝs] *vt.* *vi.* 排練 rehearsed, rehearsed

In movies, the less I **rehearse**, the better I am. (Kristen Wiig, Actress)

拍電影的時候，我越不預演，演得越好。

14. relevant [ˋrɛləvənt] *adj.* 有關的、恰當的

I never give up on anything because suddenly the thing you never thought you'd do might become **relevant**. (Joss Whedon, Writer)

我從不放棄任何事情，因為你從來不覺得你會做的事可能突然變得相關。

15. reliance [rɪˋlaɪəns] *n.* [U] 信賴、依靠

Self-**reliance** is the key to a vigorous life. A man must look inward to find his own answers. (Robin Williams, Actor/Comedian)

仰賴自己是得到有力的人生的關鍵，人必須觀看自己的內心才能找到答案。

Part 1 「趣」你的單字基礎篇

Part 2 「趣」你的單字進階篇

16. relish [ˈrɛlɪʃ] *n.* [U] 滋味、愛好； *vt.* 品味 relished relished

🐛 Think big thoughts but **relish** small pleasures. (H. Jackson Brown, Jr., Author)

想著偉大的想法，但品味小的樂趣。

17. removal [rɪˈmuvl̩] *n.* [U] [C] 搬遷、除去 removals

🐛 I am Armenian, so of course I am obsessed with laser hair **removal**. My entire body is hairless. (Kim Kardashian, TV Personality)

我是亞美尼亞人，當然我沉溺於雷射除毛，我的整個身體都沒有毛髮。

18. renaissance [rəˈnesns] *n.* [U] 新生、文藝復興； *adj.* 文藝復興（時代）的

🐛 I want to be a **Renaissance** woman. I want to paint, write, act, and just do everything. (Emma Watson, Actress)

我想要當個文藝復興時期的女人，我想要畫畫、寫作、演戲，所有事我都想做。

19. rental [ˈrɛntl̩] *adj.* 租賃（業）的

🐛 In Los Angeles, there is a **rental** service to hire fake fans to make you feel famous.

在洛杉磯，有種租賃服務提供假粉絲讓你覺得自己很出名。

20. repress [rɪˈprɛs] *vt. vi.* 壓制 repressed, repressed

🐛 I've learned never to **repress** anything in my short life. (Otto Cross, Psychoanalyst)

我學到在短暫的生命中，絕對不要壓抑任何東西。

21. resemblance [rɪˈzɛmbləns] *n.* [U] [C] 相似（點） resemblances

☞ If you look at me close enough, there's a **resemblance** to a chicken nugget. (Kevin Hart, Actor)

如果你從夠近的距離看我，你會發現我和雞塊有些相似處。

22. resistant [rɪˈzɪstənt] *adj.* 抵抗的

☞ Incapable people are the most **resistant** and unwilling to change. (Seth Godin, Author)

沒能力的人是最抗拒改變、最不願改變的人。

23. resolute [ˈrɛzəˌlut] *adj.* 堅定的

☞ He who is **resolute** will mold the world to himself. (Johann Wolfgang von Goethe, Writer)

堅定的人能讓世界轉向他。

24. restoration [rɛstəˈreʃən] *n.* [U] 恢復、修復

☞ When we choose love over anger, we are able to experience **restoration** in relationships. (Gwen Smith, Author)

當我們選擇愛，而不是憤怒，那麼我們在感情中就能復原。

25. restraint [rɪˈstrent] *n.* [U] [C] 抑制、克制 restraints

☞ Strength gains power when **restraint** and courtesy are added. (Mahatma Gandhi, Leader)

有了克制和禮貌，力量會更強大。

Unit 49

盡情翱翔

趣味字彙表

1.	retail *n.* [U] 零售	14.	script *n.* [C] 腳本
2.	revelation *n.* [U] [C] 揭示、顯示	15.	selective *adj.* 有選擇性的
3.	revenue *n.* [U] [C] 收入	16.	sentimental *adj.* 情深的、多情的
4.	rhythmic *adj.* 有節奏的、有韻律的	17.	sequence *n.* [C][U] 接續、一連串、順序
5.	ridicule *n.* [U] 嘲笑	18.	serene *adj.* 安詳的
6.	rigorous *adj.* 嚴格的、苛刻的	19.	serenity *n.* [U] 平靜、沉著
7.	rivalry *n.* [U] 競爭、對抗	20.	session *n.* [C] 會議、講習
8.	royalty *n.* [U] 皇族或王族	21.	setback *n.* [C] 挫折
9.	ruby *n.* [C] 紅寶石	22.	shed *vt. vi.* 流下
10.	safeguard *n.* [C] 保護、防衛；*vt.* 保護、防衛	23.	sheer *adj.* 純粹的
11.	sanctuary *n.* [C] 聖所、庇護所	24.	shoplift *vt. vi.* 在商店內偷竊（商品）
12.	sane *adj.* 神志正常的、頭腦清楚的	25.	shrewd *adj.* 精明的、狡猾的
13.	scenic *adj.* 風景的、景色秀麗的		

趣味字彙句 cc 🎧 MP3 49

1. retail [ˈritel] *n.* [U] 零售
🛒 I wanted to create a new way of looking at **retail**. (Tory Burch, Fashion Designer)
我希望創造一個不同的視野來看零售業。

2. revelation [ˌrɛvəˈleʃən] *n.* [U] [C] 揭示、顯示 revelations
🛒 **Minor** things can become moments of great revelation. (Margot Fonteyn, Dancer)
小東西也能成為偉大的啟示瞬間。

3. revenue [ˈrɛvəˌnju] *n.* [U] [C] 收入 revenues
🛒 My goal was never to just create a company. More than **revenue**, I wanted to build something that changed the world. (Mark Zucker-berg, Businessman)
我的目標從來都不只是創立一間公司，比起收入，我更想建立一樣會改變世界的東西。

4. rhythmic [ˈrɪðmɪk] *adj.* 有節奏的、有韻律的
🛒 The golf swing is very, very **rhythmic**. Just like music. (Justin Timberlake, Musician)
高爾夫球揮棒是很有韻律的，好像音樂一樣。

5. ridicule [ˈrɪdɪkjul] *n.* [U] 嘲笑
🛒 **Ridicule** is a weak weapon when pointed at a strong mind. (Martin Farquhar Tupper, Writer)
嘲笑對堅強的內心來說是個微弱的武器。

6. rigorous [ˈrɪgərəs] *adj.* 嚴格的、苛刻的

🐸 Tom Cruise works out every day with **rigorous** activities like hiking, biking, and riding his motorcycle.

湯姆克魯斯每天用嚴苛的活動健身，活動如健行、騎單車與其他的摩托車。

7. rivalry [ˈraɪvm̩rɪ] *n.* [U] 競爭、對抗

🐸 The **rivalry** is with ourselves. I fight against myself, not against others. (Luciano Pavarotti, Musician)

和我們自己競爭，我與自己競爭，不是和別人競爭。

8. royalty [ˈrɔɪəltɪ] *n.* [U] 皇族或王族

🐸 **Royalty** comes from what you do. (Gianni Versace, Fashion Designer)

貴氣源自於你的所為。

9. ruby [ˈrubɪ] *n.* [C] 紅寶石 rubies

🐸 There is no such thing as red. Is it apple red, balloon red, or **ruby** red? (Lady Gaga, Musician)

沒有紅色這種東西，到底是蘋果紅、氣球紅，還是紅寶石紅？

10. safeguard [ˈsef͵gɑrd] *n.* [C] 保護、防衛 safeguards； *vt.* 保護、防衛 safeguarded safeguarded

🐸 Education is a better **safeguard** than an army. (Edward Everett, Politician)

教育比軍隊能提供更好的防衛。

11. sanctuary [ˈsæŋktʃʊɛr] *n.* [C] 聖所、庇護所 sanctuaries

🐾 My bedroom is my **sanctuary**. It's where I do a lot of designing.
(Vera Wang, Fashion Designer)
我的房間是我的庇護所,我在那裏做了很多設計。

12. sane [sen] *adj.* 神志正常的、頭腦清楚的

🐾 There is only one difference between a madman and me. The madman thinks he is **sane**. (Salvador Dali, Artist)
我和瘋子之間只有一個差別,瘋子以為他是正常的。

13. scenic [ˈsinɪk] *adj.* 風景的、景色秀麗的

🐾 Rail travel for me is the most relaxing, most **scenic** way to see the country. (John Paul DeJoria, Businessman)
要遊全國的話,鐵路旅遊對我來說是最愉悅、最美麗的方式。

14. script [skrɪpt] *n.* [C] 腳本 scripts

🐾 It's possible to make a bad movie out of a good **script**, but a good movie can't be made from a bad **script**. (George Clooney, Actor)
好劇本也可能作出糟糕的電影,但糟糕的劇本卻做不出好電影。

15. selective [səˈlɛktɪv] *adj.* 有選擇性的

🐾 Not everyone can be trusted. We have to be very **selective** about who we trust. (Shelley Long, Actress)
不是每個人都可以相信,我們必須對我們信任的人有所選擇。

16. sentimental [ˌsɛntəˈmɛntl̩] *adj.* 情深的、多情的

🐤 A **sentimental** person thinks things will last, a romantic person hopes against the fear that things won't. (F. Scott Fitzgerald, Author)

多愁善感的人認為事物可持久，浪漫的人則希望克服事物不會持久的恐懼。

17. sequence [ˈsikwəns] *n.* [C][U] 接續、一連串、順序 sequences

🐤 The **sequence** of a music album is almost as important as the songs. (Dr. Dre, Musician)

唱片歌曲的順序和歌本身一樣重要。

18. serene [səˈrin] *adj.* 安詳的

🐤 The more I accept, the more **serene** I am. (Michael J. Fox, Actor)

我接受得越多，我感到越平靜。

19. serenity [səˈrɛnətɪ] *n.* [U] 平靜、沉著

🐤 Boredom is the feeling that everything is a waste of time; **serenity**, that nothing is. (Thomas Szasz, Psychologist)

無聊是覺得所有事情都只是浪費時間，而平靜則相反。

20. session [ˈsɛʃən] *n.* [C] 會議、講習 sessions

🐤 I'm not going to deny that I enjoy a good four to five hour karaoke **session**. But who doesn't? (Ken Marino, Actor)

我不否認我享受四到五小時的 KTV 時間，但誰不是這樣呢？

21. setback [ˋsɛtˌbæk] *n.* [C] 挫折 setbacks

🐛 Anytime you suffer a **setback**, put your head down and keep going. (Les Brown, Businessman)
遇到挫折的時候，低下頭並繼續往前。

22. shed [ʃɛd] *vt. vi.* 流下 shed, shed

🐛 Tears shed for self are tears of weakness, but tears **shed** for others are a sign of strength. (Billy Graham, Evangelist)
為自身留下的眼淚是軟弱，但為他人留下的眼淚卻是力量的象徵。

23. sheer [ʃɪr] *adj.* 純粹的

🐛 The ingredients of success are talent, determination, and **sheer** luck. You have to have two out of the three. (Fred Saberhagen, Author)
成功的構成要素是天分、決心，和單純的運氣，這三項你必須至少要有兩項。

24. shoplift [ˋʃɑpˌlɪft] *vt. vi.* 在商店內偷竊（商品） shoplifted, shoplifted

🐛 MAC gave me 55 lipsticks to test. These are the same lipsticks I got caught **shoplifting** when I was 15. (Eddie Izzard, Comedian)
MAC 給了我五十五條口紅試用，而它們和我在十五歲時，被抓到在商店裡偷竊的是同一款口紅。

25. shrewd [ʃrud] *adj.* 精明的、狡猾的

🐛 A wise man knows everything; a **shrewd** one, everybody. (George Norman Douglas, Writer)
聰明的人所有事情都知道，精明的人則是每個人都認識。

Unit 50

讓生活充滿喜悅

趣味字彙表

1.	shun *vt.* 躲開、避開	14.	specialty *n.* [C] 專業、專長、特產
2.	simplify *vt.* 簡化、精簡	15.	spectacular *adj.* 壯觀的、引人注目的
3.	skeptical *adj.* 懷疑的、多疑的	16.	spectrum *n.* [C] 光譜、頻譜、範圍
4.	smack *vt. vi.* 打	17.	speculate *vt. vi.* 沉思、推測
5.	smother *vt. vi.* 悶死、抑制	18.	spiral *n.* [C] 螺旋形的東西
6.	sneaky *adj.* 鬼鬼祟祟的	19.	spontaneous *adj.* 自發的、自然的
7.	sneer *n.* [C] 冷笑、嘲笑	20.	stability *n.* [U] 穩定（性）
8.	soar *vi.* 翱翔、猛增	21.	starvation *n.* [U] 飢餓
9.	socialize *vt. vi.* 使適於社會、交際	22.	stimulate *vt. vi.* 刺激、激勵
10.	solitude *n.* [U] 孤獨	23.	subjective *adj.* 主觀的、個人的
11.	soothe *vt. vi.* 安慰、撫慰	24.	suite *n.* [C] 套房
12.	sophisticated *adj.* 富有經驗的	25.	superstitious *adj.* 迷信的
13.	spacious *adj.* 寬敞的		

趣味字彙句 CC ● MP3 50

1. shun [ʃʌn] *vt.* 躲開、避開 shunned, shunned
Don't rely on men but don't **shun** them either. (Jennifer Aniston, Actress)
不要依賴男人，但也不要躲避他們。

2. simplify [ˈsɪmpləˌfaɪ] *vt.* 簡化、精簡 simplified simplified
The hardest thing in the world is to **simplify** your life. (Yvon Chouinard, Rock Climber)
人生最困難的事就是簡化你的生活。

3. skeptical [ˈskɛptɪkl̩] *adj.* 懷疑的、多疑的
When you're in your twenties, you're **skeptical** of everything. (Jamie Dornan, Actor)
當你二十幾歲的時候，你對甚麼事物都懷疑。

4. smack [smæk] *vt. vi.* 打 smacked, smacked
Every woman in her life wants to give a good face **smack**. (Mallory Jansen, Actress)
每個女人都希望能在一生中，能好好的賞人一巴掌。

5. smother [ˈsmʌðɚ] *vt. vi.* 悶死、抑制 smothered, smothered
Make the most of your regrets; never **smother** your sorrow. To regret deeply is to live afresh. (Henry David Thoreau, Author)
讓你的後悔發揮最大功用。你的悲傷，深沉的悔恨是新生活的開始。

6. sneaky [ˋsnikɪ] *adj.* 鬼鬼祟祟的

🐦 I'd be a terrible secret agent. I can't keep a secret and I'm not **sneaky.** (Katherine Heigl, Actress)

我會是個糟糕的特務，我無法保密，也無法暗中行動。

7. sneer [snɪr] *n.* [C] 冷笑、嘲笑

🐦 A new idea is delicate. It can be killed by a **sneer** or a yawn. (Ovid, Poet)

新的想法是很脆弱的，一陣冷笑或一個哈欠都可以把它殺死。

8. soar [sor] *vi.* 翱翔、猛增 soared, soared

🐦 Keep your feet on the ground, but let your heart **soar** as high as it will. (Arthur Helps, Historian)

保持腳踏實地，但讓你的心盡量翱翔，越高越好。

9. socialize [ˋsoʃəˌlaɪz] *vt. vi.* 使適於社會、交際

🐦 People use restaurants to do business, to do politics, and to **socialize.** (Danny Meyer, Businessman)

人們利用餐廳做生意、從事政治及社交活動。

10. solitude [ˋsɑləˌtjud] *n.* [U] 孤獨

🐦 When Superman wants to be alone, he goes to the Fortress of **Solitude** in the Amazon rainforest for solitude.

當超人想要獨處的時候，他就會去亞馬遜雨林裡的隱居堡壘尋找孤獨。

11. soothe [suð] *vt. vi.* 安慰、撫慰 soothed, soothed

Nothing **soothes** the soul like a walk on the beach.
沒有事情比在海灘上散步更能安撫心靈了。

12. sophisticated [səˋfɪstɪˏketɪd] *adj.* 富有經驗的、不落俗套的

The most **sophisticated** people I know— inside they are all children. (Jim Henson, Entertainer)
我所認識最成熟的人，內心也是小孩。

13. spacious [ˋspeʃəs] *adj.* 寬敞的

Nothing makes the earth seem so **spacious** as to have friends at a distance. (Henry David Thoreau, Author)
當朋友在遠處的時候，地球感覺最無邊無際。

14. specialty [ˋspɛʃəltɪ] *n.* [C] 專業、專長、特產 specialties

Starbucks created an industry that did not exist: **specialty** coffee. (Howard Schultz, Businessman)
星巴克創造了一種原本不存在的產業：精品咖啡。

15. spectacular [spɛkˋtækjələ] *adj.* 壯觀的、引人注目的

Eating well gives a **spectacular** joy to life. (Elsa Schiaparelli, Designer)
吃的健康會讓生活充滿喜悅。

16. spectrum [ˈspɛktrəm] *n.* [C] 光譜、頻譜、範圍 spectrums

🐦 Dating someone on the opposite end of the **spectrum** teaches you an incredible amount of patience. (Chris Pine, Actor)
與跟你完全不同頻率的人交往，讓你學會極大量的耐心。

17. speculate [ˈspɛkjəˌlet] *vt. vi.* 沉思、推測 speculated, speculated

🐦 I don't sit there and **speculate**. It wastes time, actually. (Kate Adie, Journalist)
我從不就這樣坐著思考。事實上，我認為那很浪費時間。

18. spiral [ˈspaɪrəl] *n.* [C] 螺旋形的東西 spirals；*vt. vi.* 螺旋形上升或下降；不斷加劇地增加或減少 spiraled spiraled

🐦 When someone is denying what they are, then that's when things start to **spiral** down. (Will.i.am, Musician)
當人否認自我，事情便會開始急遽變糟。

19. spontaneous [spɑnˈtenɪəs] *adj.* 自發的、自然的

🐦 Genuine happiness comes from within, and often it comes in **spontaneous** feelings of joy. (Andrew Weil, Physician)
真正的快樂來自內在，而且通常以自發性的愉悅感出現。

20. stability [stəˈbɪlətɪ] *n.* [U] 穩定（性）

🐦 The most important thing in a good relationship is not happiness but **stability**. (Gabriel Marquez, Novelist)
良好關係中，最重要的不是快樂，而是穩定。

21. starvation [stɑr'veʃən] *n.* [U] 飢餓

🕮 Love never dies of **starvation**, but often of indigestion. (Anne de L'Enclos, Author)

愛從不會因為飢餓而死去，但常常因為消化不良而亡。

22. stimulate ['stɪmjəˌlet] *vt. vi.* 刺激、激勵 stimulated, stimulated

🕮 The woman who **stimulates** a man's imagination gets him. (Helen Rowland, Writer)

能激起男人想像的女人就可以得到那個男人。

23. subjective [səb'dʒɛktɪv] *adj.* 主觀的、個人的

🕮 There's a point where art is not **subjective**. If you don't like Picasso, that's your problem. (Danny Huston, Actor)

藝術過了一個點就不再是主觀的了，如果你不喜歡畢卡索，那是你的問題。

24. suite [swit] *n.* [C] 套房 suites

🕮 I love doing accents. One of my friends works in hotel reservations and I'll ring her up and complain about the **suite**. Sometimes I get her. (Geraldine Horner, Singer/Songwriter)

我喜歡假扮不同口音。我有個朋友的工作是飯店訂位人員，我會打電話給他抱怨我的套房，我有時候可以騙到他。

25. superstitious [supɚ'stɪʃəs] *adj.* 迷信的

🕮 In Spain, **superstitious** people believe that you should eat 12 grapes on New Year's Eve to have a lucky year.

在西班牙，迷信的人相信你在新年前夕要吃十二顆葡萄，整年才會幸運。

Unit 51

迎向挑戰

1.	suspension *n.* [U] 暫停、懸掛	14.	transformation *n.* [U] [C] 轉變、變形
2.	swap *vt. vi.* 交換	15.	trauma *n.* [U] [C] 傷口、創傷
3.	symbolic *adj.* 象徵的	16.	trigger *n.* [C] 扳機、能引起反應的刺激物
4.	symptom *n.* [C] 症狀	17.	trivial *adj.* 瑣細的、不重要的
5.	synthetic *adj.* 合成的、人造的	18.	trophy *n.* [C] 戰利品
6.	tactic *n.* [C] 戰術、策略	19.	turmoil *n.* [U] [C] 騷動、混亂
7.	terminate *vt. vi.* 停止、終止	20.	upbringing *n.* [U] 教養、培養
8.	theatrical *adj.* 戲劇的、戲劇性的、誇張的	21.	utility *n.* [U] 效用、實用
9.	theoretical *adj.* 理論的、假設的	22.	vicious *adj.* 邪惡的
10.	thereafter *adv.* 之後、以後	23.	victorious *adj.* 勝利的
11.	threshold *n.* [C] 門檻	24.	virtual *adj.* 實際上的、虛擬的
12.	thrive *vi.* 興旺、繁榮	25.	visualize *vt. vi.* 使顯現、想像
13.	trait *n.* [C] 特徵、特點		

趣味字彙句 🔊 MP3 51

1. suspension [sə`spɛnʃən] *n.* [U] 暫停、懸掛
Intuition is a **suspension** of logic due to impatience. (Rita Mae Brown, Writer)
直覺是理智因為沒耐心而暫停。

2. swap [swɑp] *vt. vi.* 交換 swapped, swapped
Would I **swap** my success in cooking for success in football? Definitely. (Gordon Ramsay, Chef)
我會不會想把我在廚藝界的成功換成在橄欖球界的成功？當然。

3. symbolic [sɪm`bɑlɪk] *adj.* 象徵的
Presents are **symbolic**. When you give them, they show that you are paying attention to the person. (Judith Martin, Journalist)
禮物是很有象徵性的，當你給出它們時，它們表示了你在意那個人。

4. symptom [`sɪmptəm] *n.* [C] 症狀 symptoms
One of the **symptoms** of stress is the belief that one's work is terribly important. (Bertrand Russell, Philosopher)
壓力的其中一個症狀就是深信本人的工作極度重要。

5. synthetic [sɪn`θɛtɪk] *adj.* 合成的、人造的
I cannot put this poison on my skin. I do not use anything **synthetic**. (Gisele Bundchen, Model)
我無法把這毒藥放在我的皮膚上，我絕不使用合成的東西。

6. tactic [ˋtæktɪk] *n.* [C] 戰術、策略 tactics

🔢 **Tactics** mean doing what you can with what you have. (Saul David Alinsky, Community Organizer)
戰略就是用你所有的做你能做的。

7. terminate [ˋtɝməˌnet] *vt. vi.* 停止、終止 terminated, terminated

🔢 Evaluate the people in your life and then promote, demote, or **terminate**. You're the CEO of your life. (Tony Gaskins)
評估你生命中的人，讓他們升職、降級或被解雇。他，你是你生命的總裁。

8. theatrical [θɪˋætrɪkl̩] *adj.* 戲劇的、戲劇性的、誇張的

🔢 I got into a very **theatrical** phase. I wore only black: a big black hat, wild hair, wild black clothes, and I carried a sword. (Delta Burke, Actress)
我曾經進入一個很戲劇性的狀態，我只穿黑色，黑色大帽子、狂野的髮型、狂野的黑衣服，而且我帶一把劍。

9. theoretical [ˌθiəˋrɛtɪkl̩] *adj.* 理論的、假設的

🔢 If you don't have the essentials, you might as well be writing a **theoretical** essay, not a play. (Samuel Rogers III, Playwright)
如果你沒有基本的東西，那你只是在寫論文，而不是劇本。

10. thereafter [ðɛrˋæftɚ] *adv.* 之後、以後

🔢 When I was five, my parents bought me a ukulele. **Thereafter**, my father regularly taught me songs. (Anthony Visconti)
我五歲的時候，我的父母買了烏克麗麗給我，在那之後，我父親常常教我不同的歌。

11. threshold [ˈθrɛʃhold] *n.* [C] 門檻 thresholds

🏃 Hope smiles from the **threshold** of the year to come. (Alfred Tennyson, Poet)
希望站在新年的門檻上微笑。

12. thrive [θraɪv] *vi.* 興旺、繁榮 thrived thrived

🏃 I love when people think they know what I am capable of or not capable of. I **thrive** off of that. (Clifford Harris Jr., Hip Hop Artist)
我喜歡人們自以為他們知道我會甚麼或不會甚麼，我因此而成長。

13. trait [tret] *n.* [C] 特徵、特點 traits

🏃 My most noticeable **trait** is my hair. It's big, wild and curly, and you can see it from a mile away. (Becca Fitzpatrick, Author)
我最明顯的特徵是我的頭髮，既多、亂又捲，從一哩外就可以看到。

14. transformation [trænsfɚˈmeʃən] *n.* [U] [C] 轉變、變形 transformations

🏃 It's a new challenge to see how people change your look. I like **transformation** and reinvention. (Naomi Campbell, Model)
看著別人改變自己的外表是個新挑戰。我喜歡轉變和再創造。

15. trauma [ˈtrɔmə] *n.* [U] [C] 傷口、創傷 traumas

🏃 Comedy can be a way to deal with personal **trauma**. (Robin Williams, Actor/Comedian)
喜劇可以是治療個人創傷的一個方法。

Part 1 「趣」你的單字基礎篇

Part 2 「趣」你的單字進階篇

16. trigger [ˈtrɪɡɚ] *n.* [C] 扳機、能引起反應的刺激物 triggers

🐦 It gets harder and harder to find audiences in the 500-channel world. People are so **trigger** happy with their remote control. (David E. Kelley, Producer)

在這個有五百個頻道的世界，要贏得觀眾越來越困難，，觀眾手握遙控器，隨時準備轉台。

17. trivial [ˈtrɪvɪəl] *adj.* 瑣細的、不重要的

🐦 Always write your ideas down however silly or **trivial** they might seem. Keep a notebook with you at all times.

一定要把自己的想法寫下來，不管這個想法看起來有多愚蠢或多瑣碎。記得手邊隨時都要有本筆記本。

18. trophy [ˈtrofɪ] *n.* [C] 戰利品 trophies

🐦 Takeru Kobayashi received a **trophy** and $10,000 for eating 97 burgers in eight minutes.

小林尊在八分鐘內吃了九十七個漢堡，得到了獎杯及一萬美元獎金。

19. turmoil [ˈtɝmɔɪl] *n.* [U] [C] 騷動、混亂 turmoils

🐦 The best thinking has been done alone. The worst has been done in **turmoil**. (Thomas Edison, Inventor)

歷屆最好的想法都是自己想出來的，而最糟糕的是在混亂中創造出來的。

20. upbringing [ˈʌpˌbrɪŋɪŋ] *n.* [U] 教養、培養

🐦 A good **upbringing** means that you won't notice when someone spills sauce on the tablecloth. (Anton Chekhov, Doctor)

教養代表別人在餐桌上吐醬汁時，你不會在意。（安東契訶夫，醫生）

21. utility [ju`tɪlətɪ] *n.* [U] 效用、實用

🐾 Any piece of clothing should either be for **utility** or joy.
任何一件衣服應該要是實用的，不然就要能給你帶來快樂。

22. vicious [`vɪʃəs] *adj.* 邪惡的

🐾 My dog is **vicious** to uninvited guests and welcoming to invited guests. He has officially mastered the English language. (Jean Korelitz, Novelist)
我的狗對不請自來的客人很壞，但對受邀請而前來的客人很歡迎，他是真的精通英語了。

23. victorious [vɪk`torɪəs] *adj.* 勝利的

🐾 He who knows when he can fight and when he cannot will be **victorious**. (Sun Tzu, Philosopher)
知可以戰與不可以戰者勝。

24. virtual [`vɝtʃʊəl] *adj.* 實際上的、虛擬的

🐾 I like live audiences with real people. **Virtual** reality is no substitute. (Hilary Clinton, Politician)
我喜歡有真人的現場觀眾，實際的現實是無法取代的。

25. visualize [`vɪʒʊəͺlaɪz] *vt. vi.* 使顯現、想像 visualized, visualized

🐾 Make sure you **visualize** what you really want, not what someone else wants for you. (Jerry Gillies, Author)
確定你想像你真正想要的，不是別人想要的。

－考用・文法－

精心整理出10大關鍵易犯錯誤與易混淆文法，加上重點提示、表格與例句，跳脫長篇大論的文字說明，學習更有效率。

書　系：Leader 031
書　名：英文文法顯微鏡：鎖定10大易犯錯誤＆易混淆語法：
　　　　放大檢視，矯正文法概念
定　價：NT$ 369元
ISBN：978-986-92398-0-6
規　格：平裝/304頁/17x23cm/雙色印刷

創新式英語字彙背誦法，幫助考生輕鬆讀懂iBT、GRE、IELTS等的學術文章，輕易突破長難句、SAT和GRE雙填空題，邁向新托福110⁺近在咫尺！

書　系：Learn Smart 054
書　名：N倍速學會iBT字彙(附MP3)：400魔術英語句極速提升字彙力
定　價：NT$ 429元
ISBN：978-986-91915-7-9
規　格：平裝/384頁/17x23cm/雙色印刷/附光碟

四週結合英文聽力與口說的訓練課程！4大預判重點＋專業外師錄製MP3＋英聽練習題，搶救英檢新多益聽力！

書　系：Leader 038
書　名：拯救你的英檢聽力！四週勇闖英語檢定 (MP3)
定　價：NT$ 380元
ISBN：978-986-92398-8-2
規　格：平裝/320頁/17x23cm/雙色印刷/附光碟

學習其實有捷徑，只要用對方法，讓哈佛高材生Show You How！收錄50大必考英文句型，成功地在學測、指考、新多益中三試三贏。

書　系：Leader 040
書　名：哈佛高材生的英語寫作筆記
定　價：NT$ 380元
ISBN：978-98692398-9-9
規　格：平裝/320頁/17x23cm/雙色印刷

－生活英語－

用故事區分，以及介系詞的"功能概念"分類，搭配圖解例句，考試不再和關鍵分數擦身而過，也是閱讀、寫作與口說的必備用書！

書　系：Leader 048
書　名：圖解介系詞、看故事學片語：第一本文法魔法書
定　價：NT$ 360元
ISBN：978-986-92856-7-4
規　格：平裝/320頁/17x23cm/雙色印刷

獨家吵架英語秘笈大公開！精選日常生活情境＋道地慣用語，教你適時地表達看法爭取應得的權利，成為最有文化的英語吵架王！

書　系：Learn Smart 064
書　名：冤家英語（MP3）
定　價：NT$ 360元
ISBN：978-986-92855-6-8
規　格：平裝/304頁/17x23cm/雙色印刷/附光碟

享受異國風光，走訪知名美食熱點；帶著情感品嚐美食，才是人間美味；用英語表達富情感意涵的美食，才算得上是『食尚』。

書　系：Leader 050
書　名：餐飲英語：異國美食情緣(MP3)
定　價：NT$ 369元
ISBN：978-986-92856-9-8
規　格：平裝/288頁/17x23cm/雙色印刷/附光碟

文法/生活英語 001

學校沒教的趣你的英語單字（附 MP3）

作　　者	Carolin Kuo（郭玥慧）、Jin-Ha Woo (하진우)
發 行 人	周瑞德
執行總監	齊心瑀
行銷經理	楊景輝
企劃編輯	陳欣慧
執行編輯	陳韋佑
封面構成	高鍾琪

內頁構成	華漢電腦排版有限公司
印　　製	大亞彩色印刷製版股份有限公司
初　　版	2017 年 5 月
定　　價	新台幣 389 元
出　　版	倍斯特出版事業有限公司
電　　話	(02) 2351-2007
傳　　真	(02) 2351-0887
地　　址	100 台北市中正區福州街 1 號 10 樓之 2
E - m a i l	best.books.service@gmail.com
網　　址	www.bestbookstw.com

港澳地區總經銷	泛華發行代理有限公司
地　　　　址	香港新界將軍澳工業邨駿昌街 7 號 2 樓
電　　　　話	(852) 2798-2323
傳　　　　真	(852) 2796-5471

國家圖書館出版品預行編目(CIP)資料

學校沒教的趣你的英語單字 /
郭玥慧, Jin-Ha Woo 著. -- 初版. -- 臺北
市 : 倍斯特, 2017.05 面 ；　公分. -
(文法/生活英語 001)
ISBN 978-986-94428-3-1(平裝附光碟
片)1.英語 2.詞彙
　　805.12　　　　　　　106004732